GROWING UP DANISH

*Memories of life in rural Iowa during
the 1920's, 30's and beyond*

ELNA M. PETERSEN

authorHOUSE™

1663 LIBERTY DRIVE, SUITE 200
BLOOMINGTON, INDIANA 47403
(800) 839-8640
WWW.AUTHORHOUSE.COM

First published by AuthorHouse 11/14/05

ISBN: 1-4208-8883-8 (sc)

Printed in the United States of America
Bloomington, Indiana

This book is printed on acid-free paper.

CONTENTS

FOREWORD

To the reader:

    This collection of stories came from my memories of growing up in rural Iowa. They have consumed several years in their writing. I began setting these down when in my 70's, writing on a typewriter, and as this is going to print I am approaching 91, writing the last of them on a computer—the third one I have owned.

    I grew up in a Danish family and community. Some of these experiences were unique to the traditions of Denmark. Most of what I lived through was universal. Most everyone can relate to these and similar life experiences.

    They are recollections and not academic treatises. They are intended to give a flavor of what life was like for all of us who grew up in the early part of the twentieth century.

    We were always busy. We never had money in excess. Yet we lived life fully and happily. I hope you enjoy the stories, and that you may appreciate the life we now enjoy. Enjoy and be entertained.

Elna Petersen

PREFACE

This book is written as a collection of my memories, but I must acknowledge those who helped in getting it into publication. A hearty "thank you" to Elna Bellows and Marvin Jessen for their help with the Old Danish translations and writings. Another "thanks" goes to Ralph Petersen, my son, who encouraged me in writing, and who did substantial editing to put things right. Thank you also to my daughter, Marna, who taught me how to use the computer to write this and many other items. Finally, a thank you goes to anyone who has helped, but have been inadvertently omitted from this preface. Good reading!

GROWING UP DANISH

The following story is a fictional account of how my, and many others', ancestors came from Denmark to America. They all gave up much. They left family and friends behind. They left a highly structured society to live in the free and open prairies of America. They were free to make their fortune as they chose, and so they all did. Except for accident and illness all of the Danes lived long lives into their 80's, 90's and even 100's.

BEDSTEMOR AND BEDSTEFAR

The handsome young couple leaned over the rail of the sailing ship happily waving their handkerchiefs to relatives and friends. As the ship sailed away from the pier, out of the harbor and out into the dark blue water, those left standing on the shore waved and waved until the ship became smaller and smaller, then completely disappeared.

The starry-eyed bride and her handsome young husband clasped each other tightly as they stood there thinking of the promises, the hopes, and of the new place where they would build their new home. America was calling to them.

The posted bill in the village had promised wealth beyond knowing. They knew of a cousin of a friend who had written from America of how easy it was to become rich. Yes, they had been told that in a few years they would become wealthy. They would buy land. And they would have a large farm with many barns. They would build a beautiful house with many rooms that they could be proud of. And have a big family. And they would write back to their relatives and tell them of their good fortune.

For days and days the ship sailed farther west and even farther from their old home. Seasickness and loneliness overtook both of them.

The small sailing ship on which they had taken passage danced unsteadily in the stormy Atlantic Ocean. Lying in their steamy bunks their faces became pale and their bodies weak. If only the New York Harbor would appear. Then everything would be all right again.

Finally, their feet touched the boardwalk of Ellis Island. Mobs of people pushed and shoved this way, then that way. So many strangers all talking in strange languages. How could they find their way in this mass of humanity; in this huge city? Bedstemor and Bedstefar had not learned any English. Maybe just a word or two. Wasn't there someone who could understand them?

Clinging tightly to each other they followed the throngs of people standing in a line. Surely this would get them to someone who would help them. They had never felt so alone.

A husky man behind a wooden desk motioned them to come.

Cautiously, Bedstefar walked up to him, pulled a printed sheet of paper from his coat pocket and showed it to the impatient man.

With wide gestures and speaking loudly in a language they could not understand the officer in charge pointed to a ticket booth. Over there, he motioned again.

They would have to buy train tickets.

With paper in hand, the young couple squeezed their way to the ticket booth, took carefully folded money from their belongings and they were soon seated in a train coach. Yes, someone would put their big wooden trunk in a box car. It would arrive with them, they were assured, but only after much speaking in two languages and with many frustrated gestures.

The train car lurched into motion, slowly pulling away from the platform and out of the station. This was a new journey. How exciting to see so many different things. Long days of jostling and sitting in straight stiff seats would take them to their destination. The smoky train puffed and whistled over the railroad tracks through cities and towns.

Wearily, they rode on over plains and hills through woods and forests. Would they ever get there? How long was this going to take? Soot and smoke were now part of them; part of their life.

Strangers smiled courteously at the couple as they traveled along. A few laughed at them. Friendlier ones inquired where they were going.

Iowa. They were going to Iowa. A town called Cedar Falls. They finally understood and responded. In their Danish language custom they pronounced it "ee-oh-va". They had heard of the opportunities waiting for them there. Yes, they would live there. Relatives would greet them there. They would get rich, they thought to themselves. They would tell their family at home how good it was.

At last, the train conductor called out in his loud voice, "Cedar Falls, Iowa. Anyone getting off at Cedar Falls, Iowa?" Soon the train came to a screeching halt. Smoke and cinders wafted through the passenger cars, gratefully for the last time for them. Was this the place they were coming to? Was this Cedar Falls, Iowa? Who would be there to meet them? Could this really be the place they were looking for?

The two anxious young people stepped hesitantly off the train onto the platform. Wasn't there anyone there to meet them? They had written. Everything looked so different. So different. Frightened and trembling they looked at each other. The young bride's eyes were moist with tears. What would they do?

Surely, the letter had been sent saying they were coming. All alone they stood there. The young husband clutched his young wife while looking all around for a familiar face. This wasn't at all the way they had imagined it.

The wooden trunk that held their only possessions brought from Denmark was being unloaded. Just as it reached the door of the baggage car it slipped and fell to the platform. A muffled crash gave evidence that the favorite porcelain items from home were now in a thousand pieces. It was more than she could take, and Bedstemor vented her sorrow and frustration in tears. Those lovely pieces to remember home were all gone.

Just then a resonant voice by a team of shiny black horses called out above the sound of the hissing steam locomotive. His lively team of horses had been frightened by the screeching brakes and loud noises of the train. He had to keep holding them so they wouldn't run.

"Hallo, min venner. Jeg komme snark enok." (*Hello, my friends. I came soon enough.*"

Laughter and hugs prevailed for some time. It had been a long time since they had heard the mother tongue. Each looked at the other. "Saa, vi kom endelig. Ja." (*So, we came finally. Yes.*)

"Hop op," (*"Jump up."*) the man called to them. "Jeg skal tage dig til din nye hjem." (*"I shall take you to your new home."*).

Amid the scrambling of loading the heavy, now rattling steamer trunk there was too much to say. The words came tumbling out. There was so much to say—so many questions to ask. Finally, the young couple sat high up on the wagon seat. Bedstemor hung onto the seat with one hand and onto her brown velvet hat with the other as they pulled away from the train depot. It was yet another adventure.

The wind was blowing and the sun shone hot as they rode through the little town. The horses left the print of their hooves in the deep brown dust of the streets.

There was a store, a general store, it was explained. Two women were visiting together admiring the recent shipment of figured calico displayed behind the glass window.

Bedstemor observed the women and the store carefully. She would likely buy much of what they needed for their new home there. Over there was a saloon. Three men were having an animated argument just outside the swinging doors. A few gray wooden houses stood along the narrow street. There was a church--a pretty white wooden church with a bell and a steeple. The able men of the community had built the little church recently, it was explained.

And down there. There was a blacksmith shop. It was for sale. Too bad. The owner had been injured badly and would be crippled the rest of his life.

The driver looked at the passenger beside him. Would you be interested in running a blacksmith shop? It would be a place to get started. Have a little business. You might like it.

Soon they came to a small house near the end of the street. It had two glass windows and a front door that looked sturdy. The little house had been arranged for them to live in.

Was this really the kind of house American people lived in? Was this the American way? It all looked so different than from what they had left in Denmark.

Their trunk and other belongings were unloaded and placed in front of the door. Yes, they would live there. And wouldn't they like to come along and have supper with the family, the driver asked.

Between anxious laughter, smiles and tears, the two young people graciously accepted the invitation. How good it would be to sit down at a real table again. How good to be with people with whom they could talk and visit. Bedstemor and Bedstefar knew there was much work to do, but this was a grand occasion.

In a few days the matter was settled. Bedstefar would run the blacksmith shop. Fix a little harness now and then. Maybe forge some iron for repairing the meager machinery that was used in the surrounding community. Yes, he would do it. It would be a beginning.

Meanwhile, Bedstemor unpacked some of the belongings from the huge trunk. Her keepsakes from home she valued so highly were no more. But she was brave. It was a new world after all. She unpacked some bedding including feather ticks for cold winter nights, a few dishes survived, and there was the cooking ware. There a few photographs of the family left behind. They were the only remaining reminders of their former homeland. There were few spare necessities for daily living. She would go to the store and see what was available.

Time went by. They had renounced their loyalty to the King of Denmark, had sworn their allegiance to the United States of America and had become full citizens in every way. Quickly, they learned the new language. Bedstefar's blacksmithing business grew as more people needed his services. Bedstemor with her winning personality soon became a favorite in the town. She loved baking her Kaffe Kage and people were invited in for coffee and delicious pastry now and then. This became their home at last.

The happy couple coped with all the challenges of their new life in America and grew comfortable with a new way of living. Bedstefar was always asked to sing or play for wedding dances and with the town band. Bedstemor kept her house neat as a pin. She carried the water to the house from the pump in the yard. Her white clothes gleamed on wash day as they hung blowing in the wind on the clothes line in the yard beside the house. She had quickly learned the ways of living as it had to be done in this community.

The years seemed to fly by. Now there were seven growing children and another on the way. The family was growing and they would have to build a bigger house.

Bedstefar worked furiously to provide money to buy food for his large family. With so many boys with huge ravenous appetites it kept both parents busy.

Then one day tragedy struck. Bedstefar was suddenly taken ill and died soon afterward. Bedstemor, the children and their friends laid his body to rest in the cemetery that was near the little church.

Dreams were shattered. Their plans of traveling back to the Old Country to visit friends and relatives were gone. But what now? How would Bedstemor care for her family? Where would she get the money to buy food? The garden she so carefully tended couldn't provide enough produce to keep the family alive.

Money owed to Bedstefar was never paid. He had never written down what was coming to him. He was able to remember what was owed. He understood the neighbors' financial needs. He would wait until the farmers had gotten their harvesting done. They would pay then. But now they never did.

Whether by fate, or was it faith, Bedstemor was able to acquire 80 acres of land just to the south of town. There her growing boys could do the farm work. A cow or two would give the milk. Having even a few chickens would mean they could have fresh eggs daily and fresh chicken for Sunday dinner once in awhile.

It was truly a remarkable thing the way they were able to manage. The love and courage this fine woman had was remarkable. And they had made good friends who were willing to help. It was not easy, but Bedstemor and her family were able to not only survive, but thrive on their new farm. The older boys were able to farm the land, and the weather held favorably for them. Life was once again good.

Her children all grew to be good respected citizens in the community. The determination and pride instilled in them had brought out the best in each and everyone. Their father would have been so proud to see their accomplishments.

In her old age Bedstemor continued to tend her flower garden, take part in the women's work of the church, and to be a much loved and respected woman in the community.

She had not gathered large sums of money or material wealth. But she was rich. She ever loved her family and her friends. Her contributions and involvement in the growing community could not be measured by dollars alone. She gave generously of herself and was rewarded likewise.

There were few regrets in her life. She marveled at all that she had seen and done. In the Old Country she would have probably spent her life working for others in lowly rank and menial tasks. Here she had been free to choose her own life—her own way. Yes, she had done well.

She lived well beyond 90 years, most of them in the New World. She never was able to return to Denmark to see her relatives. The worn and now faded photographs brought from the Old Country were of people who remained young only in her mind. Although she wrote many letters and received letters in return, she never saw her parents and the rest of the family again. She had given up much to come to this country, but she made her life an example of courage and joy. Her legacy was in her children and by example she showed them how to live life well.

The following is a letter written to Edith S. living in Denmark, a distant relative of my mother's birth family. The letter tells the story of how my mother found her birth mother, and met and enjoyed a whole new group of relatives.

INGER

3-22-99

Dear Edith,

Thank you so much for your recent letter and card received at Christmas time. I am grateful to you for taking the time to write so that we can in some way begin to unravel our blood relationship.

I am the only granddaughter of Inger Marie Petersen who was born in Denmark. She came to live in Northwest Iowa in the 1870s and bore a child at the age of sixteen who was to become my mother. Whether her pregnancy was the result of rape or her indiscretion is not known, and it does not matter.

Inger, known locally as "Mary," kept her baby until the little girl was six months old. At that time she was forced to let her little one be adopted by Niels and Christine Hoffman. Whether it was for economic reasons or because of the social stigma of being an unwed mother we don't know. We never learned who the father of the child was. A Scandinavian equivalent of "John Smith" is listed in the birth record, but no other record or information has surfaced. Whatever the reason it must have been a terrible hardship for Mary to have given up her baby at that time.

Court records show that Mattie was adopted in Storm Lake, Iowa, a considerable distance from the Royal, Iowa area where they lived. At that time church services were held in homes, and the traveling pastor may have been the intermediary and made the arrangements between Mary and the Hoffman's. The adoption would have been recorded in the nearest office that had that capability.

The Hoffman's were from southern Jutland (Sønderjylland), Denmark, and had also immigrated to this country in this era. As many immigrants did, they had moved to northwestern Iowa seeking their fortune in securing a piece of land for themselves. This area was still a new frontier settlement. My mother recalled as a young child people in that area still talking about the savage Sioux Uprising that had occurred not long before. When the Hoffman's and my mother lived in the Newell area, they first lived in a sod house, better known as "Soddies." As soon as they were able to get lumber together they built a house of wood. However, economic conditions in the depression of the 1890's were such that they had to give up the land and move back to the Danish community west of Cedar Falls, Iowa.

The Hoffman's, the adoptive parents, lived in the area also as farm people. Mary would go into town on Saturdays knowing that most other farmers would also do so and sit or stand on the side of the street to watch for the Hoffman's to drive by in their horse and buggy. She always hoped to get a glance of her little one in this way. The emotions of this young mother must have been intolerable both from the standpoint of giving up the child as well as bearing the scorn of her neighbors for having this child out of wedlock. Seeing her only in this way must have been heart-wrenching.

Mother barely remembers that at the age of two years she visited her real mother Mary. Mattie got a bad burn on her wrist, scalded as she said, and Mary wrapped her wrist with cloth bandages. Mattie kept these bandages in a sewing machine drawer for a long, long time.

I need to backtrack a little and tell you more about Inger Marie. As an adult, Mary had married and with her husband, now lived on a farm. She had no other children, but helped many people in the area. She was known as a very kind person. Neighbors knew that they could rely upon her for help in times of need.

Now in her thirties, Mary was polishing the cook stove top one day when the stove was still hot. She used turpentine and some other flammable mixture, probably naphtha, a common mixture of the day. The mixture caught fire and Mary was severely burned. The flesh fell from her arms as she tried to call for help. The doctor was called, but it was of no use. She lived only a very painful few days and mercifully died a short time after that fatal accident. It was said that Inger Marie had a little dog who mourned Mary's death, and the little dog would not leave her grave.

Now the Hoffman's moved back to the Danish community near Cedar Falls and my mother attended a rural school there. It was known that Mother was not the real daughter of the Hoffman's and the school children chided her terribly for that. Even Mrs. Hoffman who was not known altogether for being a loving and caring parent also reminded mother on a regular basis that she was a bastard child and undoubtedly would never amount to anything. On one occasion in a fit of anger, my grandmother threw the adoption papers into the cook stove as she scolded my mother for some indiscretion.

So that is mostly what I know about my natural grandmother. I have a red plate with a picture of a white cat painted on it that belonged to her. So you see that plate is well over a hundred years old. This may sound a little dramatic but this is what really happened. My brother and I knew from overheard comments that she had been adopted. But it was not until my mother was in her eighties that she openly revealed to my brother and me that she was adopted. She still feared the stigma. She knew her mother's name was "Mary", but knew little else.

It was at that time that my brother took it upon himself to spend many months of investigation to find out who the real birth mother was and what had happened to her. Mother had been reluctant for my brother to conduct his search, but she also had an interest in discovering who her birth mother was after all those years. My brother did a thorough job of poring through all those old records. After driving to Newell and looking up court records, getting the adoption papers opened, and searching through cemetery records did he solve the mystery. She finally found out where her real mother was buried. The newspapers heard about this story and there was a major article published about it in The Des Moines Register.

My brother died some years ago and so the search stopped there for a long time. I have a copy of a letter received from the pastor in one of your local churches where I believe Inger Marie was baptized. But your letter is the first real communication we have had. So you see how thankful we are for people like you.

My mother was happy to have found another whole group of relatives. They visited many times in the subsequent years. She also seemed relieved at fully opening this chapter of her life. My mother lived to be 103 years old. She loved gardening and especially enjoyed raising flowers. She was an excellent cook and baked wonderful things. In her old age she lived in a beautiful red brick house out on the farm. She always had one dog or another that she pampered. Each year for many years she raised a large flock of chickens. She was very active in the Ladies Aid, and served the Fredsville church well. One of their projects was to help make very fine and beautiful vestments for the altar, pulpit and lectern. They are still in use there today.

Now I am almost 85 years old and am trying to keep the ties going. I regret I have not answered you sooner. I sold my home after my husband died a year ago and moved into an apartment a few months ago. I am healthy but don't see well. I rely on my computer for letter writing. My family graciously read letters to me that come in the mail.

Well, that is one chapter in our lives that I am mailing to you. The next letter will probably give you more information. I have been waiting for my sister-in-law to come and help me locate the ones you mentioned in your Christmas letter.

Wouldn't it be interesting if we could get together sometime and you could look over the material that I have on file.

If this information is of any use to you let me know. Who knows? We could become pen pals.

Can you establish our blood relationship from this information?

Hilsen from,
Elna

MY BEDSTEFAR, JØRGEN SCHMIDT

Jørgen Schmidt

My grandfather ("bedstefar" in the Danish language) Jørgen Schmidt was tall, slender, and almost regal in appearance. He had immigrated to America, and had become a U.S. citizen. Perhaps as a remaining tie to "the old country," he proudly wore a muttonchop beard similar to that of King Christian of Denmark. This distinguishing feature with his striking, now snow-white hair further enhanced his appearance.

He had farmed in Denmark, and when he arrived in Iowa, he purchased 160 acres of prime land southwest of Cedar Falls. That area had already become a Danish settlement where he knew many of his neighbors. Apparently, farming was a good business for him. He built several large buildings on the farm, including a large Victorian house and a dairy barn. Bedstefar Schmidt had retired from farming before I first remember him.

In 1913, at age 67, he moved off the farm to Cedar Falls, but continued to spend many days at the farm, helping Dad during the planting and harvest seasons. When he was there I would follow my grandfather while he was working. I was small, and it was hard for my short legs to keep up with the long strides he took when walking. But as I got older I trotted behind him as he walked out in the yard.

It was a habit of his to clasp his hands behind his back as he stood talking with the other men.

His constant companion was his sea captain's smoking pipe with the curved stem and large meerschaum bowl. He kept wooden matches dry in a silver match box which was carefully guarded in his shirt pocket. His red tin Prince Albert smoking tobacco was safely kept in his hip pocket. He enjoyed sitting on the back step cradling his smoking pipe as he sat resting after a day of work.

When working out on the farm he wore loose fitting trousers held up by suspenders, a blue chambray shirt, and a certain cap that was sure to have been brought back from Denmark on one of his several trips overseas to his homeland. On rainy days when the farmyard was muddy, he wore heavy woolen stockings inside of a pair of hand-carved wooden shoes, which also had come from Denmark. An old sweater, used on cool rainy days, hung on a nail in the back porch entry.

He wore long sleeved and long legged one-piece underwear both summer and winter. In the summer he wore fine cotton underwear and in the winter he wore underwear made from fine chamois skin.

Jørgen "helping" harvest oats

My grandfather helped Dad a lot during planting and harvest seasons. During corn cultivating time he rode a two-row corn cultivator behind a team of horses. He guided the shovels on the cultivator with his feet. The cultivator stirred the soil between the rows of corn. It uprooted weeds and piled additional soil next to the corn which strengthened its root system. If the metal plow shares happened to hit a rock, the wooden pin that held the plowshares would break. It was better that the wooden peg broke than to have a steel plowshare bent. So in the evenings, he spent lots of time whittling new wooden pegs for the following day. He carried them in a pocket and could do a quick repair in the field.

During haying season it was his job to drive the horse that pulled the hay rope behind the big red barn. The rope was attached to a large hayfork in the front of the barn, and was routed along a track that ran the length of the barn in the peak of the roof, and then through the barn by a series of wooden pulleys, then outside to the team of horses. In front of the barn, one of the men stood on the wagon full of hay. He would stick the prongs of the fork into the hay, then, signal my grandfather to pull on the rope. The fork full of hay would be pulled up to the track which held a wheeled carrier. When the fork reached the carrier it would release a latching mechanism, and the fork full of hay would travel along the track into the haymow to a place where it could be dropped. When the man in the haymow called out "Whoa!" the man on the wagon would jerk the trip-rope, which dropped the fork full of hay down into the haymow. Then Bedstefar would unhook the clevis hooked to the loop at the end of the rope, turn the horse around and go back to get ready for the next fork full while the man on the wagon would pull on the trip rope to return the carrier and fork to the front of the barn. Bedstefar again hooked the clevis to the end of the rope. It was an important bit of work and he enjoyed being there to help with the haying.

In the evening after the day's dusty work was done my grandfather would take off his shoes, go into the kitchen and, one leg at a time, he would put a foot into the basin of water in the sink and wash his feet. People were amazed that a man in his seventies was still capable of lifting his legs that high, but Bedstefar was still up to it.

He did other jobs on the farm, too. Out in the hog house he kept a "smithy", a small, hand-operated forge. Pieces of coal were placed in this shallow metal pan set on cast iron legs. A hand-cranked fan blew air through the fire to bring it to the proper temperature. He fired up the forge to do work on piece of iron that needed repair. When the pieces to be repaired were red hot he would take a pair of tongs, lift the hot iron to the anvil and hammer out the piece as needed.

He also did shoe repair at the workbench in the hog house. He would turn a leather shoe up side down onto an iron shoe last, remove the worn sole, and tack on a new piece of leather, thereby making the shoes good for a long time. There was always leather harness to repair as well.

As a kid I liked to play around the farmyard to amuse myself, probably having been told to keep out of the way. Behind the machine shed was an old horse-drawn surrey that was especially fun for me. It was a relic of earlier times, but now it sat neglected among the tall weeds. There were still some fringes dangling around the top, and the black leather seats were now torn and weathered. It was fun to climb into that old carriage, and imagine traveling far into the world. My

16

mother and father talked about the times when the surrey had been used to go to church and social functions. Now, it was a relic of their past, but became my chariot of dreams.

When the surrey was used regularly, there were times on Sunday mornings when my grandfather would not wait for his two daughters. He would put on his dark blue wool serge three-piece suit, drop his gold watch in one vest pocket and put the gold chain across his chest into the other pocket. If the daughters were not ready at the appointed time, he would put on his black felt hat and start walking to church. The women came later in the surrey. Once at church, the horses were tied in the horse shed at the east end of the cemetery that surrounded the little country church.

My bedstefar also had to deal with tragedy. Many, many years before I was born my grandmother died. This is what I was told:

Jørgen & Marie

Bedstefar's wife, Marie Kirstine Sliffsgaard, had borne five children. She died from appendicitis in 1897 at the young age of 48, leaving three living children ranging in age from six to twelve. My father was the youngest surviving child. Two little boys had died of hemophilia when they were very small, and were buried in the Fredsville cemetery. In the large house on the farm was a narrow winding staircase leading to the large attic. It was narrow and had no handrail. They had been salvaged from the small original house on this farm. Both boys, in accidents twenty years apart, fell on this staircase and bled to death. The first child's burial was the very first grave on that cemetery. His grave was just outside the front door to the church, and we saw it each Sunday morning.

When my grandmother became very ill, the doctor was called out to the farm. It was his diagnosis that she had appendicitis and that he should operate. He carried the essential tools in a little black bag. My grandfather lengthened the dining room table and my grandmother was laid on the table for surgery. With chloroform to deaden the pain, he proceeded with the surgery. I don't know how long she lived after the surgery, but it must not have been very long. Did she die of a ruptured appendix and peritonitis, or was it incompetent surgery. We will never know the answer.

In October of 1913, my mother and father were married. My father and mother stayed on the farm. In that same year, Bedstefar Schmidt built a new two-story house in Cedar Falls at 18th and Washington. The house still stands just as it was built. It had a spacious front porch

The home in Cedar Falls

and polished oak hardwood floors. The oak floor and stair steps were so highly waxed and polished that I had to sit down to come down the stairway for fear of falling. He also built a barn next to the alley large enough to keep a team of horses and a buggy. On the side of the barn was a chicken coup, where he kept a few chickens for fresh eggs and the occasional fried chicken dinner. When there was work that he could help with on the farm he hitched his team to the buggy and drove the five miles to the Schmidt farm.

I was impressed with my grandfather's new house. I had never seen an indoor toilet, and this one had a wooden tank high on the wall. I could pull the chain that hung from the tank, and a rush of water would noisily flush the toilet.

He moved there with his two grown daughters, Martha and Johanna. I often stayed with my grandfather and the two aunts. After all, I was the only grandchild at that time. Aunt Johanna became more of a grandmother to me than an Aunt. I really loved her. But she was adamant about which language I spoke. I must always speak Danish.

It was Aunt Johanna who showed me how the pansy petals could be removed and where the tiny lady sat with her feet in a tub. She also showed me how the snapdragon blossoms could really snap. Aunt Johanna had an Overland touring car, which she drove out to the farm on occasion. She never slowed down for the corners and she never rolled the car. It was amazing.

When relaxing in town on beautiful summer days Bedstefar would sit on the front porch on the wooden porch swing waiting for the 10:00 morning postal delivery. Promptly at the appointed time the postman would come walking down the street with the morning mail. And then he would return again at 2:00 in the afternoon with another mail delivery. The Rock Island and the Illinois Central railroads would each bring mail every day except Sunday. It was then possible to receive a letter in the forenoon, write a reply letter and post it in the afternoon mail.

He also spent leisurely Sunday afternoons on the porch swing watching for visitors or reading his Danish newspaper called the "Dannevirke", a newspaper published locally by friends of his, the Holst family. He could get news from Denmark from this newspaper.

The streetcar or trolley car that operated between downtown Cedar Falls and the college campus ran at regular intervals just down at the next corner on Main Street. The trolley bell always rang as it went by the corner.

The iceman came through the alley twice a week delivering chunks of ice, which had been cut from the river the preceding winter. The ice was stored in a round brick building and covered with sawdust as insulation against the hot summer months. A cardboard sign in the back window of the house was turned to signify how much ice was wanted that day. Was it 25, 50, 75, or even a 100 pounds needed that day? The iceman would chop a chunk from a larger block, weigh it on a scale that hung from the back of the wagon, and, with ice tongs, carry the ice to the house. There, he put it inside the icebox through a door on the outside of the house that opened into the ice compartment of the icebox.

Or my grandfather might hear the "old Jew", as he was known, as he slowly made his way through the alley behind the house, driving his old rickety wagon pulled by a nag just as decrepit, crying out, "Rags! Rags! Rags!" If my aunts had any old clothes to get rid of they would bring them out to the alley and dump them in the back of the wagon.

My grandfather died of stomach cancer at age seventy-six. I can still see him lying on his bed in such terrible pain. But at the moment of death he reached out a hand from his bed towards the ceiling with a smile on his face. He quietly lay back down, sighing his last breath, and died. I was seven at the time and I stayed with him during his final illness. That experience made quite an impression on me.

Did he die because of his diet, or was it from smoking his pipe? I don't know. It had always been his custom to have a cut glass salt dish at his plate during his meals. It seemed he salted everything he ate. He often dipped his bite of food into the salt before eating it.

After he died the undertaker came to the house, and after the preparations were done, placed his body in a coffin. The coffin was then placed in the living room where he laid in state for three days. Someone of the family sat next to the coffin both night and day to be with the body. It was the custom to place a floral bouquet by the front door so that passers-by would know that someone in that house had died.

From his home in Cedar Falls, the funeral procession of 70-some cars drove slowly over the dirt roads to the church in Fredsville. This was in 1922, and there were not so many automobiles at that time. This was a lot of cars! The hearse was a motorized panel truck with ornate gray panels and trim. After the services his coffin was placed in a grave close to the church building in the family plot. He had lost two sons in infancy from hemophilia, and a wife to appendicitis.

True to his nature he was brusque in speech and demanded much from those around him. He was a patriarch of the old order. For example, when his wife died, Johanna, his oldest daughter was only 12 but she was expected to run the house as well as take care of her younger brother and sister, Hans and Martha.

My grandfather came to America in search of a better life than in the old country. As so many immigrants thought, he, too, wanted to maintain the language and traditions of the mother country. In these endeavors he succeeded, and was loved and respected by all. In addition to being a successful farmer, he was very active in establishing the Fredsville Danish Lutheran church in the community.

I think it was fortunate for me to have spent as much time as I did with him, both in Cedar Falls and out on the farm. I hope these memories of mine will give you some insight into what his life was like and from whom we descended.

THE HOFFMAN'S, NIELS AND CHRISTINE

Christine "Stina" Syndergaard arrived in the United States from Fjelstrup in southern Denmark in the 1880's, probably traveling with one or two of her brothers. It is possible that her brother Chris was already here. She had other brothers, namely, Peter and Simon. Chris farmed north of Dike on the road between Dike and New Hartford. Simon and Peter went west to Clay County, Iowa.

As many immigrants did in those days, they would come to this country and seek employment with people they had known in the Old World. She must have known someone in the Fredsville community because she quickly got employment at the Slifsgaard dairy farm in that village. Stina worked there as a dairymaid, and between the twice daily milkings she worked in the house. It must have been a sizable dairy herd since the farm also had a creamery where they made and sold butter.

In those days women always wore long dresses. Aprons were worn over the dress to protect the dress from most of any dirt and spills that came that way. Aprons were much easier to wash than the dresses. I recall Stina telling about the apron she threw on over her other clothes while milking. There were many cows to milk in a short time, so spilling or splashing milk on clothing was a problem. After each milking she hung the apron on a wooden peg on the wall of the barn. The apron became stiff from the dried milk splattered onto the apron.

When no more milk could be gotten from the cow, and the pail was filled, the whole milk was poured into ten-gallon cans. After the last cow had been milked, these cans would be ready for the separator. Stina filled many pails with the warm milk.

Across the road was a creamery where the milk was taken, and where farmers from the surrounding farms brought their milk. Here a large cream separator imported from Denmark easily separated the valuable cream from the milk. The cream was churned into butter and packed in wooden butter tubs. These tubs were made in the village at a cooperage shop. The butter was then sold, some back to the farmers, the rest into the general marketplace. Cream was a good source of income for the farmers.

Niels Hoffman who had recently immigrated from Aller in southern Denmark was also employed at the Sliffsgaard dairy farm. A relationship between Niels and Stina matured. They fell in love and decided to make a life together. They left their employment at Fredsville to begin farming on their own. They took the train and moved to Clay County, Iowa. There they must have homesteaded a piece of land. They were married in Newell, probably on the way to their

Niels' & Stina's
wedding portrait

destination. I was told that their first house was a sod house called a "soddie." There they lived until they could build a proper, but small, house. Together with the brothers, Peter and Simon, they farmed land in the area, helping each other on their separate farms.

At that time the northwest part of Iowa was reasonably well settled. My grandmother told me that at that time, the local residents still talked about the Great Sioux Uprising of 1862 that had terrorized northwestern Iowa and southwestern Minnesota. Civilization was gaining a strong foothold.

They had enough money to buy a team of horses, a buggy, and a wagon. They were able to travel to the nearby small towns of Royal and Peterson, Iowa. There must have been other Danish immigrants living in the area. When they moved back to the Fredsville area they talked a great deal about the friends they had made while living in that area.

In 1893 they adopted my mother, a child who was born to a local sixteen year old girl named Inger Marie "Mary" Peterson. Mary was not married, and my mother was thus born out of wedlock, a significant social disgrace at that time. Mette, or "Mattie," as my mother was commonly known, was six months old when she was adopted.

Did the Hoffman's know the father? We will never know. There are no records to prove this.

So my mother with her new stepparents lived for a while in the Royal area. When Niels and Stina came into town, the mother, Mary,

Neils, Mattie & Stina

was often waiting in front of one of the stores in hopes that she would see her little girl with the Hoffman's. My mother had a little school friend there whose last name was Haggedorn. She talked about running across the field to play with this friend. It was she who first called my mother "Mattie," not remembering the exact pronunciation of her given name. It stuck for 103 years! For the rest of her life she was known to all as Mattie.

During the 1890's there was an economic panic on top of a drought in the area. The Hoffman's packed what belongings they could and traveled by rail back to the Fredsville area. Mattie and Stina rode in the caboose. They rented a farm near the Schmidt farm just north of the Greeley school on the west side of the road. I think that is known as the Abel's farm now. They must have lived there until after my parents were married. Then they moved to one of the four Bill Walter's farms in that area, a farm two miles directly east of the Schmidt farm.

As a very young child I remember going in the horse and buggy to their place. To get to their farm, Dad drove south to the corner, then down the diagonal road, then east of Gordon Hansen's farm on the "Green Road", a grass-covered approximation of a road. In this part of Iowa, straight roads were laid out in one-mile squares, but not always graded. Where the mile should have had a road, but didn't, it was called a "green" road. The road was undeveloped and was used as part of the farmland, most often grown over with grass. Horse-and-buggy rigs could drive these roads before farmers put up fences, but not automobiles. Or sometimes Dad drove south to the corner of the south eighty, then east two miles, and north a half mile.

As a small child I visited them often. I recall they had only one kerosene lamp. There was no electricity available at that time. During the day it sat in the center of the dining room table. In the evenings, this lamp was the only light in the house. If light was needed in another room the lamp was carried to that room.

Grandfather Niels had made a home for a family of skunks out in the pasture. He laid an old milk can on its side, half buried in the ground, and put in some straw. The family made their home inside the can. I was allowed to go out to the pasture to see them, but knew to keep my distance. Skunks were good to have, at a distance, because they kept the mouse and rat population in check.

Also, as a young child I stayed overnight with them occasionally. My grandmother would tuck me into bed, tell me to fold my hands and we would say, "Our Father, -- 'Fadervor du som er I Himmlen' -- Who art in Heaven."

A custom the Hoffman's kept was probably a custom they had begun while living in the Old Country. Every evening just as the sun was setting, no matter what they were doing, both of my grandparents would come into the house and quietly go into the living room where they sat quietly on chairs, folding their hands in silent meditation. After the sun was down they would resume whatever work they had been doing. When I was there, I sat on a wooden chair dangling my legs waiting for this quiet time to be over.

It was sometime around 1910 that Stina needed a gall bladder operation. At that time it was necessary to go to Chicago for an operation. Stina took the Illinois Central train to Chicago where she had a friend living. After the surgery Stina stayed with her friend, Helena Falk, until she was recovered enough that she could take the train home. Stina enjoyed telling and retelling the surgery event for many, many years. It was a major event! Few people survived major surgery of that type in those years.

Farming went well for the Hoffman's. It must have been in the late 1920's that they retired from farming at the age of fifty or so. They had saved up a tidy nest-egg for their retirement years. They decided to return to the little village of Fredsville where they had met. They bought a little white house just short distance down the hill from the Fredsville church. There they kept a team of fine white horses and a small flock of chickens. They also had a vegetable garden. The entire area around the house was planted to flowers. The house was furnished with fine furniture.

For his part, Niels, aside from pumping the occasional pail of water from the well just outside the door, or carrying out the ashes from the cook stove, spent his time reading the *Decorah Posten* word after word. He didn't miss one bit of the information contained therein.

Stina was still active in the Farm Bureau women's group and did a lot of craftwork. One item that she was so proud of was a terra cotta tile cylinder about 26 inches tall and about ten or twelve inches across. On the outside of the tile she had glued pieces of colored china until the whole tile was covered in a fine mosaic. The finished tile stood in front of the bay window and with a board laid across the top, and served as a stand for a fern.

Their home was beautifully furnished. The "fainting couch" was upholstered in maroon colored velvet, which she covered with a white crocheted spread. In the kitchen was a walnut drop leaf table with four little chairs. Above the table was a shelf bordered with white crocheting. The mantle clock stood on the shelf. I still have and display the white lace, so very delicately crocheted.

Each morning my grandmother had the entire house in order, including polishing the stovetop, most often by nine o'clock. She was then ready to sit down for the day doing her fine knitting which was her specialty. Her favorite chair was a comfortable rocking chair built with legs shorter than usual to accommodate her size.

My grandmother was a short woman, but was large in girth. For as long as I can remember, every morning her very long hair was

Niels, Stina, Jørgen and Elna

made up into a single braid which was then wound around the crown of her head. Each evening the braid was undone and she carefully and thoroughly brushed her long hair. Her daily apparel was always a dark ankle-length dress with a white lace collar just below her full round face. When she was working at home her dress was covered with a clean white starched full apron.

My grandmother was good at preserving fruit and vegetables each summer. She also made a lot of fruit juice and bottled it. She called it "saft", Danish for "juice". She kept the bottles in the cellar where it would be cool in the summer and would not freeze in the winter. She could have saft all year 'round.

I remember that Stine bought a lot of patent medicines for much of her life, and took them regularly. She was probably addicted to them. I suppose that some of them contained a goodly amount of alcohol, as did many of those remedies of the time. She didn't suffer any ill effects from them at any rate.

When the model T Ford came into vogue in the 1930's Stina considered the advantage of having a car instead of buying and feeding

27

a team of horses. So Stina dealt with the car dealer in Dike, brought home an open touring car, and stated to Niels that she would drive it. In her mind he would never be able to learn how to drive it. There was a practical aspect to this bargain. Someone had to turn the crank in front to start the car, so Niels, being the stronger, complied.

There was no door on the left side of the car by the steering wheel. She had to get into the car on the right side and then slide across the seat. She was so heavy that when she stepped on the running board the car swayed over to one side. She had the car dealer put an extension on the brake lever, which was on the floor, and now she could reach it from a sitting position.

There were no windows in the car, and my grandmother had only one speed when she drove. When they drove down the road my grandfather would hold onto his hat with one hand and hold onto the side of the car with his other hand. To my knowledge he never complained.

They made lots of trips to Dike for shopping and medical appointments. They shopped at Henningsen's General Store and got dental work done at the local dentist office. During their shopping trips, my grandmother always carried a small black beaded purse which she had made herself. She was quite creative.

She was not afraid to drive her car. I remember of them driving to Cedar Falls when we were living on the Waterloo Road. Because of the depression, we had to leave the farm for a few years and move to a more economical house in town. I knew she was not pleased with the situation we were living in. We were all in the depression years.

Niels and Stina remained in that little white house near Fredsville for many years. Niels had done well at farming and they had saved their money well. But then they lost all of their savings through a bad loan and they really had nothing to live on anymore. They had made a large loan to a friend, who was unable to repay them because of the depression. For the rest of their lives they lived in poverty.

When in 1940 Niels died at age 75 of emphysema, it was necessary for Stina to move to the Old Western Home, an early old people's home in Cedar Falls. I recall this was a gloomy building. It was built of dark red brick, and had tall windows trimmed in black.

Stina in her ever-
present hat and apron

There was little light inside, and it smelled of old people. There she lived through her seventies. She spent the last few months of her life living with my parents on their farm where my mother cared for her until her death in 1951, at age 80.

My grandparents were always good to me, and I loved them dearly. They taught me much about life and how to live it. Perhaps the most memorable experience was how my grandmother helped me when my little sister tragically died. She helped me understand death, and instilled within me a very strong faith. They lived their faith no matter their circumstances.

HANS PETERSEN

Hans was the fourth child born to Ebbe and Ellen Petersen near a lumber camp just north of Prescott, Wisconsin in an area known as Clifton Hollow. Hans and his three older sisters lived there with their parents. Ebbe, the father, was a laborer in a lumber camp. Hans' mother cared for the four small children with barely enough food to feed the family, and likely made all the clothing for the family. Living was difficult.

However difficult daily living was for the family, the religious background of the parents was strong enough that the children were baptized in the local German Lutheran church. That church later burned and the baptismal records were lost in the fire.

His parents were both immigrants from the southern part of Denmark who had come to settle in a new land where they would seek their fortune and be spared from serving in the German army. It is ironic that the area around Prescott was primarily German. So much so that official records were sometimes written in the German language. It was the hatred that the Danish people had for the Germans that compelled the family to move to a Danish community in Iowa known as Fredsville. They had heard of others who had moved there.

With their worldly goods, consisting of a few pieces of furniture and a trunk of clothes, they boarded the train and traveled from Wisconsin to Iowa near Cedar Falls. There they moved into another small house. It had one bedroom, a living room, a loft upstairs and a lean-to kitchen.

It was not long until Hans' uncle and family, who had lived near by in Wisconsin, also moved to the Fredsville area. There they moved in with Ebbe and his family. It was said the children all slept crosswise across the living room floor at night. It was a wonder they ever were able to feed all those growing children as well as keeping them all clothed.

When Hans was only eleven years old, his father, Ebbe, died of appendicitis. This was a great loss as that meant the loss of income that supported the family.

Hans, being the oldest boy, was sent out at age twelve to work as a hired hand on Chris Syndergaard's farm two and a half miles north of Dike. Hans often referred to the work he did as slave labor. Early mornings and late nights were required to do all the farm work both summer and winter. He was awakened at 4 am, and often worked until 9 pm. His only breaks were for mealtimes. For all this, he was paid fifty cents each month which he sent home to help feed his family.

By this time Hans had only a fourth grade education. In his teens he had no time for mingling with friends or being around his family except for birthdays and holidays.

It was his good fortune to meet Emma Nielsen during this time. We have no idea how long their courtship lasted but on February 22, 1910 they were married in Dike at the bedside of Emma's father. Emma's father, Jens, was gravely ill, and died just four days later on February 28. Pastor Rodholm drove his horse and buggy from Fredsville to Dike, a distance of five miles, to perform the marriage.

On the first of March they moved to a farm a mile north, a half-mile east, and then three-quarters of a mile north from their prior home. It is likely they didn't have much to start out with, but Hans had learned to be a good farmer. Emma told of how the water often froze on the kitchen floor when she washed it in the wintertime. Hans told of waking up one winter morning following a fierce blizzard with snow drifted across the quilts of their bed. Water in the teakettle boiling at bedtime on the cook stove would be frozen solid in the morning.

Hans's first child, Harold, was born on that farm. Shortly after that Hans heard of another farm of 80 acres that was for sale and he was able to make a down payment on it. That is the farm where Hans and his family lived for many years. Their second child, Hilma, was born on that farm.

Hans accomplished so much in those years as a farmer. He loved working with his livestock and enjoyed "feeding out" beef cattle each year. He would buy yearling cattle called "feeders" that were shipped in from the West each fall. He would grind ear corn by the wagonload. Twice daily he would mix mineral supplements into the feed for the cattle, and carry it in two-bushel baskets to the feed bunks for the waiting beasts. He could watch those white-faced cattle grow sleek and smooth as they lined up by their feed bunks on the concrete floor.

Every October Hans would contact a trucking company from Gladbrook, Iowa, and have his cattle shipped via truck to the Chicago Stockyards. There his cattle were sold at top prices and sent on to New York to be sold again for prime beef.

Hans also kept hogs, both to sell at the market and for butchering at home for the family meals. The manure from all the livestock was spread on the fields, which made the soil very rich and productive. Hans's crops were always good and weed-free. The fence-lines were carefully tended. Wild growth was cut with a two-hand scythe and the perimeter of the fields was kept weed free.

As Hans cut each swath along the edge of the field he checked his fences for repairs needed. The outside field fences always were made with woven wire around the bottom with three strings of barbed wire on top. This style of fence was called "hog tight" since hogs could not penetrate it. Corner posts were firmly braced, set deep and meant to stay forever if needed. Noxious weeds, such as thistles, were carefully destroyed, as were quack-grass patches, which were usually killed with salt. He checked the pastureland for thistles and kept the waterways green with Timothy grass or bluegrass to hold down erosion.

Hans made other improvements. When the two children were still quite young, Hans presented a plan to the Townsend-Merrill Lumber Company in Cedar Falls to have his house enlarged. The enlarged house included a bathroom in the basement, running water in the kitchen, a dumb waiter, a front porch, and additional bedrooms. It even included electricity. During the rebuilding Emma cooked

The renovated home

the meals in the old kitchen that had been pulled away from the house. The old kitchen was later converted to a garage.

Hans had a generator built into the house in order to have electricity available. There were only three farms in the area at that time that had electricity.

On a summer afternoon it was not unusual to see Aunt Anna, Emma's sister, and Uncle Jes Jepsen in their shiny black Model T Ford chugging down the long lane that led the quarter mile from the county road to the farm buildings. Hans would walk with Jes to the feedlot where he enjoyed showing off his livestock. Standing there in the shade, they casually set one foot on the wooden gate, watching the animals lazily while away the afternoon. There the men enjoyed a lengthy discussion about how the cattle were doing, when would they be ready to ship, and what they would bring on the Chicago market.

Meanwhile, Anna went in the house to help with whatever Emma was working on. It could be canning garden produce or helping with mending or other sewing. They enjoyed each other's company while working.

Hans and Emma also had a flock of chickens, but it was considered women's work to take care of them. It was Emma's job to gather the eggs and sell them for next week's groceries when they went to town on Saturdays. She also kept a trio of geese so that there would be goose dinners for Christmas and New Years.

Hans enjoyed keeping up his subscription to the Drover's Journal mailed out of Chicago, and he would also scan the Capper's Weekly. During the noon meal he listened to the radio news, weather and farm market reports and make comments on current problems.

At one time Hans owned a four-door car equipped with winter storm windows. The early cars were not equipped with glass windows. The storm windows were made of wood with a small opening at each door. I do not know how they were installed or how they were held in place. But I do remember seeing the car going by our farm with these unusual fabrications offering protection against cold and rain.

In the evenings, when Hans opened the black wooden case holding his violin, we knew we were in for some good old-time fiddle music. He would tighten the hairs on the bow, flick the strings of the instrument and before long he had the instrument tuned and ready to play.

Hans and his fiddle

He was happy when he played, and a smile of satisfaction danced on his face. His eyes looked far away to other times and memories, but they twinkled merrily. The melodies just seemed to come to him as he played. He didn't need sheet music, he just had a good ear for sound. One after another the old melodies would fill the room with toe-tapping music for the listeners. His favorite piece was "Buffalo Gals." Once in a while Hans would take out a mouth organ and play that a few tunes. However, I think the fiddle was more fun for him.

He played for family gatherings in earlier days. Then people pushed the furniture back to the walls and began dancing while he played his fiddle. Everyone would remark, "Those were the good old days." Then music was fun and everyone had a good time.

Uncle Harry, his brother, had a concertina and that made lively music too. Between the two brothers there was a lot of good music. Harry had two daughters who were good singers and they entertained the crowds as well.

None of these people needed sheet music. If they heard a piece they would play it.

Hans was a staunch Republican. He hated Franklin D. Roosevelt and everything he stood for. Hans could eloquently argue the political point or points whenever the occasion arose.

Probably the things Hans enjoyed most were the annual birthday parties for members of the family. In the summer Hans strung a light out on the lawn where the men could talk, smoke cigars, and laugh and talk about how times were going. The women, who had brought baked goodies for the parties, always stayed in the house. At the appropriate time egg coffee had been brewed on the cook stove, sandwiches made, cakes cut, and cups and trays set out for all to enjoy. Those parties were memorable and fun.

For many years Hans kept horses to help with the work of farming. One June day he was cultivating corn, sitting on the two-row cultivator pulled by the team of horses. Several summertime "popcorn" clouds gathered together, and a bolt of lightning struck the team, killing them instantly. Hans was thrown back about 30 feet from his perch on the cultivator. Other than a ringing in his ears for a day or so he was unhurt. He knew that he was very fortunate. He did keep a careful eye on summer clouds from that time forward.

In the 1940's, shortly after WWII, Hans bought a new Allis-Chalmers round-bale hay-baler. This was a very special event. It was probably the first real new toy Hans had ever owned in his life. And what a difference it made in making the hay on hot summer days.

Hans and his new baler

He was so proud to show off his new piece of machinery. It was the topic of conversation in the territory for many years, in part because the round bale was a radical departure from the traditional and easily-stacked square bale, and partly because he had purchased a _new_ piece of machinery. He was well known for his conservative nature. The machine ran well for many years. Hans knew how to care for his machinery.

Another purchase he made was a tractor-mounted two-row corn-husking machine. Just think. Two rows at one time! This new machine was a real time saver. In earlier times he and Emma with young Harold in the wagon had gone to the field to pick corn by hand. Corn was picked (or "husked") by walking along the cornrow, breaking off each ear, tearing away most of the husk and tossing the golden ear into the nearby wagon. The horses knew to walk slowly along with the family. One time, Harold was in the wrong place and was struck in the face with a thrown ear. It broke his nose and was very painful for a few days. No doctor was called, and the nose was adjusted as best they could. Harold had a slightly crooked nose for the rest of his life.

Hans kept track of dates and expenses with a lead pencil, writing the figures on the wall of the corncrib or barn. Otherwise, the remaining records' keeping was left to Emma to take care of.

Hans preferred to let Emma do the "going to church" thing. He would much rather stay at home on Sunday mornings, making minor repairs, or just enjoying some time to himself.

Life was good to him until Emma had a stroke and died when she was only 65. Then the world seemed to fall apart for him. They loved each other greatly, and had depended upon each other so much. He mourned her loss for the remainder of his life. Together, they had survived both lean and full times. He never really seemed to recover from this time in his life. He continued to live on the farm, but it was difficult by himself. For many years he had a housekeeper who cooked and kept house, and provided conversation, perhaps more than he wanted. He maintained his good health and operated the farm until he was 82 years of age.

He then moved to a house in Dike. There he kept active for a few more years tending his garden and lawn, and those of more than one widow in town. But his eyesight was failing and he was not able to drive a car. It was a bad day when he was told by the examiner that he could no longer renew his license. He lost his zest for living and was often really despondent thinking of times past and what life meant to him now.

Hans at age 91

He lived to be ninety-one and died in January. The winter was bad, the snow was deep, and the roads were often closed because of the weather. The day before his funeral a blizzard with only six inches of snow but with very high winds closed roads with great drifts as deep as ten feet in places along the sheltered roads. The strong wind left eerie snow sculptures in the fields.

Hans was a frugal man, and he never had to go into debt after his farm was sold. He had managed the business of the farm very well, and he had been a good steward of the land, the buildings and all the livestock in his care. He was recognized by all for his honesty and integrity. When he could sit down with a pipe or a cigar and casually review the world around him he was very content.

In the span of his lifetime he saw and experienced many changes in the world. He was born in a log cabin with no amenities save a fire in the fireplace. He lived through two world wars and two major depressions. He farmed using horses and hand operated equipment, yet lived to see the most modern equipment available. He was born in candlelight, yet was one of the first to electrify his farm. He embraced and used the radio, but was fascinated by television. When he watched the first landing on the moon, he just shook his head slowly from side to side in utter amazement at his good fortune to see such amazing advancement of human endeavor. He lived a full life.

Hans was a well respected man in the area, and was known for his integrity and business skills. His ability to entertain along with his wry smile drew many people to him. While he may have been born into this world in poverty, he lived a long and fruitful life leaving a legacy of wealth and stature.

EMMA PETERSEN

Born: July 20, 1887
Married: February 22, 1911
Died: March 25, 1953

Emma Margretha Nielsen was born into a large family, the eleventh of thirteen children of Jens and Johanna Nielsen. Two of the thirteen children, twin boys, were stillborn in 1874. The Nielsen family

Emma in her teens

lived in a small one room log cabin in rural Iowa near Independence. This cabin was only about twelve feet long and ten feet wide. There was a loft in the cabin where many of the children slept. The parents and younger children slept on the ground floor. The main floor of the cabin was also the kitchen, dining room and living room, all based around a large fireplace, which was the cooking area as well as the source of heat in the winter months. Thirteen people in one small area would certainly define the term "cabin fever!"

Sisters Bessie,
Emma & Anna

Emma was well educated for the era. She must have had some schooling as a young girl since she attended Grand View College in Des Moines, Iowa for one or two years in her teenage years.

This family of Danish Lutheran heritage maintained close contact, for that time, with other families of similar heritage. In order to be closer, they moved to a farm near Fredsville, Iowa, where there were several families of like heritage. There were not so many families in this circle, and over the course of time, three of the Nielsen children, Otto, Taylor and Emma, married three children of the Ebbe Petersen family, Alma, Carrie and Hans, who lived in rural Iowa near Cedar Falls.

Little is known about the courtship between Emma, a pretty young lady, and her handsome beau, Hans, but their wedding ceremony was conducted at the bedside of Emma's father. Jens Nielsen was gravely ill at that time, and died six days after the wedding.

Hans and Emma's
wedding portrait

Soon after their marriage, Emma and Hans moved onto a farm to begin their life together. The farm buildings on this farm were not of great quality, and the house was very drafty, especially in the winter time. In the cold of winter, when Emma scrubbed the floors, the water froze on the floor boards as she was still washing the floor. In the evening a teakettle would be left on the cook stove with the water boiling. In the morning it would be frozen solid. One winter morning after a particularly strong blizzard, Emma and Hans awakened with a snowdrift lying across the top quilt of their bed.

After renting two or three different farms, they purchased at auction 80 acres of prime farm land west of Cedar Falls. This farm was much better, both in quality of the buildings and "farmability" of the land. This farm home was nurtured with great care. Every square foot of their land was weeded, trimmed and groomed to perfection.

They were in charge of that piece of land, and it became their kingdom.

Much care was given to preparing the land for crops. This was crucial to making the farm profitable. As much care was given to the home and outbuildings. Repairs were made as needed. All the buildings received a fresh coat of paint on the outside, and a coating of whitewash on the inside. They took great pride in making it all the best they could. During most of 1924 the house was completely renovated. A full basement was dug (a luxury of the time). New shingles were ordered, much lumber from the lumber yard in town soon arrived, and carpenters began the task of completing the new house. An addition for a bedroom and new kitchen was added, and the stairway to the second floor was moved to create more room. The old kitchen was moved and converted to a garage. It was able to house two of the new-fangled automobiles.

Modern conveniences were employed throughout the farm and its buildings. A large cistern was dug next to the house. Rainwater was collected through a series of gutters and downspouts. A hand pump was placed next to a sink in a large room in the basement. Here laundry could be done in the comfort of any weather. The wooden tub and wringer washing machine could be powered with an electric motor. Later, it was replaced with a Maytag wringer washing machine and two galvanized tubs mounted on a metal stand that could be wheeled about with ease.

The new house was wired for electricity, a very advanced thing for the time. A space was made in the basement for a generator and batteries to store the power. Later, connections were made to the power company when the Rural Electric Cooperative built their system past the farm.

Drinking and cooking water came from a well under the tall windmill that was between the house and the barn. It was centrally located so that water could be carried with equal effort to the livestock or the people. The well was only twelve feet deep, and had been dug by hand. The water was cold and sweet any time of the year, as the well was fed from running spring water. A tin cup hung from the pump under the tall windmill, so that anyone could have a drink of the cool refreshing liquid. When the power company was connected to the farm, an electric powered pump was installed that brought water under pressure through pipes to all the buildings that required water.

With the advent of pressurized running water, the kitchen counter top was redone in fresh linoleum and chrome edging, and with a new porcelain sink and chrome plated faucet. An indoor toilet, tub and sink were installed in the basement. The new water heater in the basement allowed both hot and cold running water in the kitchen, and in the new bathtub and laundry sink in the basement.

Emma was indeed a fortunate woman, wife and homemaker. She had all the comforts to be had on the farm. Her house was as good as any in town or on the farm, and the competition was strong.

Emma and Hans enjoyed having company at their home. It was a good opportunity to show the farm with a quiet pride. Many people would gather there to celebrate birthdays, anniversaries, holidays, and the many family milestones of their lives. The arrival of guests was always a time of great anticipation. Any cloud of dust from a vehicle passing by on the gravel road was watched eagerly. When it would slow near the end of the driveway, it was time to go out to greet the arrival. The time needed to drive down the quarter-mile lane gave enough time for Emma to make the last minute check of house and kitchen, and still be there to greet the guests.

Often, Emma's sister Anna and her husband Jes would come driving down the long lane. Anna wore a little black straw hat and a dress. Jes usually wore a black suit with vest and a derby hat. He wore a pocket watch with a chain swaged across the front of his vest. They made a handsome couple. For many years they drove a Model T Ford, and their arrival was accompanied by the unique "chug-chugging" of the automobile. They came to visit often, and there was a curious mixture of dignity, love and pride in their arrival.

The social event of the year was Emma's birthday on July 20. This date usually coincided with the annual oats harvest threshing event. It could happen that the threshers would be at that farm on that date for threshing. No matter, the birthday would be celebrated anyway.

The weather was always hot and often sultry, so everyone knew that it would be a warm event.

Anna would bring a pan with a coffee cake she had baked for the birthday. Hans and Jes spent the afternoon putsying around the yard checking the cattle, fields, fences, etc; Anna and Emma were in the house getting ready for the evening event.

Emma and her sister Bessie each had a dozen serving trays made of pressed board and decorated with flowers. They were very useful for holding food and beverage in a lap. The long rectangular trays were brought out and set on the dining room table. Aunt Bessie would bring her twelve trays with the little red nail polish dot on the underside when they came. Along with the twelve that Emma had that should be enough to take care of all the guests.

The 40ᵗʰ wedding anniversary

Emma had plenty of sandwich material on hand. There would be sliced cheese bought off the Benson creamery truck, dried beef or summer sausage, and egg salad. In those days we could buy sandwich bread. The COLONIAL or KLEENMAID bakeries supplied the grocery stores with long loaves of white bread known as sandwich loaves. Each slice was a perfect square and when cut diagonally it made a triangular sandwich.

Sandwich making began after supper. There were sure to be several people coming, each bringing a cake. It was also time to fill the gray enamel coffee pot with water and get it set on the stove. It would make a good twenty five cups of coffee.

Hans and Jes had a light bulb strung from the front porch out onto the lawn where the men would sit on folding chairs and maybe smoke a cigar.

Early after supper people began arriving. Aunt Carrie and Uncle Taylor came with the girls: Carol, Mildred, Iva, and Harriet. Somehow, Aunt Alma and Agnes drove up too. Uncle Pete and Aunt Yetta arrived as well. Ernest and Esther were sure to come. Then a few neighbors such as my parents and I came.

The trays were stacked at one end of the dining room table. Emma used the cups from her good set of dishes as well as the everyday cups from the kitchen which were all placed on the table. Cakes were cut and plates of sandwiches were set out on the table.

The men gathered out on the lawn while me women sat out on the porch or in the living room. There seemed to be sitting room for everyone.

Meanwhile in the kitchen Emma and Anna had been tending the coffee pot. No matter that it was 80 degrees or more outside, the coffee must be made, so more wood was fed into the cook stove to get the pot boiling. Coffee grounds had been stirred out with raw egg and added to the water in the pot. One spoon of coffee per cup as well as one or two more spoonfuls for the pot. The pot had to be watched as it would easily boil over on the stove.

When all was ready the men came in from the lawn, filled their trays and went back outside to eat their lunch. Then the rest of the guests lined up around the table to fill their trays. More sandwiches were brought in as the supply began to dwindle.

Such was Emma's birthday. After everyone went home there were chairs to be brought in, cups to wash and a general clean up in the kitchen. No royalty ever enjoyed a birthday more man Emma did. She would savor this event for several days afterwards.

AUNT BESSIE

Our Aunt Bessie was one of thirteen children born to a family living near Independence, Iowa. Four of the children died in childbirth,

This family lived in...

but the remaining nine, along with the parents, lived in a log cabin near Quasqueton, Iowa. The cabin was very small with only one room. There was a small loft where the boys of the family slept. Meals

...this log cabin.

were prepared and eaten in the crowded single room, but I am sure they lived mostly outside the cramped structure. Her parents, Jens and Johanna Nielsen were Danish immigrants.

I saw the actual cabin in the 1980's. It was still intact and had become a very small room of a very large barn out on a farm.

Her given name was Lina Kjerstine Nielsen, but was known to all our extended family and many friends as Aunt Bessie. She was the caregiver to the family, whether from instinct or necessity I don't know. For her entire life she concerned herself with other's welfare and good health. She was indeed the family matriarch.

The area nearby had been settled with people who were not of Danish Lutheran heritage. The children were all quite young when the family moved to Grundy County, Iowa in order to be in a Danish community.

Bessie, of her own free will, studied nursing at Iowa City and after three years of intensive study became a Registered Nurse. She was an inspiration for all to see and hear wherever she went. She stood tall and erect, and when she spoke, she spoke with great authority. We knew she was right in what she said or did.

Bessie as an RN

Bessie was selected to be the supervisor of the local hospital in Cedar Falls, Iowa known as Sartori Hospital. At that time the nurses lived in dormitory unit built next to the hospital. It was part of

Bessie's job to look after the student nurses as well as to teach them the art of nursing. She served that position with distinction for more than eighteen years.

It was right after World War I that Bessie was selected to go to Finland to take part in a Nursing Seminar. She sailed across the ocean in a steam ship. When she left Finland she boarded an airplane to see some of the European sights. This in itself was unusual as the planes were not sophisticated at the time. On the way back to the mainland in Europe, somewhere over Holland or Belgium, the plane was forced down in a cow pasture. The plane landed safely, but the several passengers, as well as a quantity of mail, had to travel on by bus and rail. She then got to a sea port and sailed back to the U.S.

Bessie was a very caring person who enjoyed looking after all the nieces and nephews as they came along. One of the tragedies she experienced was when Carl and Anna Nielsen had two very young girls who became terminally ill. The roads were so deep with mud that spring that it was almost impossible for her to get to Carl and Anna's farm house a mile east of Dike. It was not really determined what the girls died of but it was a terribly sad situation.

In the Twenties Bessie drove a 1928 Chevrolet Coupe. At the beginning of World War II Bessie went to California to take up nursing duties. She gave her car to Harold which he drove for several years.

While in California, Bessie met James Boysen, a Danish immigrant, and came back to Fredsville to marry him. They purchased a farm south of Cedar Falls, and operated it for many years. Later they leased the land and lived in an apartment built over the garage there on the farm.

Bessie had an unmarried brother named Willie. He operated a farm of his own, but also was a cattle buyer/dealer. Officially he died in his sleep at age 43, but those who knew him believe he was murdered in a deal gone bad. When he died Bessie and her sisters, Emma and Anna, became the owners of Willie's farm. The farm was eventually sold and the proceeds were divided among the three girls. Some jealousy arose from that situation among the rest of the family. The Great Depression years were on them and other siblings were losing farms one after another because they were not able to meet their farm loans.

Bessie found a soul mate in her husband Jim. He was as adventurous as she. When they retired from the farm in the early 1950's, they were both about 65 years old. They purchased a brand new Dodge

Jim & Bessie

with lots of fins and chrome. They, along with another couple drove from Cedar Falls to Anchorage, Alaska over the AlCan highway. The road was still very rugged, being mostly a gravel covered road. Bridges were shared with the railroad, and difficult to traverse. They wore out two sets of tires on the journey, but had a great time. Their friends did not entirely share this opinion of the trip.

The trip was not entirely as they planned. They planned on camping and cooking their own meals along they way. At one picnic ground they had just set the food on the table when a dog appeared, jumped up on the table and ate most of the food. Bessie and Jim were able to deal with those things easily, but apparently their friends were not. It was just another minor event in life to Bessie and Jim.

Bessie was an independent mind and worked very hard all her life. For her 90th birthday she baked all the cookies, cakes and bars that were served.

Bessie & nephew Harold
at her 90th birthday.

She cared for others to the end. She died peacefully at age 91. She was a great lady who saw much of life, and who traveled much of the world. She never feared a new adventure, and could recall her adventures in photographic detail all of her life. The account of her travels by plane in Europe was recounted in infinite detail when she was 90.

She was a gracious hostess. We never left her table until she knew we had eaten enough, which was usually more than we needed. She was a gracious hostess and was loved by young and old alike. The world is better for her life and poorer for her loss.

ABERDEEN TRIP

It was a beautiful sunny May morning in 1923 when my family, including my mother, father, baby brother Hilmar, and Aunt Johanna left our farm just west of Cedar Falls, Iowa to travel by automobile to Aberdeen, South Dakota. My uncle, Alfred "A. C." Nielsen, was teaching history there at the state college. He and his wife of not quite two years, my Aunt Martha, were expecting their first child in June. Johanna and Martha were my father's sisters.

Dad & friend in the new Mitchell.

Mother and Dad had carefully planned the journey and packed our luggage. It was an ambitious trip of almost 600 miles. We would be traveling by automobile at a time when a trip of this nature was unusual. Traveling with a baby has never been easy, and we would need extra luggage in case we were delayed along the way. Since we could not count on restaurants being available, nor did we wish the added expense of paying for our meals, Mother had packed food for the trip as well.

A Mitchell

Our method of travel was my folks' black Mitchell four-door touring car. It was equipped with chrome headlights mounted on either side of the radiator, a horn just outside the left front door, and a place in the front of the car under the radiator to insert the crank used to start the car. The windshield consisted of two rectangular pieces of glass mounted in a metal frame, and the black cloth retractable top stretched over a folding metal frame was secured to the top of the windshield. Rain curtains of black leather that had openings covered with isinglass were neatly folded and stored under the back leather upholstered seat. The car had high wheels with wooden spokes. There were running boards on each side of the car between the front and rear fenders. Dad securely strapped our luggage to the side of the car along these running boards. The luggage was fully exposed to the weather and road conditions. We stepped up onto the running boards, over the luggage and got into the car. Everything was ready and off we drove leaving the farmyard behind, the wind blowing around us as we drove down the road on this fine early summer's day.

It was a grand adventure. We had no idea of what the roads would be like. There were no interstate highways in those days. There were only a very few roads in the state paved with concrete. Most roads were dirt, but a few were covered with gravel. Some roads were non-existent, and then we would drive on the grass of the fields.

Highway maps were unavailable, so the path of our journey would be marked with red balls painted on telephone poles or even trees. Dad had a good knowledge of where all the towns were that we needed to drive through along the way. He would watch for the red ball markings to guide us on our way.

Muddy roads

As our car pulled out of the driveway, we turned north onto the dirt road that ran past our farm. After about three miles, we turned westward onto a brand new road paved with concrete. It was one of the first concrete highways in the state, and was considered an experiment. The pavement ended after only ten miles, and we then were driving on dirt roads once again. Dirt roads are very dusty when the weather is dry and very muddy when wet. Deep ruts made in the mud when the weather was rainy dried into the roads when the sun baked them dry and hard. They became hazards to be avoided. The ruts were made by buggies, farm wagons and the occasional automobile or truck, each of a different size. These ruts were deep, many and often difficult to avoid.

The plan was for the journey to be made in two stages. We would drive the first day as far as Centerville, a small town in the far south-eastern corner of South Dakota, a grand distance of over 250 miles. There we would stay with Pete and Clara Andersen, friends of the family from Grand View College. The next day we would then drive the rest of the way to Aberdeen, an additional 300 miles.

We followed the "Red Ball Highway" and all was going well as we rumbled and jostled our way along the questionable dirt roads. On occasion we would stop for gasoline in towns along the way. The gasoline was pumped by hand from the storage tank into a glass

Early convenience

cylinder atop a tall metal stand. The gallons were marked on the side of the glass. When the proper amount had been pumped into the cylinder, it was fed through a hose into the gas tank of the car. It was all very new to me. Watching the flow of the gasoline into and then out of the cylinder was very fascinating.

We knew the names of some of the towns along our way. There were no signs telling us how far it was to the next town, nor how many miles left to travel. These early roads often followed railroad lines established only a few years before. It was not until we were in a town that we knew for sure where we were. The towns were identified only by the sign on the railroad depot.

Somewhere along the way we stopped off the road, and found shade under a nearby tree. There we ate the sandwiches and other food mother had packed for the journey.

Mother made good use of the supporting mechanism of the convertible top of the car. From time to time wet cloth diapers were hung over the support rods to dry in the warm wind of the summer's day. I don't think they were ever designed for that particular useful purpose, but it worked well.

The day was warm, sunny and breezy as we drove down the road. Mile after mile and small town after village disappeared in the ever billowing cloud of dust left behind our speeding Mitchell. When the road was relatively smooth, we could go as fast as 25 to 30 miles per hour!

Not long after noon, clouds began to form on the horizon. They grew and became dark, quickly blocking the sun. Lightning flashed ahead of us and soon thunder rolled over us. Puffs of wind brought the sweet aroma of wet prairie grass and clover, harbingers of the coming summer storm.

Dad stopped long enough to get out the side curtains, as they were known, and he snapped them into place along each side of the automobile. Soon large patters of rain began to fall making little puffs in the dust of the road. Then more and more rain showered down all around us. The surface of the road became slippery, making steering difficult. The wheels of our Mitchell automobile alternately fell into and climbed out of the ruts formed in the last rainy spell. It was not long until the tires were carving their own ruts in the freshly moistened road. We drove on, but the heavy rain turned the dirt of the road to thick mud, and the muddy rutted roads slowed us down. The difficult roads had taken their toll, however, and the rear axle of the car broke. There we sat waiting for the rain to end.

Fortunately, we were near Hawarden, Iowa, a small town on the Missouri River, and were able to get into the town without further mishap. There Dad was able to find a telephone, and called ahead to his friends the Andersen's to let them know of our dilemma. We were less than 30 miles short of their farm near the Vermillion River in South Dakota.

We stayed overnight in a hotel in Hawarden. This was not in our plan, but it was another new and exciting adventure. I had never stayed in a hotel before. The next morning we went downstairs from our room to have our breakfast in the hotel dining room. There we had large slices of ham, eggs, bread and coffee. I had never seen such large white heavy dishes and large thick coffee mugs. I was very impressed with all of this.

After breakfast we continued on our way on the second day of our journey. The Andersen's came to Hawarden to help us get the disabled car, and all of us, to their farm. Somehow, and I've forgotten just how, we got to the farm where car repairs could be made by my father and Mr. Andersen.

Andersen's farm

Of course, it was necessary to get the parts for the repair before we could continue our journey. The closest place Dad could get a new axle was in Sioux Falls, about 30 miles distant. Peter and Dad drove to Sioux Falls and back. They jacked up the Mitchell, and spent the better part of the week getting the car back into running order again. Meanwhile, Clara was busy cooking for us, and Mother was busy hand washing diapers and helping when and where she could.

We enjoyed Clara's homemade waffles every morning. They were baked in a black cast iron waffle iron set on the cook stove. The iron was set into the top of the stove in place of one of the lids directly over the hot fire. This heated the iron quickly and swiftly cooked the waffle batter. The waffles were light and cooked just right to a toasty brown. We lathered these tasty treats with honey collected from the Andersen's own bee hives. I did not care for the milk from the Andersen's Shorthorn Hereford cows. It was not as rich as the milk from Dad's Guernsey cows.

The Andersen's took us out to the cow pasture to show us where circles of stones lay from the time when the Indians had built their teepees and camped there. The family had found lots of flint arrowheads in the same area. We saw wild elk roaming in the distance.

It was obvious that the farm settlements were new in this area. Even the white farmhouses and red barns looked quite new.

Out on the prairie

After about a week of car repair and good food we were able to continue the trip on to Aberdeen, almost 300 miles more. This part of our journey was uneventful. Only the vast prairie stretched out in front of us with occasional trees to break the horizon. The landmarks were few and far between. I do recall that we traveled through the town of Mitchell, where we saw the corn palace.

We finally arrived at our destination, and we were very glad to see Alfred and Martha. Our cousin, the expected baby Helen, had not yet arrived. The journey had been long, and it was good to rest again.

Relatives in Aberdeen

We discovered that the water in Aberdeen contained alkali and we couldn't drink it. After the sweet, clear well water from our farm, this water tasted terrible to us. Alfred and Martha were used to it, and they kept this water for drinking in a stone jar. It was impossible to use a metal pail or dipper, as the water would eat through the metal.

A short windmill served to pump the water from the ground. We were accustomed to tall windmills built to stand above tall trees and large barns, but here on the prairie with only a few short trees windmills did not have to be very tall. Even the buildings were short. There was little but prairie grass to block the wind. The short tree growth indicated how the prairie wind blew continually.

Later, Alfred and Martha, by then new parents, and baby Helen moved away after living there only a couple of years. We did not make that journey again.

On the way home we drove through the Twin Cities of Minneapolis and St. Paul in Minnesota. As we drove south of Minneapolis, near Hayfield, Minnesota, we saw a crew of men hand-digging the trench for the first pipeline that was to bring oil from Texas to the Twin Cities.

1920's bridge in southern Minnesota

Considering the miles we traveled, the condition of the roads and with no maps to guide our way, it was a long, daring and exciting trip for us to take.

FIRST DAY OF SCHOOL

Writers and authors who have become famous always seem to have some sort of humble beginnings. I do not claim to be a great author, but I do write for pure amusement. I do remember my first encounter with writing.

It was my first day of school. On a warm, sunny September morning I left my house and walked, then skipped and did a few "whirl-arounds" along the dusty dirt road towards the "Country School" located about a half mile from my home. I was five years old, excited and ready to go to school. I was proud of being old enough to go to school. I did this great thing on my own. I did not need my parents to take me. They had other things to do. I was off on this adventure by myself.

My mother had sent me off with my lunch pail, which, by the way, was an empty Karo syrup pail, which is what all of us used in those days to carry our noon lunches. In my other hand I had a brand new "Big Chief" pencil tablet and a pencil. This was exciting. I couldn't wait to get there.

At school Mrs. Johnson met me and assigned me to one of the smaller desks. The desks with black cast iron legs and a slanting wooden top were fastened to the floor. I would not need the ink well yet even though the hole at the right hand top of the desk had a place for the ink bottle.

School began at 9:00 and I was anxious to try my new pencil and writing tablet. I had been told previously that if I needed something I was supposed to hold up one hand and wait for the teacher to recognize me.

It was not long until I needed to know how to spell a word. I held my hand high and waited. Mrs. Johnson saw me and asked in her quiet voice what it was I wanted.

I said, "How do you spell "hafta"?

Mrs. Johnson replied, "There is no such word as "hafta".

"Oh, yes, there is," was my quick reply.

Well, from there on I quickly found out the world was not ready for my vocabulary. I had been speaking Danish for five years at home, and the Danish language has a single word very similar in meaning to the two word phrase "have to".

That was my first mistake.

I then broke the point on my lead pencil, and took it upon myself to walk back to the pencil sharpener attached to the black board at the back of the room. On my return from the pencil sharpener I stubbed my bare toe on the cast iron leg of one of the desks.

"Bingo!" I called out in a loud voice. At least that was better than what Dad would have said in Danish had he stubbed his toe!

That brought about glances from the other children as well as a reprimand from Mrs. Johnson.

That first half day of school set the pattern of how things would continue for the rest of my life. Well, I have had a wonderful life in spite of all the mistakes I have made in my lifetime. Isn't if fun to look back and laugh at the dumb mistakes we have made?

CHRISTMAS AT GREELY -- P. S. NO. 8

My first eight years of schooling were in a rural country school. A few miles west of Cedar Falls, Iowa at a rural crossroads was a one-room school house known as Greeley Public School No. 8. Life and customs of the 1920's were so different compared to the turn of the Millennium. Here is a story of one instance:

There were two exciting events in this rural school each year. The most exciting was the school picnic held in the spring at the end of the term. The second most exciting was the Christmas Program. Yes, in those days we were allowed to call it a "Christmas Program."

It was the custom that each child would participate in the program by speaking a memorized "piece", singing songs and taking a part in a short play. The teacher selected poems, short verses, songs and play parts for each of us. It was our responsibility to memorize these at home. The closer the day came for the program, the more stressed and frightened I became.

The school was prepared for the program. White bed sheets were solicited from the parents' homes. A wire was strung from one side of the room to the other, and the sheets were hung on the wire. Excitement grew when we realized that the room was now divided. Our parents were to be on one side, and we would perform from the other side. It may not have been The Rialto, but it was a real theater to us.

On the day of the program, the parents anxiously arrived and found seating, uncomfortably so in our school desks. We huddled excitedly in a hallway used for a cloakroom for our winter wraps and lunch pails. The hallway was unheated, so we moved about nervously to keep warm as well as to relieve our stress. Our winter wraps were hung on hooks on the wall. The shelf was lined with our lunch pails. Emptied Karo syrup pails were commonly used for lunch pails.

The program opened when two of the big boys pulled the sheets apart to reveal the "stage" of our grand little theater. At our cue, we lined up in formation, short to tall, and marched to the front of the stage. There, as a group, we sang one or two Christmas carols.

The teacher held a sheet of tablet paper with our list of names. As our name was read, we were nudged out onto the stage to say our piece.

Soon it was my turn. My mouth was dry, my face crimson red, and I couldn't find a place for my hands. There I was. All those grownups with dour faces were in front of me. Everyone was staring at me. It was a dark moment in my life.

Hurriedly, I spoke my "piece" and ran back to the hallway. To this day I have no recollection of any of the "pieces" I may have done. Neither do I have a memory of any positive comments about my performance when I got home. I think that told me how well I had done.

My mother, when she was a child, endured similar experiences in her school. She could recite her very first "piece" until she was over one hundred years old. Her first "piece" was:

"Be kind and gentle to those who are old,
For kindness and goodness are better than gold."

But at last, for all of us, the terror was over, and there was a happier moment ahead:

Early in December we had drawn names for the gift exchange. Each child had been given a slip of paper on which to write his or her name. The slips of paper were put into someone's cap, mixed up, and we each drew one slip of paper. There was considerable suspense to see whose name we had drawn. If we were not satisfied with the name we drew, some of us would secretly exchange names with someone else, even though we were not supposed to do so.

We had explicit directions that the gifts to be exchanged should not cost more than 10¢. F. W. Woolworth's made their fortune on 5¢ and 10¢ items. Girls usually received a bottle of perfume or an embroidered handkerchief. Boys would receive trinkets of some sort.

Thankfully, now, the program was over. The saying of my "piece" was behind me. It was time for Santa Clause to appear. Santa Clause was always the oldest boy in the school. He wore a well worn, faded red flannel suit, trimmed with cotton batting pinned to the suit, well padded with pillows. Santa appeared with a gunny sack of carefully wrapped packages. One by one he pulled out a package, read the name, and with wondrous expectation we awaited our turn to hear our name. We enjoyed and appreciated these gifts as though they had been brought by the Magi. I still have one of those gifts that has survived all these years.

We were filled with excitement and relief. It was Christmas and, since the program was over, I would not have to re-live this curious mixture of anxiety and excitement until next year.

To the reader: Æbleskiver is a Danish treat that is best described as a light pancake batter cooked in a special pan to form a round ball. A special cast iron pan with seven half round depressions is heated, a small amount of lard dropped into each depression, and, when the hot fat is smoking, each depression is filled level with the batter. A small piece of apple may be placed on top of the batter. When the æbleskiver is browned on the bottom side, it is quickly turned over to finish cooking on the other side. The delicacies are served warm and may be dipped in sugar or other sweetening, and are eaten using fingers to dip and bite. Æbleskiver translated literally is "apple circle."

ÆBLESKIVER AT CHRISTMASTIME

When my grandparents were living, æbleskiver were considered a special delicacy for Christmas. This is a story about æbleskiver and one Christmas in the 1920's:

It was Christmas Day and we were going to my grandparents' home for dinner. Niels and Christine Hoffman lived in a very small white house just a short way down the hill from Fredsville Church. But before we could go, there was much to do.

Traveling any distance in the middle of winter at that time was a test of preparation, determination and skill. We lived on a farm 2 ½ miles east of my grandparents' house. The road to their house was a dirt road between the adjoining farms. In the summer, the road was dusty in dry weather, muddy and impassible in rainy weather. In the winter, it was frozen into icy hard bumps and ruts and often drifted with snow. If the snow was too deep on the road, we would have to travel across the fields. In the 1920's we could cope with that.

If farmers had cars, they were not used in the winter. Our Mitchell four-door touring car with the flapping side curtains and isinglass windows was set up on four jacks for the duration of winter. There was no antifreeze, and no snowplows to clear the roads at that time. It was easier to travel by horse-drawn bobsled when the roads were frozen and snowy. A bobsled for us was a heavy wagon, but instead of riding on wheels, there were four large sled runners that slid over the snow and frozen ground.

Early in the morning, well before sunrise, Dad had to do chores. While these were routine chores, it was Christmas, and in honor of the season, the animals were treated especially well and given extra rations. A fire was started in the heater in the stock tank of water to thaw the thick crust of ice that had formed overnight. Dried corn cobs made a quick fire that would thaw the water so the livestock could drink. The sweet smell of the smoke from the cobs was pleasant on the crisp, cold air. The herd of cows was milked, the milk and cream separated, and the cows were fed hay and grain. The squealing hogs were given extra feed as well. Mother gave "her" chickens warm grain mash on cold winter days. Lastly, the horses received their grain and hay.

After breakfast, Dad threw a generous layer of clean, yellow straw into the wagon box to help keep us warm on the journey. Some wooden boxes were loaded for us, upon which we could sit. Bob and Prince, the trusty red roan horses, were harnessed for the cold drive. Great blankets were loaded into the bobsled so that we would be warm, and, after our arrival, the horses would be covered and kept warm in the winter cold.

In the house Mother put a soapstone in the oven of the cook stove to warm. The soapstone would be set under our feet during the ride to ease the cold while traveling.

Everyone dressed warmly. Mother wrapped my little brother, who was about two years old, in a large, warm quilt. I, at eight years of age, was bundled in a woolen coat, knitted scarf, knitted cap and knitted mittens and three-buckled black cloth overshoes with my long black cotton stockings neatly tucked inside. A string passing through the sleeves of my coat secured my mittens so that I would not lose either one. A clean handkerchief was pinned to my dress with a safety pin so that it would be convenient and not be lost. Since Dad had to stand and face the wind on the journey, he wore his long black sealskin fur coat, a sealskin cap with flaps that folded down over his ears, and fur mittens that came well above his wrists.

Now that everyone was dressed for the cold, the team hitched to the bobsled, and the family seated in the straw and covered with two or three woolen horse blankets, Dad turned our little procession out onto the road towards Fredsville. Off we went at a steady pace. The horses trotted at a brisk pace to keep warm, snorting as the cold air hit their nostrils, and we bumped along over the frozen ruts and drifts of snow. The vapor from the horses' nostrils, as well as our own breaths, made tiny clouds as we traveled along.

The hooves striking the icy, frozen ground, the jingle of the harness, and the occasional snort of the freezing horses made a rhythmic music as we hurried over the icy road. The runners of the bobsled irregularly squeaked as we slid over the frozen dirt and snow, adding a surreal melody to our little band. Otherwise, there was no other sound, only a strangely dense quiet, as only the intense cold of winter can provide. We passed a few farms. The curling smoke from the chimneys and the smell of wood smoke as we drove by were the only signs of other people nearby. We huddled close together keeping the wind at our backs hoping the ride would soon be over.

Just past the Fredsville corner, Dad pulled the team down the lane, and into the yard at my grandparents' home. We scrambled out of the bobsled and ran into the house to get out of the cold. Grandfather helped Dad unhitch the horses and get them into the small barn and covered with the heavy blankets to be out of the cold. Grandmother, her round face rising above her tightly tied white apron, with her braided hair wound about the top of her head, welcomed us inside. There we could rub our hands over the stove after dispensing with all of our wraps, shaking snow and straw onto the floor.

The Hoffman's house in 2000

What a hearty warm feeling it was to arrive at our grandparents' house! Their house was tiny and white, and had just enough room for a kitchen, living room, parlor, and a bedroom. Attached was a "back hall" where there was a sink, a water pail, and a washing machine. Beside the back hallway was a narrow pantry. There was where my grandmother kept all the goodies she had made for Christmas.

But oh, the smell of cooking when the door opened! I could tell it would be a feast. The potatoes were boiling on top of the cook stove, the goose was roasting in the oven, and the simmering, pungent red cabbage all filled the air with the promise of a Christmas feast. We could hardly wait. It was all too good to be true.

As we gathered about the table to eat, Grandmother tied a large white dishtowel around my neck. After all, I would undoubtedly spill something before I was through. A table prayer was said, in Danish, and the food was served. Beautiful slices of roast goose served with prune stuffing, potatoes with rich brown gravy, the savory red cabbage, pickles, homemade bread and jams made a sumptuous feast. We were cold and hungry, and we ate well.

Dessert was a traditional Danish apple cake served with fresh whipped cream and coffee. I was only eight, but I had been drinking coffee for a long time by then.

The meal was finished, and the men retired to the living room to keep close to the parlor heating stove. Mother and Grandmother washed the dishes. My job was to clear the table, gather the dishes, and mostly stay out of the way.

The kitchen stove radiated such a pleasant warmth, and we were all so cozy after a wonderful meal. The teakettle kept a steady whistle from the cook stove, and in the contented quiet, the clock above the table steadily ticked the minutes away.

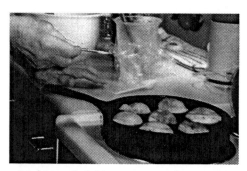

Making æbelskiver on a modern range

But I knew we would have coffee and Christmas baking before we left.

The clock was nearing three – our coffee time. The table was set again. Grandmother brought from the pantry the large blue enamel bowl filled with æbleskiver that had been made the week before. She put a generous amount of æbleskiver into a pan, set them in the oven to warm while she finished setting the rest of the table. There were cookies of many kinds – spritz, klejner, almond cookies and others, and coffee cake, pastries set in profusion on the table.

But the thing I looked forward to most was the æbleskiver.

We drank coffee, ate extravagantly of everything, but the æbleskiver tasted so good. I could never get enough. With my fingers I deftly took them one by one, dipped them in sugar and ate them as fast as I could. It would be a long, long time until next Christmas. I glanced at Grandfather, who was also dipping and eating his sugar coated delicacies. He winked at me and smiled as if the sharing of these delicacies became a conspiracy. Then Grandfather would sit back and wipe the sugar from his dark reddish beard. We knew that it

66

had been a good Christmas. And then we knew it was time for us to get ready to go home.

With our coats and other wrappings warmed, we again dressed for the cold outdoors and the men got the horses hitched to the bobsled. We gathered up our newly knitted scarves and mittens – our Christmas gifts each year. After many "thank you's" and "good bye's", we scrambled back into the bobsled and nestled in the straw under the warm blankets. It would soon be getting dark and there were chores to be done at home. The horses wasted no time on the return trip.

The wind was blowing stronger, now, and small drifts of new snow crossed our path. The runners of the bobsled alternately rumbled on the ice or softly hissed through the freshly drifted snow, leaving deep trails in the drifts to be filled behind us by the blowing wind. The stars were coming out now in a crackling cold clear sky and the full moon was just rising over the eastern horizon. Christmas would not come for another long year.

CHRISTMAS DINNER

Christmas dinner in our home was a large festive meal with roast goose as the focus of the feast. It was a tradition of long standing in our family. However, if we wanted goose for Christmas it meant starting in the late winter to raise the geese for the following Christmas, many months distant. First came hatching the eggs, which took four weeks, and then taking care of the goslings. We couldn't let them get too wet or too cold. If this happened they had to be plopped into a box set next to the cook stove until they were dry and warm enough to be on their own again.

Summer came and went and now the goslings were full-grown. In the meantime we had to put up with the old gander that delighted in tormenting dogs and kids alike. He thought nothing of sneaking up behind to take a little nip in the back of the leg. A nip from his beak on the back of a bare leg was more surprising than painful. But a beating from his powerful wings was painful. Ganders had sharp spurs on their wings, and when so moved could inflict great harm to small children.

By late fall we were all irritated enough at the whole flock that we didn't have any sympathy left for any of them, and the fattest and largest was beheaded, scalded, plucked, singed, and drawn (gutted) for our Christmas dinner. The soft downy feathers from the breast were saved for pillows.

Roast goose or duck stuffed with prunes fills the house with a savory aroma too tempting for anyone's appetite. The dark meat is rich in flavor, and a carefully made dark gravy topped the whipped potatoes with both tempting color and taste. It was delicious. Roast goose is well worth the effort and irritation suffered during the months required to raise the geese.

ROAD GRADERS

The earliest road graders I remember was the one that came by our farm. The roads were black dirt and the ditches were covered with grass, weeds and wild flowers. The dirt roads became deeply rutted in wet weather, and when the sun baked the roads dry again the ruts were dangerous to every vehicle that traveled that way. Therefore, a clerk was appointed in each township and was responsible for road upkeep. Grandfather Petersen was one of the clerks in Cedar Falls Township. It was his job to appoint a farmer in the area to do road grading. Each farmer was assigned a certain number of miles.

An early road grader

The grader consisted of two pairs of iron blades about six inches in width and about four feet long attached with iron chains to levers that controlled the depth and angle of the blades. A man stood on a wooden plank placed on top of the iron frame. He drove a team of horses harnessed to the grader. If the road were very bad it would take three horses to pull the grader. The driver controlled the angle of the blades and watched the side of the road. Sod would creep into the road so that was bladed off to keep the road from getting any narrower. The road was slightly higher in the middle than at the sides so that when it rained the water would run off. When the dirt roads had dried up after a rain the grader came along scraping and filling the ruts left by wagons or early cars.

In the summer men could work off their poll tax by using a slip scraper to bring dirt back up on the road to rebuild its crown making a run-off for the water to drain into the ditch.

After World War I cars were becoming more numerous. Henry Ford was selling Model Ts as fast as he could turn them out. Road improvement was necessary for all the new vehicles.

The road between Cedar Falls and Dike was one of the first to be improved. "Road gangs" set up large tents in areas close enough together that the men could drive the mules and men could easily walk to their job. One work tent was set up in a pasture across from Ed Refshauge's place, and another was set up about three miles away next to the road in the Schmidt's south eighty. Dad took me over there one time. It was like a real campsite. The men slept there, ate meals prepared by the camp cook, and tethered dozens of mules outside the tent. They were coarse men, and I was cautioned never to repeat their language.

Each morning, four mules were harnessed to a grader with an elevator. The scraper brought up dirt to the elevator, which dumped each load on the new road. A bell would ring when the load was full, the mules would stop, and the dirt was dumped. The dirt was scraped from the side of the road and placed onto the roadway. This elevated the surface of the road and created good drainage along each side.

Next came the road grader. This was a heavy machine mounted on steel wheels. It had a steel blade on an adjustable frame that was used to push and smooth the dirt. It was operated by a man standing on a platform at the rear of the machine. He carefully turned wheels

that controlled the angle and elevation of the blade to shape the contour of the road. Horses pulled this implement, initially. Later, the horses were replaced with an early tractor. It must have taken all summer to grade that road. When the grading was completed, it was covered with gravel.

The resulting roadway was much better to drive on in any weather. The elevation drained rainwater and snowmelt away very well, and the crushed limestone gravel surface remained smooth except in extreme wet weather. It took many years to upgrade all the rural roads in our area. Even in the early 1950's roads were still being graded and improved in this fashion.

Grandfather Petersen kept a road grader like this one to grade his long lane. Harold enjoyed running this grader and was saddened when it was sold on a farm sale.

Then there was the big yellow motorized grader where a driver sat high up and maneuvered the wide blades to maintain the then graveled roads. Graveled roads were a big improvement over plain dirt. Cars didn't get stuck as easily on gravel roads when they were muddy. Before gravel, when cars got stuck on dirt roads, some farmer would have to come with a team of horses and pull the car out of the mud.

In 1922 I was up by our windmill near the road with Dad and Anton Jensen. Anton looked over at the nearby newly graveled diagonal road and exclaimed, "They'll never pave that road." The road was one of the earliest highways in Iowa paved with concrete. It has been changed many times over the years. A major renovation occurred when the curbs were cut off, and the roadway widened on both sides. Now, this road has been reduced to a county road, and portions of it abandoned. At the turn of the Millennium, it has been supplanted with a nearby modern four-lane super highway.

All of these changes to the roads involved ever improved road grading machines and equipment. Now fewer men with larger and more powerful machines move massive amounts of earth to create smooth highways with much more gentle turns and hills.

SLIP SCRAPERS

Before there were caterpillar tractors and large earth movers of various designs, earth was moved by hand. Digging by hand, especially with wooden tools, was tedious and slow. Wooden slip scrapers were used to move dirt in this country very early in our history. In 1830, while building the Erie Canal in New York, a man fastened a strip of iron to the front of the scraper. The tool was then more efficient and lasted longer. Later the device was made entirely of iron.

Visualize a sugar scoop now expanded into a wrought iron piece of machinery about three-feet square. On opposing sides are two wooden handles mounted as on a wheelbarrow. The opposite end is shaped as the letter "U", and has a sharp edge. There are bolts and chain to which a horse or mule would be hitched in order to pull the scraper.

The driver held the two wooden handles as he walked behind the device. He could control the angle of the scraper as the horse was commanded to go forward. The scoop was held at a slight downward angle in order to dig into the dirt. The handle was then carefully controlled, as the horse could only pull the scoop when it was cutting a thin layer of dirt. When the scoop was full it was held at a slight upward angle to slide on top of the dirt. Then it was pulled to the area where the soil was to be deposited. The driver quickly lifted up on the handles letting it turn completely over, dumping the load of dirt. Then he pulled the handles back, sliding the scoop over the dirt as he drove the horse back again to scoop up more dirt.

Shallow ditches were cleared along the early roads for better run-off of water. It had been discovered that the roads would dry sooner when there was room for the water to drain away. Dirt was also scooped away from culverts where eroded soil had gathered.

My husband, Harold, as a teenager was sent out to work off poll tax in this manner.

WINDMILLS

Every mid-western farm I knew of in the early 20th century had a windmill on the farm. The tall structure of metal or wood pumped water for all the thirsty needs on the farm place.

Windmills were a big step up from hand-dug wells made by the early homesteaders. As land was opened up for settlement, the first priority was finding a source for water. Digging and setting up wells came in successive steps.

First, a likely location needed to be found. The well had to be convenient to the farm buildings since all the water had to be carried by hand in pails. Most important, however, was to "hit water" when the well was dug. Only after a lot of hard work digging would the farmer know if the well were in the proper location. It was a lot of wasted effort if the well came in dry.

Therefore, a special person was called in to find water. Somewhere in the territory would be a person who had the gift of using a "divining rod." This was a "forked" willow branch. The two branches of the fork were held in both hands and the single branch pointed straight out in front of the person. As the "diviner" walked about, the branch would tremble, or even point down, when there was water below the ground. There is little scientific evidence that this could work, but it did. Most early wells were located by this means.

In those days the well was dug by hand. The well shaft had to be dug large enough around that the person digging could wield a shovel and dig ever deeper. Digging continued until water was found or it was determined that no water was present at that site. If that happened, the dirt was put back into the well, and a different location was selected. The well showed promise when the dirt changed to mud. Then digging was done with care, for when water was "hit", it would sometimes rush into the bottom of the well. Then it was a scramble to get the digger out of the well before he was covered with the water.

The well shaft was then covered with boards. Before pumps were available, these boards were removed as each pail of water was brought up to the surface. Early wells were shallow. A well hand-dug to a depth of thirty feet was a very deep well, and a lot of backbreaking work.

Later on, mechanized methods were used to dig wells. These wells could reach as deep as 150 feet and more. These drillers were able to find water at most locations.

The well on Grandfather Hans Petersen's farm was only twelve feet deep. The men who dug the well were very lucky. They struck a spring at that depth. Clean cold water ran actively at the bottom of the well, and the water level neither rose nor fell for the many years it was used. When the earthquake struck Anchorage, Alaska in 1964, this well immediately quit, the only one that did so in the territory. A deep well was drilled nearby to reach a different aquifer. This water was never as good as the spring water of the original well.

When the hand pump became available, it was set over the well and mounted to the board top. The pipe from the pump was sunk down into the well. To bring the water to the surface the pump was primed with one or two cups of water. The pump handle was urged briskly up and down several times until the fresh water poured from the spout. This was not always sanitary as small animals could get under the boards and drown in the water. Ugh!

Then the windmill came into existence. The windmill harnessed the power of the wind to do the laborious task of pumping water for livestock and humans alike. Ours was a tower made of galvanized angle iron with each of four corners set firmly into the ground. These towers tapered almost to a point at the top, with crosspieces bracing the structure at regular intervals. Near the top a wooden platform was built, wide enough upon which one man could stand. On top where the corners met was a mechanism of gears in a heavy iron casting. A wheel with many blades set at an angle to catch the wind jutted from one side of the casting. A large fan tail stuck out from the opposite side to turn the wheel to the wind. From the casting, a long rod reached down to the pump.

A windmill at rest

The device was controlled from the ground by means of a wooden handle connected to a long heavy gauge wire that reached to the top. This was the "On/Off" switch. When the handle was pulled down, a brake was applied to the wheel and the fantail was turned against the wheel and sideways to the wind. The wheel was unable catch the wind to turn. When the handle was up, the fantail moved perpendicular to the wheel, and the brake was loosened. The wheel was then faced into the wind, and turned freely, thereby operating the gears in the casting. As the wind blew and turned the wheel, the gears moved the long rod attached to the pump up and down to bring the water to the surface.

With this device, large amounts of water could be pumped without someone doing all the work. Large tanks for watering the livestock could be easily filled. When possible, a cistern was built to hold drinking water, and a rudimentary "running water" system could be used. The water was conveyed by an underground pipeline to various buildings.

Windmills in our part of the territory were very tall structures. They had to reach above the surrounding buildings and trees to catch the wind. Towers of forty to fifty feet were common in our area. Out on the flat plains of the Dakotas and Nebraska, the trees and buildings were not as tall nor as close together. There the towers were so short as to almost reach the wheel from the ground.

An early wooden windmill near the barn.

I remember my father building a concrete cistern in the early twenties. The cistern was underneath the windmill, which was located on an elevation of land that was higher than the farm buildings. The cistern then was connected to various locations on the farm by means of underground pipes. Running water was piped to the house and barn, a distance of about 300 yards. He even ran a pipe to a field a half mile away. There he could raise pigs at a refreshing distance from the farm house. When the cistern was full, we had plenty of running water to use. As the flow of water began to slow, someone was sent to the windmill to release the brake, which controlled the wire to the wheel. The mill would then pump water until the cistern was filled. Then someone had to go back to the windmill to turn the device off.

I remember neighbors who built wooden cisterns in their barns. The purpose of that was to keep the water from freezing in the winter. These were not sanitary. Hay and straw, and the occasional small animal, seemed to find its way into the cistern. Also, these wells were usually dug near the barnyard allowing yard contaminants to enter the water system.

Windmills were successful as they could be set at a distance from the farm buildings. The biggest problem was that the windmill wheel needed to be greased occasionally. A man had to climb the metal ladder on the side of the tower, stand on the wooden platform, and then grease the gears. Our neighbors would know when our windmill needed to be greased. A piercing squealing noise could be heard for miles when the gears and bearings were dry.

This task was not the safest thing to do. Standing on that narrow platform so far above ground was precarious. It was necessary to use both hands to open the access panel and apply the grease or effect repairs. There was no secure hand hold there. Men were sometimes knocked off the platform and thrown to the ground if the wind suddenly shifted the wheel around.

On occasion there would be a spell of several days when there was not enough wind to power the windmill or pump the water. If large amounts of water were needed for the livestock, it was necessary to operate the pump by hand. Some farmers had a stationary gasoline powered engine that they would use to operate the pump.

Then in the thirties, during the great rural electrification project, electricity came to the farms. Electric motors were installed to operate the old pumps. Soon thereafter it became economical to install a pump that pressurized the entire water system allowing water to be delivered to any of the farm buildings. This was especially well greeted by the housewife who had carried water by hand for many years.

It was not long until the windmill became obsolete and the tower stood as forgotten monument to the past. Now, almost all of the towers have been dismantled. The silhouette of the tower holding the rapidly spinning fan above the trees and buildings now once more absent from rural view.

THE VILLAGE OF FREDSVILLE

The village of Fredsville was located near the crossing of two country roads a few miles west of Cedar Falls, Iowa. A number of Danish immigrants had settled in this area. Some were merchants, but many were farmers. In this part of Iowa, they found abundantly rich soil and a climate particularly suited to the style of farming of which they were familiar.

The name "Fredsville" translated from the Danish means "Peaceful Village." True to its name, it was nestled in the dale between three of the highest gently rolling hills for miles around. The village was reminiscent of those the Danish immigrants had left behind when they came to America. It never was a "town" as we would imagine with carefully structured streets. Rather it was a loose collection of a few small houses and businesses which were built near the crossing of the two rural roads. The people who lived in them had come here to support the nearby agrarian businesses. True to the custom of "The Old Country," the structures were loosely scattered, some adjacent to their business building, yet close enough that the residents walked

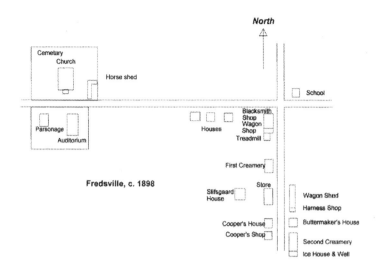

Fredsville, c. 1898

Cemetary
Church
Horse shed
School
Parsonage
Auditorium
Houses
Blacksmith Shop
Wagon Shop
Treadmill
First Creamery
Store
Slifsgaard House
Wagon Shed
Harness Shop
Buttermaker's House
Cooper's House
Second Creamery
Cooper's Shop
Ice House & Well

North

Fredsville in 1898

from house to business, house to church, or house to house. Walking a quarter of a mile to work or to church was just part of life, and had not yet become "an exercise program."

Nearby, on the crest of one of the hills, was a farm that raised many dairy cows. Along with the large barn and farmhouse was another large building. It housed a general store, a post office and had a

The creamery

large room upstairs where dances and other festive occasions could be held. The principal business of the village was the creamery housed in a large building across the road from the barn. Here was located the first mechanical cream separator brought to America. Truels Slifsgaard (Truels was my Grandmother Marie Schmidt's brother)

The general store (from a folded tin type).

and his father Jeppe operated the general store, the farm and the dairy, and, according to the story told to me, were responsible for virtually smuggling the cream separator into the country.

In about 1880, C. G. de Laval of Sweden devised the first success-ful mechanical cream separator, using centrifugal force to separate the cream from the milk. Prior to this invention, cream was sepa-rated from the milk by setting the fresh whole milk aside for at least twenty-four hours. In this time the cream would rise to the top of the container, ready to be skimmed off to make butter from the thick rich liquid. Cream does indeed rise to the top. With the cream removed skimmed milk remained, hence its name. The first separator in America was imported from Denmark by Jeppe Slifsgaard, Truels' father, in 1882. The newness of the machine and the effort to bring it to Fredsville speaks volumes of its importance and the foresight of Jeppe.

As the story was told to me, in order to bring this machine into the United States at that time would have meant paying a substantial duty tax. Being the frugal businessmen they were, they instead completely disassembled a machine, covered the parts with thick grease to protect them against the salt of the sea, packed them into several crates, labeled them as "miscellaneous parts" and had the crates shipped to their creamery. "Parts" were not subject to the duty. This story of the importation of this machine was colorful, but not the only one.

Another account tells of how the machine was held in a New York customs house for two months while officials determined whether it was made of iron or steel. Apparently this was very important, and finally a duty of $93.00 was assessed and the machine traveled on to this tiny village. In either account the bureaucracy was satisfied.

It was a large machine "...set in a frame as large as a common wagon box." It was powered by a steam engine, and would process about 2,000 lbs. of milk per hour. Quite a sizeable production for this village, but farmers from the area brought their whole milk there to be processed. This solved a major problem of refrigerated storage and distribution for the dairy farmer.

A variety of businesses were located in the village. In addition to the creamery and farm, there was the general store and post office, a butter makers shop, a blacksmith shop, a harness shop, a wagon shop, and a cooperage shop where wooden tubs for butter were made. The machinery of the blacksmith shop was powered by a horse on a treadmill. At its zenith, the total population of the village may have been as great as twenty souls, and was listed on the early maps of Iowa. Most of the population worked at the creamery, the general store and post office or the farm.

Through a series of unfortunate events, the main economic focus of the village faded, leaving the houses, the farm and the church to survive on their own. It had been rumored that the railroad would pass through this village as it reached out into the farmland in the late 19th century. Because of the topography of the area, the railroad surveyors chose to route their line elsewhere. In 1900 the Northwestern Railway founded the town of Dike nearby and other towns also competed for the farmers' business. Two blacksmiths opened shops in Dike. It was cheaper to ship empty butter tubs into Dike by rail and haul them to nearby Fredsville than to make them in the village. The building housing the general store and post office burned to the ground in 1908. So, one by one, the businesses of the village passed away into memory.

However, the church survived, and is still the home to a thriving congregation. For a time, the church caretaker lived in one of the village houses. My grandparents, the Hoffman's, lived in another village home when they retired from farming.

One by one over the years the houses were demolished. I recall my husband, Harold, and my brother, Hilmar, joined with other men from the nearby church to demolish one of the houses. It was the house in which the caretakers for the nearby church had lived. No large machinery was used; only hammers, crowbars, sinew and sweat were on this job. When the attic was open to the light, they discovered a few charred rafters and joists near the chimney. Apparently a chimney fire had ignited them at some time, but had snuffed itself out before becoming a major conflagration. My grandparent's small white house, the last of the village, stood alone near the crossroads until it, too, was demolished in 2003, nearly a century after it was built.

Today almost nothing remains of the village. Only fading memories and written stories tell of its existence. But it served a good purpose in its time, and it now lives through the nearby farms and church.

THE FREDSVILLE CHURCH

A white wooden frame church stood on the highest of the three gently rolling hills in this part of Iowa. From this place the land fell away in all directions, and it was possible to see for many miles. The church was surrounded by fields of corn, beans, and other crops typical of the farms in this area. In the summer the hill was bathed in warm sun and cooled by gentle breezes sighing through the tall pine trees. In the winter there was little shelter from the biting northwest wind.

Fredsville's second church

In 1866 conservative farm people, primarily Danish immigrants who needed a place to worship had formed the congregation. The newly formed group purchased the land and erected the first building in 1874 at a cost of $425. A second building was built in 1889. The outside of this church building was built of lap siding painted white. There were three clear glass windows on either side, each window arched to a point at the top. At the rear of the nave was a vestibule with an arched entry door. Above the vestibule rose a tall steeple that held a bell high above the rest of the building.

Church and cemetery c. 1950

In the vestibule, narrow steps curved their way to the upper chamber of the steeple where hung the bell separated from the open air by four large louvered openings in the walls. A trap door closed off this room. Two ropes were let through the floor of the belfry and hung out of the way in the entry. One rope rotated a large wheel at the side of the bell. This would tip the bell back and forth, and allow the clapper to loudly and cheerfully ring the bell. The second rope was attached to the lower end of the clapper. This provided more control, and was used to elicit a more somber tone from the mighty instrument as it was tolled. When rung on a calm summer's day, the bell could be heard five miles away or more.

Over the years, certain rigid customs developed regarding the ringing or tolling of the bell. Before each worship service, the bell pealed merrily until it had rung exactly twenty-seven times, that is, three times nine. After a pause and a change to the other rope, it was tolled nine times, three by three, in a more somber fashion. Only then would the worship begin. When there was a funeral, and as the procession reached the church, the bell was carefully tolled once for each year the deceased person had lived. The reasons for these customs have been lost to time, but woe to the man who miscounted his responsibility! Certain members of the congregation kept careful count each Sunday. Any departure from these customs caused tongues to wag, wondering what had gone wrong. The ringing of the bell was indeed an important task. It just wasn't right to do it wrong!

In good weather, most parishioners gathered outside in front of the church where many lengthy conversations prevailed. When the bell began to ring, we knew it was time to go inside for worship. In the time the bell rang out its call and then tolled its count, the pews were filled and worship would begin.

Inside the nave, the walls were covered with beaded pine boards laid horizontally and darkened with years of varnish. The boards curved to the top of the ceiling leaving the tops of the windows set deep in the walls. Several oak pews with ornate hand carved ends

The interior c. 1900

filled the room. The pews had hymnals to spare. The earliest were printed in Danish and later ones were printed in English. Early hymnals had only the lyrics of the hymns, as everyone knew the correct melody. It was not until the 1930's publication that the music was incorporated into the new hymnal. It was the custom to present a new hymnal to each young person who was confirmed at about age thirteen. These hymnals were brought to church each Sunday, young people and adults alike. Along each side wall were hinged boards that could be raised for additional seating. Milk white glass hexagonal globes trimmed with black outlines hung from chain pendants, and provided light for the congregation.

There were never printed bulletins in the early years that listed the order of service, the hymns, the sermon title, the special music and a myriad of announcements. Any announcements were given orally from the front of the church. The order of service was known by all from long repetition. The name of the day in the church year and the hymns for the day was listed on a special wooden panel in the front of the church where all could see. The name of the Sunday and the hymn numbers were displayed using moveable placards with white numbers and letters printed on a black background. These were slid in the proper order between horizontal wooden cleats on the panel.

In the early days, all the men sat on the right side and women sat on the left. Later families sat together throughout the pews. It became customary for a family to sit in the same location of the nave each Sunday. I recall my father coming home from church one fine Sunday morning muttering about how someone visiting that morning had "sat in his pew!" The muttering continued much of the day, but finally diminished. Some traditions are hard to change.

Above the center aisle, far above our heads, was a model sailing ship suspended by small chains. The ship was complete with all the appropriate rigging, and pointed toward the front of the church. Across its stern was carefully and clearly painted its name, "Hjemad" or "Homeward" in the Old Danish language, a poignant reminder for the immigrants of their homeland both in this world and the next. The ship was particularly meaningful to the recent immigrants either because of their familiarity with the fishing industry of the Old Country, or from the often rigorous crossing of the stormy North Atlantic Ocean. Memories and yearning for home was strong in the early immigrants.

Pr. Nygaard in front of the altar in the 1940's

The large carved oak altar was placed deep in a large arched niche dominating the front of the church. In the early days, the altar was graced with a replica of the famous Torvaldsen sculpture of Christ with arms extended in a welcoming embrace. The figure was sheltered in a smaller wooden niche set on the altar, echoing its larger arched image at the front of the nave. Later, a large cross of polished brass with a miniature figure of Christ occupied the center of the altar.

Also in the front of the nave was the baptismal font. It was a large bowl on top of a pedestal, and was made from a single piece of white marble.

At the rear of the nave was a small balcony from where, in the early years, the occasional very small choir sang and the organist played. It was small, and had barely room for the organ and organist. It was necessary to climb a narrow winding staircase to access the balcony. Not an easy task for the organist in the days of long dresses.

In later years, to make room for a larger choir, a small "loft" for the choir and the foot-powered reed organ was created on the front left side of the nave. This loft was little more than a raised floor with wooden folding chairs for the singers. There was much more room for the musicians, and they could walk up to the loft from the congregation when it was time to sing their anthem.

For many years a reed organ led the congregation in hymns and liturgy, as well as other musical elements during the worship service. My aunt Johanna was organist for several years. It took strength and physical stamina to be the organist. The instrument was powered by pumping two pedals operated by the organist's feet. Musical pieces were not so long in those days, especially on those warm and steamy summer mornings. In the late 1940's, after much discussion and some heated debate in the board meetings, the wheezing instrument was replaced with a brand new Hammond electronic organ with large speakers set into the wall near the pulpit and covered with green grill cloth framed in white wood. It was new, but not in keeping with the rest of the church interior.

Cleric c. 1910

This was a congregation that enjoyed singing. They were the "Happy Danes" of the N. S. F. Grundtvig tradition. They could sing the hymns and liturgy with or without the accompanying organ. When there was no organ accompaniment, someone had to set the pitch and begin the music. For many years, Jes Jepsen would begin the hymns from his place the congregation. He had a strong clear voice, and a good sense of pitch. Reverend C. A. Stub, when he was pastor there, led the hymns with a mighty voice, standing in the front facing the congregation, swaying back and forth in the tempo of the music. None of the congregation fell behind or failed to sing out with such strength of leadership.

On the right side of the nave was the pulpit. It was a raised platform surrounded by hand carved panels of oak. The top of these panels was upholstered with wine-red velvet fringed with gold braid and threads. The velvet was a convenient hand rest for the preacher, and the gold fringe twitched noticeably under the preacher's hand when he made a particularly intense point. The only access to the pulpit was through a narrow arched door from the sacristy immediately behind.

Beneath the church structure was a small cellar for the furnace that provided heat in the cold weather. A large cast iron grate in the floor discharged the heat into the nave. The girls liked to gather over the grate in the cold weather to warm themselves as their skirts billowed in the rising warm air. The furnace was hand-fired, so it was necessary for the custodian to get there very early on Sunday mornings to carry wood or coal in from the shed, light the fire, and be sure, in the cold winter mornings, that the church was warm before worshipers began arriving.

A well-kept cemetery surrounded the church. In earlier years the graves were framed with black wooden frames with a white board edging around the top. Grass that covered the entire cemetery was carefully tended all summer long, and for many years was cut entirely using a push mower. I doubt that whoever was the caretaker was paid nearly enough for all their efforts. Perhaps heaven has a special place for them.

The earliest caretaker I can recall was Jens Rodholm. He and his wife lived in one of the village houses next to my grandparent's house by the corner. I recall that in the hallway of the house was a bench. Underneath the bench a goose kept her nest to hatch her offspring. She came and went in and out of doors freely during the day. This was a common practice in Denmark, and was not out of place in the village. The Rodholm's had a son, Søren. D. Rodhlm, who became a pastor. It was he who conducted the wedding ceremony for Hans and Emma Petersen at the bedside of her dying father.

*The Rodholm's on their
golden anniversary.*

After the Rodholm's, Hans Agaard was caretaker. He was followed by an Andersen family out of Chicago, Illinois. Willie and Anna Christensen served many years there as well. Willie and Anna were well regarded by the members of the young people's group of which I was a part. I recall them making coffee for the young people's meetings at the Auditorium. They boiled the coffee in a large copper boiler in the basement kitchen. These meetings were an important part of our social life, and many romances flourished after the meetings, many of which became long and happy marriages.

Later, Carl "C. M." Nielsen filled the position of caretaker. The caretaker was most often the person who rang the church bell before services and funerals. They were on call at all times. Most of them lived in the same small house on the corner of the village. In 1950, after the new sexton's home was built near the church, it was this old structure that was demolished by hand.

Later, pea gravel was placed around the graves and crunched as people walked the cemetery remembering those there interred. In early times there were many children's graves marked with a lamb made of concrete. Stones of every size and shape marked the graves of those now only remembered. For many years, even in the early part of the 20th century, I remember there were more children's graves than adult graves due primarily to outbreaks of small pox and diphtheria. The very first grave in the cemetery was for Hans Jorgensen, the infant son of my grandparents, Jørgen and Marie Schmidt. He died in 1875 of hemophilia at the age of 16 months. In 1895 a brother, Jorgen Hansen, was buried in the family plot. He, too, at the age of just over two years, died of hemophilia

The cemetery was enclosed in its entirety by a black wrought iron fence. In front of the church was an ornate gate, also made of the wrought iron. I recall even now the unique clinking of the latch as it was opened or closed. Later, the wrought iron was replaced with an ornate woven wire fence. This was painted with a silvery paint. An arched gate replaced the old iron one.

A shed to house all the horses used to bring parishioners to the church was located along the eastern boundary of the cemetery. An "ell" at the northern end provided shelter from the often bitter northwest winds of winter and the sun and rains of summer. Imagine the time and effort it took in those days to go to church. At home, in addition to doing the farm chores, preparing breakfast and getting everyone dressed and ready for church, the buggy or wagon had to be prepared against the cold winter air. Heavy blankets and often "warming stones" were loaded into the buggy. The horses were curried and fed early in the morning and then hitched to the buggy. After the ride to church, often a journey of several miles, the women and children were set off near the entry to the church. The men then drove the horse or team to the shed, where they were unhitched and placed in stalls with blankets covering the animals against the cold winter air. Only then would the men walk to the church for the worship service. Even in fair weather much effort was required to attend worship services. "Going to church" was indeed a lengthy endeavor compared to our modern time.

Ready to go to church.

Across the rural road from the church stood two tall wooden flag poles. For many years two flags flew proudly from each staff every Sunday. The Danish flag honored the country of birth for most of the church members. The Stars and Stripes honored the new country to which they had pledged their fealty. In the early years of the church all worship services and occasions were conducted entirely in the Danish language. Later, as the use of Danish was blended with English, services were held in the English language. In the late 1940's, when the Danish flag waved proudly on the first Sunday of the month, we knew that the service would be in Danish. Memories and customs of The Old Country lived strong in the community.

Also across the road from the church was a building of equal size known to all as "The Auditorium." This structure was built in 1903, and proudly displayed this date in the gable end facing the road. The main floor was a large room with a small stage at one end and an even smaller balcony at the other. Like the church, this room, too, was finished with bead boards laid in horizontally and darkened with aged varnish. Folding wooden doors could close off a separate room under the balcony.

The auditorium

Many wooden folding chairs provided seating for the Sunday School and other gatherings there. These folding chairs were easily folded and moved or stored, but they were precarious contraptions. The legs and back supports were gently curved, presumably for comfort, and the seat easily folded, but this was also their downfall. A person had to seat themselves carefully, and remain still, for any unusual movement would cause the chair to slip out from under the seated person without warning. Then there would be someone unceremoniously dumped on the floor with a neatly folded chair laying flat on the floor nearby. I don't recall a Sunday School time without at least one episode of clatter and commotion as someone fell to the floor. Some of the chairs were grouped together in gangs of four, each seat folding separately. These were no more stable than the others, with the increased opportunity to send four at one time to the floor.

A unique feature of the main room was its gymnastics equipment. It was fitted with ladder-like devices along the two side walls. These were used for displays of physical balance and strength as gymnasts used hands and feet on the bars. There were also moveable pieces such as the "horse", the balance beam and other items used in gymnastic events. Local people would use all this equipment, but on occasion, gymnasts traveling from Grand View College in Des Moines or even from Denmark would come to perform. There was an event! They would do amazing feats of strength and balance.

The full basement was a large room with many steel posts supporting the main floor. All the posts and concrete block walls were white with many layers of whitewash. At one end was a kitchen that was used often for many different occasions, but never better than for the annual church chicken supper.

Behind the auditorium a short distance stood the two obligatory outhouses for many years. In more modern times, two restrooms were devised at one end of the basement opposite the kitchen. The basement always had an odor. It was a curious blend of musty mildew, past kitchen cooking and a heady variety of strong perfumes used to cover body odor and wet wool. The new restrooms in time added to the smell. Strangely, the peculiar pungent combination was not offensive. It was part of the era that came before deodorant, and recalling it brings back fond memories.

Each Sunday, the children gathered in the auditorium for Sunday School. The children gathered all together in the main room to sing many songs and hymns. Then separate classes gathered by age and grade at tables placed apart, both on the main floor and in the basement. It could be noisy then. After a time all classes were recalled to the main room to close the session. Closing the session consisted of the announcement of the children's offering. The offering was always an odd number such as $2.83 as pennies would be misplaced unless tied up in a knotted handkerchief. Then followed other announcements and more singing of hymns.

This building was also the social center for the church and surrounding community. Many wedding receptions, anniversaries and special birthdays were celebrated there. Often the wedding ceremony was held in the church, after which everyone would parade across the road to the auditorium to celebrate the event. There would be food, refreshments, music and dancing until late into the night. All of these items were provided by members of the church. Even the music for the dance was provided by parishioners and their close relatives. There was much talent there.

Other programs as well were held in the auditorium throughout the year. "Dane School" was convened there for many summers

Sunday School children on stage

early in the life of the church. There we learned the language and customs of our immigrant ancestors. Summer bible school brought many children to the auditorium annually. And if the weather turned inclement during the summer church picnic, what better place to gather in shelter from the rain!

The Sunday School Christmas program was always a festive occasion. After the children had performed their "pieces" in the Christmas pageant, the folding chairs were cleared away. A tall pine tree that reached to the high ceiling and mounted in a large, heavy wagon wheel was moved to the center of the room. It had been decorated festively for the Christmas season, including real candles in the early days. When the candles were lit, men would stand nearby with wet rags on long poles, ready to douse the candles as needed. Amazingly, in all those years, there was never a fire in the tree. Surely, with all the woodwork and old varnish, that would have been a tragedy. The most excitement I recall was the time the tree was brought in and erected for the holiday. As the tree warmed in the room, an owl flew out of it, and flew about the large room until it could be coaxed outside through the double doors at the rear of the auditorium.

A 1940's Christmas tree.

When the tree was ready, the children would gather in concentric circles around it. As we sang Christmas carols and hymns, the circles "danced" in opposing directions, reversing for each verse or song. The singing and dancing always concluded with a Danish folk song, "Nu hav i Yul igen" ("Now It Is Christmastime"). The song was repeated faster and faster, louder and louder, until we could move no faster. Then with much anticipation we each received a small brown paper bag filled with hard candy, peanuts in the shell and a large red Delicious apple. What a treat and treasure!

Next door to the Auditorium was the Parsonage. Built in 1889, it was a modest two-story home in which the pastor lived with his family. A small barn was located behind the house, where the parson's horse and buggy was kept.

Pastor & family in front of the parsonage.

Between the two buildings was a large grassy area with an assortment of trees that provided welcome shade in the summer months. Church picnics were held here. The caretaker had much to do as he maintained the grass, flower beds, trees, shrubs and buildings. Other members of the church also assisted in the varying needs of the property.

In so many ways the Fredsville village and especially the church served as the spiritual and social center of the nearby territory. People gathered there for business, for worship and for pleasure. Time was marked by lengthy conversations and joyful fellowship. While wintertime brought chilling winds from the northwest, neighbors gathered inside. In the warm gentle breezes of summer, there was ample time and space to gather outdoors. Truly this was the "Peaceful Village" of its founders, the village of Fredsville.

CHICKEN SUPPERS

As sure as the second Friday of October arrived each year, much like a religious holiday, everyone in the community knew that the Ladies Aid at Fredsville Lutheran Church was ready to serve another chicken supper.

All of the ladies contributed. After all, there was some pride involved! Farm wives "dressed" chickens, baked pies, dug potatoes, pulled carrots and gathered large heads of cabbage for the meal they would serve to the families of the congregation as well as friends from town.

Spring chickens weighing four or five pounds that had been foraging the entire farmyard all summer were the choice for the main course. They had eaten shell-corn and other loose grain, live bugs and crickets in the grass, angleworms and anything else edible. Chickens raised and fed on this diet grew plump and produced meat with real flavor. Two or three chickens from several farmyards were snagged, killed, plucked, singed, and "drawn" (gutted), cut up for frying and chilled in a container of cool well water. That is how the chickens were "dressed."

Some of the women dug pails of new potatoes from their gardens, others pulled bright orange carrots, and some cut large heads of cabbage. These were all carefully washed under fresh water from the pump, where the dirt from the garden was removed. Freshly dug vegetables had a flavor that was full and aromatic. All of the produce was hauled to the Fredsville church and carried to the basement kitchen of the auditorium, a large building for just such occasions across the road from the church.

Pies made from home-rendered lard, rich flour, home churned butter and filled with fresh apple slices grown in the family's orchard were baked at home in the cook stoves. Glass jars of homemade beet pickles and cucumber pickles scooped from the vinegar brine were brought to be served in glass dishes placed within reach of all who sat at the tables.

There were few modern conveniences in this basement kitchen. There was one faucet with cold running water, a few electric lights and the two cook stoves. It was all the ladies needed at the time. Water for washing dishes would be heated on the stove. The entire meal would be prepared on these cook stoves hand fired with wood. It was warm in the kitchen in spite of the cool autumn air outside. Various women filled large kettles with peeled potatoes, scraped carrots, and set the long tables with places for the guests. Others shredded the heads of cabbage and prepared the sauce that would make the coleslaw. Potato peelings and other scraps had to be carried up the steps, out the door and dumped over the nearby fence into the neighbor's field. There these odds and ends would become compost to enrich the already fertile soil.

For many, many years, it was a fact known by all that the same two women, Esther Stage and Hjerte (Mrs. Louie) Olsen, lovers of good food and how to cook it, would of course be selected to 'do the chicken'. It had been their rite for several years. Large iron skillets set on top of the stove with a goodly portion of home churned butter and fresh lard were heated. Each piece of chicken was dipped in flour, browned in the pans, and seasoned with salt and pepper. From there the meat was placed in large baking pans and put in the oven to bake slowly until serving time.

I remember one time in particular when a generous amount of flour had been spilled on the kitchen floor. Without hesitation one of the two cooks grabbed a wet mop and wiped the flour around the floor, leaving more of a sticky mess than a clean floor. They continued their work undaunted by the necessity of walking in the gooey paste.

People from the surrounding rural community and towns knew of the supper. Admission was by tickets purchased earlier or at the door. They gathered at the appointed hour in large groups in the main floor of the Auditorium or outdoors in good weather. While they were waiting before or after the meal, they could view handwork displayed nearby. During the afternoon, the annual bazaar was held where women of the congregation brought handwork that they had embroidered or sewn during the past year and offered it for sale. What was not sold in the afternoon or during the supper would be auctioned off later in the evening. The tickets also served in a lottery for a hand made piecework quilt. The winning ticket would be drawn at the end of the evening. Everyone was anxious to see who the winner would be.

When I was still very small some of the church members prepared a "play" and that was presented on stage after the meal. The plays were very entertaining. I think the entertainment value was not so much in the story line, nor in the acting ability, but rather seeing adults that we knew well act in roles that were far removed from their usual personalities.

At the appointed hour a bell was rung signifying that the food was ready to serve. As many of the hungry families as could be seated at the long tables filed down the stairs into the dining area and sat

Dining in style

down to the most sumptuous meal that was ever set before them. The rest waited their turn, enjoying the aroma of good food and lengthy conversations with friends and neighbors. It was a good time to share news and compare the yield of crops that year.

They were served platters of tender, mouth-watering, fragrant chicken roasted to a golden brown. There were heaping bowls of garden-fresh boiled potatoes, still hot and steaming from the cook stove. The tender hot buttered carrots were sprinkled with freshly chopped parsley. Bowls of hot steaming creamy chicken gravy were set on the tables for people to serve themselves. For dessert a generous slice of pie was set in front of each plate. Several women wearing white aprons poured plenty of hot coffee. The coffee had been boiled in a copper wash boiler in the kitchen, and had to be "just right."

The guests were well fed, and could have all they wanted to eat. Most of these people were farmers and had large appetites. They would not be disappointed. It was a memorable meal, and they would all return next year.

When the first setting was through eating, another line of people was standing outside waiting their turn to be seated and served.

Before the next group came to the table the dirty dishes were carried to the kitchen, hand washed, dried with large white cotton dishtowels made from flour sacks and placed back on the table. All was made ready again and again until all were fed.

When all the ticket holders at a dollar and a quarter apiece had been served, it was time for the kitchen and dining room helpers to sit down and eat their meal. Everyone was sweaty and tired, but well pleased that they had successfully served another fine meal. Already plans were discussed of how it would be done next October. At the next Ladies Aid meeting they would again review how well everything had turned out, and now how they would spend the money they had made. The annual fall bazaar, as it was called at that time, was talked about for several weeks. It would be another whole year before all of this would happen again.

No one forgot the occasion. The church suppers were legendary, and more would attend the next year. There were not so many opportunities for us to gather together like this in those days. It was a time to eat well, make friends and renew friendships. Not only did we feed our bodies, and feed them very well, but we fed our souls equally well, filled to the brim and running over. Warmth and fellowship flowed generously from the kitchen to envelope all who attended.

WHAT DID I DO?

I lived on a farm five miles from any town in northeast Iowa. There were no children nearby with whom I could play. So what did I really do?

As a child, in the summer I liked to watch the ants crawling in the dust by the side of the dirt road. They made neat little trails while carrying things. Sometimes, it might be a dead fly. Or other times it might be ant eggs. They scurried this way and that way always knowing what they should do and where they were going.

Elna & chickens

In the spring and early summer I looked for Meadow Lark nests in the grass along the fence lines. There would always be four spotted eggs. I thought their brown back, white spotted breast and beautiful song was the best one could hear.

In the summer I always went bare-footed, even in the mud. It squished between my toes. Or I walked through the wet green pasture grass to bring the cows home to the barn for milking.

When I went to the country school I carried a tin syrup pail with my noon lunch in it. I sat with the other children out on the grass in good weather eating my sandwich and orange.

I gathered the eggs in the chicken house and put them into a bucket. Sometimes, there would still be a hen on the nest and I would have to reach under her warm breast feathers to look for eggs. If she didn't want me to do that she would give me a quick peck on my hand as if to say, "You can't have my eggs, so there!"

When Dad was through milking and the milk was flowing out of the separator, I would catch the warm skimmed milk in a cup and drink it right there in the barn. It tasted so good.

If I thought there might be baby kittens, I climbed into the horse mangers and looked under the feed boxes. Sometimes I would find five or six tiny gray and white baby kittens with their eyes still closed and their little pink mouth open crying for milk from their mother. Or I would climb up into the hay mow looking for more tiny kittens.

Mother cats didn't like it when we found their babies and they would then hide them somewhere else.

The cows thought it was fun to bunt their heads at me if I walked down the aisle in front of them where they were stanchioned. One time a cow kicked me in the mouth because I got too close to her hind legs as I walked behind her. That hurt! Some lessons were learned the hard way.

When the duck and goose eggs hatched it was fun to hold their fuzzy little bodies. They were so warm and soft to hold. The mother goose was very unhappy about me doing that, and sometimes the gander or father would run after me. It hurt if they nipped my bare legs.

When I was nine years old, and therefore considered old enough, I drove the team of horses hitched to the hay wagon as the hired man pitched the loose hay around on the hayrack. There was a wooden ladder on the front of the hay wagon so, when the load was getting deeper, I had to crawl up the ladder one step at a time as the wagon filled, in order to still handle the horses. Fortunately, they were very gentle and did not mind my driving.

It wasn't much fun going into the hog house. It was always so smelly and there were thousands of flies. It wasn't safe to get too close to the hogs. They could be mean to small children.

I remember Dad's horses in the horse barn. I could go in behind the horses and take a hold of one of the horses' legs and the horse wouldn't hurt me.

I had a pony by the name of "Babe." I rode Babe to my grandparents who lived in Fredsville, which was located a little over two miles from our house. Or I would ride it to Dane school, which I attended for six weeks every summer. Babe had to be tethered along the fence and wait until school was out in the afternoon.

Babe could be very tricky. If I didn't get her bridle on before I took off the halter, she would shake her head and get away from me. Then she ran back home as fast as she could go and I would have to walk home after school.

Elna astride Babe

I went to Dane school every summer for six weeks. There we had singing, reading writing, geography, story time, gymnastics, and singing folk dance games, all in Danish of course. When we finished our studies we did embroidery work, which was displayed on the Sunday after the school had finished.

I played with my coaster wagon a lot in the summer. I put my right knee inside the wooden box, held the handle with my hands, and pushed myself with my left foot along my make-believe roads made in the black soft dirt. I must have journeyed to the far corners of the world in that wagon, at least in my mind, but not far in the farmyard.

When my mother and father went fishing on Sunday afternoons it was fun to dig for clams in the warm sand on the river's edge. We would open the clams looking for pearls. We never did find a perfect pearl.

Sometimes we would go swimming in the Cedar River. I had a black swimsuit trimmed with white edging that I wore. After a rain, the river would be high and we had to be careful in the deep water.

My best friend was my Dalmatian dog that had been shipped from Chicago. His name was Rover. We played together all the time.

Elna and Rover

One day the gander chased Rover out into the road in front of the car that the mailman was driving. Rover was killed. I cried all the rest of that day.

When the oats harvest was done, and when the threshers had left for the day I walked around the straw stack pulling out lengths of twine. I made large balls of twine from those short strings.

In the fall Dad would use a potato plow to bring up the potatoes from the ground. I followed behind gathering new potatoes into a pail and dumped them into a wagon.

It was fun to watch all kinds of holes in the field or along the dirt road. I was always wondering if striped squirrels, snakes, or bugs would come out of those holes. Sometimes a big bull snake would slither back into his hole. Or maybe it would be a common garter snake. Black beetles made very small holes.

The Fourth of July was fun because the hired men would buy packages of half-inch long firecrackers for me. I would spend the day lighting and throwing those 'crackers. Sometimes I bent the firecracker in half. Then I would light the powder and watch it blow sparks and smoke.

Sometimes when my mother baked rye bread she would give me a small piece of dough and I would make a tiny loaf about three inches long. I laid my loaf on top of the cook stove towards the back where it was not so hot and bake it there on top of the stove.

Occasionally, my father would meet the train in town and bring home a visiting pastor to stay at our house over night. One of the pastors wore a skullcap. I wondered what his head would look like without his skullcap. I would stand outside his bedroom door to see if I could see his bald head after he took the cap off at night. Somehow, I never did get to see his bare head.

In the winter I played with my sled. With warm clothes on I would go outside, grab my sled, and after running a little ways I flopped down on the sled and,, steering with both hands, I tried to outdistance myself each time I went down that little hill.

I liked to go to town with my mother and father. When the groceries were bought the grocer often gave me a tiny brown paper bag of candy. This was a much appreciated and rare treasure.

Then we would go to the candy kitchen run by two Greeks. Their display of chocolates and other candies was the most wonderful sight to see. Sometimes we got strawberry ice cream sundaes that we ate while sifting on ice cream chairs by an ice cream table. Each little bite with that small ice cream spoon was so good.

At my grandfather's house in town it was sensational to pull the chain extending from the oak box above the toilet stool in the bathroom.

Mother bought fabric to sew a new cotton dress for me. When she was ready to hem it, I had to stand on a chair or table so she could measure the length. My legs itched and tickled awfully while I stood still for that. By the end of the season I would have grown another two inches and the dress was then too small for me.

Many Sunday afternoons I sat in my grandparent's parlor floor looking at pictures through the stereoscope photo holder. It amazed me how the pictures seemed to come alive.

When my father brought home a huge square of ice bought at the ice house in town, I watched and helped as he made home-made ice cream. I could hardly wait until it finally was ready to taste and enjoy.

When visitors were entertained in the front parlor at home I sat on furniture stuffed with horse hair, which scratched the back of my bare legs.

In the winter fresh snow was heated in a copper boiler on the cook stove to heat soft water to wash our hair. My hair was straw colored and shone after washing using the snow melt.

Through all these childhood pleasures I got stubbed toes, scratched knees, growing pains, sunburned, teased and brought to tears. But I was so fortunate to have experienced these good things. They are all a gift of love.

With all there is to do these days, my life then seemed simple. But I got to see some of the details of life, and to appreciate some of the smaller things that surrounded me each day.

ELNA AND THE BOOGIE MAN

As a very young child I had an on going relationship with the boogie man who resided in the dark of the closet under the stairway.

My home was a large three story white farm house. The full sized attic was not finished off. Rough boards covered the floor and we could see the rafters and the underside of the roof. Attic windows looked out in all directions.

The second farmhouse

At the front entry of the house there was a large front hall with an open stairway to the five bedrooms on the second floor. Just inside the front door were four steps up to the first landing, then a right angle turn to the next five or six steps up, and from that "landing" were five more steps up to the bedrooms and long hallway.

In the front hall there was a closet under the stairway with a door. When the door closed it was dark as pitch inside. And that is where the boogie man lived.

The front was part of the first farmhouse

I spent many anxious hours in that closet with the door closed after committing some indiscretion or another. It was intended that I would meditate on my behavior and that when I was allowed to leave the closet I would have repented of all my sins and that thereafter I would behave as a growing young child should. However, it would not be many days before I renewed my time with the boogie man.

Inquisitive as I was I had inventoried the contents of the closet by day with the door open. There were several old items kept in that closet. All were from days long past. On a hook on the wall hung a long smoking pipe my grandfather had used while living on the farm.. Another item was my father's old brown leather jacket which he wore when riding his motor cycle. With that was a brown leather helmet much like to first aviators wore. It was also where my father kept his photography equipment. He had done extensive photography while attending Grand View College. Other items were two white heavily starched bibs which the men could put on over their work shirt to make theme appear presentable when sitting at the dining table. These bibs buttoned at the back of the neck. But what I found in there was so much fun. It was Dad's horn which had been attached to the handle bar of his motorcycle. It was chrome plated and had two separate tones. The rubber ball attached that had to be squeezed to make it sound had long ago disappeared. But I loved to blow on that horn. My, oh, my I could cause an awful lot of disturbance by blowing on that horn.

I contemplated many things as I spent my time in that dark, dark room. Truthfully, I probably spent most of the time crying. When I emerged red eyed I was sent out doors where I could work off my feelings. I would go to my ever friend, Rover, my dog. Rover and I had many things to discuss. He was such a good listener.

To further antagonize my parents I had a wooden coaster wagon. I pushed the wagon with my right knee inside the box and pushed the wagon along with my bare left foot making tracks in the dusty barn yard or lane. Having spent much of time out doors I had seen the men greasing the wagon wheels. They removed each wagon wheel one at a time, dipped a wooden paddle into a bucket of axle grease and then spread it on the axle.

So I thought I would try that with my coaster wagon. I removed one wheel of my coaster wagon with the intentions of greasing the axle. However, when the wheel came off all the ball bearings spilled out on the ground. I don't remember if the wagon was usable or not after that. I probably became reacquainted with the boogie man in the closet one more time!

Isn't it a wonder I ever grew up?

DANE SCHOOL

As part of the effort to retain the language and customs of the Danish people I attended a folk school we called Dane School from the age of six through twelve. Each summer a teacher was sent from Grand View College and classes were held during six straight weeks in the Fredsville Auditorium across from the church.

Each morning Mother packed a bag lunch for me and I walked alone a little over two miles each way to and from school. It took about forty-five minutes to walk the distance to or from Fredsville.

Classes lasted from nine in the morning until four in the afternoon five days a week. We studied music, reading, writing, grammar, geography of Denmark, and gymnastic classes.

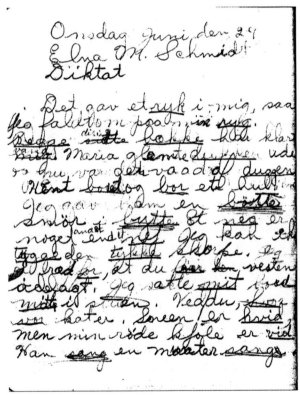

My early Danish writing

When classes began we started the day by singing. We sang lengthy songs of mythical Norse heroes. One was twenty-four verses long. We also sang children's songs, and one we especially liked to sing was how the Danes drove the Germans out of Denmark. We really sang that one at the top of our lungs. The Danes never did have much time for the Germans.

After music class we studied dictation. The teacher would read sentences to us in Danish, and we wrote them in our little blue note books. Then we had a spelling lesson. When we had morning recess we played on the lawn between the parsonage and the auditorium. During many of the recesses we did folk dances and sang the songs to accompany them. After recess we did oral reading. At noon we sat on the grass outside in fair weather and ate our lunches.

One of the requirements for the six weeks of Dane school was to sew a piece of embroidery. Whenever we finished our reading assignments, we would all bring out our sewing kit and work on our needlework. These items would be on exhibit on the Sunday following the six weeks of classes. Boys as well as girls were required to embroider.

After that class we stacked our songbooks, readers, notebooks, pencils, and sewing in a neat stack on the long tables in front of where we were seated. Then it was time for gym class.

The large room in front of the stage was fitted out with all sorts of gymnastics equipment, including the leather horse, the raised walking bar (balance beam), and at least six wooden racks attached to the walls used for various exercises. The racks had wooden bars at regular intervals so we could do hand holds or climb the rack with our feet. Then there were gym mats where we did tumbling exercises. We were all required to participate on each of the pieces of equipment. I never was much good on the horse.

Here we learned many Danish folk dances. We did not have anyone to play music for the dances, so we sang the songs as we danced. It was a common practice.

At the end of the day we gathered in our classroom and sang an evening song before we went home.

On the final Sunday of the term there was a church picnic. Each of us who had attended school dressed up in Danish costume and did several folk dances out on the lawn for the parents and friends. Our embroidery was exhibited on a table in the auditorium.

Elna in folk costume

I think this was a special time in my life that I can never forget. I wish I had retained more of the language.

My grandparents, the Hoffman's, lived down the hill from the church, and I stopped in there every afternoon on my way home for coffee and snacks. During raspberry season I would get a dish of fresh berries with sugar and cream for a snack. Sometimes I would have a glass of "saft", the Danish for juice. It was very refreshing.

After one or two years of walking the almost three miles to and from Dane School, I acquired a black pony named "Babe". I rode her back and forth to Fredsville every day. Finally, I grew so tall that I could touch my feet together around her belly. Babe was a tricky pony and had a mischievous nature. There were times when I didn't get the halter on her before I took the bridle off. Then Babe would run all the way back home, and I had to walk all the way home that afternoon.

There were three or four big boys in the school who were really mischievous. If memory serves, their last names were Nelsen, Andersen, Mikkelsen and Danielsen. One day they untied my pony and took her inside the parsonage. I don't recall if there were any punishments for their mischievous deed, but they are a part of a collection of colorful memories of Dane School. These boys were mostly good kids, but very full of life. They farmed successfully for many years as adults. There were a few quiet stories of further adventures by these miscreants even as adults "who should know better," but these were stories of people who lived a very full life.

The Hoffman house (2000) on my way home.

Dane School did keep the language and customs brought over from Denmark alive into our generation, the second in this the New World. However, with each passing generation, more of the old traditions and customs are lost to time. My ancestors who immigrated to this country strove to keep the memories of "home" fresh and alive. There were many conversations about the family left behind in "The Old Country." As much as my elders remembered a frozen moment in time, even the old country moved on. The language we learned in Dane School is no longer spoken in Denmark. Most of the holiday customs have also disappeared. While life has evolved, I treasure the memories and customs we learned in this traditional folk school. It occupied my youth and brought many happy times to all of us. Like all of us, it is difficult for me to accept the changes life brings. But I can savor the memories of Dane school.

COUNTRY SCHOOL
ERA: 1920-1930

I attended a country school at the crossing of two county roads not far west of Cedar Falls, Iowa. We knew the school as Greeley No. 8. It was a plain rectangular wooden building built of white pine lumber. In the late 1800's white pine lumber was readily available and inexpensive.

One of the Iowa governors who was in office in the 1800's decreed that there should be a school built throughout Iowa every two miles so that every child should be entitled to a free education. This was a monumental legacy to leave for the Iowa children. Greeley was just one such school, one of many, but a sample of all.

It was about a half mile from our farm, so I walked to and from school every day. I walked barefoot along the dusty road for as long as the weather would permit. It became a badge of honor to see who could go the longest into the cold months and still be barefoot.

The first Greeley school

The school yard was a patch of original prairie land. It would be covered with wild prairie flowers each spring and thick prairie grass grew tall each summer. Many kinds of wild flowers grew there including violets, shooting stars, sweet Williams, wild roses and many others. On the fence line were wild plum thickets, a mulberry tree that gave its sweet fruit and wild grapevines. Even when fully ripe both the plums and the grapes were extremely sour. There was a small grove of trees at one side of the yard which were good for playing hide and seek at recess time. These trees also served as a windbreak in the winter months. While we were sheltered in part from a strong wind, it also allowed snow to accumulate into deep drifts on the downwind side of the grove, just near the outhouses!

During the summer months the grass in the yard would grow wild. After all no one was using the school so no effort was made to have carefully groomed grass. Just before school started one of the school board members would hitch his team of horses to a hay mower and mow the school yard grass. This left a sharp, two-inch long thick stubble that hurt the bare feet at first. After playing games on the yard for a time the stubble would be worn down so that it was no longer a problem.

The Greeley schoolhouse was built thirty feet long and twenty-four feet wide. There were three small paned windows on either long side. The outside of the building was covered with lap siding and the roof had wooden shingles. There was no insulation in the walls. The building was set on a flat lime stone rock foundation with enough space underneath for small animals to live underneath. In the winter the floor was very cold, and rabbits and skunks gathered under the building for shelter. We tried not to disturb the skunks as their odor would make life unbearable in the schoolroom. Too often we did not succeed. Then it was very difficult to draw a breath in the school.

Inside the ten foot high ceiling and walls were lined with ten inch wide boards painted gray. Three of the walls were lined with blackboards made of 18 inch wide boards nailed one above the other and painted black. A chalk tray was built along the bottom board. We did a lot of our arithmetic at those boards.

Two kerosene lamps with wide circular copper shades that attempted to reflect the dim light downward were suspended from the ceiling, each by a long rod. They were up so high that it was nearly impossible to light the lamps. They were intended to be used on dark days but I never saw them lighted. To light the lamps someone would have to stand on the teacher's desk in order to lift the chimney and light the wick with a match. Cloudy days came and went and the teacher did not feel compelled to light the lamps

Two doors at the front of the building opened into two small hallways where coats, boots and other outer wear were hung on hooks with lunch pails set on the floor underneath.

A coal burning heating stove stood in the center of the room. Each morning during cold weather the stove had to be lighted in time to have heat in the room before the children came. Some children walked two miles in all kinds of weather to attend classes. In the cold of winter the hot stove was welcome relief. Often arriving children gathered near the heater to warm themselves in the radiated warmth.

High above the blackboards were large pictures of Washington, Lincoln, and more current presidents. Between the two doors to the hallway was a rack of world maps.

There was a large desk in the front of the room where the teacher sat. Children sat in rows of desks facing the front of the room. These desks were bolted to the floor. They were made of an ornate cast iron frame with a wooden seat in front and a wooden desk top in back. The seat of one unit was arranged to use the desk of the next one in front. They ranged in size from small to large. Bigger children sat in the back rows.

In one corner of the room was a wash stand with a water pail and tin pitcher. Attached to that was a shelf to hold a wash basin where children washed their hands for lunch. There was no well at the school so only one pail of water carried from a nearby farm had to suffice for the day. Our water for drinking and washing was carried to the schoolhouse by two of the biggest boys in school. To get the water they walked about a quarter mile to the neighbor's farm and filled the large steel pail from the wooden tank housed inside the cow and horse barn. I do not even want to imagine what might get into the water tank. From there the boys carried it back to school uncovered and set the water pail on a shelf built in the corner of the room. The tin dipper was placed back in the pail and we, in the beginning years, all drank the water from the same dipper.

Then came the time when we could each have our own drinking cup, which we kept on a shelf above the pail. One of the big boys in school had a tin retractable cup which all of us envied. If I forgot to bring a clean cup from home I would tear a sheet of paper from my tablet and from it fold a paper drinking cup being sure to drink the water before the paper collapsed.

At noon the teacher dipped some water into a washbasin and we washed our hands for lunch, all in the same water. We were to each bring our own towels from home.

There were two small buildings not too far from the school. One was for the winter's supply of coal and the other was known as a cob shed. If one of the farmers had corn cobs to spare he could bring a wagon load of cobs to use for kindling to start fires in the heating stove.

Toilet facilities were two outhouses behind the building, both two-holers. On cold winter days, when a trip was required, we bundled up and walked to the outdoor toilet, the cold wind whistling up behind us while sitting on the seat. We used old Sears & Roebuck or Montgomery Wards catalogs for toilet paper. We were required to use hand signals to receive permission to go to the toilet. For some reason, and I can't explain why, the teacher needed to know the purpose of going. As we sat at our desks and nature was calling we held up one hand with one or two fingers up. One, if we needed to urinate and two for you know what. If we waved our arm it meant we were getting very serious about going. The teacher nodded at us to signify we had the privilege of leaving the room. These were the only toilet facilities, but then we were all used to them. Almost none of us knew the convenience of indoor toilets. I do recall they were cold and usually drafty in the winter time.

There was a recitation bench built of one straight board set on two braced legs. Each class was called to the front to recite their lesson.

The children sat on the bench to recite their lessons. As a young child I was sitting on one end of the bench when suddenly a warm stream of yellow urine was coming towards me. Someone had not asked to go to the toilet before class.

The school was heated with a round stove set in the center of the schoolroom. In cold weather, the teacher started the fire each morning and kept it burning all day by adding more coal carried in from the coal shed outside the building. If we were too warm we opened a window.

The teacher was also responsible for keeping the inside of the building clean and neat. She, or he, made sure the floor was swept, washed the blackboards each day, and made sure the room was generally neat. With luck she would work these tasks into the teaching assignments so that the children helped as they learned.

That was about as simple as it could be. I walked barefooted to school in warm weather and bundled up in a wool coat, woolen cap and scarf, mittens and three-buckle black cloth overshoes in the cold of winter.

We carried our noon lunches in one-gallon pails that had contained Karo syrup. These lunch pails stood in one of the two entry halls. Lunch might be a fried egg on bread, an orange, and a piece of fruit. Much to our envy, one of the boys had a real dinner pail with a removable top in which he could have milk or cocoa. He could set that piece on top of the heating stove to warm it up. He was also the kid who had a slice of pie nearly every day in his lunch. We were envious.

Our library was comprised of less than a dozen books. One book was "Pride and Prejudice", and another was called "Billy Goat Whiskers," which the teacher read time and time again. We also had a Webster's Unabridged Dictionary, which was six or seven inches thick. There were some songbooks. We did sing several national songs that we don't hear in the schools today: "Columbia the Gem of the Ocean", "America", "John Brown's Body Lies a Smoldering in the Grave", "Dixie", and so on.

When I was in fourth grade we had a teacher who was rather strict, but we learned much from her. She cleared out a small store room and introduced DOMESTIC SCIENCE. She had installed a three-burner kerosene stove on which we cooked food once each week. We all brought an item of food to contribute to the cooking class. From this food we cooked soup of all kinds and other simple dishes.

The boys had a work bench with a vise called a manual training table where they learned woodworking. It was there I also learned to use a coping saw. I still have an item of woodworking that my husband made when he was in country school.

Our teacher was good at teaching arithmetic. We learned how to measure farm fields. We learned to calculate how much fence would be required to fence in a field. We also learned how to measure rooms for wall paper. That was in the old WENTWORTH textbook. She taught us practical things. She was a whiz at math and was called upon to solve math problems that other teachers in nearby schools could not.

I enjoyed school, but had problems from time to time as many others have had. I remember a spelling test where the teacher would read a word and we were required to write it in our tablet. She read the word "colonel" and being the good farm girl I wrote "kernel." I was reprimanded for my lapse of knowledge.

The Christmas program was one major event of the school year with the program for the parents and a gift exchange. The other highlight was a school picnic at the end of the school year. All the families would attend, and there would be another program where each of us students would recite a "piece" or display our knowledge in some other way. But the real highlight was the ice cream—real store-bought ice cream. It would be packed in dry ice to keep it frozen in the warm weather. We rarely had ice cream, so this was a very special treat.

In our country school we had a lot of fun at recess time with all ages of children going outside to play games. "Annie, Annie Over" was easy as we had to throw a ball over the roof of the school. When the team on the other side got the ball they would come around the ends of the building and try to catch one or more of the kids. "Pump, Pump Pullaway" was another team game we played.

Sometimes the smaller girls would play "Old Mother Witch", where we would take the name of a fruit pie. Someone was appointed to be the witch. Whoever was "IT" would whisper the name of a fruit pie in each of the players' ear. When the leader guessed the name of someone with that fruit pie name a game of tag would ensue. If the leader was able to tag the player, that tagged person would have to go to the witches "lair".

In the wintertime we played a lot of Geography games by opening our texts to a certain map. Someone would be appointed "IT", and would name a place for us to find. The first one to find the said place was then the next leader.

Sometimes on rainy days we played "Blind Man's Buff" indoors. Someone's hand towel was used to cover our eyes. Whoever was "IT" stood inside the circle as one more was chosen to be inside the ring of players. The blind man had to find that person and identify him or her.

Some of this sounds terribly childish now when I think of it but we did have fun. The games kept us active to burn off some of our energy. The games also taught us integrity and cooperation. Consider the game of "Annie Annie Over." The team on one side would throw a ball over the roof of the school building to the team they could not see on the other side. If it didn't make it over the roof, we yelled "pig tail," to let the other side know that it didn't make it over. If it did make it over, the ball needed to be caught before it hit the ground. If not, the team with the ball would in turn pitch it over the roof again, hollering "ante over" in their turn. If it were caught, the entire team would run around the building and tag as many of the other team as possible. The tagged people would then join the opposing team. How did we know if the ball had been caught successfully or not? There was no observer or referee. There was just our integrity to say it was so. How many games do we play today on that basis?

There were very strict rules of the day regarding the personal life of the teacher. The teacher absolutely could not be married in order to teach school. A friend of mine, Thelma Hansen who taught in the mid 1930's in the Benson School west of Cedar Falls, Iowa, secretly got married during Christmas vacation and the marriage was not discovered before the end of the school year. It was a wonderful conspiracy.

Following are rules enforced for teachers who taught in a rural country school. The list was included in a teacher's contract in 1913. Some of the rules still were enforced in the 1930's, particularly #1: Don't get married.

1. Don't get married.
2. Don't keep company with men.
3. Be home between the hours of 8 p.m. and 8 a.m., unless attending a school function.
4. Don't loiter in downtown ice cream stores.
5. Don't leave town at anytime without permission of the chairman of the board of trustees.
6. Don't smoke cigarettes.
7. Don't drink beer, wine or whiskey.
8. Don't ride in a carriage or auto with any man except a brother or father.
9. Don't dress in bright colors.
10. Don't dye your hair.
11. Wear at least two petticoats.
12. Don't wear dresses any more than two inches above the ankles.
13. Keep the school room clean and sweep the classrooms daily. Scrub classroom floors at least once a week with hot water and soap. Clean blackboards once a day and start fire at 7:00 a.m., so the schoolroom will be warm when the children arrive at 8:00 a.m.
14. Don't use face powder, mascara, or paint your lips.
15. Receive $35 a month for eight months.

When we finished the eighth grade we were done with the country school. If we went on to high school we would go into town. At the end of the eighth grade term we went into Cedar Falls and took an exam furnished by the County Superintendent. Somehow, everyone passed. Reality hit us when began high school in town. The classes were much larger, and the pupils had learned different things than had we. We were not as well prepared for high school work, as were the children educated in the city school system. We struggled.

The old country school houses were a link to something better. One of the positive things about the rural school was that children learned from each other. There were children in grades kindergarten through eighth grade at this school, although not every grade may be represented. This diverse age group led to lots of school yard scraps and fighting and we learned to resolve our differences amicably. The children learned to live with each other whether they were six or fourteen years old. We learned a lot at school, only a portion of our learning was in the books.

PIANO LESSONS

Of course I would take piano lessons. We had the piano, and the teacher came right to the house on the farm to give lessons. My parents had my welfare in mind, but I was young and had what I thought were more important things to do, like playing outside. If I had known eighty years ago what I know now, I would have been serious about both the lessons and the piano.

The concert piano, which sat in our living room, was built of black walnut with ivory white keys and ebony black keys. Large carved legs at each corner supported the heavy instrument. The cover could be raised and supported on a stick made for that purpose.

It was called a "square piano" when in reality it was rectangular. It had wonderful tone and likely belonged in a concert hall somewhere.

So every summer I took lessons, even though there were many times I would have rather been playing outdoors. I resented most that Mr. Leversee, the teacher, had such bad breath that I deplored sitting next to him on the piano bench.

"Have you practiced today?" "Do you know your lesson?" he would inquire, further fouling the air. "Just five more minutes," he would say. And so it went on throughout the long hot summer days. When I saw Mr. Leversee turn into the driveway in his Overland car it was time to go inside and have my 30-minute lesson.

In spite of what likes and dislikes I had for him, he must have been a good teacher. I learned "The Robin's Return", "Falling Waters", and other such pieces. My mother liked to have me play "Whispering Hope." I played it over and over for her.

Whatever happened to the piano, I don't know. In the Great Depression of the 1930's, when my parents did not have money to pay the taxes, everything on the farm was sold, including the piano. I have no idea who bought it or where it went.

I did retain some of the technique, and have played well enough for myself throughout my lifetime. That is the legacy of Mr. Leversee in me.

MUSIC

In the 1920's the Charleston was a very popular dance among the younger and more daring generation. I was accustomed to dancing Danish folk dances, and they were lots of fun, but this was different. I remember trying to dance the Charleston, in our house, although I don't recall with whom. It was a new type of music in our house to which we were unaccustomed. Dad had always insisted on all of us listening to classical music.

We had a Brunswick phonograph. Dad had purchased many good recordings. Among them was "The Poet and Peasant Overture", "Santa Lucia", "Humoresque" by Dvorak (one of my favorites), "Il Travatore" and several other recordings of opera music. Dad had studied in Denmark after high school and had attended the opera in Copenhagen, where he developed his appreciation of the opera. There were recordings of selected marches by John Philip Sousa's band and others. Of course, we had to turn the crank on the side of the phonograph once in awhile to keep the spring tight.

For me he bought two little records about four inches across. I enjoyed these records especially because they contained the songs that I learned. The words to one of the songs are as follows:

The Carrion Crow

A carrion crow sat on an oak
Day dee day dee day dee day oh
A carrion crow sat on an oak
Watching a tailor shape his cloak
Sing hi ho for the carrion crow
Day dee day dee day dee day oh

Oh wife bring me my old bent bow
Day dee day dee day dee day oh
Oh wife bring me my old bent bow
That I may shoot yon carrion crow
Sing hi ho for the carrion crow
Day dee day dee day dee day oh

The tailor shot and missed his mark
Day dee day dee day dee day oh
The tailor shot and missed his mark
And shot his own self through his heart
Sing hi ho for the carrion crow
Day dee day dee day dee day oh

The old man died and the bells did toll
Day dee day dee day dee day oh
The old man died and the bells did toll
All for the sake of the old man's soul
Sing hi ho for the carrion crow
Day dee day dee day dee day oh

The other song was about a sow that had three little piggies that said "WEE WEE WEE".

The phonograph was a wonderful device. Its fidelity was not even close to what today's equipment can reproduce, but it was a marvelous device to us. It brought professional entertainment into our home. It enabled us to hear music that was outside of our usual fare of volunteer talent, no matter how talented they were. What a new and amazing experience!

BARBER SHOPS

I was still a young kid in the early 1920's. My parents always had my reddish hair cut short with bangs in front.

Going to the local barber shop in Cedar Falls is still memorable. There were three barber chairs with a brass spittoon set in front of each chair. These chairs were made of heavy cast iron with a soft finish of nickel or chrome. The seat and arms were upholstered in leather.

To cut my hair the barber placed a board across the two arms of the chair and set me up on the board. Then a huge white apron was tied around me while I got my hair cut.

When I was a ninth grader in Cedar Falls high school I went to Julius Ostergaaard's barber shop on College Hill just west of the Berg Drug Store. It was 25 cents a hair cut in those days.

BATHROOM

The farmhouse I grew up in had a bathroom inside the house, that is, a room in which to take a bath. This was a few steps ahead of the times. Farm bathrooms were not necessary by the standards of the time. Most baths were done in the nearby laundry shed in warm weather. In the cold weather baths were given in the kitchen next to the cook stove. It was the warmest room in the house.

Our bathroom, located in the far corner room of the unheated cellar, did not have hot running water, or a sink, or a toilet stool, just a tub. This farmhouse was newer, and had a large furnace in the basement to heat the upstairs, but the bathroom was not heated. In the winter the heat pipe from the wood fired furnace was turned on into that room. The floor was still cold, but we had a bathroom.

Our tub, shaped like the old four footed white porcelain tubs, was made of tin or zinc on the inside boxed in with wood wainscoting around the outside. The metal pieces were cut and shaped to tub size and soldered at the seams. There was a drain with a plug stopper to hold the water in the tub. Around the edge at the top was a five-inch flat piece of wood where the bather laid the soap.

At the time our farm had a water distribution system powered by gravity from a cistern under the windmill on the hill. The tub did have a single faucet from which cold water could be drawn. There was no hot water running into the tub. My mother heated the water on the cook stove upstairs in the kitchen and carried the kettle of hot water down the cellar steps all the way back to the bathroom. Then she heated another kettle for more hot water.

Because I was a child I bathed first. Then the older ones bathed next. We did not change the water after each bath. This was to conserve water and work.

When the last bath was done the water would be drained from the tub. A plug at the bottom was pulled, and the water flowed onto the concrete floor. There was a channel made in the floor that led the water across the bathroom floor, under a partition wall, then across the rest of the basement floor to a floor drain. From there, the sudsy water drained through an underground tile to the ditch alongside the road. Since there was no septic system, this drainage left an unpleasant odor in the ditch. It probably wasn't the most sanitary, but we never suffered any ill effects.

In today's world that sounds very unlikely. Improvements to farm homes were very slow to come. It was not until after WWII with rising farm profits that new and modern farmhouses began to replace the old houses. The newer farmhouses had running water from a pressurized system. Then it was possible to combine the bathhouse, toilet and sink into a room inside the farmhouse. It was also necessary then to add a septic system to deal with the waste. This was a major effort and expense to the farm business. It took a long time for all of that to happen.

The farmer's view was that no money was made from the farmhouses. Only the field crops and livestock deserved the investment or expense of excess capital. They would be profitable. From very early times there was always running water for the livestock.

SATURDAY NIGHT BATHS

Saturday night was known as bath night on the farm. A lot of time and effort was expended in this endeavor, and we usually bathed only once each week. This custom remained true until after World War II, when a few farmers began building new houses, replete with running water and indoor toilets, to replace the original 1800's houses.

There were no real bathrooms as we know them now. For many years after I was married, taking a bath meant bringing in the large galvanized wash tub from the wash house or from the back porch where it hung on a nail. The tub was placed in the kitchen near the cook stove. In front of the stove was the warmest place to undress and do our bathing. The tub was about 30 inches in diameter and about fifteen inches deep.

Pails of water were carried from the well, and then heated, either on the cook stove or on a kerosene-fired stove. The water was poured into a copper wash boiler where it was heated. Then the hot water was dipped into the washtub. Cold water was mixed into the tub to make a comfortable bath.

When the children were small, they were bathed first. The children enjoyed playing in the water, both because it was warm and also that they could stretch their legs full length in the water. You can imagine what we adults had to do to get ourselves folded into the tub. Nevertheless, it was good to be clean, and we enjoyed it. There were no alternatives.

Of course, the water had to be carried outside afterwards, which in the winter was not too enjoyable.

126

Saturday night bathing meant that everyone was clean, with clean clothes from the inside to out, to go to church and Sunday school the next day. Also, we might be making a Saturday night trip to town to see the sights and walk with friends on the sidewalks.

In the 40's the Fuller Brush salesman came around selling a bucket with a hose attachment that could be hung on the wall to make a shower. There again one pail of water was all we had to shower and rinse. So that bath didn't take long to do. That worked well in the summer when the bucket could be hung inside the washhouse.

We were married twenty years before we had our first bathroom with running hot and cold water. It was another experience in learning to appreciate the good things in life.

BARN FIRES

Barn fires were a common sight at night during haying season. There were no electric lights to illumine the dark summer nights, and there was no air conditioning or television to keep us in the house in the evening. We often sat out on the spacious front porch talking or sitting quietly listening to the sounds of the night. In the haying season the sweet smell of fresh clover hay wafted on the night air.

Suddenly, a bright reddish glow could be seen in the distance, sometimes as far as twenty miles away. Someone's barn was burning and there was no way to extinguish it. Hay that had just been put in that barn had not been thoroughly cured while in the field and was put away too green. A terrible heat from the great pile of green hay in the haymow of the barn resulted in spontaneous combustion and had set the barn on fire.

This was long before there were modern-day fire departments that could be called upon to bring the big fire trucks. Neither did we have telephones with which to notify the fire departments. Even when there were fire departments in town and with telephones available, there was little they could do to save the barn. By the time the firemen arrived at the scene several miles from town, all they could do was to save other buildings.

We would stand out in the yard, watching the bright glow. Some time later, it would die down and we knew the barn was gone. In times when there were no electric lights on the farms barn fires were a very eerie sight.

There were those few times that the men would be forking hay from the haymow to the mangers in the winter time. The men would find a small black area in the hay where a fire had started, but smothered and choked itself out. We knew then that we were indeed very fortunate.

GATHERING EGGS

When I was growing up, and when I, too, was a farm wife, it was my duty to gather the eggs every day. We had between 100 and 200 laying hens at any one time. That was a lot of eggs! The incentive for doing this job was that it meant cash money for me to spend on Saturday nights when our family went to town.

So with a pail or basket I would trudge off to the hen house to see what the count would be that day. For the most part the hens had finished laying their eggs by late afternoon and picking them out of the nest boxes not a problem. But there were always a few hens that claimed setter's rights and were reluctant to give up their spoil.

The uncooperative hen's first inclination was to make a frontal attack by driving a nasty peck on my bare arm as I reached into the box. Then her feathers fluffed out and she continued the attack by constant pecking and squawking. This was the time to show how masterful I could be in that sort of situation. Through the noise and pecking I would ignore the attack and reach under her warm body and retrieve the eggs she had claimed to be her very own. Then I would move on to the next nest.

When the eggs were all gathered, I washed them in clean water on the back step and packed them into the egg crate. It is not a great effort to do this, but there was some satisfaction in knowing there was some income for the effort. During the depression we sold eggs at 10 cents a dozen.

In the spring hens had a mothering instinct, and they hid their nests. If they were clever enough by finding such faraway places as some hay in a forgotten corner, or under a feed box in a manger, they would hatch out a nice clutch of baby chicks. Mother hens were so proud of their offspring, and kept them very close to their own bodies. If there were any danger the mother hen flew after the tormentor.

She taught her young clutch to forage for food, which was mainly small insects. She showed them how to scratch the soil with their feet and peck at the exposed food. When all had their fill she gathered her family around her and snuggled each of them under her warm body. Tiny heads poked out from under her body or from around one of her wings. There was much contentment in that little family of ten or twelve babies.

ONE NICKEL

There are certain events in a child's life one memorializes more than others. Mine was the day each summer when we had the annual Sunday school picnic.

Where I lived, the old wooden frame church stood on one side of the road surrounded by a cemetery. On the other side of the road were the parsonage and the fellowship hall, which we called the "Auditorium". These three buildings were graced by tall trees and green grass. It was there in the grassy shaded area between these structures that the annual picnic was held.

The picnic was preceded by a program of accomplishments we children had been working on for the past six weeks of summer school.

In our Danish settlement the children attended a summer session of "Dane School," learning to read, write, spell, and sing Danish songs. We also had sessions each day of Gymnastics. Outdoors we played Danish "round games." During the time when our schoolwork was done we were required to do needlework, which was displayed for our parents to look at on picnic day.

On the appointed Sunday afternoon we held an exhibition of Danish round games in Danish costume. For the girls it was a colored skirt, a white blouse, a vest that laced across the front, and an embroidered cap that we wore on our heads.

When the program was over we children were allowed to go to the stand to purchase our bottle of pop.

Now for this purpose the men had erected a "stand" something like a retail store counter made of white pine boards with another board across the front where we made our purchases. Behind the stand the men had a galvanized stock tank filled with three fifty pound chunks of ice that had been brought out from the ice house in Cedar Falls, placed into the tank and covered with some water. Into this water were placed several cases of pop in glass bottles. The pop was put into the water a few hours before purchase time to cool.

Then the time came when my father placed a nickel into the palm of my one hand and admonished me to hang onto it and don't lose it. I felt as if I were the proud recipient of the grand prize.

I strolled up to the stand, thumped my nickel on the board counter top and waited my turn to make my marvelous purchase.

Young Ole Johnsen and Chris Syndergaard clerked and dispensed the precious beverages. I had to decide between Strawberry or Cream Soda. I liked both. But then there was Lemon Soda and Root Beer, too. I could get root beer at home. My parents made that every summer in our basement.

"I think I'll take strawberry," I decided after considering the selection. I could imagine the fresh strawberry flavor and the tingling of the carbonation playing on my tongue.

The clerk snapped the cap off the bottle and handed the cold, dripping-wet treasure to me as I gave him my nickel. I strode away from that stand and stood with the other children as we each proudly tasted, relished, admired, and loved each mouthful of that rare and precious pop. It was more than ample reward for those hot days spent in classes.

As we drove home from the celebration, we knew, sadly, that there would not be another nickel or another bottle of pop for one whole year. It had been a wonderful day.

CARLA CHRISTINA SCHMIDT

Born April 4, 1919
Baptized May 25, 1919
Died August 8, 1920
Buried August 9, 1920

I was born and raised on a farm about five miles west of Cedar Falls Iowa. This was normally a peaceful, quiet life, so unusual events stood out in great contrast. When I was four years old, a sister, Carla, was born to our family. I don't remember much about this time, so I presume this brought much happiness to our family. But tragedy soon followed. When Carla was not even two years old, she drowned

Jørgen, Carla & Elna

in the livestock water tank near the barn. Children have always been drawn to water, and from time to time children from other farm families were lost in this fashion. The death of a child has always been a particularly sad event, and sympathies for the loss were given in profusion by others. But when the child was of my family, my

Carla

sister, our daughter, it was devastating. Even now, eighty-five years later, the memory of this event is very painful and this story is very difficult to write.

Carla & Rover

I believe that the day my sister Carla drowned, our family's life changed completely. This was certainly true for Mother, Dad, and especially for me. Up until then we had been a happy family, enjoying life with a new child and sister. Suddenly everything was different.

It was a warm August day in 1920 and, as usual, Mother was busily working in the house. She was preparing for her birthday party to be held that very day, and many guests would be arriving later. There was much cleaning and baking to be done, and small children were just in the way. My friend, 13-year-old Caroline and I, now a five-year-old, were to watch my 16-month-old sister, and to be out of the way of all the work. We were to play just outside the kitchen.

Caroline and I were busy playing and we didn't notice Carla wandering off by herself. When my mother came to the door to ask about Carla, we didn't know where she was. A frantic search took place and soon my mother found her floating in the stock tank, which was between the barn and the house, her body face down, her skin now turned pale and blue.

My mother screamed and cried all at the same time and began calling for Dad. Dad rushed to see what the commotion was, since on the farm sounds like this were an alarm. In a rush of frantic action, Dad called the doctor on the telephone, got us all into the Mitchell automobile and drove off as fast as we could towards town to meet the doctor. The road that is now a little used highway was under construction so the going was difficult. We did not notice, nor did we care. When we got as far as Refshauge's farm place, about halfway to town, we met the doctor coming from town, but there was nothing anyone could do to help little Carla. We sadly drove back home, taking the now lifeless body of Carla with us. My grandparents, Niels and Christine Hoffman, were called on the phone and they came to our house right away. It was all a terrifying experience. No one would be consoled. It was a time of great sorrow.

I shall ever be grateful to "Stina" Hoffman, my grandmother. That same afternoon, she sat down with me to explain that God was taking care of Carla now, and that she was now one of God's little angels. "Now," my grandmother said, "she is with God in Heaven." She comforted me and, pointing her hands to the ceiling, told me that God's angels were very likely right there watching over each of us. In fact, Carla might even be flying right above us there in the house. I have never forgotten how lovingly she talked to me. At my age of five she was able to help me deal with an incomprehensible event. I have never forgotten what she told me about God, and even now I carry that strong belief with me at all times.

The undertaker was called and Carla's little body was laid on the ironing board placed between two chairs. The undertaker soaked pieces of cotton in a bright pink fluid. He then placed them on her, covering her whole body with layers of it.

When he had finished, we all went into Cedar Falls to Dahl's furniture store where coffins were kept in the balcony of the store. A small coffin was selected. The next day Carla was carefully dressed in a little white dress for the last time and then tenderly laid in her little coffin. Mother and Dad sat with her body both night and day, keeping a vigil until the time of the funeral.

Portrait of Carla for
her first Christmas

When it was time, we drove to the church for the funeral service. The casket in which Carla's body had been laid was taken to the church in a hearse, an ornate gray early automobile. Four teen-age neighbor girls were selected to carry the casket from the hearse into the church. Another girl carried a basket filled with arbor vitae leaves. She scattered these leaves on the carpeting in front of the four girls carrying the coffin as they processed down the aisle to place

Carla's body at the front of the church. The funeral service was given in the Danish language. Pastor Jens Holst gave the sermon, preaching on how God gives us hope even as He calls his children to Him.

After that I really don't remember much about this time. But I do know that there never seemed to be much happiness in our family following that horrible event. Unknowingly, I have always felt that I was held responsible for that drowning. Such a tragic event is still vivid in my mind even after all these years.

Pastor Holst typed out his notes for the sermon using a Danish language typewriter. I still have that single page of linen paper after all these years, and, with the help of Marvin Jessen and Elna Bellows, have provided a translation of it.

Carla was buried in the cemetery surrounding the Fredsville Lutheran Church. A small stone marker was placed there – one of the early graves in the cemetery. Now, many years later, Mother and Dad also rest from their earthly toil, and are buried there next to little Carla's grave. I believe Pastor Holst was right. As their mortal bodies now rest next to each other, so they are reunited in eternal life through salvation in Jesus Christ. Perhaps I, too, someday soon shall be reunited with my little sister and be able to erase the scar of guilt and pain on my soul.

Elna Marie (Schmidt) Petersen, 2004

To the reader: For those few of you who read Old Danish, you will recognize that the following text is not complete. It is more of an indication of what Rev. Holst actually preached, a guide to his thoughts. Therefore, the translation that follows the Danish has been filled in to complete each thought as best as can be determined from what is actually written.

Luk. 8 40—56.

Vi har en Beretning I vort Nye Test. hvori der fortallesoom en Fader der kom til Jesus Kristus for at bede ham komme og laage Handerne paa hans lille dødsyge Pige. Det er Beretningen om Synagogeforstanderens Vandrigg fra Kana til Jesus. Jesu Deltagelse i hans Sorg. Budskabet der kom fra Hjemmet og Herlig gørelsen da Jesus traadte ind over Hjemmets Tarskel. og under dets Tag.

Det er em Fader der beder for sit døende Barn. Og hvem kan bede som en Fader ogen Moder bare deresSmaa hen til Børnevennen stor trygle ham om Bistand og Bevarelse for de han har velsignet Liv Livet med. I saadanne Stunder læres maaske først tilfulde Jesu Ord om Barnets Ret hos ham. Lader de smaa Børn komme til mig formener dem det ikke thi Guds Rig hører saadanne til. Maaske var det det der drog hin Fader hen til Jesus Kristus maaske var dot hvad han byggede sit Haab paa da han forlod Hjemmet for at søge ham der nu var den eneste der kunde hjalpe. Det forstod han i det mindste at intet her paa Jorden havde Magt over Dødaen uden Jesus Kristus og fik han like ikke Hjælp hos ham da var der kun den baælmørke Fortvivlelse der ventede ham. Hans Haab blev ikke skuffet Jesus Kristus hørte deltagende pa Faderen Bøn villig fulgté han med ham mod Hjemmet, men det Haab den Tro hvormed har kom til Jesus den skulde luttres for at han kunde modtage det han had om og det skete da Budskabet kom fra Hjemmet du skal ikke ulejlige Mesteren din Datter et død.

Aa jag forstaar hvad at saadan Øjeblik betyder i at Menneskes Liv hvilken Srnerte der ligger deri hviken haabløshed indeholder ikke disse Ord. Alt der havde baaret bin Fader under Rejsen den kærlige Deltagelse han mødte hos Jesus dat blev med et borte han stod alene omgiven af Sorgens dybe fortvivlede Mørke. saa saa var det alligevel sket det han havde haabet at afværge. Jeg forstaar i Forældre i mine Venner hvad det Øjeblik betød for eder da i iGaar erfarede eller det gik op for eder at lille Carla s Liv var udslukt her paa Jorden. Hvor kan det knuge og lamme og stivne al Glæde Haab og Tro i en saadan Stund. Men lad os saa lægge marke til hvad mere der skete for hin Fader. Beretningen ender ikke med at han gik ud i Sorgens mørke Nat men at den Sorg og Smerte han modtog gennem det tunge Bud-skab det blev forvanlet til en Glædens og Lykkens Stund. Jesus kom ikke til Jord for at sprede Mørke for at lade Dødens spor til-bage nej han kom for at lyse op og vidne om Livet lindre den Smerte sam Døden efterlader i sit Spor.

Der er et andet Billede som jeg, gerne vil pege paa ved denne Lej-lighed. En af de store Malere gengivet det der skete i Jairus s Hus. vi ser en Østerlandsk Stue Jesus staar yed Fodenden af Sengen hvorpaa den lille Pige liger kold og død, Moderen æer sunken i Knæ ved Siden af SengenHovedet er bøjet hele hendes Skikkelse bærer Præg af Sorg. Jairus staar lidt tilbageon D Desciplene er i Baggrunden. Jesus rakker den højre Haand ud over Sengen hans Blik er rettet mod den sørgenda Moder som ve__e han paa at hun skal løfte Ansigtet op mod ham og han kan udtale Livsordet til Pigen.

Ja saadan er Jesu Stilling han venter paa at vi skal se op til ham fulde af Tro og Haab. Han staar ogsaa eders Sidde i Dag i som nu for sidste [han?] her paa Jorden skal?? lille Carla, han Haand er ogsaa udrakt over eder ikke for at i skal stirre ned i den lille Grav men opad mod Livet og Lyset deroppe hos Gud Fade Fader skal det I drø??e om blive fuldkommet for hende derv skal Livets Herlighed udfoldes for hende. Aa Venner kan vi saa ikke smile gennem Taarer thi Jesus Kristus har jo selv overvundet Døden den Sejr har han givet os Ret og Adgang til. Lad det væra Trøsten i Sorgens tunge Tid . Herren gav,Herren tog, Herrens Nave være Lovet.

Amen

Luke 8: 40-56

We have in our New Testament an account which tells of a father who came to Jesus Christ to ask that He come and lay His hands on the father's deathly ill little girl. This is the account of the ruler of the synagogue, who walked from Canaan to Jesus, of Jesus' sharing of the man's sorrow; the message which came from the home of the little girl; and the wonderful event when Jesus crossed over the threshold and stepped under the roof of the home.

This is a father who is praying for his dying child. And who can pray like a father and a mother as they carry their child to the Friend of all children; who beg Him for help and protection because He has blessed life and the living. At such a time one learns perhaps for the first time the truth regarding Jesus' words about the child's right to be with Him. "Let the little children come unto me; do not forbid them, for to such belongs the Kingdom of God." Perhaps it was this that drove her father to Jesus Christ; perhaps it was this upon which he built his hope when he left home to seek Him, the only One who could help. This at least he understood: that nothing here on earth has power over death except for Jesus Christ, and if he didn't get help from Him, only the darkness of despair awaited him. He was not disappointed. Jesus Christ listened sympathetically to the father's request, and willingly followed him to the home. But this hope, this trust which brought him to Jesus was to be dashed to nothingness when a message arrived from the home indicating: "Do not bother the Master, your daughter is dead."

Oh yes, I understand what such a moment means in the life of a person, what pain, what hopelessness these words express! All that had compelled the father to make the trip, the loving sympathy he received from Jesus, all disappeared as he stood enveloped by the dark despair of sorrow. That which he had hoped to prevent nevertheless occurred.

I understand you parents, my friends, what such a moment meant for you yesterday when you experienced, or it became evident that little Carla's life on this earth had been snuffed out. How it can crush and paralyze and harden all happy hope and trust during such a time. But let us also consider what else happened to the father. The story does not end with the father wandering out into the dark night of sorrow. Rather, the grief and pain he experienced upon receiving the devastating message was transformed into a time of joy and gladness. Jesus did not come into the world to spread darkness and to allow the power of death to return. No, He came to bring light and to bear witness for life, relieving the pain which death leaves in its path.

There is another picture which I would like to call to your attention at this time. One of the great painters has rendered these happenings which occurred in Jairus' house. We see an Eastern-style room with Jesus standing at the foot of a bed upon which lies a little girl, cold and dead. The mother is kneeling at the side of the bed, her head bowed, and her entire body bears the mark of sorrow. Jairus stands slightly behind, while the disciples are in the background. Jesus holds His right hand over the bed, but his attention is focused upon the grieving mother, waiting for her to lift her head toward Him so He can speak the words of life to the girl.

Yes, such is Jesus' stance today, waiting for us to raise our gaze toward Him who bears hope and trust. He stands at your side today also, you who today for the last time will see little Carla here on earth. His hand is also outstretched over you so that you do not concentrate on the tiny grave, but rather be lifted toward life and light with God the Father. With Him will be the glory of eternal life, and there you will again meet her. Friends, can we not smile a little bit through our tears? Since Jesus Christ himself has defeated death, that victory He has made available for all of us. Let this be our comfort despite sorrow's heavy shadow.

The Lord gave; the Lord took away, the Lord's name be praised!

Amen.

Composite translation
Elna Bellows and Marvin Jessen

APRONS

There was a time back in the twenties and thirties when every respectable housewife kept a supply of aprons. In those days, indeed into the 1950's, housewives always wore dresses. Most meals were prepared "from scratch" which meant spattering grease, spilled flour or powdered sugar and the like. An apron caught the clutter of cooking rather than the dress. Housewives could prepare the meal or wash the dishes, remove her apron and join the guests in the parlor with her dress still clean. Since laundry was such an effort and aprons were far easier to wash than the dresses, it only made sense to use aprons all the time. Besides, they made convenient hand towels and hot pads.

Each day upon entering the kitchen the housewife slipped an apron on over her dress before she began the day's work. Aprons were sewed from cotton print fabric and hemmed on the edges with either rickrack, a wavy decorative ribbon, or bias tape, a plain strip of ribbon. These items would make the seams and hems less obvious. At that period of time fabrics came in 36 inch widths only so seams were often made part of the design of the apron. Often a good apron pattern was copied onto newspaper from a neighbor's apron pattern, then pinned to the cotton print, cut and sewed.

When soiled, aprons were washed, starched, dampened after drying on the clothes line, and ironed to remove any wrinkles. On the kitchen wall there was a long nail where aprons were hung when the kitchen work was finished.

On Sundays after a splendid meal, often with good friends for company, the women would gather in the kitchen to "do up the dishes". If there were not enough aprons for each guest a large white dish towel could be tied around the waist and the corners tied in a knot in the back.

There were several styles of aprons. They all covered the front of the wearer from chin to knees or lower. Then there were those that had a back reaching to the waist line. They slipped over the head. Often the design and decorations of the apron reflected the personality of the housewife. No matter what their design, they served a very practical purpose for many generations.

COFFEE GRINDERS

Before the already-ground and hermetically sealed Folgers and Starbucks and Caribou and Nestlé's and Sanka and espresso, there was freshly ground coffee. We ground it ourselves.

From the grocery store we bought coffee beans in the bulk from round wooden barrels. These barrels were not as large as the tall wooden barrels which held a hundred or more pounds of sugar or flour. The beans of coffee were measured into a cotton cloth sack which was then neatly tied closed with a length of string.

Coffee for drinking is not made from whole beans. They need to be ground to release the full flavor. Old time cowboys out on the range could not carry a coffee grinder and lamented in song, "...I boiled my own coffee without being ground."

At home a coffee grinder was attached to the wall. It was a small wooden box to which was attached a wrought iron mechanism that ground the beans. On top of the grinder was a glass container for the beans. A foot long handle operated the grinding mechanism. The whole assembly was tipped to one side to unscrew the glass jar. The jar was then filled with coffee beans and then screwed back onto the grinder. The apparatus was then set back upright, and we had coffee available for many days. A few turns of the handle would grind out enough coffee to fill a small drawer in the bottom of the grinder. These grounds then were measured and placed in a coffee pot.

Early coffee making meant boiling the coffee grounds in water for several minutes. The resulting brew often poured the coffee and the grounds into the cup. The last cup of coffee contained mostly grounds, which was often called "sump," which in Danish means "swamp." On special occasions the coffee grounds were mixed with egg whites before putting them into the cold water. After boiling, the coffee would taste the same, but the grounds would remain in the pot.

Coffee made from beans freshly ground is particularly flavorful. In the days before percolators, filters or lattés, I learned to enjoy this flavorful beverage at a very young age. To this day I still grind coffee from beans, just not by hand.

MAKING BUTTER

When I was a young girl we didn't know that butter would ever be sold in quarter pound sticks. We knew it as something we made when we needed it. Emergency butter was butter we hurriedly made when there was not butter left to put on the table for the next meal.

To make a small amount quickly, mother brought out a clean glass quart jar and filled it half way with cream. After the lid had been screwed on tight it was then my job to sit and shake that jar until it turned to butter. I would look several times to see if the granules of butter had begun to form on the sides of the jar.

At last, after many minutes of vigorous effort, there would be a mass of butter in the jar. Next the buttermilk was drained from the butter. The lump of butter was placed into a wooden bowl where cold well water ran over it and rinsed it. The cold water tended to harden the butter. It then had to be worked with a flat wooden butter paddle running cold water over it several times, then draining it. When the butter was finally at a stage where no more buttermilk ran from it, salt was added and mixed in with the paddle. When the salt was thoroughly blended, the new butter was set in a bowl ready for the next meal.

There was also the gallon glass churn with wooden paddles at the bottom of the jar and a handle that turned the iron gears on top of the jar. That was easier, and it was the method we used most of the time. The jar was filled half full with cream, then the handle was turned to activate the wooden paddles inside. These paddles stirred the cream rapidly and vigorously. The handle was turned it until butter formed. Then the same process of draining off the buttermilk, washing with cold water, working the ball of butter with the wooden paddle made for that purpose, and finally adding the added salt was performed.

Larger amounts of butter could be made using the wooden barrel churn. The barrel was mounted on a wooden stand. An opening on the top of barrel allowed five gallons of cream to be poured into the container. The cover was latched down with an iron latch so there would be no spillage.

Then my mother or I sat beside the churn turning the crank or handle at the side of the barrel. After turning for a length of time we listened for the splash inside the barrel to change. It finally came to a time where the butter granules began to combine and be a lump of butter. Then it would be more difficult to turn the crank until the butter became a lump. We didn't often use this device often as it made more butter than we could store, especially in the summer weather. Butter kept too long in the summer would turn rancid.

My dad liked the buttermilk, and many thought it a special drink available only when butter was churned. We usually made butter in the glass gallon jar, so we had buttermilk from time to time.

Making butter was hard work, and we learned to be patient in operating the churn. Butter was our only bread spread. Every sandwich was made beginning with bread and butter. A slice of homemade Danish pumpernickel with only butter was a tasty treat. Butter and lard were the only shortening used in all of our baking and other cooking needs. In these days of attention to diet and health it seems strange to many. However, this is what we ate and used, and we were still very healthy and lived long lives. Maybe we lived long because we worked hard at everything we did. Could it be that our genetics were favorable? Perhaps these are healthy foods after all.

FANCY WORK

Fancywork was the term used to denote knitting, crocheting, or fine embroidery. Most women had some kind of fancywork to pick up and work on when work and time allowed. Women did not go visiting or go to any function without taking their fancywork along. Each woman sat and worked quietly at the piece while visiting. Patterns were exchanged when something special appealed to someone's eye.

As a young girl I stitched a sampler which gave me practice using the needle and embroidery floss. Most of these stitches were cross-stitches. Samplers were a good way to learn the craft, and my mother and grandmother could critique my efforts.

Embroidery was also an easy stitch to learn. Patterns were transferred to plain cloth such as pillows or dishtowels. Using needle and floss, a chain stitch was carefully laid out along the pattern lines. We used many colors of floss. Otherwise plain items would thus be decorated in some fashion.

A display of fancy work done by Grand View College girls.

Women always embroidered a set of seven dish towels, one for each day of the week, to keep on hand when visitors came to help with the dishes. Patterns were available in magazines or at the local five and ten store. Patterns were applied by placing the pattern face down on the white towel and pressing the pattern with a hot iron.

Crocheting was an advanced item of fancywork. Women who were expert at this art made items of beauty and grace. Fine linen thread was repeatedly looped into designs that astounded the imagination. My grandmother made many beautiful items, many of which still exist. She made doilies to decorate and protect tables large and small as well as upholstered chairs. She made collars and other decorative lace for her clothing. She made lace that decorated shelves. Good original crocheting is very valuable even now.

Knitting was another form of fancywork. We knitted all of our scarves, mittens and sweaters and hats for adults and children alike. Fine knitting for table runners also made beautiful decorative fancywork.

Fancywork of all kinds was needed and appreciated. Women always had a basket of some project close at hand. This work occupied any free moment of time, and was often done while carrying on conversations with family and friends. This work was not done on a competitive basis, although we all knew who could make very fine work.. It was a symbol of the worth of a woman who made good use of her spare time.

FREDSVILLE KVINDEMODE
OR
LADIES AID IN THE 1920'S

In the 1920's we were living on a farm in Iowa. Our area had been settled by Danish immigrants. Now, second-generation families occupied the farms where their parents had homesteaded before the turn of the century.

It was the intent of the families to continue using their native language and customs. The white frame Danish Lutheran church, which the families had built, sat on a hill five miles from any town. The church was the center for worship and social activities.

The women of the Fredsville congregation had organized a Ladies Aid some years before. These were sturdy farmwomen, all with Danish backgrounds. They could have met at the church auditorium; however, the women had decided to have their meetings in each other's homes. This played to their pride in keeping the home clean and neat. It was customary for them to meet monthly, rotating their meeting places on an alphabetical basis. What better way to display their talents as a "good" Danish homemaker? Nonetheless, it was a challenge to meet the discriminating eyes of each person as she crossed the threshold of the meeting place. They would each assess the home and homemaking skills of the hostess with a discriminating eye.

The following account is what I recall as a very young child. I was born in 1914 and this took place in the 1920's.

When Mother left Annie Olsen's house that cold wintry day in February, she knew it would be her turn to have the women at her house in July. That meant the weather would be hot and the men would be right in the middle of oats harvest. It would be the busiest time of the summer.

Esther, the president, had read the names in alphabetical order of the upcoming meeting places: first, Camilla Petersen in March, then in April, Karen Petersen, Otillia Petersen in May, Inger Rasmussen in June, and then my mother. Her last name began with the letter "S".

The months would pass all too quickly and all too soon it would be my mother's turn to host a meeting. I remember the hectic days and weeks that preceded the event. Everything would have to be just so! A slow-moving tornado might describe what took place during that time of preparation. Without any doubt the house would be ready for the most discerning guest.

It might be well to note at this time that modern conveniences as we know them now had not been invented. There were no radios, TV's, microwaves, automatic washing machines, dryers, or dishwashers. There were no so-called "fast meals", either. Gas stoves, bathrooms with hot and cold running water hadn't yet invaded this community. Anyway, I started out to tell you about the Ladies Aid.

It didn't take long for Mother to begin the task of a very thorough cleaning and decorating for the forthcoming event. There was housecleaning to be done from the attic to the cellar. We had a full-sized attic where mother hung clothes to dry in the winter. The wide boards in the floor would have to be washed with lye soap and hot water carried up from two floors below. That task done, there were all the second-floor bedrooms to be cleaned.

All the bedding was washed, and quilts aired. One bedroom had rag carpeting, which had straw under it for cushioning. The carpet was carefully taken up, and the old straw removed. After the floor was washed, fresh straw was carried in, and the carpet carefully tacked in place again.

Lace curtains from every bedroom window were taken down, washed, starched, and stretched to dry on curtain stretchers. As the curtains were drying, the windows were washed with the old stand-by Bon Ami. Bon Ami came in a can as a powder. It was wiped on the window with a wet cloth, left to dry and then wiped off with another clean cloth. Now we had instant clean windows. Never mind how much "elbow-grease" had been used by that time.

When all the windows were washed, woodwork cleaned, and furniture polished it would be time to begin on the downstairs rooms. The entire process was repeated on the main floor. There were more lace curtains, woodwork, furniture, walls to dust and clean – where would it end? Carpeting had to be swept clean, and the kitchen made spotless.

The living room would need new wallpaper. And while they were at it, the kitchen should be papered too. The flyspecks on the ceiling from last summer's pests were noticeable.

The new Sears Roebuck wallpaper catalog had arrived just a week or two earlier. An order was sent via the rural mail carrier as soon as the selection of papers had been made. Mother could expect the bundle of paper to arrive in about two weeks.

The papering would have to wait until the early spring butchering was all done. There was meat to cut up, meat to can in glass fruit jars, lard to render, sausages to make, and the liver loaf baked for future rye-bread sandwiches.

Fieldwork had not yet begun, so Dad would be able to help with the papering. The dining room table was stretched out to its full length of six table leaves, then covered with layers of newspaper. The brushes and scissors, tools for the task, were also set out.

Mother made a paste from flour and water that had been brought to a boil, then cooled and stirred to the right thickness. Dad brushed the paper and mother usually did the hanging. It was amazing what a difference new paper would make to the "look" of the room.

In the meantime, there were meals to prepare, loaves of bread to bake, butter to churn, chickens to feed and care for, and hired hands coming in from the field or farmyard for meals three times a day. We would go down in the cellar and bring up a jar of canned pork that had been processed the winter before. That would make the meal easier to get ready.

The garden had to be planted and weeded. It was my job to run to the garden and bring in fresh potatoes, carrots, parsley or any other fresh produce as was available in the season.

When the day of Ladies Aid finally arrived everything was in absolutely perfect order. Curtains hung stiffly, windows shone in the bright sunlight without a single streak, furniture gleamed with polish and all the floors were freshly broomed and scrubbed. Hand-embroidered doilies, cleaned and starched, were tastefully and strategically placed on open flat areas. Even the porches were swept clean.

The chickens had been fed, the cream separator washed, wood had been stacked in the woodbin beside the cook stove, and the men were fed and "shooshed" out of the house.

At the appropriate time mother was ready in her neat cotton print dress with a pretty apron tied in back. I, too, had been washed, combed and brushed for this occasion.

Early on, Little Esther arrived. She was the president, and as such, had the responsibility and privilege of arriving early. Little Esther was a misnomer. She had more inches around her midriff than she had in height. But she was a good president and a good organizer.

Soon, the rest of the ladies arrived in their open touring cars-- Overlands, Mitchells, Fords, and a Buick. The ladies filed in, were escorted to the bedroom where they took out their hatpins, removed their hats, and laid them carefully on the white bedspread. A glance in the mirror quickly put any stray hairs in place.

Then they moved on to the living room where chairs were placed around the room. Soon the pastor and his wife would arrive. The pastor's wife--may her dear soul rest in peace--was always the object of particular scrutiny. She was held to the highest, often impossible, standards.

When all had arrived, the pastor opened the meeting with a song, a prayer, and then talked about something theological and esoteric. It must not have been meaningful to me because I don't remember what he said. The ladies, however, listened with appropriately solemn faces. Afterwards, everyone stood and recited the Apostle's Creed, and then all filed towards the dining room. I think that this was what the ladies really wanted to see.

There, on her finest white linen tablecloth were Mother's best china cups, saucers, plates, and spoons, all carefully arranged. Farther along the table, very attractively placed, was a Lady Baltimore white cake, butter cookies of at least two kinds, and freshly baked coffee cake. These mouth-watering refreshments were accompanied with coffee that had been made in the large granite coffee pot, the fresh grounds having been stirred out with a fresh egg. The women had a delightful time, enjoying the coffee and pastries, catching up on news, gossip, and the affairs of the day. No comments about the housekeeping were made, but nothing escaped the notice of the gathered ladies.

It had turned out to be a wonderful occasion, my mother stated as she collapsed into a nearby chair when everyone had left. The tension was gone until next year. Now it would be her turn to observe the housekeeping at the next meeting. The Ladies Aid did provide a valuable service to the church, and it was a meaningful social event for the ladies. And it certainly kept us on our toes to maintain a clean home.

BEES

On the Schmidt farm where I grew up back in the 1920's there stood two very large soft maple trees between the house and the barn. The trees were shedding bark and were showing their advanced age in other ways. The tree trunks also sounded hollow. It was only a matter of time before they fell or were blown down.

It was time to cut both of them down. The firewood from them would be useful. One late winter day, Dad and the hired man got out the tree cutting tools. They used hand saws, axes and wedges. This was long before powered chain saws and hydraulic log splitters.

When they dropped the first tree, I remember how Dad ran to the house to get large pans. They had sawed into a "bee tree" and the hollow inside of the tree trunk was filled with honey. The men scooped at least two large dishpans full of honey from the trees. Mother would have to pick out all of the bees that were barely alive because of the cold temperature.

What a treasure this was! We had honey on bread and pancakes for the rest of the winter.

No hive can have two queen bees for long. So if a new queen bee was hatched in a hive she would fly away, settle at a new place, and the worker bees would come and swarm around her.

It was not uncommon to find a hive of bees gathered on a wooden fence post along the roadside. If we knew a beekeeper, he would be notified. He would then come equipped to gather the swarm and take them home.

STRAW MATTRESSES

As a young kid I got a "new" mattress once a year. Our mattresses were straw-filled and by the time summer arrived the old straw was well settled and the mattress had gotten very thin.

Each summer at threshing time when the straw stacks were finished, my mother would empty the blue-striped ticking and wash it. The ticking was a heavy cotton fabric with a top and bottom side. Down the center of the topside there was an opening almost the full length of the fabric. It had large buttons on one side and buttonholes on the opposite side. It closed like a shirtfront. Now with a clean ticking my mother took it out to the straw stack and filled it with fresh, sweet, bright yellow straw. It was filled to about a two-foot thickness. The straw mattress was then buttoned and put back on the bed. The bedsprings were a flat wire mesh.

The first night crawling into bed, the mattress was very high. How it crackled with each turn one made. Later the straw became worn to the point that it would dip in the middle and be high on each end.

That new straw smelled so sweet. It was exciting to crawl up into that fresh high bed.

Can you imagine the sight of my mother carrying the new mattress across the yard and up to the bedroom where it would stay for another year?

POTATO BIN

There were five sizable rooms in the basement of our farm house. One room was the place to store the potatoes. It was a room large enough to store our supply of potatoes to last our family for one year.

Each spring Dad had half a dozen rows of potatoes planted at the edge of a field just north of the grove. Each row was almost a half mile long. These were all planted by hand using a tool we called a potato planter. The potato planter was a tool used just for that purpose. It hung on the wall of the potato bin from one planting season to the next. It was a metal pipe made of tin about five inches in diameter and maybe 24 or 28 inches long. This tube was filled with the pieces of potato that had been so carefully and laboriously cut. At the top was a mechanism, which released a piece of potato when the handle was squeezed. Near the bottom of the planter were two flaps that formed a wedge. This wedge was pushed into the soil by stepping on a foot piece. This would also pry the wedge apart, allowing the potato piece to fall to the bottom of the hole.

At potato planting time it was common for my grandfather and Dad to sit on the back porch steps cutting seed potatoes, leaving at least one eye in each piece, and throwing the pieces into a bucket. When enough potatoes were cut and the ground was ready, one man walked the row with the potato planter. Every twelve to eighteen inches, he would push the planter into the soil and release a potato piece. The potatoes were always planted before Good Friday.

Not long thereafter, the green leaves of the potato plant would be up in visible rows. When the potatoes were grown to about six inches or a little more they were sprayed for potato bugs. Without the spray, it was probable that the potato bugs would eat many of the leaves from the plants during the summer thereby reducing the yield. Rows were planted far enough apart so that they could be cultivated with the corn cultivator. The cultivator would push the soil up onto the base of the plants, making a long mound in the field. This increased the yield of the crop. In the rich soil of the farm, the plants would grow large and bushy.

As early as August, we would be able to dig a potato hill and gather up the small new potatoes, enough for a family meal. It was always good to have potatoes fresh from the soil. They had a special flavor. In late September, or even the first week of October, the potato harvest would begin. By then the potatoes were full grown, and the vines were withered and brown. The children would get a week off from school for picking the potatoes.

Dad would take the horse drawn potato plow to the field and turn up the long potato rows exposing most of the potatoes. Just behind the plowshare was a series of iron rods that would let the soil fall through as it moved along in the rows, leaving most of the potatoes exposed on top of the soil. We followed along behind the plow, picking up the potatoes and putting them into the pails we carried with us. We would dig a little in the dirt with our bare hands to make sure there were no buried ones. By the end of the day it would take some effort to wash off all the dirt.

At the end of the row, an empty wagon had been parked. As our pails were filled, we emptied them into the wagon. It was a back-breaking job to bend over the rows and carry our pails all day long.

When the potatoes were all picked up and in the wagon, Dad pulled the wagon along side of the house. The basement window was opened and the potatoes were shoveled and rolled down a wooden chute into the basement storeroom. Some wooden fencing in the cellar kept the potatoes from rolling all the way across the floor.

At the door to the potato room, the pile grew to almost two and a half to three feet deep, sloping higher toward the back wall of the room. The potatoes would have to last all year until the next harvest came in. In addition we had to have enough potatoes to use for seed in the spring. Each day through the winter we went to the potato bin and brought back a large pan of potatoes to peel and cook for the meals.

By spring the potatoes began to get soft and wrinkled and were hard to peel and use. The best ones were saved and used for next spring's planting.

We had potatoes with many of our meals. They were usually peeled and then boiled, although Mother did cook quite a few of them with the peelings on. They were rarely mashed, but rather served simply in a bowl. Occasionally Mother would prepare a cream sauce from flour and water to cover them. Fresh parsley sprinkled into the mixture added a little color and flavor as well. No matter how they were served, the potato was a staple in our diet.

SOAP

I grew up in an era when nothing was thrown away. There were times when we had no money to buy even what we needed, but even when we did have money, it took lots of time to go into town to purchase the desired item or to order through the catalogue process. It always seemed that on those occasions when we did throw something away, we would be sure to need it the next day.

So, as I have been reading and sorting papers from fifty or more years ago, I have found some recipes that may seem strange to those growing up in the twenty-first century.

For example, what young housewife would consider making homemade laundry soap when, today, it can be purchased at the local grocery stores in brightly colored plastic bottles or gaily painted cardboard boxes either in liquid or powdered form?

In the early part of the last century, and even before that time, making soap was an annual event. My mother always made soap after the hog butchering was done in late winter. The meat had been canned or brined and the lard had been rendered. Rendering cooked the slabs of fat to separate the lard. The residue, called cracklings, was then used in making soap.

In the hog house was a large cast-iron bowl-like kettle about three feet across and about twenty inches deep. Under this kettle was a place to build a fire. The bowl was surrounded by sheet iron both for keeping the bowl stable and to contain the fire. The fire was usually fed with corncobs. They made a hot, quick fire.

The cracklings were poured into the iron kettle along with water and lye. The contents were cooked and stirred with a heavy wooden paddle. When the soap had cooked long enough, the fire was left to go out on its own, and the soap cooled for a day. It was then cut into square or oblong pieces and stored in cardboard boxes.

We would then have enough soap to last the year. It was crude soap, but it was very strong and it did clean what we washed.

Here are a few modern recipes for making homemade soap. Our soap was made similarly:

From "Ask Mary" column (Mary Hart) of the Minneapolis Tribune, Thu., Jan. 10, 1980:

Methods for preparing homemade soaps of all kinds arrived after Phyllis G. asked for help in making laundry and hand types.

M. Janecky supplied this information and recipe. She wrote that the type of fat determines the quality of soap.

Beef fat (tallow), she said, produces a harder, longer lasting soap than does lard. Vegetable oils make a nice hand soap, she added. Soap making is an entertaining project, Janecky said, and never fails when properly done. However, she advised, homemade soap is less sudsy than commercial kinds.

This is the recipe she sent, cautioning to use glass or earthenware bowls only.

HOMEMADE HAND SOAP
13 oz. lye
5 c. warm water
6 lb. warmed vegetable oil
(coconut, palmseed or soy oil are good choices)

Dissolve lye in the warm water. Have ready a 6-quart bowl and add oil. Add dissolved lye in a slow steady stream and stir until mixture is creamy. Add a fragrant oil, a tablespoon or two, or food coloring at this point. Pour into a wet mold.

A shoebox lined with wet paper works fine. Wrap the box in a towel for the mixture must cool slowly until it sets. When set, cut into cakes and let the soap cure for a month before using.

More soft soap

Eighteen years ago, Cordelle M. Collins and her sister began making soap when they had a "lot of lard to use."

"We mixed this in a large stone crock outdoors and used a large wooden stick," wrote Collins. "Don't let any splash on you. Lye will cause burns on the skin."

"This makes a granulated laundry soap and did a great job of cleaning."

LAUNDRY SOAP
3 qt. minus 1 c. lukewarm water
1 can Lewis lye
¾ c. borax
9 c. melted lard
1 c. ammonia
½ ox. citronella

Put water in a large stone crock. Add lye and borax and stir to dissolve. Pour melted lard slowly into lye water. Stir for 15 minutes. Add ammonia and citronella. Stir often for 36 hours. Then pour into a box to dry.

Another laundry soap recipe arrived from Mrs. T. Seltz.

HOMEMADE LAUNDRY SOAP
5 lb. waste fat
1 can lye
1 qt. hot soft water
2 tbsp. sugar
1 tbsp. salt
3 tbsp. borax
½ c. cold water

Melt and strain the waste fat into a 3-pound coffee can (filled one inch from top). Let cool until it is of a creamy consistency. In a two-

or three-gallon crock, dissolve the lye in the soft water. Let this cool several hours.

Mix sugar, salt, borax and cold water. Stir into lye mixture slowly. Add the fat slowly, stirring with a wooden paddle. Stir occasionally for about 15 minutes. Let stand about 12 hours.

Cut into pieces. Remove when pieces are firm. Store in a wooden crate for about a week. Let age three weeks before using.

World War II recipe

Mrs. H. Hoover said that she made soap (similar to the recipe above) during World War II and if the price of soap continues to rise, she may make it again.

She said that she ground the soap in the meat grinder and then used the product in the washing machine. However, she doesn't know if this would work in an automatic washer.

Perfume often was added to her recipe, she said.

Here's a laundry soap recipe given to me by a friend about a year ago. I figured the cost to be about 75 cents. The soap is soft but keeps in a covered container for ages.

J. Andrews

ECOLOGY SOAP
3 gallons lukewarm soft water
1 can lye
7 c. melted fat
½ c. ammonia
½ c. white vinegar
½ c. liquid bleach

Place water in a 5-gallon crock. Add lye slowly and then mix in other ingredients. Stir (be careful of fumes while mixing). Let stand and mix every hour for six to eight hours. Mix often the next two to three days until thick. Use ¾ cup per laundry load.

CANNING SEASON

Preservation of food was of utmost importance on the farm. Food preservation was referred to as "canning". Early in the 20th century food staples such as flour, salt and sugar were available in bulk, either barrels or bags. There were few prepackaged foods available. In order to have a wide selection of food the year 'round it was necessary to preserve produce grown on our farm. There were no freezers available until after World War II. Electricity to operate them or even early refrigerators did not reach most farms until the rural electrification project of the 1930's.

Canning season began as soon as there was food growing that could be harvested. In early spring there was rhubarb from which jam could be made, stored in jars with melted paraffin poured over the top to seal it. Then all summer long other fruits were picked and some were made into sauce or jam. We canned homegrown apples, pears, peaches, cherries, elderberries, grapes, currants and gooseberries. Sometimes the larger fruits were sliced and canned in a sauce. Berries could be canned in their juice or made into jams and jellies. Later on in the summer garden vegetables likewise were preserved. All of these items had to be picked or dug up, then washed and prepared for canning. From spring to fall there always seemed to be canning to be done.

Most farm wives made a variety of pickles from cucumbers and beets. Recipes were exchanged to see who could make the crispest cucumber pickles. Even the ripe cucumbers made a good pickle. Watermelon rinds also made an excellent sweet pickle.

Most vegetables were canned by the cold-pack method, which meant that the glass jars were filled with uncooked produce. Then the jars were sealed, set in a seven-quart canner or wash boiler where they were covered with water, brought to a boil and simmered for three hours. This cooked the vegetables and sterilized the containers. Then the jars were gently lifted from the hot water and set out to cool. Some lids had to be retightened when they came out of the hot bath to ensure the seal. We knew that the jars were hermetically sealed when the center of the lid would suddenly indent making a metallic "plink." If the jar did not seal properly, it would not keep. We would use these jars of food right away.

Dad would on occasion make wine from the grapes. I was told that it was very good. Mother had a girl in our home to help her with the housework. She was there at the direction of the Red Cross as what we now call foster care. Her father had been put into the state penitentiary on a very long sentence for stealing twelve chickens. The girl found the wine to be very good, too good, perhaps, and that had to be stopped. She lived with us for many years and received no pay. Her sister lived on a neighboring farm. She became a part of our family in most respects. My brother and I traveled on the Rock Island railroad to stay with her and her new husband for a few days. We kept in touch with her and her family until she moved to Washington State. Then we lost track of her, and heard nothing from that time on.

By the end of the growing season dozens and dozens of glass fruit jars had been filled with a variety of produce. They lined the many shelves in the basement by the hundreds, clearly displaying their contents. With a good supply of fruits and vegetables, jams and jellies, and pickles there would be food for the family throughout the winter.

When a hog was butchered much of the meat was canned. Ground pork made into meatballs was particularly good eating. Sometimes, meat packed in jars could be preserved by setting the jars in the cook stove oven and baking the meat for three hours. The flavor was very good.

The pork hams were usually put into a brine solution in a large stone jar. Some people had smoke houses and smoked their own hams. They would then be hung in our cellar where it was always cool.

It was sort of a status symbol when visiting with other women to tell how many jars of food had been put away in the cellar. Of course, there were always those who had done a few more quarts than the others. Canning was a lot of hard work in the heat of summer, but it was necessary to have the food available that would not only sustain us through a long cold winter, but also maintain our good health. It was always a proud moment and comforting to see the many, many jars of produce all lined up on the shelves in the cellar.

We knew that while we enjoyed fresh produce during the growing season, the canned fruits, vegetables and meat would be there to provide good food during the winter. Our diet thus followed an annual cycle that we don't experience in modern culture. When canned and cooked properly it all tasted very good.

Canning was a learning process as well. We learned the responsibility to take care of ourselves and our families. We learned to be prepared by planning ahead in times of plenty in the summer for the lean times of winter. Those who failed to can enough food went hungry in late winter. It was a tough lesson about life. We knew it was necessary to prepare more than enough food for our family to have for the unknown length of the winter season. It was not possible to predict exactly when we would have fresh produce again. We knew by faith that it would be sometime in the next year. Perhaps these lessons need new vehicles for our edification.

BLACK WALNUTS AND BUTTERNUTS

Every fall Dad gathered up two or three gunny sacks for the annual nut gathering event. Gunny sacks were made of coarse burlap and were large enough to hold 100 pounds of livestock feed or potatoes. We always seemed to have plenty of these sacks on the farm. They were used for many and varied purposes, including dousing grass fires, of all things. Of all the uses none was better than harvesting these nuts.

The family got into the car and we drove to the Beaver Valley Woods that grew along the Beaver Creek northwest of Cedar Falls. These woods had many butternut and black walnut trees. It was the same area where we had gone for fishing and swimming during the summer.

The woods were thick and the green nuts were on the ground ready to be gathered. After an afternoon of stooping and picking up nuts one by one the sacks were full. We drove home with the bountiful harvest. The bags were emptied on the cellar floor and the nuts were spread out to dry. After a couple of weeks, the green husks turned to dark brown when dry.

After the nuts had dried it was time to peel the husks from the nuts. This was tedious work. As we peeled the husks from the nut our hands turned to dark brown from the stain. If you have ever wondered where walnut and butternut stain comes from, try peeling husks for an afternoon!

Both butternuts and black walnuts had a thick, wrinkled shell that was very hard. These shells required at least a hammer and hard surface to even crack. When Mother needed walnut nut meats for baking, a pan of nuts could be taken out to the tool shed where there was a vise and the nuts were gently squeezed in the vise until the very hard shell was broken. If the weather was too cold to go outside to crack nuts we could squat on the cellar floor and crack the shells with a hammer. These broken pieces were gathered in a pan, taken up to the kitchen where we tediously picked the nut meats out with a sturdy nut pick until we had enough to flavor a cake or a batch of candy.

The flavors of these nuts in a cake or in candy were well worth all the effort it took to crack the nuts. Nothing tastes so warm on a cold winter's evening than fresh popcorn accompanied by rich fudge flavored with black walnut nuts!

CURTAIN STRETCHER

An abominable piece of equipment in each household was the curtain stretcher. It was made of four long lengths of narrow boards precisely marked at one-inch intervals with sharp menacing ¾-inch prongs of steel protruding at each inch. The boards had holes drilled in them at intervals so that a bolt and winged nut attached each corner sized according to the measurement of the curtain. The curtain stretcher would be set up in an area where anyone walking by would not be scratched by the protruding pins. It was dangerous for children to get near and injure themselves on the stretcher. No one really enjoyed having the stretcher set up for any length of time. The pins were as sharp as needles, and it was difficult to pin a lace curtain on the device without drawing blood and ruining the clean lace.

No matter how small or how large the house was there would be lace curtains hanging in each window. Once or twice a year the curtains were taken down from the rods across the top of the window. Carefully, these curtains were washed and, if coloring was needed, the rinse water was diluted with strong coffee. When the curtains were dipped in this solution it would give them the color of ecru. The previous color application had long faded from the curtain while hanging in the sunshine. After the color rinse solution, the curtains were dipped in a solution of Argo clothes starch. The bulk of the starch was squeezed out by hand.

First one corner was pinned, then a few areas of the curtain were temporarily pinned to the frame. Inch by inch the curtain was stretched to its correct size and left for a day to dry. If fingers were pricked, pinning had to stop until the blood flow ceased. When the curtain was dry, it was then removed from the stretcher and hung in the window again. For the first few days the curtains seemed to strut stiff as a board from the starch, but before long the humidity in the air would allow the curtains to hang freely again, but now free of wrinkles.

When all of the house cleaning was done and all the curtains had been stretched and hung once more, the apparatus was disassembled. The bolts were removed from the stretcher and the four long pieces were bound together with strips of cloth rags torn from old shirts or other old pieces of clothing. This bundle was carefully set away in the attic or closet. It was good to wrap those four cumbersome boards in some strips of old cotton shirting until the next stretching season.

CARPETING

The largest of the five upstairs bedrooms in our white frame farmhouse had wall-to-wall carpeting. This was in the World War I era.

The carpeting consisted of cotton rags woven into 30-inch wide strips made into the length of the room. These strips were sewed together along their sides to complete one piece that covered the area of the room.

Once a year my mother pulled out the carpet tacks around the edge of the carpet by the walls. The tacks were carefully saved to be re-used. She then carried the carpet outside to be brushed clean. I don't remember of it being washed.

Underneath the carpet was a layer of straw that over a year's time was worn to shreds from people walking on it. This straw was swept up and carried outdoors. The eight-inch pine boards of the floor were washed thoroughly and left to dry for a day.

Then Mother went to the straw stack in the farmyard and carried in armfuls of clean straw to scatter over the clean floor. This was done right after the oats harvest when the straw was fresh and clean. When there was enough straw to make some cushioning the carpeting was brought back in and spread over the straw. Then began the tedious task of tacking the carpeting back to the floor along the walls. My mother used a carpet stretcher to pull the carpet taut and at the same time, with a tack hammer, she would tack the carpet every two or three inches all around the room. It meant hours and hours of work. When the tacking was finished the furniture was brought back into the bedroom.

The living room and parlor on first floor each had wool area rugs. In the winter mother would bring in fresh clean snow, scatter it over the wool carpeting and, with a broom, sweep the entire rug. The snow would cling to dust particles and freshen the rugs. The floors were not very warm and the snow would not quickly melt. This method of cleaning with snow was quite effective.

EVERYDAY CAKE

In the era after World War I and before World War II we made our own desserts. Cake mixes were unheard of, and during the depression we couldn't afford them even if they had been available. Cakes were an easy dessert to make, and were a good ending to the large meals we served on the farm.

Almost every day my mother baked a cake. When the men stopped their work for afternoon coffee, as they always did, there was always a fresh cake and sandwiches ready for them.

During the weekdays my mother baked chocolate, spice or other dark cake. And they were very good. I remember the burnt sugar cake she made where she caramelized white sugar in an iron skillet until it was a dark brown and used it to color the cake batter.

But for Sundays there was always a white Lady Baltimore cake. It stood two or three layers high and was frosted with a boiled white frosting. The frosting was made from a sugar syrup that was boiled until it spun a thread when lifted by a spoon. Egg whites were beaten until stiff, then the sugar syrup was poured into the egg whites making a sweet, rich frosting.

If the sugar syrup was boiled to just the right temperature it made a nice white fluffy frosting that remained soft. But if boiled too long the frosting was hard and brittle. One neighbor said he didn't like it if, when he put a knife into the frosting, the whole top would crack and break.

White cakes were always baked for the company who visited on Sunday afternoons. It was a tradition. I don't know why it was so, but most families in our area made white cakes only for Sundays. My mother often chopped raisins and nuts together to make a filling for a white layer cake.

Cakes were often good examples of the housewife's baking ability. Other people compared the various attributes of the cake to their own efforts. But no matter the quality, everyone seemed to enjoy these desserts whenever they were served.

HOME BREW

Dad liked his home brewed beer made from hops. On the Schmidt farm, there was a woven wire fence around the lawn area next to the house. On the fence out by the road, there grew a hops vine. From this vine, Dad gathered the light-colored flat seed clusters for making his beer.

I don't know his recipe but he did have a large stone jar in the basement where he used water, yeast foam, and hops. There must have been some sugar in it, too. When the liquid had fermented long enough, the beer was ready for bottling.

Dad had glass bottles, a device for clamping on bottle caps and a supply of new bottle caps. Before he had bottle caps, he used corks to seal the bottles. When the bottles were filled, leaving an inch or two of air space at the top of the bottle, the bottles were capped. The beer had to "season" for a week or two before it could be drunk, so the filled bottles were left on the cellar floor during this time. Once in a while a bottle cap or a cork would hit the cellar ceiling and we knew another bottle of beer had exploded. Everyone laughed when the cap hit the ceiling. We knew that was one less bottle of beer for Dad.

When the beer was finally ready, the bottles were cooled in cold running water that was collected in a washtub in the basement. At that time we had fresh running well water from a gravity fed system.

Wine making was common in the neighborhood with the bounty of homegrown grapes that were produced each fall. However, Mrs. Lauitz Christensen made a wonderful wine from dandelion blossoms. It made a delicate light-colored wine.

The beer and winemaking was popular back in the 1920's. There was a time when in the later 1960's, people made "gallon jug wine." It was done as follows:

Into a clean, clear glass gallon jug, pour the contents of two large cans of grape juice. (I do not know the exact size, but there was a time when juices came in tall round metal cans.)

Add ¼ teaspoon dry yeast.

Add 5 cups of sugar.

164

Cover the jug and shake the contents to dissolve the sugar and yeast.

Instead of capping the jug tightly, slip a large rubber balloon over the neck of the jug. Set the jug out of the way, but at room temperature, moderately warm. The balloon will expand, and then later it will deflate. Then the wine is ready.

Of course I had to try this easy recipe. I got everything ready and set the jug on top of our refrigerator ("out of the way, but at room temperature, moderately warm"). However, at that time our refrigerator was an old model, and it had a top that was slightly curved from side to side.

Early one morning, about 4:00, we heard a terrible crash. From the vibration of the refrigerator motor, the jug had eased off the top of the refrigerator and crashed to the floor. Can you imagine the mess there was to clean? That ended the winemaking for me.

HOG BUTCHERING

The lowly pig was the source of much of our meat and shortening necessary for cooking. It even provided our soap for all of our washing needs. These noisy and nasty smelling animals provided excellent meat that we could make last all year long.

Pigs are noisy. They grunt and snort and squeal for no real reason other than making themselves known. They smell badly. A walk through the hog pen or hog house was an assault to the nose. The smell also lasted on clothing that would remain for some time. Even their food smells bad. We fed them potato peelings and other scraps from our food preparation, even when not so fresh. A common food was oats or shelled corn soaked in water or milk and left to ferment. It smelled worse than sour milk. No wonder they smelled bad.

The older pigs were ill-tempered and dangerous to children and adults alike. Sows with a litter of piglets became very protective. Boars were just nasty and not to be trusted. Injury and even the death of the farmer from a mad boar were not uncommon.

But the pig was the source of many valuable items. We had delicious ham and bacon. A savory pork roast with apple or prune stuffing made a very tasty meal. Ground pork provided relatively quick meals when seasoned and made into meatballs. Pork liver was considered a delicacy, but not by everyone. The lining of the intestines was used to make sausages of all kinds. Lard rendered from the fatty tissue was used for cooking throughout the year. The leftover cracklings from the lard was used to make soap.

The rite of butchering on the farm came when the nights were frosty in order that the carcass could chill overnight without spoilage. Cold weather made it possible to process the pig without any contamination of the meat.

To begin with the hog to be butchered was paneled off into a corner of the barn with wooden panels. With rope and pulleys the hog was raised off the ground for the procedure. The animal was hung by its hind legs from a 'single tree' (the wooden bar with attachments at either end for hitching one horse to a vehicle). I was never present for the actual killing, so I don't know each of the steps in order. I do know my father took the big butcher knife from the kitchen for the actual killing. I heard the squealing as the hog hung in mid air. I knew my father had stabbed the jugular vein to bleed the hog.

After the blood was drained from the hog it was dipped into a barrel of hot water to loosen the bristles on the hide. The hot water also cleaned the dirt from the hog as well. The hog was then scraped removing the stiff hog bristles. A hog scraper was a moon-shaped piece of steel about 6 or 7 inches across, razor sharp on the curved edge, with a wooden handle across the points of the steel.

After that the hog was gutted with a slash through the underside of the hog. From these entrails the fresh liver and heart were set aside in a clean pan. The carcass would then hang outside overnight for the meat to chill.

The next morning the carcass was split down the middle lengthwise and the halves were brought into the kitchen and laid on the wooden kitchen table.

The hind legs were severed to be made into hams. The ham could be cured by immersing it in a salt brine made in a ten gallon stone crock. The meat would take on a very salty taste. A twine string could be inserted through the Achilles tendon and the hind leg hung out in the smoke house. The smoke house was a small wooden building the size of an outhouse. Burning coals were laid on the dirt floor. Small pieces of wood, preferably apple wood, were placed on the red embers to smolder, making lots of thick smoke. The hams were hung in the smoke house to partially cook in the heat, take on the flavor of the smoke and be ready to store in a cool location.

Slabs of side pork were hung in the smokehouse with the hams. The smoked side pork became bacon. Smoked hams and bacon had much better flavor and color than the brine-cured items.

After the hams and slabs of bacon were put away the rest of the hog was cut up into serving pieces. As other pieces of the pig were cut from the carcass, the fat was trimmed from the meat. The slabs of fat were laid aside.

The smaller trimmings of selected pieces of meat were packed into one quart green glass jars. A red rubber ring was placed over the top of the jar and a zinc metal top was screwed lightly on the jar of meat. When the jars were filled they were placed in the cook stove oven to cook. The jars of meat were baked in the hot oven for three hours. Then they were removed and the lids tightened on the rubber ring. The jars were set aside to be cooled, and then stored in the basement on shelves for future use throughout the year.

On occasion a jar would explode in the oven creating a terrible greasy mess to clean. The cook stove had to be fired for the three hours baking time, which meant lots of firewood had to be ready. The cleanup of broken jars had to wait until the oven had cooled sufficiently to do so.

Some women roasted the pieces of meat, then placed those pieces in one gallon stone crocks, then covered them with melted lard. When they wanted to use some meat it was picked out of the lard and heated in an iron frying pan. These stone crocks filled with lard and meat were stored in the cool basement.

The cast iron meat grinder was attached to the edge of the wooden table. The meat grinder had a crank on one side that operated an auger mechanism. As we turned a long crank by hand, the auger forced cuts of meat or pork fat through a mesh that ground the meat or fat into small pieces suitable for further processing. The ground meat became sausage and the ground fat was used for lard.

The fat or lard of the pork was trimmed away from the lean meat. The fat was cut into pieces of a size that could be sent through the meat grinder. After the fat was ground, it was placed in large kettles, set on the cook stove and heated to the point where the lard turned into liquid form. Lard melts at a fairly high temperature, so this part of the process held some danger of burns or fire.

The liquid fat, now called lard, was drained off into stone jars. The remains in the cooking kettle were called cracklings. The cracklings were placed into the lard press to squeeze out the remaining liquid. A lard press is made of wrought iron, with a round container of about a two gallon size. On top of the machine is a gear system by which when turning the handle a flat iron plate presses down on the cracklings, squeezing out the remaining lard.

The lard, having been poured into the stone crocks, was set in the basement where it would keep through the next summer. It would be used frequently for cooking and baking, and had to last until the next butchering time.

Some of the cracklings were then saved to use when frying potatoes. These crisp brown nuggets were actually very tasty and gave a rich flavor to the fried potatoes. In the winter or cold weather heavy meals were served. Men husking corn especially needed food that would give them energy and keep them warm in the bitter cold. We would say that this was a meal that "would stay with them until the next meal time."

The other cracklings were set aside in a container to be made into laundry soap. They were put into the large cast iron kettle stored in the hog barn. The kettle was set on a ring of stones outside in the yard. A large fire was started under the iron cooker. Water was added to the kettle along with a generous amount of lye. As the cracklings and lye were cooked they were stirred with a wooden paddle. The fire was allowed to go out, and the mixture cooled. We could then scoop the freshly made soap into containers to use at laundry time, for washing dishes, for bathing and for any other soap needs in our life.

The remaining scraps of meat were ground, seasoned and made into sausages.

Another use for the lard press was for stuffing sausages. At the bottom of the press was a round opening. On this opening a round closed spout was attached to the press. Casing for the sausage was placed over this spout.

Sausage casing was made from the pig's intestines. The pig's intestines were carefully washed and scraped with a wooden blade. This hand made blade was about six inches long and slightly curved. The soft intestines were held between the fingers as the knife stripped away the lining.

The wet, clean intestines were slipped over the spout. Ground sausage already placed inside the press was slowly forced through the cone and into the casings allowing the casing to slip forward as the meat filled into it.

These sausages were then placed in glass fruit jars and processed the same as the other meat.

The liver would be sliced and dipped in flour. Then it was fried in an iron pan until done and served with boiled potatoes and a milk gravy. Liver had a unique flavor, and not everyone acquired the taste for it.

There were some who trimmed the meat from the hog's head. That meat was made into head cheese.

After all the meat, sausage and lard was cut from the carcass there was much cleaning to be done. The kitchen was usually a greasy mess by now, and would need thorough cleaning. The hog's hide would be tanned, or taken to someone who would do the tanning. It would make good leather. The bones would usually be fed to the dogs. Some larger bones might be added to baked beans for additional flavor. Many bones were used to add flavor to vegetable soup. We enjoyed the richly flavored soup in the now cold weather.

The whole process of butchering took a tremendous amount of energy. The whole process would take several days. There were meals to prepare anyway, in the midst of cooking meat and fat. Chores needed to be done and children needed care. It was a lot of hard work.

The lowly pig gave us much for which we were thankful. Imagine all that from the nasty smelly ugly pig!

WALL PAPER CATALOGS

Along in the latter part of January the rural mail carrier delivered wallpaper catalogs to each farm house along his route. Sears & Roebuck and Montgomery Wards were the two companies who mailed them to potential customers. The catalogs measured almost half the size of a standard sheet of typing paper and were one to two inches thick. Each page was a sample with its accompanying border. The most expensive papers were at the front of the book and became less expensive as one neared the end of the catalog.

A section of our grade school arithmetic texts dealt with mathematical problems on how to measure a room for wallpaper. Schools were practical so most people knew how to measure and order from the catalog. As I remember my mother ordered wallpaper from the back of the catalog, enclosed a check with the order blank, and waited for the delivery in a week or two. Wallpaper arrived in single or double rolls and had to be trimmed on the side with a scissors. There was about a ¾-inch plain edge on each side of the roll.

Most farm kitchens were papered with fresh new paper each year in early spring. Kitchen ceilings were covered with fly specks from the previous summer as well as the soiled areas around the cook stove that needed to be replaced with new paper.

A thick paste was made from a flour and water mixture that was brought to a boil on the cook stove, and then cooled. Dad brought a couple of wide planks from one of the farm storage buildings, laid them across the backs of two dining chairs, and covered them with newspapers. Here the wallpaper pieces would be laid out, paste would be applied and then made ready for hanging.

Dad was delegated to paper the ceilings. More planks were laid across chairs so that he could walk along the plank while hanging the ceiling paper. It was a little tricky to get the pasted wallpaper stuck to one end of the ceiling while walking across the board to line up the other end. The chairs and planks were moved for each successive strip. The walls were easier to do. Carefully matching the edges was the most important.

We had a six-inch wide wallpaper paste brush to spread the paste and an even wider brush to smooth the paper. Always we needed a rag to wipe the extra paste that oozed from the edge of the wallpaper. The newly applied paper always brightened the room.

I was about twelve or thirteen years old when on one spring day my mother had been papering the walls of a bedroom. It was time for her to make the noon meal. She said, "Elna, you go ahead and keep hanging the wall paper." For years I had been hanging around when it was papering time and I pretty well knew how to do it. Anyway, I did continue hanging paper and it must have been all right.

When I lived in one old farmhouse I thought it would be a good idea to remove the layers of old paper. By count there had been twenty-six layers of paper applied to the kitchen walls. It was a lot of effort to remove the paper, but the fresh paper looked very clean and bright. The following winter the kitchen was a very cold room. Apparently, all those layers of paper had been good insulation.

WASH DAY

The most labor intensive and backbreaking work the farm wife had was doing the laundry on washday. Mondays were the most logical day to get that work done. Because of the lack of plumbing for bathrooms and bathtubs, people bathed only on Saturday nights. That meant lots of soiled clothes needing to be washed, but not on Saturday night or Sunday. Now that seems very strange to us in the era we are living in now.

Water in five-gallon pails had to be carried a distance and then heated and carried again. It involved strength and determination to get any of these necessities done at all.

Early on Monday mornings, in wintertime, the washing machine, two rinse tubs, a copper boiler and all of the other equipment needed was brought from the washhouse into the kitchen. Water was brought into the house and poured into the copper wash boiler set on the kitchen stove. In the warmer weather, we placed the copper boiler on a kerosene-fired stove in the washhouse. The copper pot held about 25 gallons of water so it meant three or four trips to the well or cistern to fill the boiler half full. Then the fire had to be kept burning to get the water to the boiling point. Firing the cook stove meant carrying wood or cobs as well.

The first washer that I remember was made of wood, probably maple, and had a gear system underneath with a wooden handle on the side. When the cover was put on the machine, someone had to pull the handle back and forth, back and forth, for at least ten minutes. The "dolly" inside the machine was agitating the clothes in the hot water. There was a wringer attached to the side of the machine. It, too, was hand operated by turning a crank on the side of the mechanism.

While the water was heating, the housewife, with a large knife, pared a few shavings from a bar of homemade soap into the tub to be dissolved in hot water. Then, when the soap had been dissolved, one or two tablespoons of Lewis Lye would be stirred into the water. The combination of soap, lye, hot water and the washing machine did get our clothes clean. It was a potent concoction. We dared not put our hands into the wash water. We needed another tool.

The wash stick was made of a piece of hardwood, about 18 to 20 inches long, and shaped with a cutting tool to make a smooth handle at one end and a flattened area at the other end. It was a very important tool on washday. Wash sticks were most often homemade and strong enough to hold the weight of hot wet clothes. My mother-in-law had a commercially made wash stick, made of two long sticks about an inch thick at the upper end and somewhat narrower at the other end. The two thickest ends were fastened together with a metal pin so that the stick was used with a pincer like fashion.

Meanwhile, the dirty clothes from the whole past week had to be sorted according to color. Bed sheets first, then dish towels, next bath towels, another stack for house dresses and aprons, and last of all the men's overalls, the dirtiest of the lot. Prior to World War II the most commonly used fabrics were made from cotton or wool. So when bed sheets, white clothes and towels were washed, they were also boiled to whiteness in water held in the copper wash boiler.

When the water in the boiler was hot it was bailed over into the washing machine and the first batch of clothes was put in. The boiler was then refilled with water to heat, and some lye was added to this water. With effort, the handle on the side of the washer was moved back and forth to operate the agitator. The washer whoosh whooshed away, agitating the white sheets to cleanliness. When the sheets had washed for the ten-minute time, and the water in the boiler was hot, the sheets were picked up with the wooden wash stick and transferred into the boiler where the sheets were boiled for five or ten minutes. This was dangerously hot hard work. The wash stick was essential to keeps hands from being scalded. It did happen that some of the lye water would splash over onto the woman doing the laundry. This could cause a serious burn.

While the sheets were boiling, a wooden bench that held the two galvanized washtubs for rinsing was then lined up next to the washing machine. The sheets were rinsed twice in the two round metal tubs. They were filled with clear clean water. Some Mrs. Stewart's liquid bluing was poured into the first tub. The white clothes would look brighter with a little bluing in it. The second tub would also have a dash of bluing added to the water in insure even more whiteness.

Then, at great risk of being scalded by the hot water, the sheets were lifted with the wash stick from the boiler over into a pail or wash basin. With the wooden wash stick we lifted a corner of the wet sheet from the basin and got it started through the wringer, as someone else was turning the handle of that device. If we were alone we had to turn the crank at the same time. The sheets were sent through the rubber rollers to wring out the hot water. The trick was to keep the sheets from wrapping around the rubber rollers. If they did that, the roller was reversed. Then the housewife deftly caught the tip of the sheet with the stick as it once again proceeded through the rollers. As the hot sheet came through the wringer it fell into the first tub of rinse water. There the sheets were doused up and down several times to flush out the soap.

Next those sheets were sent through the wringer once more and then into the second rinse tub. When they had been doused up and down several times, the wringer was swung around on a pivot. Then the sheets were put through the rollers again, falling this time into a wicker clothesbasket.

As the sheets were then rolled into the wicker clothesbasket waiting to be hung on the clothesline, the next batch of white dish towels were being agitated in the washer. Hopefully, one of the children would keep the agitator going as the mother was lifting the clean sheets up and down to rinse the soap from them.

The clothesline was carefully washed to remove whatever dust, grime and bird droppings had accumulated. Then the sheets were carefully hung in a rectangle, matching corner to corner, and were secured to the line with wooden clothespins. It seemed important to bring corners to corners so that the sheets hung in envelope form on the line. When clothes were hung on the lines in the winter they would of course freeze stiff as a board. Then little by little the clothes were brought in and hung on lines strung across the kitchen to finish drying.

By that time the second load of clothes was washed and the identical procedure was carried out. The process continued until all white clothes and towels were washed, boiled, wrung, rinsed, and hung up to dry. Blue chambray shirts and denim overalls were never boiled, as the dye would be leeched from the fabrics. The bib overalls were last to be washed since they were the dirtiest and were dark colored.

If there were white dress shirts in the wash they would be dipped into a pan of starch, which had been cooked on the stove. Next the aprons were starched and hung on the line.

After all the clothes were washed rinsed and hung up to dry, all the water had to be emptied from the tubs. Again it meant bailing water out of the containers to be carried away to the yard pail by pail. After all the water had been emptied the machine was rinsed with clean water. The washtubs were rinsed and hung on nails on the wall of the washhouse.

As the clothes dried they were folded and readied for ironing. Bed sheets were folded into four and ironed while slightly damp. Dishtowels were meticulously folded corner-to-corner and ironed. White shirts, house dresses, aprons, and men's everyday shirts had to be dampened and set away for ironing the following day.

My mother took pride in having clean clothes for the family. She did very well and was known in the neighborhood as having the whitest sheets around. Washday was a major chore for the housewife. It would take most of the day. In addition, there were meals to prepare, babies to tend, chickens to be fed, etc. We were always busy.

The earliest washing machines I remember were hand operated. It kept everyone busy to do all of the operations of washday, and housewives developed very strong arms. In the 1930's small 2-cycle gasoline engines were available to power the washing machine. The Rural Electrification was begun in the last half of the 1930's, and as it spread into our area electric motors took over the noisy, smelly 2-cycle engines. These made the physical effort of washing and wringing the clothes much easier, but with the additional power the housewife had to be more careful of being injured by the machine.

It took a long time and plenty of effort to do what a modern washing machine does automatically in less than 30 minutes. As a housewife I'm glad for the newer devices. What I miss, however, is the fresh smell of bed sheets that have gone through the old process and then hung out in the sun and fresh air to dry. This fresh aroma is or was unique, and has not been duplicated with modern machines.

IRONING DAY

No doubt about it. Tuesday was always ironing day. On the Saturday night before, the whole family had bathed and got a complete change of clean clothes. Come Monday morning, water was carried to the wash house, heated, and the clothes were washed, boiled, rinsed, starched and hung out to dry. That same afternoon the clean clothes were sprinkled and rolled up tightly and tucked away in the wicker clothesbasket ready for ironing on Tuesday morning.

First of all, the fire in the cook stove needed to be kept burning to heat the "sadirons". How the flat irons got the name I do not know. Usually, there were three heavy irons smooth and flat on one side. The hot irons were designed to be used with a "holder" which was a device with a wooden handle on top. When the holder was attached to the iron it looked like a standard ironing device. The top of the sadirons had two prongs to attach the holder. The irons were used alternately so as to keep one iron hot at all times.

The ironing board was a 16- or 20-inch wide board covered and padded with an old blanket, then wrapped in a white sheet fastened underneath with safety pins. If the board did not have legs it was balanced on the backs of two dining chairs.

To test the irons for the right temperature we clamped the handle on one of the irons. Then with a quick lick of a pointer finger tapped the bottom of the iron. If the iron was hot enough it would sizzle from the saliva. When it tested hot enough the iron was brought to the ironing board where it was rubbed on a piece of newspaper to make sure that the iron was clean. Sometimes it helped to put some coarse salt on the paper and rub the flat piece back and forth to make the flat piece smoother. If some starch had gotten stuck to the iron the salt would remove the spot.

When the fire in the cook stove was burning well and the irons were ready we could begin ironing. One piece at a time each item was unrolled, smoothed and then ironed. If any piece needed mending it was laid aside to be mended later. Often buttons needed to be sewed back on, shirtsleeve elbows and overall knees patched, or tears on clothes repaired.

Handkerchiefs and dishtowels were matched corner to corner before ironing, then folded again, being careful to match corners.

It was uncomfortably warm to iron in the summertime. There were many, many trips back and forth to the cook stove to get another hot iron. The cooled one was set in rotation so that while it was heat-

176

ing, the other two were used one at a time. If the iron got too hot, and it did sometimes, it meant the garment would get a scorched spot. In order to avoid this, the iron was always tested on the white sheet at the far right hand side of the ironing board. If it were too hot there would be a short waiting spell for the iron to cool.

Besides the ironing for the day, there were the meals and coffee breaks to prepare for the men coming in from the fields or other farm work. The children also needed attention and care. The housewife was kept very busy.

When the day of electric irons came, however crude the first ones were, it was a work saver for the person doing the ironing.

The first electric irons had a cord to plug into the iron. When the cord began to fray it could cause an electrical short and burn. My own hand and wrist got badly burned one time from just such an event.

In our family ironing was as important as bathing or wearing clean clothes. It was a matter of pride to wear or display well ironed and wrinkle free clothing. High standards were set, and we learned the satisfaction of doing our job very well.

FLOUR BINS

Between the dining room and the kitchen there was a cupboard with shelving that opened into both rooms. On the kitchen side below the cupboards there were two built in wooden bins. One was for flour, the other for sugar.

The bins were constructed so that when we pulled the handle on the front, the bin would tip out only to a certain distance. It worked on some kind of rocker underneath.

The flour bin held at least a fifty pound bag of flour at one time. The large flour sifter remained in the flour bin at all times. Because home made bread was a staple food many loaves of bread were baked each week. The bread sponge was set the night before with a cake of "yeast foam" the only yeast able to be purchased at that time. Some women relied on "bread starter", a liquid yeast growing continually in a glass fruit jar. It had to be kept in a warm place usually on top of the shelf on top of the cook stove. Potato water was added each time some of the yeast was poured from the jar to provide food for the yeast culture.

The flour bin was a 'modern' convenience of the time. It made baking easier by having an ample supply of flour close at hand. It also represented an era when we made all recipes from scratch. There were no pre-packaged cake mixes nor were there any other pre-mixed items to be purchased. We all knew how to cook, and we appreciated the flour bin.

FRIED CHICKEN

Somehow the term "fried chicken" has an altogether different connotation now than when I was kid growing up on the farm and even for many years after I was married.

If we wanted chicken for dinner we did not go to the Super Market to get a package of chicken. We had to hatch the eggs, feed and care for the chicks, and watch them grow until they were big enough to butcher.

Brooding chicks

Along about March my mother would gather eggs from the hen house. There were plenty of roosters in the flock, so she knew the eggs were fertile. With a pencil she scrawled an "X" on one side of the egg, and placed them on a rack in one of the three incubators which she kept in one of the basement rooms

With a thermometer placed on the rack, the temperature was kept at a constant 108 degrees. Each morning and night each egg was turned. Part of the day the "X" was up, and for the next 12 hours the "X" was underneath. It would be 28 days before the eggs hatched, but the eggs were turned each day without fail. We listened for the chicks inside of the egg the day before they hatched. Then the eggs would begin to have tiny holes in them. Soon a wet ball of down would emerge from the shell, lie for a while, begin to dry off, and then the little chick would stand.

By then the brooder house, kept warm with a stove surrounded by a metal cover, had to be ready for the new arrivals. Often sand was scattered on the floor or a layer of straw was also used for the bedding. Sand was better because chickens need grit for their gizzards to digest their food.

Fruit jar fountains with fresh water and long metal feed troughs were provided. Then it was watched constantly to check heat, water, and food.

Young chickens in their pen

In a day or two a nub on the tip of the beak would drop off. That nub was what broke through the eggshell when the chick was inside. In about two weeks the wing feathers began to appear.

Gradually the chicks grew. When they reached the weight of 2 ½ pounds they were ready to slaughter.

By now the chickens were running outdoors finding and eating bugs and worms. How to get hold of them was the next question. We used a piece of heavy gauge number 9 wire, bending a hook at one end and a loop for a handle at the other. The loop was also used to hang up the wire tool when not in use.

The flock scavenging

Valiantly, we would try to catch one or more chickens as they ran wildly about the farmyard. When we finally caught them, we would weigh them and then behead them. A stump of wood out in the yard with two nails about one inch apart protruding from the top was the chopping block. To quiet the nervous chicken we would tuck their head underneath a wing and move them rapidly in a circle. This made them disoriented. The neck of the chicken was placed between the nails, the head was chopped off with an axe, and the chicken held until the blood had all run out.

Next, the chicken was scalded in boiling-hot water and all the feathers plucked off. Then we crumpled up a newspaper, lighted it with a match and singed the hairs off the naked chicken.

The chicken was washed clean with soap and water, then cut open, gutted and cut into serving size pieces. The meat was chilled in cold well water.

Finally, the pieces of meat were coated with flour, and browned in a large black iron skillet that had a generous amount of butter in it. Salt and pepper were added.

After all that time and work of preparation, the aroma of fresh fried chicken served up with wonderful chicken gravy was one of the best treats we could have. It was also one of the easiest meals to prepare, taking less time than roasting beef or pork or turkey. Besides, raising a pig or a steer took much longer, and butchering was far more complicated. Fried chicken was popular for picnics as well as more formal meals. It was good anytime.

THE RAIN WATER CISTERN

A cistern is defined as any container that holds water. Whatever the 'container' may be, in order to collect rainwater it has to be close enough to a downspout so that when rain falls on the roof of the house, the water will run through the downspout and, through a connecting spout, into the barrel or cistern.

It was convenient to have rain water available close to the house. As a young child my grandparents, as did many of the early farmers, had a large wooden barrel situated under a rainspout so that whenever it rained the rain water would run into the barrel. My grandmother would bail water from the barrel with a pail, carry it to the copper boiler on the stove and heat it to use in the washing machine.

What I remember about the barrel is that in the summer, after a dry spell, there were squiggly mosquito larvae moving about on top of the water. Then the water then had to be strained through a dishtowel before it could be used.

At my husband's home place there was a deep cistern in the yard not far from the house. It was lined with red bricks and covered with a firm top made of boards. A long piece of waterspout was attached to the house and then fed into the cistern. That was much more efficient than the rain barrel.

My father dug a large cistern next to our house about eight-feet square and just as deep. The walls were lined with concrete and a piping system was run into the house. A small hand pump by the kitchen sink brought rainwater directly into the kitchen.

There were advantages to using rainwater. It was a source of naturally soft water free of dissolved mineral contaminants. Homemade lye soap dissolved quicker in rainwater and clothes seemed to wash cleaner. Rainwater was also good for shampooing hair especially when pine-tar soap was used for sudsing. A rinse with rainwater left the hair very shiny.

The disadvantages were few and easy to remedy. In addition to gathering mosquito larvae in the summer, the water would have very fine particles of dust in the water, dust washed out of the air and off the roof as the rain fell. These settled to the bottom of the cistern. On occasion we would have to drain the cistern and clean the layer of fine mud from the bottom.

Collecting water in a barrel was good in the warm and rainy weather, but not possible neither during the winter months nor in an extended dry period. We used the rain water sparingly. It had great value. With the large cistern we had at home we were able to have rainwater available not only through the warm weather rainy season, but also through most of the winter months since it was below ground and did not freeze.

CORSETS, BLOOMERS, AND COTTON STOCKINGS

World War I was probably a turning point in clothing fashions. The Victorian style for women of long dresses and artificially narrow waists gave way eventually to the "flapper" for formal occasions or simpler long dresses for daily use and a more natural form. Outwardly, formal wear went from elegance to flamboyance. The daily wear for housewives changed very little.

Undergarments for women also changed.

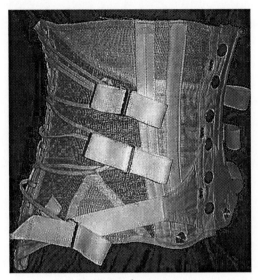

Typical corset

My mother as well as everyone else was not completely dressed unless she was wearing a corset. The corset was made of firm pink fabric stabilized with whale bones and metal loops from which long pink laces were laced back and forth all the way down the back. Taking hold of both sides the corset was pulled on and placed just below the arm pits and down over the buttocks. There were metal hooks which connected both sides down the front. Laces on the back of the corset tightly pulled the figure into form. I remember my father bringing home a new corset for my mother. It was packed in a long white box. When mother put on the corset, it was necessary for my father to lace it in the back so it would conform to my mother's body.

THE CORSET COVER

When a woman wore a corset she then wore a corset cover made from white cotton fabric with built up shoulders. The cover had buttons and button holes down the front.

It was shocking when women began wearing bloomers in the 1920's. This was an improvement over the one piece cotton under suits worn before that time. Bloomers were cut and sewed from black sateen with elastic around the waist and knees. Some women were so daring as to sew bloomers from purple sateen. This fashion tended to lift eye brows among the neighbors. My mother was chastened for wearing such daring apparel. I'm not entirely sure how this information got around, however.

Together with the one piece under suit, the corset cover, and corset waist, the woman also wore a cotton underskirt with built up shoulders over which she wore a loose fitting cotton print dress.

Then to complete dressing women wore cotton stockings that came just above the knees. Garters were attached to the corset and reached to the stocking tops. For dressier occasions cotton lisle stockings were available which had a softer smoother appearance.

The laced corsets with bone stays gave way to girdles made of latex rubber. These were easier to use since no one had to help tug on the laces and tie them. They were uncomfortable, however. They also smelled "rubbery." In spite of a sweet scent like baby powder applied by the manufacturer, a walk through the girdle area of the department store was an assault on the nose with the strong mixture of rubber and perfume.

Men's undergarments changed very little until the 1940's. For many years men wore a one piece union suit which buttoned all the way down the front. There was also the ubiquitous buttoned flap over the buttocks. Although red flannel was popular, others were made of cotton fabric in white. My grandfather wore long underwear made of thin chamois. Later, boxer shorts and briefs supplanted the union suit style for most men.

New methods combined with modern materials have changed the undergarment industry and styles. Now that homes are warm and diets have less fat the new fashions are appropriate for the times.

HOME CURES

In the days when there were few doctors, drugstores and hospitals, we used time-honored methods of curing various illnesses and maladies. These methods kept our medical expenses very low, and most often we recovered. I'm not sure if we recovered because of the remedy, or in spite of the remedy. We were very healthy, however.

Here are some memorable methods:

- When Harold's cousin Duane Petersen was sick with the croup, and was beginning to turn blue because he couldn't cough anymore, his mother, Lillian, gave him a teaspoon of sugar with a drop of kerosene in it. Duane did get well. In olden times a bad chest cold was called the croup.

- "Don't bite your fingernails on Sunday or the devil will be with you all week," Grandma Iversen told the children.

- If anyone was sick, Grandma Iversen gave those who were ailing a dose of baking soda dissolved in a glass of water.

- One of the first years I was in grade school I got head lice from someone at school. My mother washed my hair in kerosene and that ended my head lice.

- When I had a cold my mother would make a cup of hot lemonade to drink. Then I would get my chest rubbed with Mentholatum, and a flannel cloth was placed over my chest.

- The first winter we were married, Harold got a really bad chest cold. His mother brought an iron skillet filled with fried onions and placed the concoction on Harold's chest. His cold did get better.

- If I got a toothache I put some dry cloves on the tooth to ease the pain.

There is probably no way to prove the worth of these medicinal "cures." Perhaps the cure was in the mind of the patient or the care giver. Maybe some did help scientifically. It was the best we had, and we not only survived, but thrived. Was it because of, or in spite of the cure?

PEDDLERS

In the early part of the twentieth century there was a small segment of people who eked out a living by peddling wares of one kind or another. Most of them carried a pack on their back and walked the dusty or muddy roads from one farm to another. If the farmwife were good-natured and kind she would give the peddler a meal. The farmer might offer him a place to sleep in the barn on some hay. It was a different style of living, but for those who were driven by wanderlust it must have served its purpose.

My first recollection of a peddler was when I was about four years old. A tall man with a long white beard walked into our farmyard unannounced. He was dressed in clean blue overalls and a matching blue chambray shirt. He was carrying a pack over one shoulder. His name was Jens Juhl, and I later learned that he walked a very large territory, even beyond the state of Iowa.

My mother met him out in the yard where he displayed needles, pins, and beautiful Swiss-made white laces. Mother could select any of the items if she wanted to buy any of them. When his sale was finished he slung his bag over his one shoulder and walked on to the next farm place

Another kind of peddler was the rag man. When I stayed with my aunt in town, I heard the rag man coming through the alley with team of old horses and a broken down wagon. The driver called out loudly, "Rags. Rags. Rags," as he drove slowly along. If anyone had old rags that they wanted to get rid of they would hail him and throw their things into his wagon. He in turn sold them to a paper company.

Once when I was about seven or eight years old we had had a three-day rain. It was one of those times when the rain kept on falling straight down both night and day. Out in our barnyard was a covered wagon that had been there all that time. It was evident the team of horses couldn't pull the wagon through the mud out on the roads. After a couple of days my mother sent me out in the rain to do a little exploring to find out what was going on in that wagon.

There was a husband, wife, and a young girl sitting inside the wagon. Both parents were weaving baskets from green willow twigs. The baskets were really well done. At least that is what they looked like to me. In my way I tried to strike up a little conversation with them. It seemed they had come all that way from Missouri. For us it was a unique way of living. How they cooked any meals inside that wagon through that rainy period I do not know. Anyway, when the weather was better they moved on. I did not find out where they were going. I wonder if they were sure of their destination.

Another kind of peddler was the meat man. He drove from farm to farm with a supply of fresh and smoked meat. I can still see the wieners and sausages dangling from the back of his truck. This business was good as long as he could keep the meat from spoilage. There was no refrigeration available so his business didn't last very long. His business dwindled off quickly with warmer weather.

A few years later the "spice man" traveled through the country. He drove an automobile. Now the automobiles were built better and he was able carry more merchandise and to reach more people in a day's time. He could travel a large territory.

One such peddler was Mr. Hollipeter, the "Watkins" man. He would drive into the yard unannounced and when both husband and wife were there to greet him, he would bring out his leather cases, lay them open and display his wares. He specialized in many spices, liniments and other home cure medicines, and a few products to use on the farm animals. I bought mostly cinnamon, pepper, and vanilla.

He didn't use any sales pitch. He mostly sat quietly while we inspected his wares. If we saw something we needed we set it aside. One by one he took the things out and one by one he placed them back into his bags. What we had set aside was purchased, and he collected our money. Without much conversation he would then move on.

His competition was the McConnon and Raleigh Spice man who came out from Dike. His name was Jens Tunnesen. He was ample of girth and wheezed some when he talked, but was always kind. He brought out his spices much like Mr. Hollipeter. He had a good product but never seemed to be as successful as the Watkins man.

Mr. Hollipeter and Mr. Tunnesen continued to come long after World War II. They both were old men by then, and they either retired or died, I don't know. We didn't see any traveling spice men after that. They were the last of their kind.

Then there was man who drove the Grocery Wagon. He came in a more modern paneled truck. From his store in Benson he carried a line of grocery items. He couldn't bring everything in his wagon, but we could order some things and he would bring them the following week when he next came. We bought several things from him when we were first married. Mostly we purchased items such as flour, sugar, soaps, and etc. from him. After a few years his deliveries stopped.

The Fuller Brush man made his appearance at regular intervals, convincing his buyers that the Fuller brushes would outlast any brush on the market. And we did buy some articles from him. One valuable item was a metal pail with a shower hose attached at the bottom of the bucket. We used it out in the wood shed in the summer time. We filled the bucket with water in the morning and by evening the water was warm enough for a shower. Of course, we knew the bucket would quickly run dry so we timed the shower with the outflow of water. It worked.

I know I bought a wall brush, which was used to sweep spider webs from the ceilings in the house. A clothes brush that we purchased worked well, too, and has lasted my lifetime.

These peddlers were a convenience for those of us who did not often go to town. Those were years right during and after the Great Depression of the 1930's. Things changed after people had more money and now owned cars to more often and more easily get themselves to town.

The Montgomery Wards and Sears Roebuck catalogs were also an important part of how business was transacted. They were a very good source, and I ordered a lot of things from them. I remember as a very young child that Mother and Dad ordered wooden boxes of dried prunes, peaches, and salt fish from one of the companies. These items were stored in one of the upstairs bedrooms along with the wooden barrel of sugar that was kept up there, too. As a small girl, I remember leaning over the edge of the barrel trying to reach the sugar that Mother needed.

One group, which was not selling anything, was the Gypsies, who drove in large black automobiles from place to place.

One summer afternoon when my mother and I were alone home, we saw the gypsies drive into our farmyard. We knew they were gypsies by the way they dressed. They wore bright colored clothes. Several of them dashed out of their two cars and immediately scattered in many directions. They darted in and out of the farm buildings. They didn't bother to come to the house to announce themselves. Anyone who was friendly would have come to the door.

We never really knew how much or what they took, but I don't believe their entrance into the henhouse was for sightseeing purposes. One gypsy came to the house to ask for food for the baby. I'm sure they were not in the yard very many minutes, and soon left.

My mother and I stood just inside the screen door, frightened to death. My mother had grabbed a large butcher knife and stood there with it in her hands. I don't know why she did this, but she must have thought it would protect the two of us. At the very least we knew they were not friendly.

There were tales of how gypsies stole produce from the farms. There were even rumors of how they stole children, and what else I don't know. After I grew up we learned that the gypsies liked to camp near Waterloo, Iowa. It was their way of living.

There was another wanderer in our area known by the name of Gammel Soren, or "Old Soren". Where he came from and where he eventually went we don't know. He had a very old covered wagon that was his home, a decrepit horse that could barely walk and a dog that fit the scenario. The clothes he wore were equally threadbare.

Old Soren wandered throughout the neighborhood from one place to another, relying on the generosity of the farm wives. There were times in warm weather we would see his wagon sitting in the school-yard. We knew he was there for the night. If the weather were cool, he would open a school window and climb inside for the night. Discretely, in the morning he would be gone before either the teacher or children arrived, and not a trace of his presence would be known.

There was the time he asked my mother for butter. He offered her a glass to put it in. My mother remarked that the glass wasn't very clean. Old Soren apologized by saying his dog couldn't reach any deeper in the glass. My mother washed the glass, gave him butter and probably threw in some other food to go with it. He must have made his living off the goodness of the people of the community, as he had no wares to sell. Farmers provided grain for his horse and housewives gave him food.

Old Soren must have been an immigrant as he spoke Danish to everyone. Somehow he must have been disillusioned by what the New World had to offer him. I believe when he was found dead that he was buried in the Fredsville cemetery.

Our farmhouse was very large and had five bedrooms in the upstairs. One of these rooms was quite small. My mother referred to it as being the "tramp room". It is probable that when my grandparents lived in the house that they might have kept some transients in that room overnight. I never saw them.

Once in a while Dad would come in from doing chores early in the morning and announce that a tramp had slept in the haymow over night, but we never saw them.

I also remember of Dad telling of when he was a child that the Indians passed by the farm on their way to a summer camp. Mother told about being afraid of the Mormons who were dressed in their black suits. They were on their way West.

The days of the so-called peddlers were coming to an end. However, after World War II a new kind of peddler stopped at our home. Young GI's, fresh from the war and brash as can be, sold magazine subscriptions from house to house. At that time we had two dogs on the farm who loved to greet any car that came onto our farm. One was a large St. Bernard, a very gentle dog that loomed large over the driver's side car window. The other was a small dog of unknown lineage. This dog would sit on the other side of the car waiting for the salesman to get out of the car. This dog was very protective and would have chased off any dangerous person. We rarely went out to greet the salesman unless we knew them. The dogs did the trick. The salesman would look at the St. Bernard looking him in the face through the car window, and wait. After a time, he would give up and drive on to the next farm.

More in the style of the old peddlers, but with much more beautiful merchandise, was a couple representing the Minnesota Woolen Company. They came around once a year. They drove into our farmyard in a good car and asked to come in.

We welcomed them eagerly. They had such an array of blankets and outerwear that was irresistible; at least at our place we couldn't put up any resistance.

We bought woolen blankets, which to this day, sixty years later, are still in good condition. We bought jackets and mittens for both children and adults. Those people must have had us targeted as good prospects. We loved their colorful display of goods.

We "ooohed" over the quality, the good price, and in general, were taken by what they had to offer. We saw them once a year for some time.

Peddlers fit a need in the economy of the early 1900's. But like the buggy whips, they were no longer needed. Other economic outlets took their place. What is missing is the colorful people and the testing of our good business sense and benevolence as required. They also now live only in memory.

HIRED MEN

On Dad's farm, as on several larger farms in the area, the tasks of farming was more than one person could manage. Farming involved long hours of heavy work. It was necessary to hire helpers to accomplish all the chores involved in farming. These helpers were called "hired men", or sometimes "hired hands".

My earliest recollection of a hired man was a man from Denmark who could neither speak the English language nor relate to the customs of a new country. When he had earned enough money to move on, he went west to one of the Dakotas. He may have homesteaded there. I'm not sure.

Then there was Martin Westergaard, a Danish Jew who lived with us from time to time. He had several remarkable traits. He was a small, slender man but wiry in muscle and strength. I doubt he weighed 150 pounds. His voice was also thin and he spoke broken English laced with Danish. In later years when he had few teeth his speech was often difficult to understand. He worked outside daily and his skin was a dark tan and had a leathery texture from the exposure to the sun. He drank alcohol often, but never caused harm to himself or others in so doing. When he was sober he was a hard worker, and willingly did each task well no matter how long it took. Dad did keep an eye out for him to make sure he was generally okay and not bothering anyone. From time to time Dad searched all the hiding places on the farm to collect the hidden liquor bottles. No amount of convincing ever got Martin to cease drinking. It was said when Martin finally died at a very old age, that the undertaker did not have to use any embalming fluid since his body was pretty well pickled naturally.

Among his several talents, Martin was a tile digger and moved from farm to farm, digging ditches in the fields for drainage tile entirely by hand. He dug tirelessly and steadily all day long in the heavy loam and deeper yellow clay. The trenches he dug were as much as five feet deep and sixteen inches wide. Six or eight inch diameter red clay tiles were laid in the bottom of these ditches to help drain away excess rainwater. There are many farms in the area that still are successfully drained by the tile he dug and laid by hand.

When he didn't have a place to live he often drifted back to our farm. Mother and Dad always found him a place to sleep and gave him good food. Martin's great delight was in teasing me in a cruel way. I was not very old. On a daily basis he would threaten to shoot my dog. I believed him and cried many tears as the others in the room laughed. They thought it was funny. He was a kind man by nature and probably did not mean the cruelty of his comment. But at that age it terrified me, and left a sour memory of him lasting all these years.

Then there was Stanley Graham, a World War I veteran, who owned an open touring car and a bulldog. The car had a starter button on the floor of the car, which had to be pushed by one foot to start the car. Whenever Stanley would attempt to start the car, the bulldog would growl and grab at the starter button. However, the dog did enjoy going for a ride in the car. Stanley wore khaki-colored leg bindings that he deftly wrapped around each leg every morning and likewise rolled them up at night after work.

I was about eight when Stanley moved on to a place near Cedar Falls, where he had a strawberry bed. I was hired to pick strawberries that sold for 25 cents a quart. I was not successful in berry picking and that job soon ended.

Then came a man by the name of Mickaelsen. I don't remember much about him nor how long he was there.

After that Terry Hansen came to work for Dad. He was a Barber School graduate but never had a shop of his own. During his stay at our farm he cut hair for all of us in the kitchen.

Terry fell in love with the schoolteacher who was boarding at our house. They married and moved to a farm north of Denver, Iowa. This may have caused many tongues to wag. Schoolteachers were not allowed to be married in those days. Marriage meant immediate dismissal. Furthermore, the two were living under the same roof – in our house!

The parade of hired men who came and went, who lived and worked on the farm, were often young men from Denmark. They knew to come to our farm through some lengthy connection of friends and relatives in The Old Country. They were given meals, a place to live, their laundry, and a monthly pay. I have no idea what their pay rate was. Their bedroom consisted of a bed and a table. The men shaved at the kitchen sink with their long shaving blades of straight razors. When they had been with us for some time, they moved on to seek their fortune elsewhere in the New World.

One young fellow from Denmark did well. He stayed with us a short time, and then went on to the university at Ames. He later became the chief engineer for Illinois. Others stayed with us long enough to learn enough English to make their own way in the world. Many went on into the Dakotas to set up farming operations. Only one returned. I think he came back because he had a romantic interest in me. I was sixteen years old at the time, and I had no interest in him. He moved on.

The hired man's room was the far northwest corner bedroom in our house of five bedrooms upstairs. I never liked going to that room. In the early days men didn't bathe very often and the room had an odor that I highly disliked. I think it was the sweaty socks that did it.

The men who were hired to work on our farm were many with varied capabilities. The farm was relatively large for the area, and Dad operated a large dairy business for some years complete with milk delivery routes in town and a few of the surrounding farms. The dairy herd required help to milk all those cows by hand. In addition there were the other livestock plus the field work annually. I am sure they earned their keep.

THE WOOD BOX

Next to the cook stove in the corner of the kitchen was the wood box hopefully filled with dry stove wood. The box itself was built strong enough to hold several armloads of wood split and ready to build a good fire in the stove. It was about as tall as a chair back in the back, shorter on the front and the sides were angled to fit between the front and the back. Our wood box had sides built of wainscoting boards.

This feature of the kitchen seemed simple enough, but it represented a great deal more than what could be seen in its rough appearance.

Cook stoves used wood as fuel for cooking almost every meal as well as for baking all of the bread, cakes and other pastries that were served in our home. Wood was the fuel of choice for a variety of reasons. It was readily available in our area since we had a sizeable grove of trees around the farm buildings. These groves were a windbreak for the yard from the cold prevailing winter winds, and later the trees became a source of firewood for heating and cooking. Wood was a renewable resource. Many of the trees were planted as part of homesteading the farm in earlier years, and Dad planted additional trees from time to time. Wood was a clean fuel rather than using coal or oil, both of which produced a lot of greasy soot.

Firewood was harvested from dead trees and trees damaged in the summer storms. During the winter months, when it was cold and no field work was being done, the trunks and branches of the trees were cut into usable pieces about twelve to sixteen inches long. These chunks of wood, some of them quite big around, were brought to the wood pile by the fence that encircled the lawn and not far from the kitchen door. There they were split into pieces that were large enough to give heat but small enough to fit into the cook stove. These became the "stove wood" required in the cook stove.

Filling the woodshed

All of this was done by hand. In those days there were no power tools to do this work. Large trees were cut by a saw that required two men to operate. They pulled the saw back and forth, each in turn, being careful to only pull and not push the saw. Smaller logs and branches would be cut using a bow saw with a coarse blade. The logs were split into the proper size using wedges with a large hammer or with an axe. The proper tool was selected depending on how easily the wood would split. A sturdy block of wood was left by the pile to set smaller pieces on for splitting.

The saying of the time was, "When you heat with wood, you are twice warmed." No wonder. Since we needed the cook stove all year 'round, it was necessary to have firewood on hand at all times. The heaviest work was done in the cold of winter, when the effort was a welcome out door exercise.

The wood was allowed to "season" or dry for some time, at least through one summer season, hence the term. A fresh green tree might take two years to season. Wet wood did not make a good fire that was hot enough to cook our meals, and it would fill the chimney with soot creating a danger of a chimney fire. Many homes were lost to these hazards. Wood properly seasoned made it possible to maintain an even temperature for baking as well as keeping the chimney clean of soot. There were no thermostats on cook stoves – only the cook's ability to maintain a constant fire of the right temperature for the time it took to bake or cook the cake or meat or meal.

The heat from the cook stove was welcome in the winter. It gave enough heat to warm the kitchen and nearby rooms to be comfortable, except on the very coldest days of winter. We kept warm, cooked our meals, dried our outdoor clothing, and even dried our laundry near the cook stove. Putting on a nightgown freshly warmed by the cook stove made getting into a very cold bed in the winter almost enjoyable.

In the summertime it was a different story. Cooking and baking on the hot sultry days of July and August were a test of endurance to the hot weather. Some farms had "summer kitchens" for just these times. At least the heat of cooking was confined to another building.

The housewife, however, always worked in the heat of the kitchen no matter the season.

The wood box indeed was an important fixture in our kitchen. It needed to be filled every day of the year. Keeping split wood in the wood box also helped keep the mess off the floor as bark and small pieces could do. It was hoped the men would bring in an armful of wood whenever they came in for meal time.

While the box itself was simple and functional in design and use, it represented a great deal of planning and physical effort to keep sufficient dry fuel for the cook stove.

CORN PICKING TIME

There was a time before hybrid seed corn, tractors of any size, mechanical corn pickers and corn shellers that human beings actually hand picked the fall crop of corn each year, one ear of corn at a time. On the farm I grew up on corn picking usually began in late October or as soon as the corn was dry enough to pick. Harvesting 40 to 80 acres of corn would require more than one wagon.

We had several wagons that would hold the ears of corn. They had all four sides enclosed, and the top of the wagon would have been about five feet above the ground. On top of the one side of the wagon were two or three rows of "bang boards." Bang boards, each at least twelve or more inches wide and as long as the wagon box, were attached to the wagon side with wooden cleats. The cleats were fastened so that those of one board could fit on top of another. Sometimes as many as three boards were attached to one side of the wagon, effectively making that side of the wagon much higher. The purpose of the bang boards was to keep the ears of corn from going over the wagon and falling to the ground.

Harvesting corn was called "husking." A man usually husked two rows of corn at a time, pulling each ear of corn from the stalk, quickly tearing off the dried husks and throwing the ear into the wagon box. Husking was made easier by the use of a "corn pick." The corn pick was a metal hook fitted into a piece of leather then worn over one hand. The metal hook helped pull the husks from the ear of corn.

As the person husking each ear broke the ear loose from the stalk and the removed most of the husk, he tossed it into the wagon box without looking to see where it would fall. Hence, the bang boards guided the corn down into the box and prevented the ear from flying entirely over the wagon.

At our farm, the hired corn husker got to our farm about four o'clock in the morning, went out and fed and put the harness on a team of horses. Then he came into the house where Mother had prepared a hearty breakfast. When finished he took his corn husking pick, hitched the team to the wagon and went to the corn field.

He would drive the wagon into the corn field and stop at one end of the half-mile long row of corn. Then he would dismount from the wagon and begin husking corn. As the stalks were freed of the corn and the husker moved down the row, the wagon would have to move forward to be within tossing distance. Without mounting the wagon, he could command the horses to move forward. Horses quickly learned the rhythm of how many steps forward to move in the row on their own or by voice command before stopping again.

By noon a lone man could have husked a wagon load of corn. There were a few men who could husk three loads of corn in one day and they were valuable help, if they could be hired. It would go even faster if more than one wagon were used. With the wagon full, and being noon time, he drove the team and wagon home to the corn crib where he hand shoveled the load of corn into the crib. Then took the team to the watering trough for a drink, unhitched the team and took them into the barn for some feed.

By then, it was time for the noon meal which meant a hearty warm meal for a very hungry and often chilled man. Working outdoors in late October in that climate created a very robust appetite. When finished with the meal the man got the team out of the barn, hitched to the wagon and back to the field to continue the husking. He would spend the entire afternoon picking another wagon load of corn.

Two rows of corn by two tedious rows of corn, the work continued for the next two or three weeks until at last the fields were cleared.

Foul weather rarely interrupted the harvest. Huskers just wore more clothing and stayed as warm and dry as possible. There were times when the husker would come into the house at the end of the day and stand near the hot cook stove to warm the bone-deep chill of the day's effort.

One hazard among corn pickers was a sprained wrist. That usually meant the man could not continue the job. Some wrapped their wrists enough so they could continue their job. It was imperative to bring in the harvest before winter set in.

Schools would often close for two weeks in the late fall so that the children could help however they could with the corn harvest. Older boys went into the fields to husk corn. The girls and young boys stayed at home helping with meal preparation or whatever they could do. My mother-in-law was expected to go to the field to help my father-in law husk the corn. My husband, a young boy at the time, got a broken nose when an ear of corn hit him in the face. A good husker rarely looked up to see where the thrown ear was going. My husband was just in the wrong place at the wrong time. He received a broken nose for that lapse of attention, and for his lifetime his nose had a curious kink in it.

Now, the years have passed and corn is picked, husked, and shelled in the field. The shelled corn is elevated into a dryer to finish the process of drying the corn so that it would not spoil. The harvest that used to take days or even weeks is now completed in just a few hours. Life on the corn farm is much more efficient, but perhaps not so colorful as in the days of husking by hand.

OAT THRESHING DAY

The most exciting day of the summer was oats threshing day. We knew when it would be our turn to have our bundles of oats threshed because the separator and its attending crew had already been to the neighbor's place. It would be our turn next.

A week or more before, the horse drawn binder had been out in the field to cut the grain and bind it into bundles wrapped with sisal twine. Men had followed the binder to stack several bundles into

The horsedrawn binder

"shocks" that would shelter the grain from inclement weather, and allow the grain to easily dry thoroughly for harvest. The field was full of row upon row of shocks in their orderly ranks.

The binder was a wonderful invention. The machine had an awkward appearance, an example of function over form, but it became a living being when in operation as it went about the field cutting the standing grain. A very large steel wheel called a "bull wheel" powered the mechanism as it was pulled by a team of horses. A six-foot long sickle bar full of sharp cutters moved rapidly back and forth cutting the stalks of the standing grain. Guided by a large rotating wheel of thin, wide boards, the stalks carrying the hooded kernels of grain fell back onto a wide conveyor belt made of canvass with wooden slats attached. The conveyor carried the grain and stalks of straw up into a gathering area where, like magic, at regular intervals the mechanism whirred and twine spun while a huge needle wrapped the stalks full of grain into a bundle and neatly tied a knot in the twine. The bundle of grain was then discharged onto a carrier at the side of the binder that looked like an overgrown fork raised above the ground.

When nine bundles had accumulated, the operator triggered a lever that carefully deposited the bundles in a heap on the straw stubble, just off the ground. The men walking behind would then stand the bundles on end with the kernels on top, the first two bundles leaning against each other, then two more to make a square. Four more bundles were fitted to the corners of the square, and, lastly, the ninth bundle was spread fan-shaped over the group as a shelter from birds and weather. This was hot and back-breaking work.

A different horsepower

The operator was very busy and very skilled. As he drove the team of horses, guiding them so that the machine always cut all the grain in the six-foot width and yet left none standing, he also had to raise or lower the cutter to cut only the stalks of grain and not the new crop of clover growing near the ground. He was also responsible for counting the number of bundles and to release them at the proper interval. Being sure that the machine was well lubricated, and that it always had a reservoir of twine were also crucial to the successful harvest. On top of all this it was a matter of great pride for the farmer that the machine leave a clean straight row the length of the field without missing any of the grain. A well-disciplined team of horses made the job much easier.

My husband owned his own threshing machine commonly known as a "separator" because it separated the oat kernel from the chaff and straw. He had put together a group of nine, sometimes ten, neighboring farmers who were part of the threshing "ring". The group of farmers in this "ring" would travel to each of the nine or ten farms to help each other harvest the crop of oats. It was necessary to have a number of workers available to complete the operation of the harvest. It was never considered a barter system. It was simply a part of farm life of the era.

In one year he began threshing at one end of the neighborhood. The next year he began at the other end. Harvest time in late July and early August was bound to be the hottest, and hopefully the driest, weather of the year. It meant the beginning of exciting days.

Threshers on parade

Very early in the morning of a beautiful clear summer's day, with the sun barely up, everything and everybody went into action. We watched as the dinosaur of a machine came slowly towards our farm place pulled by a huge softly chuffing steam engine in the early years, later by a gasoline-powered tractor. It was a hulk of a machine put together with sheet metal and angle iron held together with bolts and rivets. A long large cylindrical pipe that would blow the straw into a stack was slung across the top and another spout on the side let the oat grain flow out into a wagon.

Tractor power

The wide farm gate was swung open to let the two machines enter accompanied by the clink and clatter of iron wheels passing over stones in the road and driveway. Thereafter followed a parade of wagons pulled by horses or tractors. Some wagons would haul the bundles of grain from the field. Others would carry the separated grain to the granary. In the days of horse power, this parade marched to the jingling of harness hardware, the snorting of the horses and the creaking of straining leather.

Neighbor women came in to help cook the noon meal and the men came with their teams of horses or with their tractors, pitchforks and wagons. The wagon axles had been freshly greased with thick dark green axle grease. As the men gathered in the barnyard waiting for the dew to dry off enough so that they could go to the field, they talked and laughed. Some exchanged the latest jokes. Others relived experiences they had at other times when they were threshing. Often these tales would begin by someone saying, "Do you remember the time...?" And that would then remind someone else of another happening, and so the stories went back and forth.

Out in the yard, the dogs were having a great time barking and seeking out the attention of all the new faces. The farm cats had early on taken refuge somewhere in the depths of the haymow in the barn and likely wouldn't come out until everyone had left.

The thresher was set into position so that the straw could blow into a neat stack at a location convenient for the farmer. Small trenches were dug for the wheels as needed, so that this leviathan would stand level. Steel stakes were strategically placed and driven deep into the ground to securely anchor the thresher.

Threshers in action

When all the men had gathered, the discussion began as to who was going to be bundle haulers, bundle pitchers, and the straw stackers. Someone would haul the harvest of grain from the separator to the granary. Harold would operate the thresher and the engine that drove the mechanism.

Two men with forks were needed to pitch the bundles onto the wagons in the fields. Although they would be done with their task first, they would be in the field most of the day except for the noon meal, so they filled a stone jug with water to take with them to the field. It would be hidden in an oat shock to keep it reasonably cool. Their task was to stick a pitchfork into a shock of oats and lift it into the wagon fitted with high sides to hold the bundles. The wagon was driven between the rows of shocked grain so it could be loaded from both sides. The stronger men could pick up the entire shock of several bundles at once. Others took two or three forkfuls to pitch the bundles into the wagon.

Another farm, another harvest

When the wagon was filled, it would head for the thresher, and an empty wagon would take its place in the field. At least five bundle haulers were needed so they could keep a steady flow of wagons lined up two at a time at the machine.

Those assigned to do the straw stacking knew they were in for a very dirty dusty job besides being very hot and sweaty. These men would work in the discharge of straw and chaff all day long. The chaff would stick to their sweaty skin and itch constantly.

The empty wagons, drivers and loaders headed out to the fields after the morning dew had lifted. In the meantime, the steam engine had to be lined up precisely so that the long, eight-inch-wide flat leather belt from the main pulley on the thresher was in a straight line with the fly wheel on the side of the engine. Harold had to move the steam engine ahead or back it up so that the belt was just the right tension and alignment. This was particularly difficult since the belt had to remain on the engine's fly wheel and the thresher's drive pulley to be aligned, but the fly wheel had to turn one way or another to move the engine. All of this took time and was done with great care. When in operation, the belt ran unguarded between the engine and thresher at a high speed, and if the tension or alignment were not just so, it would fly off, possibly causing great injury or even death to anyone nearby. When the engine was finally aligned properly, it was anchored in place ready for the task of driving the thresher.

The thresher was carefully checked and prepared for the day of operation. All of the many belts and chains were inspected, tested and, if needed, repaired. All bearings were greased or oiled. Perhaps an hour or more was required to carefully check all adjustments and moving parts. After all, every belt, pulley, chain and gear was fully exposed on the outside of the machine. There were no guards. Any breakdown was a potentially dangerous event. Not until all this was accomplished was the machine ready to thresh oats.

Starting the machine was an exciting moment; for it was then that all the careful preparation bore its fruit. The drive wheel on the steam engine or tractor was slowly and carefully engaged. The engine strained mightily to bring the great machine into life. The great belt began to move, at first very slowly, then faster and faster, slapping against itself with the strain, as all of the parts of the machine were started at once. After a few tense moments, it was running smoothly. Then, making sure all was operating as it should, the throttle was advanced to operating speed, the belts traveling around and around their loops with dizzying speed. Although snorting loudly during the startup, the steam engine chuffed quietly as it awaited the effort of feeding the hungry thresher. The separator swayed slightly with a soft shuffle, shuffle rhythm, humming contentedly, waiting for the bundles of grain to be fed into its hungry maw.

Threshing on our farm (my dad on top of the machine)

When a gasoline powered tractor was used to drive the ungainly monster, it, too, would growl at the immense load of starting all those many moving parts at once. The tractor, too, would purr when all was running well. The sound of the engine was often an excellent gauge of how well the equipment was operating. Any unusual noise often called for a quick shutdown. "Quick" meant several minutes while the grain completed its journey through the machine and all that running gear coasted to a stop. The sound of either engine was a good measure of how dry the grain was, how heavy was its yield or how many bundles were being fed into the thresher.

Under steam power

By this time, the first wagon had come in from the field, swaying and creaking across the uneven ground under its load of bundles. It was carefully parked beside the intake apron on either side of the thresher. The horses could not be skittish as the wagon on one side was right next to the speeding main drive belt. A second wagon, when it arrived, would be on the opposite side of the apron. One man on each wagon would pitch individual bundles onto the apron of the separator with a soft thud, making sure the grain end of the bundle went into the machine first. They worked in an easy rhythm pitching bundles alternately, being careful not to overload the machine. Wooden slats mounted to iron chains moved the bundles up the apron toward its mouth. Just as the bundles entered the machine, sharp knives rotating like strange flailing claws cut the twine holding the bundled straw together. As the loosened bundles of grain disappeared into the gaping mouth of the machine, a cylinder rotating at high speed separated the grain from the twine, chaff and straw. As the materials traveled through the innards of the machine, grain was discharged at the bottom, cleaned and separated from the straw and chaff by "straw walkers" and a large blower. The rest of the material traveled on to the rear of the thresher and was blown through a long large moveable tube onto what became the straw stack. There, two men standing in that dusty discharge helped to guide the straw into a neat pile that would grow to an immense size during the day. In the morning only a flat patch of ground was there behind the machine. By the end of the day, a large pile of straw occupied the space. There would be enough straw to provide bedding material for humans and animals both until the next year.

By means of an elevator made from a flat belt with metal cups attached, the grain was raised to the top of the thresher. It fell into a one-bushel scale that measured the volume of grain harvested. A counter kept track of the number of bushels of grain. It then traveled through a spout into a waiting wagon. The spout was hinged so that it could be swung back and forth filling the wagon evenly. When the wagon was full, there would need to be an empty wagon right behind to take the next load. Each full wagon was taken to the granary where it unloaded its burden into an elevator that carried the grain to its bin, and then returned for another load.

The organization and effort that went into the activity of threshing was phenomenal. It was hard work, and not long into the day, red or blue handkerchiefs were pulled from a hip pocket to wipe away the dust and sweat. From time to time words of encouragement or advice were shouted above the noise of the harvest, but for the most part they worked quietly and steadily. It was dangerous work as well and there was an understanding among the men of each one's responsibility. Each man did his job well and yet kept track of all that was happening so that the operation was safe. It was important for everyone to work together as a team to keep safety at the highest level possible.

The work was constant with few breaks so that the harvest would be finished that day.

And they would have to be fed.

Thresher's meals are legendary. Threshing was heavy work and the men would be hungry by noon. Fresh baked chicken with gravy whitened and thickened with flour or a large savory beef roast with rich dark gravy were the centerpiece of the great meal. New potatoes and carrots freshly dug from the garden, or tender green beans just picked, or whatever vegetable was ready in the garden, all sprinkled with fresh parsley, accompanied the meal in abundance. Jars of home canned beet and cucumber pickles brought up from their shelf in the cool and musty cellar provided a sweet or tart contrast to the main dishes. Fresh dinner rolls yet warm from the oven were served with home churned butter and homemade jellies and jams. Cool well water, chilled milk and plenty of strong coffee would help replace liquids lost to sweat in the hot sun. Fresh baked pie filled with freshly ripened fruit would provide a sweet desert. Sweet rolls and cake also needed to be prepared for the morning and afternoon coffee break.

The meal was carefully planned. We knew that the selection and quality of the food would be a topic of conversation among the neighbors. There was great competition to fill the table with the best of food. We were determined that this meal would be memorable. None of the women would ever be shamed by serving a poorly prepared meal!

None of this began without careful attention to the signs of weather. No convenient forecasts were available, so the farmer and his wife would reach their decision to harvest or not based on their best judgment that they could muster reading the sky. Should rain occur, the threshing would be delayed until the grain was once again dry, perhaps for several days, and the huge meal would not be prepared. This decision needed to be made before the roast beef was purchased or the chickens caught and butchered. Food for the threshing crew needed to be fresh, and in the heat of the summer, could not be easily stored. If there was to be rain, there would be no fresh dinner rolls nor roast beef, nor garden vegetables. Careful thought went into this decision and preparation.

If the day was judged to be favorable, very early in the morning in the house there was a flurry of pots and pans rattling, stove lids and oven doors opening and shutting, and the aroma of wood smoke and cooking food beginning to flow out into the yard. By 5:00 in the morning, either a large beef roast was acquired from the butcher in town, or several chickens were butchered to be served at noon. Chickens were caught, killed, plucked, singed, drawn and then chilled in cool well water. Oven time and heat was carefully planned and controlled to bake pies, dinner rolls and pastries, and to roast the beef to a deep dark brown or the chicken to a flaky tenderness.

New potatoes needed to be dug from the garden, washed, peeled and placed in a pot of water for cooking at just the right time. Green beans needed to be picked, snipped and cleaned, or carrots dug, washed and scraped and also made ready for cooking. Yeast dough for the fresh rolls or pastry was carefully timed and prepared for the oven. The women began their work very early, and worked into the heat both of the day and of the kitchen like an efficient army. It was often crowded in the kitchen, but they were large rooms, and much conversation and laughter accompanied the efforts there.

By the middle of the forenoon it was important to have a bench set up outside where the men could wash their hands and face when they came in for noon dinner. The wash bench pulled out of the washhouse was just the right height. It was placed close to a tree so that a nail could be pounded into the trunk of the tree and a mirror hung on it. A cake of homemade soap, a tin wash basin, a clean towel and a comb were laid out. Now all that was needed was the water. If the pump were close by there would be fresh water for each man. Otherwise they would have to bail water out of a bucket with a dipper into the wash basin. It helped the men remove some of the accumulated dust, dirt and sweat, but as my father said, "It was a poor towel that couldn't remove the other half of the dirt." We knew that the men would sit down to the meal with clean arms, hands and face and freshly combed hair, but their clothing mostly still dusty and sweaty.

The dining table was extended to its fullest to seat twelve at a time by pulling apart and adding all the table leaves there were. Then the table pad was laid down. For some reason, the best white linen tablecloth was used to cover the table and pad. The dust and dirt of the field always made its way onto the cloth, which would need a thorough washing, bleaching, bluing and ironing after the day was done. Then the table was set with plates, cups, glasses, forks, knives, spoons, salt and pepper shakers, pickle dishes and all the other necessary items to serve this grand meal.

There were often more than twelve men, plus the women and children, so two or more settings were required. After each setting, of course, dishes were washed and dried by hand, and the table was reset. Plates and bowls and dishes of foods were replenished and placed on the table for the next group.

After they finished eating, the men would sit outside in the shade awaiting the others to finish their meal. The rest was welcome with quiet conversation and a few nodding heads. But soon they would be back at their assigned tasks to complete the harvest.

In mid afternoon everyone took a break time. The machine was again stopped and everyone gathered for coffee, sandwiches, sweet rolls and cake. Even the men in the fields came in to relax their tired arms and backs. It was a wonderful time for a little rest and relaxation. There was much bonding and fellowship that took place on a day like this.

Cleanup

211

By late afternoon and sometimes early evening the field of oats was cleared, the last of the bundles were fed into the machine, the oats were in the granary's bin, and the straw was neatly stacked in the yard. The great machine was stopped at last and quiet returned once more. The men were hot, tired, and exhausted. And the women? They too were so tired, but could still laugh and have some good conversation together. But on the whole it had been a good day and oats threshing was done at our farm for another year. With the same clatter and commotion of arriving, the neighbors paraded out of the farmyard to make their way home. All this would happen at another farm tomorrow.

Another inspection

When everyone had gone home the dogs flopped down on the back step all stretched out and panting. The cats slowly and cautiously came out of their hiding places, perhaps wondering how long it would be before there was fresh warm milk for them to drink. The dogs were too tired to give chase.

But there were still chores to do this night, a quick supper of leftovers from the noon meal, and breakfast would be needed early the next morning. If the weather was good, the family would need to be up very early to follow the thresher to the next farm.

As a child, oats harvest meant a lot of fun and excitement. Other children came with their families, and, when we did not have to help with the meal preparation, we could find some time to play. We didn't often have that opportunity. For several weeks after harvest, the straw stack was a great playground. There were no other playgrounds nearby. If we could, we would climb to the top of the stack and then slide down the side. Fresh straw is very slippery, and it makes a fast slide. If we could not climb the stack, we would walk around the pile looking for the pieces of twine that had been cut going through the thresher. They were often hard to find because they were the same color as the straw.

The new way

It was a very sad day when Harold sold the threshing machine. Even though he purchased a new modern "combine" that would harvest the oats far more efficiently requiring fewer workers and far less effort, we knew instinctively that the sale of the thresher meant the passing of an important era. Threshing time meant a lot of hard work for many people, but we did it happily. It was a time for strong fellowship. It was a time when many people worked together for a common and good purpose. It brought our neighbors close. I can think of nothing that compares to what happened in those days of harvest. I miss the laughter of the conversation. I miss the many sounds and smells of the horses, the men and the machines. The smell of the fresh straw and clean grain cannot be erased from my mind. Likewise, the kitchen produced a pleasant aroma that invited all to gather around a table groaning with good food. This was a communion of all who raised small grain crops that is now lost to time.

But we always brought the threshing days to a close feeling good about what had been accomplished. We were exhausted, but happy, and relieved to have brought in the harvest once again. Days of a good harvest are valued no matter how it is done.

HAYMAKING

Next to oat harvest, haymaking was one more significant rite of summer on the farm. It was not as intense as harvesting oats, but the process required several men to do the job effectively. It was another opportunity to work together with good friends.

Raising and harvesting a good crop of hay required some planning and considerable good fortune. It was customary on our farm to rotate crops from corn to oats to hay, and then back to corn. This was in the era before high test fertilizer and refined hybrid seed for planting crops. Clover put natural fertilizer into the soil, and the other grasses also provided humus to further enrich the soil. Raising hay was a form of composting. It enabled the farmer to raise a good crop of corn.

Hay was also very important as a food crop for cows and cattle. Their natural food staple during the summer was grass, which they found in the pasture. In the cold weather months, hay was the only alternative to grass. It was their principal food during the winter months.

Clover and timothy seed was sown at the same time as the oats, usually in mid March. Oats, in addition to being a food crop for the animals, was considered a nurse or cover crop for the clover seed. Both would grow in the first season, but the oats would reach well above the clover and ripen in late July. After the oats was harvested, the clover and other hay seeds would be free to grow unchallenged for the rest of the season. The hay crop would reach maturity and then winter over.

Loading loose hay

In the following season the hay crop would grow unchallenged until it was mature enough to be harvested for the hay crop. Haymaking was often done in mid June or early July. After cutting a single crop of hay, the field would be left to grow again until fall. It might then be plowed under at that time, or left until early spring when the field would be plowed and made ready for a crop of corn. Later when alfalfa was grown there could be more than one cutting of hay.

Haymaking depends on weather and the maturity of the hay crop. The crop of hay must be cut and allowed to dry down to a certain moisture content. It would then be raked into "windrows". The hay was then loaded onto a wagon and hauled to the barn where it was put into the hay loft or hay mow. All of this had to be done without rain falling on the hay.

If the hay dried too long it had no food value and became worthless. If gathered up too soon it would be too wet. Wet hay will spontaneously combust and often a barn was lost to fire after haying season. Try collecting green grass from the lawn mower and putting it into a pile. Then the next day carefully put your hand into the pile. The center of the grass pile should be hot enough to burn flesh. A wet season can be devastating in trying to mow hay in the barn without excess moisture in it.

With eyes of the farmer on the sky and the direction of the wind as well as the maturity of the hay clover, he would assess all the conditions before making the decision to start making hay.

Along in June when it seemed there would be a few days of dry weather, a team of horses was hitched to the hay mower and my grandfather drove off with the well oiled sickle bar standing upright at the side until he entered the hay field. One five foot row at a time he cut a swath of hay around and around the 60-acre field. The hay lay flat in neat rows on top of the stubble ready to dry.

On occasion a pheasant nest would be uncovered while mowing. The hen's natural defense would become a curse to the hen. It was her nature to run on the ground to lead the "enemy" away from the nest. If she ran in front of the sickle bar, her legs would be cut off. This was always a sad occasion for the farmer. If possible, he would dispatch the hen to end her misery.

Some days later, when the hay had dried sufficiently, the team of horses was hitched to the hay rake and the swaths of hay were gathered into fluffy rolls ready to be picked up. The hay rake was a series of iron rods mounted on a bar about eight feet long. The rods were curved into large two-thirds of a circle arcs. By driving the rake across the field, it would gather the cut hay into the iron rods. When enough hay was gathered, a lever was tripped. The rods would rise up, leaving the gathered hay to become part of a larger row. The rods then lowered to the ground, gathering up the next collection of hay to be deposited in the next row. A good farmer would leave neat rows across the field. The less careful would leave ragged and broken rows of raked hay strewn across the field.

Up to this point the process was a one-man job. On the day the hay was to be put into the barn, neighboring men would gather bringing wagons and teams of horses to help in the event. As soon as the dew dried from the hay the team was hitched to a hay rack, a box-like wagon with slatted sides all around and a short ladder at the center front.

Almost full

The hay loader that stood behind the machine shed all the rest of the year was hitched to the back of the wagon and taken to the hay field. One of the wheels had a large sprocket mounted to it. A chain mounted on the sprocket activated the rack. As the wagon pulled it along the row of hay, iron rods like fingers mounted on long wooden slats grabbed the hay from the ground and moved it to the top of the loader and dumped the hay into the wagon rack.

There the hired man forked the loose hay first to the front of the wagon, then to the back, filling it up until he had a sizable load. It was often my job to drive the team out in the field. I climbed the ladder in front of the wagon as the load got higher and higher. When the wagon was heaping full, the loader was unhitched and the wagon load of hay was hauled home and pulled up alongside of the barn just under the gaping hay mow door.

At the barn the unloading of hay was synchronized so that one or two men were in the hay loft, another man drove the team of horses that pulled the long hay rope, and the third man was on the wagon load of hay. This required good communication and cooperation to put the hay into the barn loft.

As each forkful of hay was dumped into the haymow, it was the job of the first man to move the hay around the loft so that the hay was evenly dispersed. This was back breaking work using a pitchfork exclusively. Walking on the fresh loose hay was also difficult and tiring. As each forkful of hay came into the loft, it was also his job to call out loudly to the man on the hay wagon when the fork was in the proper position to drop its load of hay.

The second man driving the team of horses had to listen carefully for shouted commands as well. A very long length of ¾" hemp rope was strung through several pulleys placed at crucial points throughout the barn. The rope was long enough to reach from the team of horses, through to the back of the barn, then up to the steel rail in the peak of the roof at the back of the barn, then along the rail to the front of the barn, with sufficient length to reach down to the wagon and back up to the rail where it was finally fastened.

The team of horses pulled on this rope to lift the forkful of hay up from the wagon to the rail. There the fork would latch itself to a wheeled carrier. As the team continued to pull the rope, the carrier would roll along the rail into the barn loft, sometimes as far as the very back of the barn. When the carrier reached the desired position to drop the hay, the first man would holler "Drop it!" and the man driving the team of horses would halt the team.

At his point the third man, the one on the hay wagon, would jerk on a ½" rope called a trip rope. This rope reached loosely from the wagon to the fork that carried the hay into the barn. The fork would then release the load of hay. After the forkful of hay was dropped, this rope pulled the fork back along the rail to the front of the barn. There the carrier would latch itself in place on the rail, and the fork would lower itself to the wagon.

The third man brought down the hay fork from the pulley mounted on the hay rail. He set the four massive tines of the hay fork into a bundle of hay, alternating fork locations first in front of the wagon, next in the back. After jumping up and down on the hay fork to make as big a bundle as possible, he called loudly so that both men, the one in the loft and the other back of the barn would know that the next forkful was ready to go. The man with the horse in back of the barn led his horse forward until the man in the hay loft shouted for him to stop. The forkful of hay was dropped, and the process repeated until the wagon was empty.

Then it was back to the field for the next wagon load of hay. When there were more men to work, the unloading of the wagons would go much faster, and the crop of hay would be "put up" for the season. A surplus of hay meant stacking hay out in the barnyard. This haystack would be stacked carefully to shed as much rain as possible. Hay exposed to the elements would not keep its food value for long and this haystack would be used first.

Making hay was a hot sweaty job. The men stopped for drinks often and ate hearty meals at noon. Both forenoon and afternoon coffee breaks with cake and sandwiches were served in the field and at home. The brief respites from their labor were greatly appreciated.

It was always good if some homemade hops beer or root beer had been made ahead of time. The bottles of beer were cooled in running cold well water. At the end of the day and of the harvest these refreshments were most welcome to slake their thirst and wash the dust of the hay from the throat.

After World War II mechanical hay balers displaced the storage of loose hay. They made firmly packed "square" bales which took up less space and were easily handled and stacked. The process of filling the hay mow in the barn remained unchanged except bales were moved in the hayloft by hand or with hooks instead of pitchforks. However, out in the field the process was different.

Making square bales

Early balers had their own gasoline engine mounted on the machine as the source of power. They were not well muffled, so they were loud and could be heard all day long at home and at the neighbor's farm as well. As the hay was gathered into the front of the machine, a very large iron arm compressed the hay into a square channel that led to the rear of the machine. The arm was powered from a rotating fly wheel, and with each rotation the engine would snort even more, creating a rhythmic pulse that could be heard a mile away as it traveled around the field. The arm was a nasty looking device as it flailed in and out, up and down. It was also dangerous and was known to take off the arm of a not-so-careful farmer.

In the very early machines, there was a seat mounted on each side of the compressed hay channel. A man sat on each of the seats often under an umbrella for shade. Their task was to tie the ends of the baling wire together in order to form the hay bales.

Later machines tied the wire automatically, and even later used twine, first sisal and then poly, to tie the bales. With more powerful tractors, the balers were then powered from the tractor via a power take-off shaft. Gone was the pulsing roar of the engine.

As the square bales traveled to the rear of the machine, they were pushed up to the hay wagon. The wagon now a flat bed with a tall slatted back. Here, one or two men grabbed the bales with a large iron hook, dragged them to the rear of the wagon and stacked them carefully. The bales were stacked so that the large hay fork at the barn would be able to grasp eight bales at a time.

Around 1950 Allis Chalmers developed a baler that made "round bales", that is, the hay was rolled tightly into a cylinder about 24 inches in diameter and about four feet long.

Loading round bales

These bales were more difficult to handle and stack, but they kept the hay fresh for a longer period of time. My father-in-law purchased one such machine as a brand new item – the first new machine in his lifetime. This type of baler caused much conversation among the neighboring farmers. They were all convinced that it would not last. Perhaps they were right, but perhaps Grandfather Petersen was just ahead of his time. As this is written most hay is now baled into massive round bales using the same concept.

No matter how hay was baled, it was a fun time to get together with the neighbors. Like the threshing season, it was a time of fellowship, a time to be out in spectacular weather, and a time to eat well. The fresh hay smelled so sweet. It was a time to enjoy life on the farm.

STONE BOATS

Much has been written about the struggle of the pioneers in cutting down forests of trees to make land tillable. In Black Hawk and Grundy County Iowa where I lived the pioneers not only cleared the land of trees but also of rocks and stones.

When the immigration of farmers came to the Midwest lands, they found very fertile ground left from glacial deposits. The land had gently rolling hills, and grew generous crops each year. But just underneath the surface, the glaciers had also deposited granite stones and boulders of varying size. The stones were a hazard for the machinery. No one had ever bothered much about the rocks and stones before. But as the newcomers tried to plow the fields for planting, they often discovered these stones the hard way, most often resulting in damaged equipment.

Even years after fields had been plowed and cultivated, the winter freezes would push additional rocks to the surface. Each spring it was necessary for the farmer to walk the fields to gather up the stones. The smaller stones were carried to the side of the field where they would be out of the way. They were often very heavy, and it was hard work. The stones too large to carry would have to wait for the stone boat to be carried out of the field.

The stone boat was then devised by joining heavy planks together with heavy iron bolts and then set on cast iron skids. Eyebolts were attached to each side of the sled in the front. By means of iron loops, steel chains and leather harness, one or more horses were hitched to the sled and they would pull it over the ground like a snow sled without the snow.

Every spring on our farm a team of horses was hitched to the stone boat. Out in the plowed field the team was driven back and forth as the farmer loaded the rocks onto the boat. Rocks were of all sizes, many were eight to twelve inches thick or larger. The rocks were then piled up in the corner of a field or taken back to the farm place and dumped in a pile out of the way behind some building. Smaller stones were usually spread out in the farmyard.

Because only a small portion of the stone might be visible, when we found a rock, we never knew how large it might be. Some stones might be the size of a small potato, or they could be as big as a muskmelon. Others were as large as three or four feet tall. Once, Dad and my brother struck a stone in the field. From all outward appearances it was of a moderate size. After digging around it for a day, they had laid bare only a portion of a huge granite boulder in a hole fifteen feet across. Realizing the futility of further digging, they bought some dynamite and blew the top off the giant stone. They then covered it over with sufficient soil that it no longer posed a threat to the machinery. They never did discover the entire girth of that massive boulder.

The granite stones left from the glacial deposits were all well rounded from the glacier's activity. They ranged in size from just a pebble to the size of a modern refrigerator, or even larger. When a stone was discovered that was too large to move by hand, it was common to call in a man who was an expert in the use of dynamite. There were only two or three men in the area who were known for their ability to use the explosive efficiently.

Martin Westergaard was just such a person. He would in early spring dig an area around the large rock, place dynamite as far under the rock as he could place it, set a cap and a fuse, scratch a match, light the fuse, then walk away from the rock. Martin had done this enough that he knew about where the small pieces of rock would fall, and stand there accordingly waiting for the blast. He had a habit of talking to the dynamite as he walked away from the area. When he had finished blasting all the rocks, a wagon or stone boat was brought to load the small rock.

In the days before concrete blocks and poured concrete foundation walls, these rocks became the basic material that held buildings above the soil. Large rocks as much as two feet across were used in building foundations for large barns.

A good stone mason could place rocks so that they fit close together. He would sort through the accumulation of stones, selecting carefully those that could be laid up into a foundation wall. To further strengthen the wall the cracks were filled with a cement mixture called mortar.

The basement of the large farm house built in 1913 had a stone foundation. The wall of rocks was so carefully laid that it was nearly smooth. I never knew who our local stone mason was, but whoever he was he knew how to cut or select a stone so it could fit neatly next to another.

GRIND STONE

An essential piece of equipment on the farm where I lived was the grindstone. Our grinding stone was a solid sandstone wheel about three inches thick and twenty-four inches in diameter that was mounted on an iron stand with three iron legs. Underneath the stone was a foot treadle with an arm reaching up to the side of the stone wheel where it was connected to a rod bent to the shape of a crank. A metal seat was situated so that the man sharpening tools could sit as he turned the wheel with his feet pushing on the treadle. Directly beneath the stone was a shallow trough, which was filled with water when the wheel was in use.

To activate the wheel the man on the seat gave the stone a slight push to start it, then he pedaled to keep the wheel in motion.

The grinder was used to sharpen all manner of blades, including those on scythes, axes, and knives, even scissors.

Scythes were essential to cut tall grass and weeds around fence lines and around buildings. The wooden handle was curved to a unique shape. It was held with two handles that could be adjusted to fit the user. At the lower end of the handle was a very sharp curved blade. With a sweeping motion a man could cut a swath of grass and weeds. It was time consuming hard work, and tired both back and knees.

Axes were used to cut and chop wood. Wood was used as fuel for the kitchen cook stove and various other heaters used on the farm. Early farmers had planted large groves of trees around the farmyard. Storms often blew trees down during the summer months. It was a winter job to cut this wood for firewood. When a tree was old and had died, it needed to be cut down. A sharp axe was used to chop out a wedge on one side of the trunk. From the opposite side the tree was cut with a saw until it would fall to the wedge side. After felling the tree the logs were cut into short lengths suitable for firewood.

The kitchen had a supply of knives for cutting meat, bread, and at butchering time for killing and butchering hogs. These needed frequent sharpening. The farmer needed to be skilled at this task at the grindstone so that the many cutting tools worked well and lasted a long time.

224

CREAM SEPARATORS

Writing about cream separators is not exactly an exciting topic. Few of us even know that cream and milk come from the cow already mixed together and need to be separated. There are those that even believe that milk just comes from the carton in the store.

Many Iowa farmers milked cows, and the cream was a good source of steady income. Cream was used to make butter and other products, and had good value. Dad had a large dairy business on the farm with as many as 20 or 25 Guernsey cows. There was a bull as well, so from time to time there were also calves. He had studied dairy husbandry in Denmark and was anxious to have a good herd of cows when he was farming.

Milking meant sitting on the right side of the cow next to the cow's udder, either on a one- or three-legged stool. From that perch the cow could be milked by hand. Milking required strong and gentle hands with good stamina. A good cow could give enough milk to almost fill a five gallon pail. If the cow was calm it would go easily. Sometimes, however, the cow would be skittish. Then the milker had to be nimble to avoid being stepped on or knocked over backwards sending milk and milker flying.

When no more milk could be gotten from the cow, and the pail was filled, the whole milk was poured into ten-gallon cans. After the last cow had been milked, these cans would be ready for the separator. The warm whole milk was poured into the top of the cream separator. Farther down the machine, two spouts poured out skim milk and cream separately.

Before the invention of the mechanical cream separator, the cream was separated from the milk by allowing the whole milk to stand for one or two days. The cream would rise to the top, where it would be skimmed off, leaving the milk. Cream does really rise to the top! In about 1880, C. G. de Laval of Sweden devised the first successful mechanical cream separator, using centrifugal force to accomplish this task quickly.

The cast iron stand for our de Laval brand separator was bolted to the concrete floor in a room separated from the area where Dad milked the cows. A large stainless steel bowl was attached to the top, into which the fresh whole milk was poured. Below that, a series of numbered discs were inserted on a spindle in a heavy steel cone-like shield. As someone turned the cast iron crank at the side of the machine, the warm milk would flow through the discs spinning at a high speed. The weight of the cream separated the heavier liquid from the lighter liquid. Hence, cream was separated from milk.

Turning the crank handle was hard work. The crank turned slowly, just a few revolutions each minute, but was geared so that the discs spun at a very high speed, 6,000 to 9,000 rpm's. The speed needed to be constant during the time it took for the milk to flow through the machine. As someone quipped, "Do you know how many verses of 'Onward Christian Soldiers' it takes to separate a pail of milk?" Years later an electric motor was attached to the cream separator so that the hand crank was no longer needed.

Our family was uniquely proud of the fact that my great-grandfather, Jeppe Sliffsgaard, had brought the first cream separator to this country. It was not shipped assembled in one piece, but each separate piece was heavily greased and the parts were sent to his dairy operation in the village of Fredsville to be assembled. In the early 1900's there was a creamery in Fredsville where farmers brought their whole milk by horse and wagon. I have a faint memory of going to that creamery once when I was very young.

After each milking time the separator was taken completely apart. Each piece was washed, rinsed, and dried. Racks were built on walls to hold each of the pieces. Milking was done twice each day. That was a lot of washing. Somehow, it was always the farmer's wife who had the duty of washing the separator.

The separated cream had to be stored. The cream was poured into separate ten-gallon cans that were made just for that purpose. Farmers kept a tank where they could keep cold well-water running all of the time. The ten-gallon cans of cream were kept in the tank to keep them as cool as possible.

Cream haulers had regular pick up routes. The cream was hauled to the Benson Creamery in our area. Each can of cream was weighed, and at the end of the month a check was presented to each farmer.

Cream cans were initialed with paint so that the cans were returned to the proper owners.

The skimmed milk was considered a low value commodity. Many farmers just fed the product to the hogs. We did not drink skimmed milk. We only drank whole milk, so that had to be collected before it went into the separator.

For a time, Dad had a milk delivery business. The customers could order whole or skimmed milk and cream. Skimmed milk was a special order as most people drank whole milk. For that purpose we had a room in our basement of the house filled with the required equipment to put the milk into glass bottles.

The milkman, my dad

There were the tubs in which the bottles were cleaned and sterilized. One tub held a strong soap which washed the bottles. This was aided by a mounted bottle brush which washed the inside of the bottles. They were then rinsed in hot water, and then dipped into a final rinse that left the bottles sterilized. The clean bottles were then put into a wooden case that held twelve one-quart bottles. The case was placed under a tank full of the milk. By pulling a lever, four bottles at a time would be filled. When all the bottles were filled, another machine would place paper caps on each bottle. These bottles had to be kept cool in cold well water.

Each day Dad would load the cases of milk bottles into his delivery van, and set off on his route. It was a lot of work every day, but it provided another source of income.

The dairy business, along with the cream separator, lasted for many years. It lasted until the early 1920's when the government made a great push to test for tuberculosis in the cow herds. Veterinarians were required to test and certify herds of dairy cows all across the country. When the vet came to our farm, he used the same needle and syringe on every cow for his test. I do not know if the needle was a fresh one or not. The result was that entire herd, cows, bull and claves alike, was certified as positive for tuberculosis, and had to be destroyed. They were all "put down", and the truck came from the rendering plant and took the carcasses away.

This was the worst day of Dad's life. He loved those docile dumb animals, and had taken great pride in the care and husbandry of the herd. For a time he was very despondent, even to the point of considering suicide. It was a huge financial loss for our family. We lost a good source of income that was very difficult to replace. The loss of the herd was also a huge capital loss for the farm for which there was no reimbursement. But the greatest loss was the animals themselves. They were friendly beasts, and had become part of the "family" on our farm.

Farmers are accustomed to raising animals for food. They are used to the birth and death of animals in the normal course of life. They come to us as small things, are fed and cared for, and then sent off to market for slaughter and entry into the human food market. But there was something special for Dad in these cows. They had been on the farm for several years, and I suppose it was the expectation of a long term relationship with the animals interrupted by purposeful destruction that caused Dad so much pain. After a time we had a cow or two on the farm so that we had fresh milk and cream for our use, but the dairy business was gone forever. It was never the same again.

The equipment for bottling milk disappeared from our farm, hopefully to some useful purpose. The cream separator, however, was retained. It was moved to our basement in the house at some time, and was used only on occasion for its intended purpose. These hand cranked machines are now probably antiques, but the principles are still in use in the dairy business.

SUICIDE

Children probably don't need to see death or be near death but I saw it often while I lived on the farm. Life and death of animals is a part of farming. Life and death of people is also a part of the normal course of events. But self inflicted death is so terribly unnatural, and even the possibility of suicide leaves scars that last a lifetime.

When I was about seven or so and my younger brother, Hilmar, was still a small baby, I observed something I don't ever want anyone else to see. Things must not have been going well on the farm. However, at the time I was not aware of what was going on. It was in the middle of the forenoon when my mother took me in one hand and Hilmar in her other arm, and she took us to a shed not far from the henhouse.

There was my father crouched in a corner, holding a double-barreled shotgun in his hands. We stood pleading with my father to keep from killing himself. My mother stood outside, pleading and crying at the same time. After sometime there was resolution, and my father put the gun down. We all walked back to the house and life thereafter continued as normally as possible.

It is still a horrid memory, and is clear in my mind after all these years. I can never erase memories such as these.

FAIRS

Dad had an excellent herd of Guernsey cows. He was proud of his herd and would show them at several fairs around the state. The competition was strong at the fairs he attended held in Cedar Falls, Waterloo, and Des Moines.

When going to the several fairs, blankets, grooming tools, electric clippers on a stand, and other needed things were placed in those big wooden trunks that have survived all these years.

The fairgrounds in Cedar Falls were at the northeast corner of what is now Main Street and University. There were cow barns, food stands, and a track for horse racing. Tiers of wooden boards for seating were on one side of the racetrack.

Dad's prize beef

Dad walked his show cows the five miles to town and tied them up at his designated stalls in one of the cow barns. The cows from several owners were paraded in front of the grandstand, judged, and ribbons awarded according to how they placed in the judge's opinion. I remember Dad having a Grand Champion purple ribbon to bring home.

Dad showed his cows at the Dairy Cattle Congress in Waterloo, and again at the State Fair in Des Moines. To get the cows to the State Fair they were shipped by rail car to Des Moines. From the depot area, Dad walked the cows up Court Avenue, which meant walking them under the Court Avenue bridge, and then on to the Fair Grounds a number of miles away.

Those were memorable times for Dad. He was very proud of his herd of Guernsey cows.

Going to the fair in the 1920's there were lots of new and wonderful things to see. There were horse races, automobile races with strange looking vehicles, and airplanes flying above the crowds. They were the open cockpit biplanes. Dad was always the adventurous fellow, and made friends with the pilots and race drivers alike.

The part I liked best about going to the Fairs was that there were always fireworks in the evenings after the shows.

At the Dairy Cattle Congress I liked getting the tiny loaves of Wonder Bread and eating the tiny pancakes made by Aunt Jemima. She was a lady dressed in black make-up, long skirts and a red kerchief around her head.

When we went to the fairs, mother always prepared food for our noon meal. That included warm fried spring chicken, potato salad, pie, coffee, and sandwiches. We spread a cloth on the grass and ate our noon meal, as did other neighbors. One time, Pete Jensen, sister-in-law Jeanne's father, ate a chicken dinner with us at the fair in Waterloo. Pete served in the county sheriff's department, and may have been assigned to the fair as his duty. The Dairy Cattle Congress days were full of enjoyment for the whole family.

The several fairs we attended were an important part of farm life. The fairs were not for seeing the side shows or attending the carnival rides. Farmers and their wives brought in the best of their animals and produce to be judged for its merit. They learned from the experience no matter the placement. It was always good to place well in the judging. It made the exhausting task of farming worth while, and of course there were always the bragging rights. Fairs were important as well as fun.

FARM ANIMALS

I would like to share with you a few of the hazards of growing up with farm animals. I lived with my parents on a typical mid-western Iowa farm complete with cows, chickens, horses, etc. I want to relate to you what it was like being a free-running young child. I had many good times with the great outdoors, but there were some pitfalls I encountered.

For example, gathering eggs in the hen house should have been, and was, a rather simple job, no matter what my age. I would take a basket or pail and trot off to the henhouse. I had to reach into each nest-box attached to the wall and carefully place the eggs into the pail or basket. But then there would be a hen that was reluctant to give up any of her clutch of eggs tucked carefully under her soft warm feathers. We called this type of hen a "cluck hen." She would stare at me with those tiny glassy eyes with complete defiance. Having been told to gather all the eggs, I proceeded to reach into the nest and feel under her for one or more eggs. With the speed of lightning she pecked at my wrist or forearm with her dagger-like beak, and settled back into her warm box of straw. What to do next? I could walk on to the next box or I could grab the hen very quickly in the back of the neck, and pull her out of her secure nest. Well done. She would fly off in a huff cackling at the top of her lungs. Oh yes, I did get three eggs in that nest! It was my victory.

Elna astride a friendly bull

Then there was the gander with his harem of three matronly looking gray and white geese. He walked about the farmyard as if he were the sole owner of the estate and that he had the right to fight off anything that might look aggressive. I could be playing clear across the yard, enjoying myself in the brown dusty earth, when all of a sudden there would be the rapid running of webbed feet coming towards me. He would stretch out his neck and, with his bright orange beak, take a nip at my bare legs. I could scream for help but it would be too late. He would then return with great dignity to his patriarchal duty and would pride himself on doing such a magnificent job of warding off such a formidable foe.

The three mild-looking geese would have their day, too, when they had a nest of goose eggs that they are hatching. I suppose 28 days is a long time for any being to set in one place, but that doesn't mean that they should vent their anger on someone like me looking in to see how things are going. The geese loved to fly at me and beat their wings on my body until I again ran for help. They have an amazing amount of strength in those beautiful wings.

My coal black Shetland pony named "Babe" loved to harass me. Ponies have a sense of knowing the how much and what they can get by with. I was told many times to whip the pony, but I didn't want to hurt her. I always rode her bareback. If I got too far back on her spine she would bounce on her hind hooves until I finally slid off. She would then swish her long tail. She had won again. Or, if I went to the pasture to catch and halter her, she played the game of "hide and seek". The large workhorses were also out there. Babe would run behind one of the big horses as if for protection. On hot summer afternoons this was not fun for me, only for her. I would pout all the way back home because I just couldn't catch her.

I rode my pony to Fredsville a lot. I had to remove the bridle and in the same process, get the halter slipped on without her getting away. She was tricky and knew just at what split second she could break free. There was many a time I walked the two-plus miles back home when the summer temperature and humidity were at their highest.

The workhorses seemed to be very gentle as well as sensible and I could get around them without being afraid. When I was maybe three or four years old I remember putting my arms around one of the horse's hind legs. The horse stood perfectly still. I was not hurt in any way. I could climb in and out of the manger where the horses ate their hay. They didn't mind.

Dad with a new member of the herd

Dad had a herd of Guernsey dairy cows. I worked with them a lot. I didn't do the milking, but I was always around at milking time. Cows raised around humans are generally docile, but still they seem to have a built-in intuition to do some very dumb things. Swishing their tail so that it would hit directly across my face was one thing they did exceptionally well. Or stepping on my foot was the most painful thing they could do. And once their foot was planted painfully on mine they didn't want to move to set their foot somewhere else. Walking in front of the cows at feeding time had yet another amusement for the cows. They loved to butt their heads out and see if they could frighten me. Even as a child I walked the cows back and forth to the pasture up across the highway many, many times. I didn't have much trouble with them then. They were either going home for a drink or going back to the green pasture for more grass, perhaps thinking only of the food or drink.

Cows are also creatures of habit. Out in the pasture they stay together as a herd most of the time. When the herd moves across the pasture they walk in single file. At milking time the cows are let into the barn where they put their heads and neck into stanchions

234

to hold them still. Each cow always goes to the same stanchion. If a new cow is added to the herd, she will not know which stanchion is not used by the others and may take another cow's place. When this happens there is great consternation and the cows become nervous, milling about the barn until the new cow is pushed away and the others find their usual place. Most often they are gentle beasts and seem to enjoy human attention.

There is perhaps one exception to this: the Ayrshire cow. They have a unique personality that has tested the patience of many a farmer. The Saturday Evening Post for years ran a cartoon called "Ada, the Ayrshire." The cartoon centered around the misadventures of Ada, an Ayrshire cow. They were the source of much laughter until we owned one. For a few weeks my husband had an Ayrshire cow purchased at auction. She had a penchant for not staying in her pen no matter how well it was enclosed. She had an instinct about how to get free no matter what my husband did, even hurdling her large body over the fence. She would roam the farm and had no intention of going back to captivity. This misbehavior lasted until she led my husband on a "merry chase" that covered most of our 400 acre farm, retracing her path more than once. When finally caught, she was tied to a stout post on a short, heavy rope, and went off to the auction shortly thereafter.

Sometimes I helped feed the calves. Dad put warm milk from the separator into a calf pail and I was to hold it for the calf. The calf would take a few sips and then shove his head into the bottom of the pail with amazing strength. At that, pail and milk went sprawling across the floor.

I must not forget about the bull that belonged to the herd of dairy cows. He was a very dangerous animal and could never be trusted. They were born mean and looked mean. I could never be too careful with the bull.

Then there were the hogs. Nothing smelled worse than hogs. The odor would get into the air, into my clothes, and even walking in or near the pigpen left an awful smell on my shoes. Besides smelling bad, the sows were overly fat and mostly disagreeable. The piglets would squeal their piercing scream and the old boar hog would have liked to corner me and to have killed me. I kept my distance. Yet, we enjoyed pork chops, ham and bacon.

Sheep were a very stupid animal, and needed lots of help during their life. The life of a shepherd must have been, and probably still is, a life filled with patient care of each of the flock. The sheep seemed to have a fancy to stick their heads through a woven wire fence. Then they would not know enough to back out of it. They would have stood there until they died unless someone came to get them out of their situation.

I have written about as much bad stuff about farm animals from my childhood as I can think of. But I like the animals. It really wasn't that bad. It just seemed so at the time. Animals are wonderful creatures. It is necessary to know their characteristics and know how to get along with them. It is like getting along with people. You have to get to know them and find their good qualities. Animals' contribution to the life and health of humans is necessary. Just being able to live with these living creatures is a wonderful learning experience. Animals taught me a lot about the cycle of life and death, and about the value and importance of food.

What a dismal place this world would be without animals. Life as we know it would not exist without the contributions animals make to our lives and well-being. If I had a farm again I would have all of these animals, and enjoy each and every one of them.

DYNAMITE

In our area of farming the sounds of dynamite explosions were a common occurrence in certain times of the year. In the late winter or early spring of the year, series of explosions lasting several days were not uncommon. We knew to find a secure location for the best china and glassware. We, or the neighbors, were blasting rocks or stumps.

Although the soil in this part of Iowa, near Cedar Falls, was very rich, certain parts also had many granite boulders left from when glaciers had advanced through the territory leaving behind their well-polished and rounded debris. These pieces of granite could be as small as pebbles, and as large, or larger, than anyone could imagine. When a boulder was found that was larger than could be moved by hand or by horse, the expert in blasting with dynamite would be called in to solve the problem.

In the south eighty of our farm there was a rock about as large as a small paneled delivery truck for lack of a better comparison. I remember of driving by other large rocks of similar size that were left where they were for lack of equipment to move or destroy them.

In the rich soil of this area trees grew quite large. Many very large cottonwood trees had been cut for firewood, but the large stumps remained. When a tree was toppled by storm or disease the tree was cut for firewood leaving a stump well anchored in the ground. Dynamite would easily remove the stump.

We purchased dynamite sticks and blasting caps by the wooden crate. These would be used on whatever rocks or stumps required removal, and the remainder was carefully stored in the cool cellar until next year. Many farm homes such as ours kept a box of dynamite and a box of dynamite caps. Caps were kept at a distance from the dynamite box. As children we knew to stay away from the box of dynamite and never to touch the box labeled 'CAP'. One young man I knew had a finger blown from his hand because he handled a dynamite cap.

There were two or three men in our area that were truly experts at this most dangerous endeavor. They were hired to apply their skill and expertise at using this powerful explosive. It was amazing to watch them as they worked, and what they could accomplish. They would be called upon for their expertise to move or remove both boulders and large tree stumps.

Stumps were relatively easy to remove. It was necessary to dig around the entire stump, and then to dig down on one specified side deep under the stump. The dynamite expert would show the farmer where to dig this hole and how deep to dig, or often dig it himself. From a wooden box of dynamite sticks set nearby, the expert would pick the amount of dynamite that he determined would be sufficient for the task. This might be a quarter, a half, a whole stick or more of the explosive.

From his jacket pocket, where he kept a generous supply of such items, he would attach to the dynamite stick a blasting cap with a length of fuse, and place the assembly under the stump. He would then casually reach for his pipe and tobacco, and fill the pipe. After striking a large wooden match, he would carefully light the fuse. Then, as he stood down in the hole watching the burning fuse, he would light his pipe with equal deliberation. When he was satisfied that both were well lit, he would slowly walk away, but only a short distance.

After a brief interval there was a loud boom, and the tree stump would leap up out of the ground a short distance, and settle back to earth ready to be hauled away. He always knew how far to walk, and in what direction. Dirt might fly, but he always seemed to know where the stump was going to go. We would watch from a distance this daring dance, and be amazed at his audacity and his success equally. On rare occasions, after lighting the fuse, he would run from the hole. We knew then that the stump could fly in any direction.

He used this technique on the rocks as well. With the blast, they too would be blown free of the soil or broken into smaller pieces ready to be hauled away.

Some boulders, even when free of their place in the soil, were still too large to handle easily. Then he would use a different technique. He would place an amount of the dynamite on the top of the boulder, and then cover it with a few handfuls of dirt. He would again reach for his pipe, and after lighting the fuse, would also light the tobacco. Once more, when both were well lit, he would walk away, but this time he would stand behind a nearby tree or another large stone. The blast would send the dirt flying in all directions, but also crack the boulder into smaller pieces that could more easily be taken away.

He never seemed to get nervous or excited about his profession. He was the calmest person in the group. His task would continue until all the tree stumps were removed or boulders freed from the ground and made small enough to handle. This might take several days.

Housewives grumbled as the blasts rattled windows and china alike. The farmer did not take this lightly either. The animals suffered the most. Cows gave less milk and chickens quit laying eggs. Children and dogs needed extra comforting. The use of dynamite was kept to a minimum, but it was necessary from time to time in the process of clearing the farm land. These men who were proficient in the use of dynamite were remarkable people, and worth whatever their fee might be.

BLIZZARD

The winter of 1936 will be remembered by the old timers as the coldest, the stormiest, the snowiest, and the most miserable of winters they have ever known. For weeks the windows rattled night and day as the wind howled and the snow swirled. There was no transportation to speak of because all the roads were closed under large drifts of snow. The rural eight-party telephone line was the only way anyone could communicate with one another.

December and January of that winter had been rather mild as winters go in the Midwest. Dad had even been doing some plowing out on the north 80, which was very unusual for this time of the year. He came in from the field one noon and said in his usual hearty voice, "Well, I guess the winter's broke." It was only a few days later until winter really began in its worst fury.

It was late January when we began getting some snow. Every day after that it snowed a little more and before long it became a full-blown blizzard storm. The wind blew, and the drifts got deeper and deeper. Neighbors were wondering if it wouldn't soon let up. We were truly snowbound.

I was teaching in the country school just half mile north of the farm. For a time, I bundled up each morning with my lunch in hand and walked the long, cold stretch to the schoolhouse. The building would be icy cold. I needed to get the fire going before the children began arriving. Most got rides to the school in bobsleds. When the kids got there we spread out mittens and overshoes to try to get them dry by the time they were to go home. We huddled around the heating stove to keep warm.

It was a very stormy day the first of March when Dad came with the bobsled and we bundled all the children up and took them to our house for fear we would get trapped in the schoolhouse. Parents came and got their children from our house, and they all got safely home.

For the entire month the school was closed. Snow removal equipment was inadequate to open roads, and if they did get any roads open, they blew shut right away. In the large farmhouse in which we lived there was no way we were able to heat the whole house. We finally ended up living only in the kitchen close to the cook stove. Each night I ran up the stair steps to a very cold bedroom and huddled under the feather ticks to make a warm place. Once I had the bedding around me warmed I would not move all night long. Every day the thermometer would read 35 or 36 degrees below zero. The frost on the kitchen windows became so thick we couldn't look out. With our fingernails we scraped a hole in the frost the size of a half dollar so we could peek outside.

It was especially hard on the livestock. They needed water and the stock tank was frozen over. Dad would go outside all bundled up in his warmest winter clothing, and with corncobs and kerosene he lit a fire in the tank heater for quick heat. Even then the ice thawed an area only about two feet across. Dad would bring the cows out and they would try to drink as the water froze on their faces. They wanted to get back into the barn as quickly as possible. Mother heated water in the teakettle and stirred hot water into the chicken mash, then carried the warm mash to the henhouse for the chickens to eat. The water fountains for the chickens froze solid. The red combs on the roosters and hens also froze and turned black.

Day in and day out the fire had to be kept going in the cook stove. Mittens and overshoes were hung to dry around the stove. Any laundry that was done was hung up to dry on lines strung across the kitchen.

The wood pile out by the fence was covered over with deep snow, but it was necessary to bring in firewood for the cook stove. Dad would shovel enough snow to find the wood, split what was necessary, and bring in arms full of wood covered in snow. This wood needed to dry before it could be used in the cook stove. When we ran out of coal, it was our only source of fuel.

I spent a lot of days next to the cook stove doing a piece of embroidery, which I still have. I think of the blizzard when I look at that piece of handiwork. It was a linen piece done in all blue embroidery floss.

There was no television in those days, so on the long evenings we sat around the kitchen table playing card games and checkers until it was time to go to bed. Everyone dreaded going upstairs to the frigid bedrooms.

It seemed like the weather got worse each day. No one could get to town or anywhere else for that matter. For food we relied on the several bushels of potatoes in the bin down in the cellar. We also had canned fruit and vegetables as well as canned meat. Last summer Mother had wisely filled several shelves with these preserved canned goods in the basement. For as long as the flour in the big wooden flour bin lasted, Mother baked bread for sandwiches, and made stacks of pancakes for breakfast every morning. We ate well in the cold.

As the weeks went by everyone's coal supply began to get low. The dealers in town couldn't deliver any coal to anyone. Finally, when the weather began to wane, neighbors called other neighbors and it was decided that they would cut the wire fences and drive through the fields in their bobsleds. One neighbor said he would go to town with his bobsled and bring back coal to divide with the neighbors. He may have brought a few grocery items, too.

On one day when the sun was bright and the wind was not blowing as much, Erik Christiansen, who lived on the first north-south road east of Dike, put on a pair of ice skates and skated on the frozen surface of the road from Dike to Cedar Falls, a distance of several miles. There was no traffic and he had the whole road to himself.

Some of the neighbors burned ear-corn in their stoves to make heat. Corn was only ten cents a bushel at that time so it was not that expensive to burn. Another factor with which to contend was that the cream haulers couldn't get around to pick up the ten-gallon cans of cream. The cream was probably fed to the hogs.

My school was closed for four weeks before we could get back to school. It was my responsibility to get the school functioning again. I went down in our cellar at home, and with an axe, chopped some kindling, carried the kindling to school, and started a fire in that icy-cold schoolroom. Out in the coal shed I again broke up coal chunks with a sledgehammer to make pieces small enough to catch on fire. I had to carry it inside in a coal bucket and then tease the fire along. The floor never did get warm until late winter, when warm weather finally set in.

The frozen drifts were six feet or more deep between the school-room and the outhouses. My school board president called to see if I had shoveled a path to each of the outhouses. My answer was that the children would walk over the top of the drifts whenever they needed to go out there. For 45 dollars a month, which was my pay, I was not going to try to dig out a path that deep and that far. I still remember how cold the school floor was. I got chill blains so badly. Also, I can't forget that there was a den of skunks that lived under the floor, and the scent in the schoolroom was almost unbearable. They must have enjoyed the fire in the stove as well. The building was built on a flat lime rock foundation, leaving just enough space under the floor for small animals. Rabbits lived under there too.

There is one nice memory I have of that winter. On Valentine's Day, my husband-to-be walked the two miles to our house with a heart-shaped box of chocolates for me. He had to walk over the frozen drifted snow to get there.

I have the big brass key from that school building hanging on the wall in my living room in memory of that spiteful winter. I doubt if any of my visitors who see it can know what that key means to me nor the memories that are called to mind.

BOBSLEDS

Even up until WW II the automobiles were not built to withstand Iowa winters or rural Iowa roads. During the winter auto owners used wood alcohol for anti-freeze to keep the water in the radiator from freezing. It was not nearly as effective as modern antifreeze solutions. Passenger compartments of these cars were not enclosed early on, so driving or riding could be a very cold adventure. Oil and gasoline were not right for that kind of bitter weather. The oil turned to the consistency of molasses and made it very difficult to turn the crank to start the car.

The alternative in winter was to hitch a team of horses to the bobsled. What was used as a wagon with wheels in good weather could be changed to a bobsled by moving the wagon box over onto a wagon frame with two pairs of sled runners instead of wheels.

When driving to town in the bitter cold weather to sell a crate of eggs, or to bring back coal for the furnace, the driver was often dressed in a long fur coat, a seal skin cap, and fur mittens with gauntlets reaching well above the wrist.

Passengers, if any, sat on wooden boxes inside the wagon box. There would be a deep layer of straw on the bottom of the wagon box and heavy blankets to place over the laps. Often, a large piece of soapstone was heated in the cook stove oven. That heated stone was then placed under the feet to help keep passengers warm.

When snow made the roads impassable the bobsled was put into use. Bobsleds were quite heavy, and could not be driven through, or over, very deep snow. Even if the snow had a thick crust, horses and bobsled might break through. That would be dangerous for the horses, and the bobsled would be stuck in the drift. If drifts were too deep to drive over, fence lines were severed and the driver took the sled across the open fields where snow was not as deep. The winter of 1936 was a good example of bobsledding and fence cutting. The cold was so intense and lasted so long that neighbors ran out of coal used to provide heat in the home. Many got together to bring home a jag of coal to keep houses more livable.

After the war, automobile manufacturers built more efficient cars. Roads and highways were rebuilt, and a new way of traveling evolved. More powerful machines could clear the snow from the improved roads. Bobsleds became obsolete.

THE TILE DIGGER

Most of the farms in our part of Iowa were homesteaded in the 1800's by European immigrants. In the early 1900's these farms were still relatively "young." Most of the efforts of the farmer were to raise crops and make a living.

But it became apparent that the rich soil with clay underneath did not drain excess moisture away quickly enough. This meant that the farmer could not use machinery in the fields when he needed to, and often the crop yield was impaired in a wet season. For that reason, it became apparent that fields needed drainage. The soil moisture level was still too high for crop farming.

So the fields were tiled. That is, deep trenches were dug, reddish brown tiles were laid end to end and an open end of the tile was drained to a creek.

One very notable person by the name of Martin Westergaard, an immigrant Danish Jew, made a profession of tile digging. My father would arrange to have him come to our farm to tile certain fields. Martin was a good worker as long as he was sober. He was more inclined to go on a long "drunk" and the digging would have to be postponed until he was sober enough to go back to work.

When it was decided that a field needed additional drainage, Dad would have a load of tile brought to the farm, unload the tile at the edge of the field and then wait for Martin to continue his digging. The trenches were dug with a special spade about 20 inches long and eight inches wide, slightly curved on its width to "cup" the soil. There was a thick edge at the top of the spade on which to set a foot to push the tool down into the thick, rich soil. Trenches were often dug to the depth of a man's height and wide enough so that a man could dig to the bottom of the trench and the tile could be laid at the bottom. The depth of the trench would vary so that the water would drain away into a lower place such as a creek or other natural drainage method.

Digging tile was hard and tedious work. It required some strength, but a lot of stamina and determination. When he was working, Martin could dig trenches all day long. Spade full by spade full, he would inch the trench across the field in the proscribed path. Working like that in the full sun, his skin was always deeply tanned. He stopped only occasionally for water or coffee, and of course noon lunch. His wiry stature and dogged determination seemed to be just the features required for this task.

When the trench was dug, the baked clay tile was laid in place, end to end, at the bottom of the trench using a long pole. A special attachment at the end of the pole would allow a metal rod to slide into the end of the waiting tile. Then it was carried to the trench where it was laid next to the last one in the line. After all the tile was laid, the ditch was filled with the dirt that lay at the side of the trench. All of this, of course, was done by hand.

To this day many of the farms in this area are successfully drained of excess moisture from the long and hard physical efforts of Martin Westergaard and others who dug the trenches and laid the tile entirely by hand.

MACHINE SHED

Between the barn and the hog house on our farm stood a building which was open on the long front side facing the rest of the buildings. The dirt floor might indicate that it had been one of the original buildings on the farm place. It was not worth the effort or expense to put a finished floor in this building. The roof provided adequate water-proof shelter. The wooden boards on the three sides were painted barn red as were the rest of the buildings. Around the foundation were small openings where wild rabbits could duck in and out.

Inside this building were stored a number of out-of-season pieces of machinery. There was a two-row corn planter equipped with check wire, a two-row corn cultivator, a hay loader with the rack of heavy wires that pulled the hay into the hay wagon, a machine set with curved rods to turn the hay to dry it, a sickle mower, and a one bottom plow. Later a two-bottom plow was purchased and stored there too. All of these were horse-drawn machines.

At about the time of WW I Dad bought one of the earliest farm tractors built in Waterloo. It was called a "Dart". It had wide fenders, large steel wheels with lugs, and a flywheel on the side. The tractor could be used to power the threshing machine. The tractor was kept in the shed, too.

As I write this in the year 2001, these pieces of machinery would be considered obsolete, miniature, and be noted as antiques if there were still any in existence. To my knowledge, only a few have survived, now owned by collectors of antique farm machinery.

MODEL-T FORDS

When automobiles were first brought to our rural area there were some unusual events. In the twenty-first century we would label these events as "unintended consequences."

It was the norm that automobiles had no battery or electrical system to start and operate the car. Instead, the spark was made with a magneto, the same method in use today on most lawnmowers. It was necessary for one person, usually a strong fellow, to turn a crank from the front of the car. The crank connected directly to the crank shaft of the engine. Further, the crank had to be turned fast enough to make the spark hot enough to work.

A second person needed to sit in the driver's seat to manually advance the spark and to operate the manual choke and throttle. In modern automobiles the advance and choke is now done automatically, even using computer technology to gain efficiency. In the early days, these operations required some level of skill and practice. Between the two people the engine could be coaxed into sputtering and coughing life.

It was new technology of the era. To some it was like learning to operate a computer or program a VCR in our day. While most farmers were excellent mechanics, some members of the older generation were used to horse drawn vehicles.

For example, the early model T Fords used a crank that securely coupled to the crankshaft. The person operating the crank had to know which direction to turn the crank in order to start the engine. In addition, if the engine backfired, the crank would snap back in the opposite direction breaking the forearm of the operator. Later crank-started engines corrected this defect.

Then there were all the levers and pedals to operate while steering the car. Some needed attention simultaneously. There was the spark lever, the throttle lever, the choke, the brake lever, the clutch and the transmission lever. It was much different than having a horse who understood verbal commands.

Cousin Elmer decided to buy a new 1919 touring car. He and Grandpa Iversen drove the team of horses and wagon to town to bring home the automobile. Somehow Grandpa Iversen drove the new car back to the farm while Elmer brought home the team and wagon. It had been decided to park the new automobile in the corn crib alley way, where it would be sheltered. Grandpa Iversen did very well until he pulled into the corn crib. The doors on the far end of the alley way were closed. He must have been very nervous or excited. As he pulled into the shelter of the crib, he hollered "Whoa!", as if driving the horses. Of course the vehicle did not stop and ran into the door before it came to a halt. The front end "…was all messed up." It didn't do the door of the corn crib any good either.

My grandparents, the Hoffmans, had retired at the age of fifty, left the farm, and moved into a cozy little white house just down the hill from the country church they attended regularly.

My grandmother mulled over the idea of how nice it would be for them if they bought and owned a Model-T Ford touring car. I can see my grandmother rubbing her fingers together as she always did when making great decisions. They would be free to drive to town or go visiting at their leisure. No longer would they need to keep, feed and care for the horses to draw the carriage. Life would be a lot easier.

My grandmother controlled the purse strings, and it wasn't long before the idea quickly became a reality. They were off to the Dike Garage where new cars were sold and repaired, and soon she wrote out a check drawn on the Dike Savings Bank. Suddenly they were owners of a brand new shiny black Model T Ford. It wasn't long before the horses and buggy were all sold.

It was immediately decided that my grandmother would be the driver of this black marvel. Besides she thought my grandfather would never be able to learn to drive it anyway. And most of all she needed him to crank the car every time they started it. Starting this flivver was a two person task.

My grandmother learned what the two handles under the steering wheel were for, the three pedals on the floorboard, and how to put gas in the tank. The only thing my grandfather had to do was stand in front of the car and, at her signal, turn the crank to start it. Hopefully, the car would not backfire. If that happened, the crank would suddenly snap backwards.

They were ready. Grandmother put on her ankle-length black dress with the white lace collar, wound her long gray braid around and around on top of her head, then, with two long hatpins, the little black straw hat was firmly fastened to her hair. Grandfather, of course, wore his navy blue wool serge suit and covered his head with a brown felt hat.

They were ready to hit the road. It didn't bother them that the roads were graveled, dusty and rough. All she had to do was grasp the steering wheel turn up the gas lever, let out the clutch and they would be off.

The Model-T did not have a door on the left side where the steering wheel was. To get into the car my grandmother first stepped on the running board on the right side causing the car to tilt at an awkward position because she was so heavy. Then, reaching for the steering wheel, she slid across the seat and grasped the wheel while waiting for my grandfather to crank the car from in front under the radiator.

When the engine was running he took his place beside her, grasping his hat with one hand and with the other, clinging to the door so tightly his knuckles turned white.

Because she was so short and heavy my grandmother was unable to stoop down to the floorboard to grasp the brake. So the Dike mechanic installed an extension so that my grandmother could reach to the side and brake the car.

The two of them often drove to Dike to buy groceries and dry goods at Henningsen's General Store, or to see the doctor or dentist, and then stop at the meat market. Sometimes they would go visiting on sunny afternoons. They enjoyed traveling about the countryside in this new-found method of travel.

What they hadn't considered was that when winter came they couldn't take the car out. There were side curtains to cover the open sides but no heater. And the water in the radiator might freeze up. So in the cold weather the car was jacked up, set on blocks, the water drained out and there it would stand until the following spring. They spent the cold weather entertaining at home, relying on others to bring needed groceries.

Their driving was a source of amusement for people in the community. "There goes Stina," they would say and turn and chuckle to themselves.

GENERAL STORES

The old time general store was pretty much what the name implied. Almost everything we needed was sold there.

I remember well that there were two thriving general stores in the town of Dike. One of the stores faced Main Street on the corner to a side street. In my days this was owned by Hans Kelsen. He had purchased the business from his father-in-law in 1910. There were entrances to this store on the front and on the side. The building was a two storey structure. Business was conducted on the main floor, and the Kelsen's lived in an apartment on the second floor.

Double view of Dike

Inside the store, the high ceilings were finished with squares of decorative tin. There were tall shelves around the walls of the store holding all manner of goods. Counters fitted with glass fronts and shelves displayed smaller items. Wooden barrels and kegs that contained large amounts of a variety of goods littered the floor in every available place. Many were open and the contents could be measured into smaller containers as the customer required. Glass jars of cookies and candy sat on the counter tops tempting children and adults alike. Mr. Kelsen would, if the child were fortunate, reach into a jar of cookies and hand one over at no charge. We learned to say "Thank you." A "store bought" cookie was a treat.

The back of the store was stocked with groceries. The front of the store displayed cotton goods. Women could buy yard goods, 36 inches wide, and sew wonderful aprons, cotton print dresses and other garments. The men could buy shirts, socks, and shoes there.

The store always had a unique aroma that was apparent as soon as the customer stepped inside the door. It was a combination of tanned leather goods, vinegar, smoked fish, dried meat and so on. It never was offensive, and was a special characteristic of the store. Some-

250

times a similar odor even today, eighty years later, can still trigger a fond memory of the store.

Kelsen's store had a competitor not one block away, also on Main Street. This store was the same in almost every way. Pete Henningsen, who began operating this store in 1905, was the owner. He always wore a white full apron as he stood behind the counter gathering up the items the customer needed. This was before the days of bags, paper or plastic, in which to carry the merchandise. All purchases were wrapped in plain paper.

On the counter was a device which held a large roll of the paper. Mr. Henningsen would pull out a suitable length of paper, neatly tear it from the roll and lay it out on a vacant spot on the crowded counter. A large cone of thin cotton string sat above the roll of white paper. The string was strung through a couple of metal rings above the counter, and the loose end hung on the counter near the paper roll. After wrapping the purchase in paper he wound the package on four sides with the string. He would then twist the string around his fingers and break it off. Then, after tying a neat knot, he would hand the package over with a smile and a "Thank you."

Vinegar was dispensed from a large wooden barrel that stood out in the back of the store. Customers brought their ceramic or glass jugs and had them filled. Corks were used to "stop" the liquids in bottles. Flour, coffee beans and sugar could be scooped out of the barrel into a cloth bag, the neck of which would also be tied up with the string. There were a few items in metal cans available, but we had our own home canned goods and did not buy them.

Store owners gave small lined notebooks about 2 ½ x 5 inches in size to customers as a form of advertising in the early 1900's. I have copied some pages from one of those notebooks showing what people paid for groceries at that time. Note how the word "bread" was misspelled. On the cover the following was printed:

C. A. GRANT & SON
ROLFE, IOWA

LUMBER
COAL
BRICK
SEWER PIPE
PAINTS

Sept. 1909		October		October		Following page:	
Coffee	.20	Sugar	.25	Meat	.10		
tea	.10	Soda	.10	Meat	.10	Cookies	.10
cookies	.10	Chocolate	.25	Meat	.10	Coffee	.20
soap	.10	p.sugar	.15	Meat	.10	Cheese	.05
tooth p	.05	lemon	.05	Meat	.15	Sardines	.10
pepper	.10	cookies	.10	Meat	.10	Crackers	.10
Brid	.10	bread	.05	Lard	.18	Sugar	.25
P flour	.25	coffee	.20	Meat	.20	Molasses	.10
Syrup	.25	cookies	.05	Meat	.05	Eggs	.11
B Powder	.10	mince meat	.10	Lard	.35	stove p	.10
Bread	.05	panC flour	.20	Meat	.10	cookies	.10
Cookies	.10	ginger	.10	Meat	.20	coconut	.10
Yeast	.05	cookies	.05	Meat	.10	sugar	.20
Lye	.10	cookies	.05	Meat	.10	peas	.10
Farina	.13	crackers	.05	Meat	.05	bread	.10
Soap	.25	mustard	.10	Meat	.10	bread	.05
Lye	.10	oil	.20	Meat	.10	bread	.05
Cheese	.10	bread	.10	Meat	.15	syrup	.25
Raisins	.10	meat	.10			salmon	.25
Blueing	.10	lard	.36			eggs	.10
Closepins	.05	meat	.15			crackers	.05
1 Foot(?)	.05	meat	.10			bread	.05

STREETS

Some of my memories from early childhood are the trips of going to town for shopping. I was born in 1914 so this relates some of the impressions I have of going into Cedar Falls, a midwestern town located in northeast Iowa.

252

My parents had and drove a Mitchell automobile. I rode in the back seat sitting on black leather hard seats. There were no glass windows on the sides of the car. There was a leather top that covered the otherwise open car. The road to town was covered with gravel smoothed by horse drawn "graders". The grader consisted of two blades of iron set in an almost vertical position and drawn by two horses. The blades were set at a slight angle. The grassy roadside ditches were almost level with the road.

The absence of any windows in the car made for an open-air ride. The ride was windy and dusty as we sped along at a rapid 30 miles an hour. My father always seemed to have lead in his foot whenever he drove any vehicle. Once in town Dad parked the car at an angle to the sidewalks. The sidewalks were cemented but the main street was still a dirt street.

In the dry weather of summer the streets would become very dusty. Horse or auto traffic would send clouds of fine dust into the nearby stores. This was before anyone even thought of air conditioning, so doors and windows stood wide open to catch any breeze. Some relief from the dust was achieved by wetting the streets.

A wagon with a large wooden round tank braced with iron bands was situated on high wooden wheels rimmed with iron and was drawn by a team of horses. The driver drove back and forth up and down Main Street. On-lookers looked up as they heard the steady clip clop of the horses hooves as the driver let the sprinkler from the back of the wagon spread water on the dusty street. When the wagon was empty he drove to the Rock Island Depot and filled the tank again at the place where the steam locomotives filled their tanks. In the dry season it was a monotonous and endless task to try to keep the dust settled.

There were still farmers who drove their team and wagon to town. This was so the men could haul grain or coal. Some bought special feed at the grain elevator. Some hauled coal for the winter's supply to use at home either in a coal-fired heater or a coal-fired furnace.

With the wagon teams in town it was also necessary for the city to hire another man, usually the local bum who couldn't do much of anything else. He pushed a two-wheel cart with a wooden box mounted between the wheels. The box was about 12 inches deep. He pushed the cart back and forth scooping up horse manure. It was a useful, but thankless and smelly task, but somebody had to do it.

Another feature on Main Street was the white ceramic water fountain with the bubbler in the center dispensing cool clean water. There was one on each block in the downtown area. It was such a big treat to turn the handle on the side of the fountain and drink that water.

A WW I veteran who had one wooden leg patrolled Main Street. He was the lone policeman. He didn't seem to have many problems to take care of. He always had his faithful German shepherd dog beside him. Mr. Enlo, resplendent in his police uniform, was an exact copy of the police in the old black and white movie films, and he carried a stick at his side. He did little more than patrolling.

There was a livery stable a block off of Main Street to accommodate the teams of horses while in town. And there another city employee kept the stables clean of manure, the stalls supplied with straw, and for a little coin would feed and water the horses.

As a result of so many horses along the streets, there was an abundance of flies. About the only fly control were fly swatters and twisted rolls of sticky flypaper suspended from ceilings in the stores. They were never enough. There always seemed to be flies.

There were two memorable places on Main Street. One was the Candy Kitchen owned and operated by two Greeks. Their display of homemade candies was awesome. They dispensed 5-cent ice cream cones and 25-cent banana splits. Another was the popcorn wagon, which sold large bags of popcorn at 10 cents a bag. Off Main Street was a Chinese laundry. I wonder if the proprietor ever really did learn the American language. His family stayed in China, but he kept his business here.

Had we driven to Dike, Iowa, the sidewalks were built of wooden boards with wooden plank benches in front of the stores. There, patrons could sit and rest and exchange the news with other shoppers. Otherwise, the streets were much the same. There were fewer people in this small town, so some duties were combined. I don't recall if there was a policeman or not. It was a very quiet and peaceful town.

254

RURAL TELEPHONES

In the 1920's and 1930's the rural telephone was the link to the outside world. Not everyone had a phone. Some still thought of the phone as an extravagance.

Throughout the countryside, telephone poles about 12 feet high were set along the fence lines spaced so that the single wire could be strung from one pole to the next. The wire was attached to the pole on a green glass insulator. The usual arrangement was to have eight farms families on a line. In order to distinguish who the call was for, there was a signal arrangement. On our farm the ring for us was "long short long." Some might be three long rings, three short rings, and so on.

To place a call within the eight-line group we just rang their code ring by the appropriate turns of the crank on the side of the box. To call outside this line we turned the crank on the side of the telephone for one long ring, the code to get the operator. The operator at the telephone office in town answered with, "Number please." She then made the proper connection and rang the person we wanted to talk to. The operator had to know the ring code on the other line as well.

There was no privacy on these local phone lines. When the phone rang it could be heard on all of the eight member phones. That was an invitation for many to hear the latest news or to just know what the neighbor was doing. This caused consternation among the neighbors. Then there were those who loved to call a friend and talk for an hour or more. When that happened no one else could use the telephone.

If there was a fire in the neighborhood, the crank was turned for about a minute. This alerted the neighbors to go and help another neighbor where the fire was happening. Sometimes, the operator gave important news. She would initiate a "General Ring" – a long, continuous ring. We were then alerted to some important message.

Our telephone was what you may have seen in old movies or old pictures. The brown oak telephone box was fastened to a wall. The crank was on the box on the right side, the ear piece on a long cord hung on the left side, and the adjustable mouth piece was directly in front.

The party line phone was in use until after WW II. Then gradually came the two-party line and finally the single-party phone. This meant that our conversations were private, and no one else could listen. As the telephone system evolved there was less and less ability to listen in on other conversations. This was both good and bad. When we used the telephone we knew that others would most likely be listening to our conversation. We had nothing to hide, but it was an irritant. Perhaps in our day the party line phone might keep some of us from wrongdoing. We have lost some information about our neighbors that lets us live much farther apart, even when we live next door.

DID WE SAY THAT?

We had many sayings that I have heard most of my life. Some were old and may have been translated from Danish. Others seemed to be of modern sources. They all worked their way into our conversations at one time or another.

Here is a sampling of those quips. Most of them should be self explanatory.

- He doesn't know beans when the bag is open.
- Somebody let the cat out of the bag.
- She's been tied to her mother's apron strings all her life.
- Clean up your plate. Just think of all those starving children in China.
- Eat your spinach. It'll make you strong.
- Well, I'll be switched.
- That'll knock your socks off if anything will.
- If the chickens stay out in the rain it will rain all day.

- She's got a bee in her bonnet.
- He isn't worth a tinker's dam.
- I think he's got himself up to his eyeballs in trouble.
- That sure cooked his\her goose.
- Wow, she's some slick chick.
- Everything's going to Hell in a handcart.
- He kicked the bucket.
- Like a cat on a hot tin roof.
- Knuckle down.
- That sure hit the nail on the head.
- As big as a goose egg.
- Don't put all your eggs in one basket.
- Skinny as a rail.
- Like buying a pig in a poke.
- He skee-daddled out of the country.
- It isn't worth a hoot.
- I don't give a hoot about it.
- That party was quite a whing-ding.
- It's as plain as the nose on your face.
- You'd think he/she is old enough to know better.
- Well, when I was their age.
- He got left sucking the hind teat.
- You can wait till the cows come home.
- The mice will play when the cat's away.
- I'd be ashamed to show my face if I were she.
- I think he has mud on his face. Or, I think he has egg on his face.

- Looks like the table's turned.

- Sure too bad it had to go that way.

- You're old enough to know better.

- Watch out or the cat's going to get your tongue.

- Don't count your chicks before the eggs are hatched.

- Looks like he's been on the wagon again.

- You ought to be spanked within an inch of your life.

- I've said it a thousand times if I've said it once.

- I think there's something rotten in Denmark.

- Why don't you listen?

- I think she got up on the wrong side of the bed.

- Well, I'll be.

SOPHIE

Note: This is an imaginary telephone conversation between two middle-aged farmwomen who enjoy keeping abreast of neighborhood happenings as well as any other information that comes within hearing distance. Was there ever someone in your neighborhood about whom you can now chuckle?

"Hello, this is Sophie?" Sophie spoke with conviction and firm determination. She didn't mince words.

"You're home? Thought you might have gone to town or some-thing, today rainy and all. The way those flies were hanging on the screen something awful yesterday you knew it was going to rain. It was coming down cats and dogs in the night. And now I see the chickens are running around with their tails hanging down. You know, they always say if the chickens go out in the rain it's going to rain all day. I don't know though. If it stops this morning and you know what they always say, 'if it rains before seven the sun will shine before eleven.' Guess we'll have to wait and see. Sure could use the rain, but it didn't have to come down in buckets."

"Say, did you hear about your neighbor's daughter Emily? Whoop-de-doo. I think somebody let the cat out of the bag. You know that they should never have let her go like that. That girl of theirs has been on her mother's apron strings too long and now. Look what's happening. You heard about that guy she's been going out with. Doesn't amount to hill of beans, if you ask me. Well, they'll pay for it. Wouldn't doubt if she gets herself into a family way and then what?"

(pause)

"You don't say. Well, I'll be switched. I thought it would go the other way around. Just goes to show you what some people will do. I don't know what this world's coming to. Some days I think the whole thing's going to Hell in a handcart. Don't you think so too? Well, she'll pay a plenty for that. Just you watch and see."

You know, we got that new hired man. I don't know about him. Sometimes I wonder if he knows which end of the hoe handle he should use. He really isn't worth a hoot sometimes, but you know how it is to get any help these days. You have to put up with an awful lot sometimes. We'll try him for a few more days. I was wondering one day if he knew enough to come out of the rain. He's supposed to be cleaning the hen house now. Good job for a rainy day, I guess. There wasn't much else to do."

"I suppose you heard about little Jimmy. You didn't? He got hurt on the school grounds. Got a bump as big as a goose egg. Guess he'll be all right. They put ice on it right away. You never know what kids will do. I'm glad mine are as old as they are."

(pause)

"Say, I think you know who has been on the wagon again. He's been coming home pretty late they say. Been hanging out with wrong crowd. I thought you knew about that. I feel sorry for his wife and all those kids. They're the ones getting hurt. Too bad."

"My grandchildren are coming for dinner Sunday. There's one thing they'll not get by with this time. I'll tell them to clean up their plates. Carrots are good for you. Makes your hair curly. They heard me say a thousand times if I've said it once. You'd better think of all those kids in China who are starving to death. They'd be glad to get some of these good things to eat if they had a chance. I'm going to tell them. You watch and see."

(another pause)

"You say you saw her coming out of the bar? I'd be ashamed to show my face if were her. Of all the nerve! You'd think at her age she'd know better. Mark my word if she does that very many times she'll hear about it from her old man. And then what? It sure isn't like it was when we were young. We had rules and believe you me we'd better listen or we'd get a good lickin'."

"Say, we couldn't go to that big party at the Odd Fellows Hall. I hear it was quite a shindig. The music was getting pretty loud before the evening was over and the way I heard it, that one gal with the red hair, you know who I mean, I think, she kicked the traces and she and that guy did a little partying of their own. I don't know. You tell them one thing and they do another."

"Yeah, we took time to go to the funeral parlor last night. My, he looked good. He looked so natural. They sure did a good job on him. Too bad he had to go the way, he did but maybe it's better this way. Who knows? It'll be a big funeral with lots of flowers and all that. He'll be missed. He was a good man. You don't find 'em more honest than he was."

"Oh, and I almost forgot to tell you. You'd never guess what my brother-in-law did this time. I couldn't believe my ears when I heard it. He had the nerve to go out and buy one of those big computer tractors. The kind you know that does everything but wash the kitchen sink. Did you ever hear of anything like it? He just went out and bought it like it was nothing. Mark my word, my sister's going to hear about this. Of all the nerve! He had to borrow money to pay the taxes last year. And the best part is, they weren't the ones to tell me. Oh, no, I had to hear it from someone else."

"I said to my husband the day they got married. You just mark my word. That man's up to no good. I always say you can't tell by looking at a toad which way he's going to jump. Well, there you have it. They can spend money like it was growing on trees."

"Oh, Sophie, I see those neighbor kids coming up the drive way. They'd better not come in here stompin' mud on my clean floors. I tell you sometimes I'd like to whip that oldest one within an inch of his life. He gets into more trouble than you can shake a stick at. I can't tell you the trouble he gets himself into. And their mother not paying any attention. I sometimes think she doesn't have all her marbles or she'd do something about it."

"I suppose we'd better shut it off. I've got to get them 'shooed' out of here. I'll give them each a couple of cookies and send them on their way. I really ought to stay home this afternoon and do some cleaning. I'll bet the dust's and inch thick some places. Oh well, it can wait till tomorrow. I need to get a couple of things in town."

"It sure's been nice talking to you. I think I'll get some curlers in my hair. We might go to town after dinner. Rainy day like this we can't get much done around here. We might bump into somebody we know. So long Sophie. Be sure to call me sometime. We'll think of something to talk about. If I hear anything juicy I'll be sure to let you know."

Any reference to anyone you or I know is purely imaginative. I grew up hearing this kind of language. We can laugh at it now.

HALLOWEEN PARTY

I wasn't very old when Mother and Dad invited all the neighbors to a Halloween party to be held in the attic of the old house. The "old" house was really the second house on the farm. The first was a modest storey and a half structure. The second house was a very large Victorian style with five bedrooms on the second floor. The attic was a full height single large room above the five second floor bedrooms. In the attic there were three windows on each of three sides and a full stairway on the fourth side. The floor was unfinished pine boards.

The ceiling was not finished and there were no walls but it was very usable. A ladder could be set up to go up on the roof by lifting a heavy cover on the roof. That would have been more than thirty feet above the ground! I had strict orders to never go up on roof by myself.

The neighbors all came in costume. They entered the house through the door and went up to the attic by walking up the stairway to the second floor. This set of stairs turned twice on the way up. Then they walked down the full-length hallway past the bedrooms to a second stairway which led to the attic. There were three bedrooms on one side of the hallway and two on the other. The stairs to the attic were in what could have been a sixth bedroom. These stairs had been salvaged from the original small house and were very steep and narrow. They too turned on the way up, and they had no banister! No one seemed to mind. We had all learned to be careful and responsible in those days.

The attic was prepared with areas of entertainment created to be spooky in the spirit of Halloween. When the guests arrived, they would be led from one area to another while blindfolded.

I remember a few of the spooky things they did. One was a bowl of Concord grapes that had the skins squeezed off. This made a slippery gooey mess! With their eyes covered, the people were to feel the "eyeballs" of the ghost or witch. There was also a fresh hog liver that people were to touch. I think that represented the heart of the witch. It was all scary and gruesome, but everyone expected that and had lots of fun.

After everyone had felt all the gruesome wonders, they played several party games in the attic. There was lots of room there, and we all had lots of fun. Afterwards everyone paraded downstairs to the first floor dining room for refreshments that guests had brought to share. Kids and adults alike shared in the fun and games. We all enjoyed the company of each other. There were the children of all ages, parents, grandparents, aunts and uncles and friends and neighbors. What a joy it was to have all the ages playing together. It taught us much about respect and appreciation.

EGG COFFEE

In the days before paper filters and electric coffee pots, even before stovetop percolators, making coffee was an art. Whole roasted coffee beans were purchased in bulk at the general store. The beans were ground in a small hand operated grinder, making ground particles of varying sizes, some as fine as powder. The coffee grounds were put into a pot of water and then boiled. As the brewed coffee was poured into the cup for drinking, coffee grounds often went into the cup as well. The bottom of the cup of coffee was most often full of gritty grounds.

For special occasions, the ground coffee beans could be mixed with egg, which would "bind" the grounds. The result was brewed coffee that was clear of coffee grounds.

Grandmother Emma Petersen's egg coffee was the best to be had. Maybe it was because she only made it for large gatherings such as birthday parties or when it was threshing day at their farm. No matter how hot or how cold the weather was outside she always made the coffee in the 25-cup gray enamel coffee pot with the wire bail handle. True, the wire was strung through a wooden dowel for safe and easy carrying.

Ordinarily, the pot was stored down cellar in the pantry. For the special occasions it was brought to the kitchen, washed and then filled with 25 cups of cold well-water. The pot was set on the cook stove to boil. Sticks of firewood kept the fire going. In the hot summer time when 15 or 20 men were working out doors at threshing time it was really hot in the kitchen to make the coffee. No matter, it was made anyway.

In a separate bowl 25 heaping teaspoons of coffee grounds were measured out, putting in two or three more just for the pot. Into the coffee grounds Emma broke and dropped one fresh whole egg. If it seemed to need a little more liquid to get all the coffee grounds moistened, a little cold water was added. When the grounds were all moist she scraped all of the mixture into the water, which was now beginning to get warm, but not yet hot.

Now it was necessary to use a long wooden spoon to stir the pot every few minutes. As it reached the boiling point she stirred the pot almost continuously as it tended to boil over if not watched. It was not long before the rich aroma of good fresh-brewed coffee filled the air.

In the meantime as the gathered guests were preparing and setting food on the table, cousins and other guests talked and milled about either in the kitchen, dining room or living room, keeping up a constant chatter and generally enjoying the event.

When the coffee had come to a good rolling boil, it was set to the side of the stove where it was not quite as hot. The coffee grounds gradually settled to the bottom of the pot and the coffee was clear and good. Of course, different ladies in the kitchen had to taste it to see if it was just right.

So coffee was served to one and all, along with fresh open-faced sandwiches, homemade cakes, and cookies. The table was set with rectangular serving trays, cups, forks and napkins. People could fill these trays with food, pour a cup of coffee and then find a place to sit down and enjoy the party.

Coffee and pastries were staples of our diet, and became the centerpiece of communion with our friends and relatives. Good conversation and fellowship flowed freely as we enjoyed these treats. Egg coffee was the best and most affordable and satisfying beverage of our time.

SUNDAY FISHING

Sunday afternoons could be long and dull unless we used our initiative to do something about it. On a hot lazy Sunday afternoon Dad would get the long bamboo fishing poles down from the rafters in the corncrib. The long green cotton fish line with a cork for a bobber was wound around the pole. The hook was deftly stuck into the side of the pole. Dad had dug for worms out in the garden earlier so the tin can with some black soil in it contained a generous amount of bait.

Dad tied the poles to the side of the Mitchell touring car as my mother was packing sandwiches, or often fried chicken with potato salad, cake, and coffee into a picnic basket for the four of us. I got the black cotton swimsuits, knee-length and trimmed with white, out of the hall closet and threw them into the back seat along with the white rubber swimming caps and towels.

We headed out of the farmyard and headed over the country roads north about seven miles towards the Beaver Creek. Everyone in the area knew that the Beaver was a good place to go for fishing. It was a small river that eventually flowed into the larger Cedar River. There was a thick woods that grew along the riverbank and into the pastureland that adjoined it.

We stopped at a gate that led from the road into the pasture, got out and unhooked the barbed wire gate, laid it back so that we could drive through, and then hooked the gate up again. After driving into the woods, following a grassy wagon track, we were close to the river.

Dad brought out the tin can of worms that he had dug from the garden at home. He then untied the poles, unwound the green fishing line, and baited our hooks with the worms. There was neither rod nor reel, so Dad swung the pole wide and let the string down into the water out as far as he could reach. The poles needed to be long to get the line far enough out into the river.

Everyone stretched out on the grass and silently watched the cork out on the water. When the cork made little tiny squiggles we knew that some tiny fish were nibbling at the bait. If the cork went down, it was for sure that a larger fish had taken the bait.

It did happen that once in awhile a snapping turtle would take the bait. Then it was hard to take the hook out. Turtles draw their heads inside the shell and it is a struggle fraught with danger to get the hook out of their mouth.

Fishing might be good or it might be bad that day. If we were not catching anything, we put the poles away. Then we would duck behind the car and put on our swimsuits. The river had a sandy bottom and was fun to walk on. We could never depend on how deep the water was. If there had been a rain, the river tended to be much deeper. Also, we had to watch for holes where the sand had washed out. It was dangerous to swim in a river.

I spent time along the river's edge looking for clams. There were usually a lot of clams, which Dad opened, and we looked for pearls. It was exciting to expect to find a pearl, but we never found one.

In the middle of the afternoon Mother would spread a tablecloth on the ground and set out the picnic lunch of fried chicken, potato salad and cake. There was coffee in a jug that was still fairly hot. We sat on the grass quietly eating the food while watching the bobbin on the end of the line of the fish pole. Dad figured we might as well throw in the line again just in case there was a bite.

It was enjoyable sitting there eating while hundreds of birds were singing in the trees overhead. It was relatively quiet, but the air fairly droned with the hum of bees and other insects.

We also discovered a very small one-room tarpaper shack hidden in the thick of the woods. A man, his wife and small boy lived in this dilapidated structure. His name was Joe Kern. Dad struck up a conversation with him, and found out he was running a bootleg operation there. He uncovered a place in the ground where the still was at work. The coiled copper tubes were in place as well as the rest of the workings for a still. I remember of being impressed with seeing all that copper tubing. There was never any word of what happened to that family. We never saw any of his contacts or any of his dealings.

The afternoon droned on. Finally, at the end of the afternoon, we packed up all our belongings and drove home. It was quiet and peaceful, but we had had a good time.

Sometimes we would go to the Cedar River where there was more water. Dad's cousin, Herman Henningsen, had a motorized boat. Herman would drive the boat and Dad would strap slats on his feet and he would water-ski up and down the river. He was very good on the skis, and we all enjoyed the event. By the beach house in Cedar Falls there was a water slide, perhaps 20 to 25 feet high. It was great fun to go down the slide into the river.

There was also a water slide out in the river. I could go down this slide and land in water that was only knee-deep to me. One time my future uncle Alfred, who was courting my aunt Martha at the time, invited me to go with them to the river. I went down the slide, not realizing that the river had risen from the day before when I had been there. I struggled in the water for a while, but finally made it to shore without further incident. I was frightened, and did not use the slide anymore that day.

On rare occasions we would travel the distance to Clear Lake, Iowa. There we could swim in the still water of the lake. It was much safer. There were small beach houses where we could change into our swim suits. It was a long drive, and we did not go there often.

One trip we stayed too long, and Dad was tired. He lay down in the back seat of the Mitchell touring car to sleep on the way home, while Mother was to drive the car. It was dark and it became foggy. Several miles had passed us by when we discovered that we were traveling in the wrong direction. It was a much longer trip home than had been planned.

Now this doesn't sound exciting considering what we do with our time in the twenty-first century. We didn't have radio or TV. There really wasn't much of anything else to do. But just being somewhere besides our day-by-day home was a pleasant way to spend a beautiful Sunday afternoon.

PICNICS

A favorite summer Sunday pastime was attending or hosting a picnic. Picnics were often held in city or state parks where tables and small fireplaces were provided. Just as often we held picnics out on the lawn at home on the farm. Summertime birthdays and anniversaries were often the focus of the picnic. It was also a good way to meet with relatives who lived some distance away. Then we would meet at a park in a town about halfway between our respective homes.

We had picnics everywhere. We were not constrained to developed park locations. Picnics were held on our farm. We had picnics along streams or rivers, usually on someone's private property. When there were no tables or fireplaces we spread a tablecloth on the ground and built our own fire on the ground. Most everyone did picnics in similar fashion. Everyone cleaned up after the picnics, and property owners did not mind sharing their scenic places with strangers.

The coordination of good food was an important centerpiece of the picnic. A neighborhood or group picnic meant some planning a few days ahead. Who would bring what food and beverage and so on?

Picnics at home on the farm took less time to get ready. The family would gather and food was brought out to the white wooden table. Everything had to be covered as flies were always a problem.

Food served at a picnic had to be good, easy to prepare and easy to transport without spoilage. A typical picnic meal consisted of fried chicken, potato salad or creamed boiled potatoes, home baked beans, and pie or cake for dessert.

Fried chicken no matter where the picnic was held, at home or in the park, meant going to the barnyard early in the day, snagging a chicken, tying its legs together and hanging it upside down from the scale in the barn where Dad weighed the milk. If the chicken weighed between three and four pounds it was big enough for eating.

So off to the chopping block where the chicken was beheaded, then plucking the feathers, singeing the pin feathers, scrubbing the skin with soapy water, then rinsing. Finally drawing the entrails (cutting the chicken open and removing the innards), and a quick cooling of the carcass in cold well water. Then after it was cut into serving pieces, it was dipped in flour and fried in butter in a large iron skillet where it finished cooking after about an hour. The chicken would be full of flavor and tender.

In the meantime, potato salad was prepared from potatoes boiled the day before and then diced. Two or three eggs could be boiled, cooled and shelled, chopped or sliced, then added to the diced potatoes. A little fresh garden onion added zest to the salad. A sprinkle of parsley fresh from the garden completed the preparation.

A salad dressing to be poured over shredded cabbage was made by combining:

- Two eggs.
- One half cup of sugar with one teaspoon flour.
- One fourth cup of vinegar and three-fourths cup of water.
- Boil and cool

And of course one or two cabbage heads were picked and shredded just before we left. In the hot steamy weather of the summer it would easily start to ferment and soon give off a bad smell like sauerkraut.

Raw dried beans were soaked overnight and combined with tomato juice, brown sugar, and a little pork, either bacon or ham. The beans were baked slowly in the oven for several hours until they were plump and tender.

For dessert pie or cake was included with the meal. The pie or cake would be baked the day before the picnic.

Getting the food ready to take to the picnic grounds was another task. Baskets and boxes were used to pack the food, serving dishes, plates, cups, utensils, napkins and whatever we thought we would need. To be sure to have a picnic table it was often necessary for someone to go ahead of time and reserve one or more tables as needed.

Sometimes the twenty five cup granite coffee pot was taken along and the coffee was boiled on the little fireplace in the park. That way there was enough coffee for the afternoon break. As children we drank coffee as well as the adults. Water was the only other alternative, but we never transported the water. We used the water from whatever source we could find at our picnic location. We never served pop or beer.

Men often brought along two iron stakes and a set of horse shoes to play horse shoe after the meal was finished. Sometimes balls and bats were brought and some good ball games followed the picnic meal. Most often there were not enough people to make teams, but we played and had fun anyway.

In preparation for the picnic it was my job to take a spool of colored sewing thread and wind the thread around each piece of silverware that would be taken to the picnic. I tied the string in a knot and marked each piece in that way. After the picnic meal was finished each family recognized his or her own silverware and packed it away in the lunch basket.

The afternoon was spent sitting in the shade visiting, playing, and enjoying being out of doors. Coffee and a choice of cake or pie were served before going home.

When the picnic was at a park, we would often wash some dishes under the drinking fountain or in a stream so we could re-use them. We did not always have soap, but we would scrub the food from the dishes using mud, rinsing with clean water. It worked and no one seemed to suffer any illnesses from this practice.

Having the picnic in a city or state park was always interesting. There we were able to observe people who were not of our Danish community. We observed that they were not so different from us, and their picnics were much the same as ours. Families large and small occupied other tables and open areas nearby. Their children also laughed and shouted and played just as well as we did. Couples had much quieter picnics by themselves, and even a few single people came to the parks for their solitary picnics.

I recall one portly fellow who drove his ancient auto as near as he could to a table. As he brought his pots and pans and dishes of food to the table it quickly filled as if for several people. He was alone, however, but when he went to sit on the bench of the table, his weight was too much and the other side of the table tipped up as he went to the ground. All the containers of food fell to the ground or into his lap. He spent the rest of his time at the park cleaning up the mess and putting everything back into his car. He was unhurt physically by the mishap, but I'm sure his pride was severely wounded.

Our picnics were occasions where our family relaxed together. The family would be just our immediate family, or it might involve our extended family as well. Once each year there would be a family reunion attended by a larger number of people. Close to a hundred people attended these reunions after World War II. Picnics were indeed fun, and we were always well entertained no matter the place or the families involved.

FARM BUREAU MEETING

The folks (my parents) were very active in the Farm Bureau organization and attended meetings held countywide. One summer the members met at our farm. Dad had strung lights on the lawn and had set up some kind of seating arrangement. A business meeting was held and then there was to be entertainment.

Mother and Dad had rigged up a shadow play. There was a large bay window facing the audience. The window was covered with a white bed sheet. The scene was to be a surgical procedure. Someone would lie on a table, which was probably the ironing board supported on each end by chairs. Behind this set up, a bright lamp had been placed so that the figures would show outside as solid figures.

The "patient" lay on the table, and two other people draped as doctors, proceeded with an operation removing all sorts of objects from the patient. Each piece was held up so that it showed as a shadow. The doctors removed large knives, hammers and all sorts of strange items.

I guess it was quite entertaining. In those times, people were very creative and made their own entertainment.

SUNDAY NIGHTS

Oh, how we waited for Sunday night to come. Sunday nights meant fun, bonding with other young people our age, and best of all, if we were lucky, we would have a date. During the school year (fall, winter and spring) we met regularly in the Auditorium, a large building for just such a purpose across the road from the Fredsville Church.

There were sixty of us, all in our teenage years, from the farms surrounding the Fredsville church and from Dike, a nearby small town. That was a large number for so small an area, but there were some large families in our parents' generation. I recall the Nielsen and Petersen families were well represented. Most of our group had grown up attending Fredsville Church. We knew each other as friends, and many were related in some manner.

Confirmation class

It was the early 1930's, during the Great Depression years, and we were glad to find entertainment at all. If our families were fortunate we had food, clothing and shelter, but there was no money for anything else, certainly not for entertainment. But we were teenagers and we needed to have fun and to be with others of our age. This was the only opportunity for us to socialize for many, many miles around.

We were so fortunate to grow up in a Danish Community, a "Happy Dane" group of people at that, and to have a pastor who was one of the Happy Danes, as well as being an excellent leader for our group of teens. He was the Reverend Holger O. Nielsen. He knew how to challenge our minds, and how to reward us with celebration of life. He helped us burn our teenage energies, and gave us a place to dance and sing to our hearts' content. He led our "Ungdom's For-rættning", roughly translated as "Young Peoples' League" very well.

The girls came in freshly ironed cotton dresses. These were all handmade by us from yard goods that we could purchase with a few coins of hard earned money. They might not have been the height of fashion, but they were clean, pressed and presentable dresses.

Elna at 13

The guys often wore long white wash pants and smelled of shaving lotion. For most of the fellows this was all new. In the custom of the time, boys as well as girls wore what were essentially long dresses until they were age four or five. Then the young boys wore knickerbockers with legs buttoned above the knee and long socks that came above the knee. At the time the boys were confirmed, about age thirteen, they were presented with their first pair of long legged pants. It was a significant rite of passing and a symbol of adulthood. The younger boys in our group were just learning about shaving as well.

Most of the fellows had cars, and, if they didn't, they'd borrow their dad's car for the night. We learned at an early age on the farm to drive a variety of machines, including the family car. This was before we had to have a license to drive. Our parents were concerned about how far we drove the cars, in part for economic reasons and in part for our safety and well-being. One of the fellows would drive his father's car backwards on the way home so that his dad couldn't see how many miles he had put on the night before. In those days the odometer would roll backwards while driving in reverse. Harold, my future husband, drove a '28 Chevy that his Aunt Bessie had given him. Most of these cars were of 1920's vintage when economics were substantially better.

Pastor Nielsen would call us into the Auditorium where we sat on those flimsy folding wooden benches, four folding chair seats ganged to a set. We sat carefully as these chairs tipped easily causing a great commotion. After we all sat down, the Golden songbooks were passed around and we would open our gathering with singing a variety of songs, both secular and sacred. In those days we all knew how to sing and it was a common form of entertainment in any gathering. After singing a few spirited songs, the pastor got up in front of us and gave a talk. He spoke of serious things, but he was an engaging speaker and we listened well. We closed this part of our meeting with one or two more songs.

Then it was time for refreshments and fun. Out in the kitchen while we were listening to Pastor Nielsen, Willie and Anna Christensen, the church caretakers at that time, had coffee ready that they had boiled in a copper boiler. Girls took turns bringing cakes. While the kids were lining up for coffee, and we all drank coffee in those days, some of the guys folded up the chairs and benches and pushed them back against the walls clearing the floor for the rest of the evening's entertainment. With lots of visiting and enjoying of refreshments we were ready for folk dancing.

We danced energetic folk dances, such as "The Crested Hen", "The Sextour", and "Comin' Through the Rye". These were a few of the popular ones. There were many more. I still have a book of Danish folk dances listing more than sixty different dances, complete with music and instructions for each dance.

Another popular dance was sung while we danced, and the words were as follows:

"Happy is the miller as he stands by the mill
He hasn't gone away for stands there still
With a hand in the hopper and the other in the sack
The wheel turns around and the ladies turn back."

Couples walked in a circle as they sang the words. At "the ladies turn back", the girls did so, and when the song began again everyone had a new partner. I played the piano most of the time for these dances.

At the appropriate time the pastor announced it was time for us to leave. Then we sang a good night song and left for home, looking forward to next week when we would all meet again.

Noisily and with much conversation, we all left in cars, the dust rolling up behind us as we sped off in different directions, driving as fast as 25 or 30 miles per hour, a break-neck speed in those days on dirt or graveled roads. Hopefully, there were no younger brothers or sisters that had to be taken home. This was our only time to be alone with our "date." There was a lot of lovin' that took place on those back roads going home.

We did not often have an opportunity to drive the family car. Gasoline cost money. But many of us lived a number of miles from church and it was our mode of transportation. Our parents knew that our age group needed this time together. They also knew what time the pastor had closed the meeting. So we made our way home, already looking forward to next Sunday night.

On warm summer evenings we would take turns meeting at farm homes of our group's members where we could play outdoor games such as "Two Deep", "Slap Tag", and other games. In the game "Two Deep" we would gather in couples in a large circle, one person standing in front of the other two deep. Two people were selected to start the game, one chasing the other about the outside of the circle of couples. When the one being chased was close to being caught, he or she would dart in front of a couple and stand still. The back person in this group would then become the person being chased, and would have to make their escape as best they could. When a person being chased was tagged, they would then become the one who chased the others. It was great fun for us, and allowed us to burn up our energies as well as the excitement of calculating how we could make different couples.

The routine of these summertime gatherings was similar to what we had done indoors at Fredsville except we could play games instead of dancing. Electric lights would be strung throughout the grassy lawn area, giving us light as we played into the night. What a great way to spend a warm summer evening.

I must say that those were very happy times. Everyone gathered for fun and fellowship. There was neither smoking nor alcohol nor other drugs involved. It was just a really good time.

Most of us have kept in touch in some fashion over the years. Some of these budding romances blossomed into long and happy marriages. The Nielsen and Petersen cousins supplied a substantial number to this group. Many met their future spouses here. These cousins and their spouses gathered annually for reunions until the few remaining were no longer able to do so.

Pastor Nielsen moved on to another church, unfortunately not of the Happy Dane tradition. There he was forbidden to have any type of gathering that included dancing and games. They could only sing hymns and speak piously. These were the "Sad Danes." We were very fortunate to have had his leadership in that time of our lives.

It didn't matter to any of us that there was a depression. We had nothing, but we were full of life's energy. So we found ways to celebrate life, to have great fun, to enjoy each other's company, and to forget our plight. We had such good times in those years. I doubt if any of us ever forgot those times.

WILD THINGS

As a red-headed kid running around in bare feet most of the summer I had no idea that I was living in a "Magic Kingdom". I lived with my brother and parents on a Mid-Western Iowa farm just a few miles west of Cedar Falls. My world seldom exceeded five miles from home. And yet I experienced a world that children in the year 2001 pay money to see. Now, the things that I enjoyed as a child are no longer there.

Between my home and the now weathered gray, once white wooden school building, I saw wild life each day of the year along the dirt road. In the wet weather or in the morning dew, I walked through the tall, wet grass in the shallow, wide ditches, feeling the cool and wet sopping skirt against my legs. If I walked on the narrow dirt road, the mud would squish up between my toes as my feet slid along the way. In dry weather, the dust covered my feet in brown talc.

About halfway to or from school I crossed a small ditch where there would sometimes be running water draining off the field. As I trudged back and forth between home and school, it was difficult to believe that so much life existed in so many varied forms. The grassy green ditches were full of wild growing things.

Meadow Larks built their nests on the ground in the tall grass. There were four eggs in a nest. The eggs were about the size of the end of my thumb and covered with brown speckles. Bob-O-Links sat on the barbed wire fence singing happily away. It seemed they sang "bob o link, bob o link, chink chank chink," or at least I thought they did. Red-winged Blackbirds teetered on cattails growing by the little ditch of water.

Above, little sparrow hawks perched on the top of telephone poles watching for moving things on the ground. With a swift dive the mouse was caught and the tiny hawk cherished his mid morning meal. Pheasants could be heard crowing or squawking out in the field. Black and gold finches teetered on thorny thistles pulling out tiny tufts of dry thistle blossoms to be used for building their nests in nearby shrubs. Fragrant and delicate wild roses with sharp thorns grew profusely along the fence lines. Mourning doves sat in pairs on telephone wires cooing their delicate song.

Far overhead, red-tailed hawks circled on fixed wing, looking for and hoping to catch the fearful white-bellied field mouse trying to hide in the grass. Crows raucously cried out from the treetops in the grove nearby. One day I saw a crow that had caught a garter snake. It was writhing in the clutches of the claws of the crow. He was flying overhead and on his way back to his nest to feed his young family. Other black snakes and garter snakes slithered through the wet grass and slipped quietly into holes where they were out of danger.

Red-breasted robins built their nests in trees and shrubs, each nest containing four bright blue eggs. Killdeer cried out intending to lure danger away from the proximity of their ground-level nest. Redheaded woodpeckers drummed on telephone poles, hollow tree limbs and empty silos. They were so brilliantly colored in red, white, and black. They loved to announce their presence with their loud, booming tattoo. Smaller birds winged their way through the countryside but never got close enough for me to see their actual colors. Their songs however were very evident as I trudged through the otherwise quiet countryside.

In the fall of the year, as corn was ripening in the fields, blackbirds came in droves to light on the now dry brown corn stalks. These birds, as well as those I may have forgotten, all were less than a quarter of a mile from my home.

There were bull snakes that usually stayed close to the buildings, and I did see them often. They were always on the outlook for bigger prey such as rats and mice. In the spring when new ducklings and goslings were venturing too close to the woodpile, the bull snakes would come out and snatch a duckling or gosling, swallowing it whole. Bull snakes could somehow increase their size and look threatening. How they did it I don't know.

Frogs jumped from the grass back into the running water that flowed through a culvert. Their shiny green backs shone in the sunlight. Toads, with their dark brown knobby skin, stayed closer to areas where they could catch insects.

Then there were all the furry creatures that scampered here and there. Striped gophers stood very erect beside their holes. Their beady eyes constantly watched for intruders. How quickly they retreated into their little underground homes when danger seemed to threaten them.

Along the way, pocket gophers laboriously brought mounds of dirt to the surface in the little pockets on each side of their head. More elusive were the ground hogs that made their homes in the hayfields leaving huge holes for entrances. These holes were dangerous for horses. If a horse got a leg down one of those holes he could break that leg.

It was usually in the winter when I saw the jack rabbits loping in huge strides across barren fields. In winter their hair was white. In summer their hair turned brown. Their huge long ears distinguished them from the little cottontails that ran bounced hither and yon. Jack rabbits could leap and run very fast. They almost always outran their predators. The only protection for the smaller cottontails was to freeze or stand absolutely still in hopes that no other animal would see them.

Squirrels stayed closer to the farm buildings. Food was more accessible for them there. They liked to rob their meals from the corncrib.

Not only were there birds and animals in the dirt roadsides, but there were insects of all kinds. Bumblebees and honeybees flew from blossom to blossom in the red clover fields gathering pollen to take back to their hives to make their sweet, fragrant honey. Everywhere bumble bees and honeybees droned their buzzing sound all through the day during summer weather. Bumblebees nested below the ground and honeybees found nests in old trees. Hornets and wasps made the homes of self-made paper or mud in the crevices or under the eaves or peaks of the buildings.

Grasshoppers made huge leaps from one tall stem of grass to the next. Crickets kept close to the ground, rubbing their legs on their wings to indicate the temperature of the day. At least that is what I was told they did. Black beetles clicked their wings as they moved about the ground.

Tiny brown anthills sprang up along the roadside by the dozens. Occasionally there would be an old anthill that must have been there for years. They could be almost a foot high and two feet across. I never wanted to step on one of those anthills. The black ants could and would bite if their home were threatened. Gnats flew in swarms, and mosquitoes were more irksome at nightfall.

Out on the dry black dirt road, fuzzy brown and black caterpillars slowly made their way in the warm sunshine to the other side of the road. After a rain, pink angleworms made winding tracks through the soft mud.

The grassy ditches brought a profusion of wildflowers all summer long. Wild roses with their sweet delicate scent grew all along the ditches against fence lines and bloomed all during the summer. In the fall there were red seed berries on their stems. Closest to the ground were the violets. Sweet Williams were the most fragrant of all. Golden Rod and Purple Gentian bloomed during the fall. Out on the schoolyard, which was native prairie, we would look for a blossom called "Shooting Stars." They grew on a very slender stiff short stem. I have recalled only the most common of all wild flowers.

Quietly flying from blossom to blossom, the Monarch butterflies and yellow Swallowtail butterflies thrived on the nectar from the wild flowers. The Monarchs quietly laid their eggs on the milkweeds. Their colorful caterpillars could be found later by checking for the milkweed leaves that were partially eaten. Flocks of white and yellow sulphur butterflies gathered on the pastureland on their way to the south.

As the fall days approached I was more aware of spiders. Webs drifted daintily in the breeze and often touched my face as I walked along.

On the fencerows, thickets of wild plum shrubs grew, their white blossoms so fragrant each spring. In September, masses of sour purple plums dropped to the ground. Tasty wild strawberries ripened in early summer. How good they were with cream and sugar. Wild grape vines, planted from bird droppings, stretched across the fence lines. The deep purple, but very sour fruit ripened in early fall.

Skunks were in evidence with the musty odor they left. Skunks with their little black and white kittens were cute and could be tamed.

My grandparents, the Hoffman's, had a ten-gallon milk can lying on its side in the pasture where the mother skunk and her young ones lived. We would go to see them being careful not to make quick moves to frighten the mother.

The farmyard was also an area with a variety of sights and sounds. In the spring, fuzzy yellow ducklings scurried about, but never too far from the mother duck. Gray-green goslings stretched and fluttered their tiny wings, and little yellow baby chicks made tiny contented peeping sounds as they hovered under the brooder stove.

Pink piglets squealed and tumbled over each other hunting for their place at the sow's nipples, hogs grunted as food drooled from their jowls. Brown and white calves bawled loudly, cows chewed their cud and switched flies with their tails, while horses stomped their hooves and whinnied. Barn swallows dashed in and out of the hog house catching their meal in flight, and pigeons sat high on the hay rail cooing.

Out in the farmyard, hens cackled and clucked as they scratched the dirt for bugs and worms, while roosters crowed and walked about as if on stilts. Hidden away in the haymow or manger in the barn, tiny kittens mewed, their eyes not yet open. The mother cat was hunting for mice and would soon return with a mouse.

Then there were always the English sparrows dusting themselves in the dry dust. Dozens of them gathered where there was grain spilled on the ground. They were always building nests inside buildings from trash found in the yard such as feathers, grass or string. They were a messy nuisance bird.

On warm summer evenings after the sun was down, there were other creatures that surrounded us. Cicadas made their loud buzzing noise, purportedly letting us know that it was now ninety days till first frost. Bats with webbed wings flew above our heads looking for mosquitoes. Little screech owls hooted softly in the big trees in the grove. Even tiny tree frogs called in loud croaking sounds throughout the night. In the quiet of the countryside, all these combined to create a symphony with wave after wave of contented sounds that lulled us to sleep.

There were very few noises to interfere with nature's sounds. There were no radios, TV's, very few tractors and cars, and no airplanes overhead. It is a time long past. The sounds were never recorded, and now these wonderful harmonies of Nature live only in my memory.

I lived in a Wild Animal Kingdom and didn't know it at the time. Now there are only those of us in our late eighties that have those wonderful memories.

WALKING HOME

Time: winter of 1931 and 1932. It was in the depths of the Great Depression. The business of farming had failed for my dad. My folks sold almost everything they had and had moved to a house in town. There was very little food to eat and coal with which to heat the home, and nothing else.

When I was a senior in high school, and by some arrangement unknown to me, I was sent, bag and baggage, to the Andrew Jacobson farm a mile west of the college campus at Cedar Falls. The Andersons were strangers to me. Mother, Dad and brother Hilmar had moved from the house in Cedar Falls to the Walter's farm adjacent to Grandfather Petersen's farm, about six miles west of town.

As a hired girl for the Jacobsen's, I was expected to help with meals, wash the dishes, and do some of the cleaning. I did all of this before and after school hours for fifty cents a week plus room and board.

I walked the mile or so back and forth to the school in Cedar Falls on frozen ground in the winter and deep mud in the spring thaw. Imagine what my shoes and boots were like by the time I got to school.

One winter Sunday afternoon after the work was done I was lonely and wanted to go home. It would mean a walk of between four and five miles. So I put on the warmest clothes I had and began walking the four plus miles towards home by heading west on 27th Street. It was a cloudy cold wintry day but I was determined to go home just for a few hours.

After walking a little over three miles, I got to the corner north of Grandfather Petersen's farm and started the mile long trek south. The air was very cold and the snow was crunchy as I walked along.

By the time I passed Grandfather Petersen's lane, about three quarters of a mile, and started up the hill towards where my parents were living, I began to feel drowsy. I wanted to lie down on the road and take a nap. But some instinct told me that if I lay down I wouldn't wake up. I would freeze to death there on the road. So I trudged on for that last quarter mile or so, just putting one foot in front of the other, and finally got to mother and dad's house. Oh, my, it felt so good to be home!

I stayed the afternoon, and prepared to return that evening. Dad had an old Dodge coupe and somehow he had enough gas to take me back to the Jacobsen's house that evening. It is strange what can be done if desperate enough. It was an experience I would probably never do again, but somehow I can't forget that day.

I stayed and worked at the Jacobsen's until I graduated from high school. Then I got a job working in Cedar Falls for a Dr. Hearst. From there on I kept working wherever people needed me.

NICK NAMES

If I called out one of the following names would you know who I was talking about? All of these people lived in the Cedar Falls and Dike area and if their name was mentioned we all knew who they were.

None of the names were considered derogatory. We lived in a close Scandinavian community with many common or close to common last names. It was part of the colorful conversations of the time, and helped us to know of whom we were speaking.

Hay Anton
Big Pete
The Irish Dane

Hans C
Hans P
Hans K

The three "Hans's" all had the last name of Petersen, and we needed some way to mark them differently in our conversations. The second initial was from their middle name, but one had no middle name, so we assigned a letter to him.

Cray Hulda
Stinky Lenora (this was not so complimentary, but accurate)
Fat Anna (she was)
Smitty
Haakon
Four Eyes
Big Ole
Little Ole
Blue
Howdy
Little Louie
Big Louie
Flying Pete
High Pockets

I knew each of these people as neighbors or friends. As I write this a few are still living using their very respectable names.

I REMEMBER WHEN...

I remember when:
- We went to town riding in a buggy drawn by a team of horses.
- In the winter we rode in a bobsled to go to the neighbors on a dark night.

- At the depot in town we could hear the telegraph key clicking away its messages.
- Going to the candy kitchen...
  * to choose from the dozens of candies all stacked in glass cases.
  * to cool ourselves under the ceiling fans.
  * To have an ice cream soda.
  * To order a huge banana split for 25 cents.
  * To listen to music from the player piano by inserting a nickel in the slot.

I remember when:
- going to town on Saturday night meant...
  * Trading a case of eggs for $2.25, buying the week's groceries and getting change back.
  * A work shirt could be purchased for 25¢.
  * Blue denim overalls were less than a dollar.
  * Hamburgers were 5¢ apiece.

I remember when:
- a dry goods store was a wonderful place to go. There were cables running from the various counters to a mezzanine. Money for purchases was put into metal containers and they flew to the balcony via the cables. There, correct change was made and returned to the clerk, who would then give the change to the customer.

I remember when:
- a button hook was necessary to button our shoes. The hook was stuck through the hole and it neatly hooked the shiny black ball button to pull it through the hole.
- A razor strop always hung by the kitchen sink and we could hear the "slap, slap" of the razor being honed on the strop.
- Long black stockings were held up by an ingenious garter that was held at the waist with a safety pin slipped through a tiny one-inch tube of metal that was sewn into the under waist.

- Long underwear that had to be folded just so at the ankle to make the black stockings lay smoothly over it.
- Multicolored hair ribbons at least four inches wide.

I remember when:
- The road near our farm...
  * Was predicted to never be a paved highway.
  * When it was a grassy dirt road.
  * When hundreds of men and mules came and camped in large tents. They operated slip-scrapers, elevators and wagons as it was graded and covered with gravel.
  * When it was paved with concrete.
  * When it was replaced with a four-lane divided freeway.
  * When it was reduced to a county road once more.
- Red balls marked the route of cross-country travel.

I remember when:
- The church bell tolled when someone died.
- We counted the tolling bell to know the age of the deceased person.
- The funeral hearse was an ornate gray paneled wagon drawn by horses.
- Girls dressed in white spread garlands of arbor-vitae on the walk from the hearse to the altar of the church.

I remember when:
- People came to church in buggies drawn by horses.
- The horses were tied in sheds near the church.
- Men and women sat on opposite sides of the church.
- The pastor wore a long black robe with a stiff white ruffled collar.
- Offerings were collected in a velvet pouch hung from the end of a long pole.
- We visited the graves of friends and ancestors after church every Sunday.

I remember when:

- I walked a quarter mile to a rural school in all kinds of weather.
- Mud or dust squeezing between the toes while walking on the dirt road.
- Wearing cloth 4-buckle overshoes in winter.

I remember when:

- We got one day off from school to attend "Cattle Congress."
- We got one day off to pick potatoes.
- We got a week off for corn husking.
- We got two weeks off for Christmas.
- After examinations in May, we closed school with a picnic.

I remember when:

- Two Methodist families moved into our Danish Lutheran neighborhood. Oh, My!
- We were not allowed to play with these children because the families spoke "Amerikansk."

I remember:

- The threshing machine and crew coming to our farm.
- Setting up the washstand in the shade for the men to wash, using two washbasins, two bars of soap and two towels.
- Carrying a copper wash boiler full of water to refill the washbasins by using a dipper.
- Hanging one mirror and laying out one comb for all the men to use.
- The men coming into the house at noontime, clean hands and faces and hungry, smelling of fresh straw.

TIDBITS

Fancywork

Growing up, and even after I was married in 1938, it was the norm for all women, when gathered for Ladies Aid or other afternoon gatherings, that each woman brought her "sewing" with her. Sewing meant a piece of embroidery or "fancy work", as it was commonly known. Some embroidered pillowcases, some dresser sets, and others small tabletop covers. Some women carried sewing baskets and some had sewing bags. It was politically correct to bring crocheting or knitting too. Patterns and embroidery designs were shared and copied. Silent observers noted how fine and straight were the stitches of the next person. For shame, if anyone made stitches too large.

Fancy work sessions ended when WW II broke out. Many women went to work in the factories and shops to replace the men who had gone off to war. For many, sewing became necessary to make dresses, aprons, shirts, and even some underwear.

No one ever brought men's socks to mend or any other mending. That was done at home.

White Cake for Sunday

In the era after World War I and before World War II we made our own desserts. Cake mixes were unheard of, and during the depression we couldn't afford them even if they had been available. Cakes were an easy dessert to make, and were a good ending to the large meals we served on the farm.

Almost every day my mother baked a cake. When the men stopped their work for afternoon coffee, as they always did, there was always a fresh cake and sandwiches ready for them.

During the weekdays my mother baked chocolate, spice or other dark cake. And they were very good. I remember the burnt sugar cake she made where she caramelized white sugar in an iron skillet until it was a dark brown and used it to color the cake batter.

But it was an established fact that everyone had white cake for Sunday. The rest of the week it was all right to have chocolate, spice, or other kinds of cake, but not on Sunday. In the event someone dropped in for a Sunday afternoon visit it was only proper to have a fresh white cake ready to serve. And the cake had to have boiled frosting on it.

If the sugar syrup was boiled to just the right temperature it made a nice white fluffy frosting that remained soft. But if boiled too long the frosting quickly became was hard and brittle. One neighbor said he didn't like it if, when he put a knife into the frosting, the whole top would crack and break.

There were no cake mixes, electric mixers, ovens with thermostats, nor detergents with which to wash mixing bowls and pans after the cake was ready for the oven. Elbow grease was required in liberal amounts.

Often as not, fresh eggs were brought in from the chicken house, butter was brought up from the cellar, and cream was skimmed from the tops of bowls of fresh milk that had been set aside to cool.

Oven temperature was regulated by the amount of firewood or cobs that was burned in the firebox. If an angel food cake was in the oven it took only two or three cobs at a time to bake the delicate mix.

The most popular white cake made was called the "Lady Baltimore." It was a two-layer cake filled with ground raisin and nut filling mixed with some of the frosting. It was a very rich and tasty dessert. Little did these Danish Lutheran women realize that Lady and Lord Baltimore were devout Catholics, and that a church still standing in Baltimore was built for this couple. Lord Baltimore demanded a Catholic church be built for him and his followers.

Cakes were often good examples of the housewife's baking ability. Other people compared the various attributes of the cake to their own efforts. But no matter the quality, everyone seemed to enjoy these desserts whenever they were served.

Shirt Collars

Another little task the farm wife did was making men's shirts good for several more weeks of wear.

Men's shirt collars seemed to wear more than the rest of the shirt. When the collar showed significant wear, it was necessary to carefully separate it from the shirt. Stitch by tiny factory stitch, usually three rows, they were painstakingly picked out until the collar was free from the rest of the shirt. The collar was turned, pinned or basted back in place and machine stitched once more to the shirt. This way the shirt was good to wear several more times or until that side wore out as well.

Preserving Cabbage

Back about 1920 I recall my father putting away cabbage for winter use. Out in the garden, he dug a hole deep and wide enough to sink a clean wooden salt barrel fully into the ground.

Just before freezing weather, he placed some straw in the bottom of the barrel. Then he gathered the fresh heads of cabbage and wrapped each one in newspaper. He placed these packages into the barrel. When the barrel was full he placed the cover on the top of the barrel, then covered it with a deep layer of straw. Possibly he put a little dirt over the straw.

In the winter, the straw could be brushed aside, uncovering the barrel. Then we could easily take out a wrapped head of cabbage. The outside leaves were a little dark, but otherwise the cabbage was just like fresh cabbage. After retrieving a head of cabbage the barrel in the ground was then covered over again, preserving the remaining cabbage.

Mail Order Items

Montgomery Wards and Sears & Roebuck did a brisk business back in the 1920's. Mother would make out an order and in a few days receive in return prunes, dried peaches, and dried fish, which were each shipped in wooden boxes. The cartons were about 24 inches long, 16 inches wide, and 8 to 10 inches deep. The boxes were stored upstairs in a cool room. Items were removed as needed.

Sugar Barrels

I was about five or six years old when my mother would send me upstairs to get some sugar. In those times the folks bought sugar in large clean wooden barrels, almost as tall as I was. I remember getting sugar one time when I had to lean well over the top of the barrel, my legs sticking straight out, and scooping up some sugar.

Spoon Jars

Glass spoon jars set on the dining table were popular in my Grandmother's time. The jars were ornate. Some were cut glass, some were colored, decorated with gold, and others would be plainer. These holders held teaspoons. If we needed a teaspoon during a meal we asked for, or reached a spoon.

The reason for spoons set on the table this way very likely was because of lack of dishwashing facilities. The fewer dishes and pieces of silverware to be washed the better. Running hot and cold water was not available, nor was there dish detergent. They were washed using our homemade soap. Fresh water had to be brought from the pump outside and heated on the cook stove. When the dishes were washed, the pan of water had to be carried outside and poured on the ground.

Hair Receiver

Well into the 1920's my mother wore her hair in long braids, which reached down over her shoulders. Each morning before braiding her hair and each night after taking her braids apart, she brushed it thoroughly.

After brushing her hair with an ivory brush she gathered the long strands of hair from the brush and put them into her ivory hair receiver. The receiver was a round box about five or six inches across with a cover that had a hole in the top. The hair from the brush was gathered into the box. When the box was full, mother took the loose hair to town and had the hair straightened and gathered into a "switch".

With the switch she could attach it to her braid and hence make a thicker braid. Mother wore her braid curled at the back of her neck.

In the 1920's Mother was captivated by the era and cut her hair short. The family was shocked and practically disowned by Dad's sisters. It was considered sinful to wear short hair. It did cause a stir, but mother enjoyed keeping abreast of the times.

Silent Films

This was the era of black and white silent films. Cedar Falls had two movie theaters, and the black and white films were well attended. It probably cost a dime or so to see the movies. There were Charlie Chaplain movies as well as a film showing Harold Lloyd dangling from a clock several stories above the street, and many more. One of the first productions of "Ben Hur" was shown in that era. I remember how the pianist, who sat down in front of the Regent Theater stage, playing faster and faster as Ben Hur's horses and chariots raced across the screen. I'm sure that he was very tired by the end of the film.

A Mr. Marcussen played the violin for some of the movies. There was no sound track accompanying the films, only the written captions between scenes.

Rin-Tin-Tin films were very popular. I enjoyed these films very much. Perhaps it was the larger than life German shepherd dog, or perhaps it was the excitement of the drama. It was good.

Sounds from the 20's

From the barnyard:

Wind blowing
Loose barn door swinging
Chopping ice on the stock tank
Opening and closing tank heater lid
Cows mooing

Newborn calves bawling
Horses stomping hooves
Baby pigs squealing
Cats meowing at milking time
Dog barking
Sparrows constantly chirping
Hogs grunting for place at feed trough
Milk squirting the empty milk pail while milking cows
Corn sheller shelling corn
Feed grinder grinding feed
Wheels spinning on ice
Roosters crowing/hens cackling
Baby chicks peeping contentedly under the warm hover
Geese honking in the yard
Pigeons cooing in the hayloft
Woodpeckers drumming on the silo
Model T horns
The soft rhythmic shuffle of oat bundles going through the thresher

Sounds from the house:

Stove grates being shaken
Cook stove lid lifted and set back
Stovepipes crackling when heated
Teakettle singing
Coffee grinder grinding coffee
Coffee percolator perking
Pump handle pumping rainwater from cistern
Wind howling outside
Windows rattling
Feet stomping snow just outside back door
Hands slapping to get warm
Boots being kicked off
Chunks of stove wood dumped into wood bin

HAROLD NIELSEN PETERSEN

Harold was born October 17, 1912, the only son to Hans and Emma Petersen on a farm five miles west of Cedar Falls, Iowa.

He attended a country school about a mile and a half from home. He carried an empty syrup tin pail with a lunch to have at noon. Most days he walked to school. It had to be bitterly cold or very rainy weather before his father would drive a team of horses hitched to a wagon to take him to school

At the time he entered school he did not know a word of English. The Danish language was always spoken at home. He must have overcome that barrier in a short time. The other children at the Hearst school spoke English. So it was up to him to learn the language quickly.

The teacher let him skip either grade two or three. He must have been very good at reading to be able to do that.

However, arithmetic was very difficult for Harold and he spoke of it many times in later years.

He was about ten years old when it was decided he should take violin lessons. On a hot summer threshing day Harold had to get dressed to go to Cedar Falls to get his half hour lesson from a Mr. Smoldt. It might have gone better had he not had to wait for two other students to have their lesson. Then he rode back home in the neighbor's four-door open Model A Ford. By the time he got back home the threshers were nearly finished for that day and he had missed a good afternoon of boyhood fun of threshing oats.

Harold, his sister Hilma and his parents were very often together for various social events with Aunt Bessie and Aunt Anna and Jes Jespsen. Anna and Jes had a son Ernest. They lived on a farm five miles west of Cedar Falls on First Street. So many social activities centered around these people.

Harold at 13

Harold at age 12 or 13 then entered Lincoln High School in Cedar Falls. The transportation problem of getting Harold to the high school was solved by having Harold live with Anna and Jes at their home. Then Harold could ride with them the five miles back and forth to school. That road had been newly paved so riding would be easy. In later years I asked him how he could ride when there was snow. Harold said he rode many times through the snow. When weather got too terribly cold he lived with an older couple in Cedar Falls.

Early twenties

Harold enjoyed the woodworking shop classes. In those classes he built a beautiful fern stand and an oak library table. Woodworking seemed to come naturally to him. When he farmed as a young man, he built wagon boxes tight enough to hold small grain, large hayracks for carrying hay bales, heavy and durable feed bunks for the livestock and many other items. Later in life he returned to cabinetwork and carving, and was able to make many fine items before his eyesight failed. For his entire life he enjoyed working with wood.

Harold and Elna engaged

But his failing came in studying Social Studies, and Harold had neither patience nor understanding of Ancient History. His high school career lasted only two years. He got no encouragement or help from home. It was decided it would be best for him to work with his father on the farm. He left school at the end of ninth grade and studied formally no more. His learning did not end, however, and he could converse with anyone on almost every topic. He did enjoy a cup of strong coffee and a good conversation.

Our wedding portrait

MY IMPERFECT WEDDING

I was 23 and Harold, my fiancé, was 25. Harold was farming the Walter's farm next to his parent's farm. I was teaching and living at my parents' home. We had been dating for a period of several years. Now it was time we got on with our lives and get out on our own. So we thought.

It was June of 1932. I had just finished the school year and was exhausted as I always was at the end of a school year. We were still in the midst of the Great Depression. Things had been especially tough for my parents. They had had to move from the farm. Harold's parents were better off in that they had been able to stay on their farm.

At an earlier time I had been earning $45 a month teaching school. At the next school I received $75 a month. During the course of the spring months, I had bought and paid for all the furnishings of our new home to be.

In the living room I had a new couch, a matching chair, a wool area rug, and a new heating stove. In the bedroom I had a bed with matching dresser, and nylon curtains to match the birdseye maple and mahogany bed and dresser with the large round mirror. For the kitchen I bought a small table and chairs, a set of china, Wearever cooking utensils, a linoleum rug and blue and white checked curtains. Besides all of this I had purchased towels, linens, and other things needed to keep house

When I told my mother we would like to get married on June 10, her response was that that was impossible. Her house would not be ready and I would have to remove the paint from the living room and bedroom floors. At that time we lived in a large white frame Victorian style farmhouse. The large living room double pocket door opened into what was once the parlor, but was now made into a bedroom. Each room had large bay windows as well as other windows and doors.

The floors that my mother was concerned about were six-inch wide white pine boards that had never been sealed and were now painted a strange dark yellow with oil paint. Around each wall was an exposed area close to three feet wide. In the middle of the room was an area rug.

Other people would think that I was old enough to reject this demand. But I was brought up to always do what I was told. Wedding plans would automatically be postponed until June 23. Subject closed.

Harold had planned a wedding trip to California, and that had to be dismissed. I suppose that was when we should have eloped.

With batch after batch of a paste from flour and water with a can of Lewis Lye dissolved in it, I began the job of paint removal. Hour after hour I worked at the project. With a flat steel scraper I scraped up the softened pain and swabbed it into old newspapers. It seemed such an endless task. I had to scrape it down to the raw wood.

The skin from my fingertips was eaten off. I was not happy.

Then I suggested a wedding cake like I had seen in the bakery window in town. It was decorated so nicely and I thought that would be fun to have. Our two mothers got together and decided they would bake the cake, which was a two layer white cake – a common dessert item in our home.

Finally, when the day came for our wedding, I wanted to go with Harold to the courthouse in Grundy Center to get the marriage license. No. Our two fathers would do that, and I would have to clean the whole house. Amid tears, I cleaned. In the meantime I had gone to Waterloo and bought a wedding dress, not traditional, but adequate. Hilma, Harold's sister, was to be my attendant and I wanted to buy a dress for her, too. Harold's mother said no. The one I had given her earlier would do. It was economical.

There were only ten or twelve guests to be invited, so I wrote invitations in my best penmanship on blank note cards and had sent them out earlier. When she discovered this, my grandmother was in a state of fury. Why had we not gotten traditional invitations at the print shop? I couldn't win.

I had wanted to serve a 24-hour salad with the cake. So the night before, mother and I struggled in the kitchen trying to make the salad, which was to have whipped cream in it. The cream would not, and did not whip.

The wedding was to take place at seven o'clock at the Fredsville church. Harold had bought a wedding bouquet for me. Being new at this, he had not indicated what the ribbons were to be like. When I saw the bouquet, my heart sank. It was trimmed with wide funeral ribbons.

The marriage took place at seven o'clock on a hot, humid sunny evening. We stood before the altar with my brother Hilmar on one side, and Harold's sister Hilma at my side. Pastor Kjaer didn't understand how the exchange of rings was to be done. Mercifully, and with some disappointment, the ceremony quickly ended.

We all went to my parent's house for the white cake and soft salad. My mother gave me a wedding gift of a brand new stiff bristle scrub brush with a flat wooden top.

Harold's mother wanted us to spend the wedding night at their place. That was one thing we did not do. We took a short trip to Minnesota and got home in time for hay making a couple of days later.

Should I add, that by the time of the wedding I was in the midst of my menstrual period?

I don't know what I have left out. It seems nothing else could have gone wrong. In spite of all these trials, and of those to follow, or maybe because of them, Harold and I were very happily married for nearly sixty years. It does seem now like a "Cinderella" story in part, complete with the happy ending.

THE IDEAL FARM WIFE

My, how things have changed over the years of my lifetime! Women of today have no idea how difficult life was for the farmer's wife, nor how hard the work load was.

There were certain qualifications necessary to be accepted by the community in order to be a truly ideal farm wife. These qualifications were part of my growing up, and had been handed down through the generations of my ancestors. In those days no one thought much about the condition. Wives just did what was required, not of the men in their lives, but by life itself.

Her qualification was measured in part by how early she got up in the morning. She began her day by lighting the fire in the cook stove. This was more than just striking a match. Ashes needed to be cleaned from the grates and firewood needed to be carried in from the woodshed. Small pieces of kindling or dry corn cobs had to be found and placed just so in the firebox. The addition of a small amount of kerosene would help the fire to grow quickly.

That done, she would have to carry a large pail of water from the pump outside into the house to make the morning coffee. She would then continue her tasks to prepare a hearty breakfast and have it ready on the table when the husband and hired man came in from doing their early morning chores. There would be eggs fresh from the hen house and bacon or ham from the cellar with homemade bread and jam or pastry with freshly ground coffee and milk to drink.

The morning meal over, she would have water heated in the tea-kettle to wash the dishes and frying pans. That finished, the beds were all to me made. Then when more water was heated there was the cream separator to be washed. All and each of the many parts were carefully washed, rinsed and hung on the wall to dry.

There was the flock of chickens that needed fresh water to fill the water jars and feed to fill the feeders. There were also fresh eggs to be gathered and cleaned. Each of these jobs needed more water pumped and heated. There was more wood to be carried into the house to keep the stove going to heat the water.

By that time the men were likely ready for their forenoon coffee which meant having something home baked to set on the table to eat along with the coffee.

If chicken was on the menu that day she had to catch a suitably sized chicken, kill it, then scald, pick and clean it, setting it in cold water to chill. The chicken was dipped in flour and fried in home-made butter. To balance the meal there was the vegetable garden where she dug the potatoes and carrots or gathered other vegetables in season to serve at the noon meal. These needed to be washed, peeled snipped shucked and cooked.

The newlyweds

On wash days she would hang out the laundry as early as possible being careful to hang sheets, towels and dark clothes in their order. This of course was after the job of heating water, churning the clothing by hand in the sudsy water, then rinsing and wringing the hot water out of them. The next day there would be much ironing to do. There was the ironing board to set up, and then the heavy flat irons weeded to be heated on the cook stove, which meant more firewood. Whew!

There was homemade bread to be baked using yeast foam to make the dough rise. That was a slow-acting yeast and bread was often set in a warm place the night before it was to be baked to rise. Besides baking the bread there were cakes and pastries to be made ready for afternoon coffee times. On Sundays there should always be a white cake baked in case visitors arrived. The cake was always frosted with boiled frosting.

There were always clothes to be mended. Buttons had to be sewed back on shirts, men's socks were darned, and overalls to be patched.

An efficient wife made cotton print aprons to wear at all times. She also made her own cotton house dresses.

When babies were born, the mother had white cotton flannel diapers hemmed and folded ready for the new arrival. It was the wife's responsibility to take full charge of the care and feeding of babies and small children.

The new family

During the summer she canned and preserved much of the crop of garden vegetables, made jam from fruit and covered it with melted paraffin.

Some women were expected to help milk the cows both morning and evening.

In her free time she could go to town on Saturday nights to buy groceries and a few other necessities. She was expected to have the family ready for church on Sunday mornings, being sure there was a roast in the cook stove oven and the potatoes peeled so that Sunday dinner would soon be ready after church.

And last but very important, have the house neat and tidy for unexpected visitors.

Visiting neighbors enjoyed making comments about how light the cakes were, how flaky the pies crusts were and that the cookie jar was well filled at all times. These compliments were likely the only reward for all the efforts of the farmer's wife. Neighbors could also be cruel by passing judgment on how much better one woman's work efforts were than some of the others.

Then came the advent of modern appliances and running water, both hot and cold. Things changed slowly, but labor saving devices did come into the house. Most wives were up to the challenge of long hard hours of work and did quite well. They raised good families. Many lived to be quite old and enjoyed their later years in better circumstances.

Perhaps their hard labors contributed to their long lives, or perhaps it was there staunch determination to succeed. Whatever the reason or cause, the farmer's wife was a very significant part of the success of the rural landscape, and perhaps the advancement of our entire society. No wonder the saying: "The farmer works from sun to sun, but the woman's work is never done."

THE OUTDOOR TOILET

The various things I have experienced while living on Iowa farms cannot be complete until I tell you about the outhouse.

There were several names for the outdoor toilet, outhouse being only one. They were also known as the privy, Aunt Sally or Susie or whatever name they chose to call it.

Typically these wooden structures were built of wood, and had a raised seat with either two or three holes. The one I had at home had one extra seat built lower for the small children.

I have lived with toilets so old that the floor was about to cave in. I lived at one farm where the garter snakes took up residence in the outhouse on sunny days. Visualize the frantic screams that could be heard when entering this particular toilet.

These structures were most often equipped with a choice of Sears Roebuck or Montgomery Ward catalogs, from which we tore out one page at a time for private use. When paper dress patters were ready to be discarded they were also torn into proper sized sheets and used.

On the way...

Toilets were always located within walking distance from the back door of the farmhouse. Imagine what it was like when the rain was pouring down. Or when the snow was blowing a gale and the drift was well inside the toilet. Or imagine the summer time when it was hot and odorous. I won't elaborate on that.

At the country school there were two toilets. One was for the boys and one was for the girls. We had to signal to the teacher when we needed to go to the toilet. Now remember there were all eight grades in the one room and it was embarrassing.

The signals were: One finger held up high was a water job. Two fingers meant, "We had to do number two." And when we were waving our hands in a desperate motion the teacher knew there was urgency.

I was teaching in a country school when we had the big blizzards of '34 and '36. The snowdrifts were six feet deep between the schoolroom and the toilets. My school board president called to ask me to shovel a path. My reply was that the children could walk over the top of the drifts and they did.

When my children were all small they would go to the toilet by themselves. When I could hear them calling "Paper!" from inside my kitchen, I knew that I was needed to go out and help them.

All I can remember now is that it was gross. It was pure inequity from what our counterparts were having when they lived in town. There they had modern bathrooms, bathtubs, etc.

It was particularly difficult for women, although we had no other options. The outhouse was just part of life. After World War II women and their personal needs were better met. But it was really slow in coming. Indoor toilets were considered a luxury on the farm. In addition, it was not until the farm had a pressurized water system that we could even consider an indoor toilet. After WW II when electricity was available on most farms, many outhouses disappeared in favor of indoor toilets. What a welcome happening that was!

THE INCREDIBLE FEED SACKS

It is really a very unexciting topic to write about in the year 2003. For an introduction I have to make note that the era of this story is of the Great Depression back in the 1930's. It is impossible today to get any kind of feeling of what it was like living in those times. In our modern day and age we have so many discount stores that bargains can be had in an instant.

But to write about feed sacks brings back a lot of memories. It began when the feed companies found a new merchandising tactic. They began bagging chicken and other farm animal feeds in printed cloth bags. The bags were 100 percent cotton printed in small floral prints. The idea swept the neighborhoods like wild fire. Women ran to see what bags came home from the feed mill. As quickly as the feed bags were emptied, the bags were shaken out to get the fine feed grains out of the sack. Next the bags were washed, hung out to dry, then ironed and ready to be opened. The bags were always sewed with a chain stitch which was carefully and easily raveled after finding the right string to begin the raveling.

Then our creative minds took action. Bags were quickly made up into everyday cotton dresses, aprons, sheets, pillow cases, etc. There was much conversation via the telephone or at local gatherings to show off one's new print garment. Even if a bag had a small tear in it, the bags were patched and then made up into a garment.

Often the feed elevator managers knew what print pattern a certain housewife was waiting for. He would set aside feed bags of the proper print until that particular farmer would purchase feed. The housewife was thus rewarded for their repeat business.

If plain white bags were brought home, as they sometimes were, the bags were washed, opened, ironed and made ready for sewing. By pulling a thread all across the ends of the bags we could get a perfectly square piece of fabric. The white bags were good for making bed sheets by sewing four squares together, then spitting the fifth bag in half and sewing those two pieces to the end of the sheet. That gave more length to the bed sheet.

Other white bags were squared, using the pulling a thread method, then hemmed and made into good dish towels. In the winter sacks could be laid out on the snow to be bleached white by the sun.

What a wonderful development cotton feed sacks were. It made our life much better when we had no money to buy extras such as cloth for sewing. These sacks were a credit to the feed companies and their local dealers. Many friendships and business loyalties were formed in these years.

RENTERS

My husband and I were always renters while we farmed. In those days it was not a good thing to rent the farm on which a family lived. It was acceptable to rent nearby farmland as long as the farmer owned his own farm. This was just good business practice, and made the relationship with the banker much better.

When we were married in 1938 we moved onto and rented a farm owned by Bill Walters. It was well kept in every detail. The fences were in excellent condition, the buildings although not new were painted and in good repair. The farm was weed free and tiled. The soil was rich, and would produce consistently good crops. It was a good place to start our new life together.

Bill Walters owned four farms in the area where we lived in Black Hawk County. My grandparents, the Hoffman's, lived on one of his farms exactly two miles east of the Schmidt farm. The second was just north of the Hoffman's. The Walters were a very frugal couple. In Cedar Falls, where they lived, there was a five-dollar minimum on electricity each month with extra charges for usage above that amount. The Walters couple, concerned they might exceed this limit, would sit by a kerosene lamp by the kitchen table in the evenings.

The other two farms owned by the Walters' were next to Harold's father's farm. Harold and his father farmed all three of the places, that is, two of the Walters' farms and the farm owned by his father, Hans Petersen.

Our first farm home

In the next year or two after our marriage, Bill Walters offered these two farms to us for three hundred dollars and acre. In 1940 that was a great deal of money, having just survived the Great Depression and with rumors of a looming war. Even so, it was an excellent offer. But because Harold's parents said we would never get them paid for, we were not "allowed" to buy them. In those days we never defied what our parents told us. It was in that decision that we began the trek of rented farms going from bad to worse and back again. How differently things would have turned out for all of us if we had asserted ourselves.

So we looked for another farm to rent.

A farm owned by the Branhorst family was the only farm available in the area to rent. It was close to our families, and still within the boundaries of our Danish friends and family. Just across the road, however, was the boundary of the German neighborhood. Our families still lived in close ethnic bonds, and our Danish ancestors never did have much time for the Germans. But Harold and I got along well with them and made good friends and business associations within this neighborhood, much to the questioning gossip of those so inclined in the Danish neighborhood.

The buildings on this farm were old and greatly in need of repair, the stock yards were muddy, the fences needed rebuilding, and the outhouse was about to collapse. There were at least two large thistle patches in the fields, which either bothered the cows grazing in the pasture or depleted the crop yield in that area. There was no hot or cold running water. The yards needed cleaning up. But there we were. Our two children were three years and five months old when we moved onto the place.

By then our country was into World War II and we, as was everyone else, were subject to wartime rations. We relied on stamps for fuel and sugar. Other commodities as well were in short supply. There was no hired help available to help with the farm work, and we now farmed 240 acres.

Harold was not drafted because our crops were essential for food. But he worked alone apart from the little help I could provide. Busy seasons meant long working days from early morning, about 4:30 a.m., to ten or eleven o'clock at night.

There were two acres of land in the far back corner of the farm that grew marijuana. We didn't know that marijuana was a drug or that it could be smoked. We knew that it was a desired crop required for the wartime effort. It was used for making rope. We called it hemp. The best thing about that particular area was that the jack rabbits were free to live there. It was great to see them with their long ears and legs loping across the fields.

This farm had no septic system, which was common in those days. The outhouse located about 20 yards from the back door to the house. It was in great need of repair. The drain pipe from the kitchen seeped through the ground just outside the back door of the house. Our children both got impetigo on their skin from the drainage water just outside our kitchen. That meant many trips to the doctor. Soon after we moved there, Harold rebuilt the outhouse. It wasn't heavenly, but it was much better than its dilapidated predecessor.

Livestock did not do well on that farm. A good feed lot for the livestock had a concrete floor which was solid and easily cleaned. The yards on this farm were only dirt, and became so muddy in the spring thaw or in wet weather that the cattle couldn't gain their required weight well. Their legs sank down into the mud, almost to their bellies, making walking very difficult. Hogs did not do well either. When cleaning the manure from the feed lot it was difficult to know when to stop since it was well mixed into the mud and dirt.

Theft was rarely a problem in those days, but one night chicken thieves stole most of our chickens that were housed in the barn. That was a loss of both capital and income. We had to replace the chickens so that we would once again have eggs to sell for the little cash they brought, and to have the occasional chicken for a meal.

In the economic boom after World War II we made many improvements to the farm. A new corn crib was built to hold the generous crops. Some new farm equipment was purchased. Harold's threshing machine was sold, and a new bold red Massey-Harris combine proudly replaced it.

A pressurized water system was installed, allowing us to have running water in the house. We were able to purchase and use brand new appliances such as a washing machine that spun the water from the clothes rather than wringing the water out. We purchased a gas kitchen range to replace the wood fired cook stove, and a chest freezer that meant we could store more of our food on the farm rather than driving to town to the locker plant where we could rent cold storage space.. We even had a new kitchen sink in a new cabinet complete with a fresh countertop made of linoleum. Harold devised a simple shower near the back door. This made life much easier.

Then the Branhorst farm was for sale and we needed to find a place to live again. Harold's parents generously offered us their chicken house to live in and farm there, but we politely chose not to do so. By some method, we made contact with a representative of a landowner group from Chicago. He offered us a farm of over 400 acres north of Indianola, Iowa near Carlisle, and so we moved there.

Some of our farm equipment was sold, but the rest was loaded onto a 1920's vintage truck that belonged to Harold's father. It took more than one trip of over 100 miles in this fragile and unpredictable rig. But we made the move, arriving with our family at the new farm just before Christmas.

There was still the large combine to move. It was too large to carry by truck. It would have to be driven the distance to the new farm, so the next spring Harold made the journey back to prepare it for the long drive. Very early one morning, about 2:00 a.m., Harold drove out onto the road to maneuver this machine, twelve feet wide in front, to its new location. He drove all day long on the 100-mile journey to the new farm, trying to avoid as much traffic as possible. We met him in our car late in the day about 40 miles short of his destination. He pulled into a nearby farmyard, where he made arrangements with the farmer, a perfect stranger, to leave the machine overnight. We took him home, and the next day, drove him back to the combine. He arrived at the new farm later that day.

The new farm had a house that reflected the look of the plantation mansions in the south. The house was very old and in need of much repair. The outbuildings were in reasonable shape. The farm yard was on a hill that looked out over a large area of river bottom land. This land raised good crops, but the soil was difficult to till. It required different equipment than we had.

For the first time we lived outside the close community of Danish relatives. We were a Danish family living in a solid Scottish neighborhood. The people were kind, and did many things to make us feel welcome and a part of the neighborhood. Nevertheless we felt like outsiders. It was strange living so far from our roots. Besides we were renters.

We did make friends there – friends that we met again some years later.

There were good times and celebrations. One of the neighbors built a new barn for his dairy herd. Before he put hay into the loft, he organized a celebration that included a real barn dance. Corn meal was spread on the boards of the floor. Musicians were gathered – fiddle, guitar and bass. A "caller" (the local auctioneer) came to call square dances. The barn was full of people and we danced until the wee hours of the morning.

One of our nearest neighbors, an old timer, took great pride in being the first neighbor up in the morning to turn on the yard light. One morning Harold got up very early to make the trip to move his combine and turned on the yard light long before the neighbor. Later that same morning the neighbor was so upset when he discovered that he was not the first in the neighborhood to turn on his light that the next night he left his yard light on all night. This really conflicted with his frugal Scottish heritage.

This area of Iowa is primarily clay soil. In rainy weather the yards were next to impossible. One time, our two oldest children were carrying a pail of grain across the yard between the house and barn to the chicken house. This was in the spring just after frost had gone out, so the yard was all mud, "brickyard clay" at that. They got their overshoes stuck out in the middle of the yard and had to have help to get out of the mud.

Harold again made several improvements to the farm, both to the land and to the buildings. However, after only one growing season, highlighted by the greatest river flood anyone around could remember, this farm, too, was sold. This flood took place in the middle of the growing season, and the crops drowned in the flood. All of the effort at tilling new land, adding ample expensive fertilizer and purchase of new farm equipment was for naught. We learned that in the following year, the next farmer on the land had record breaking crops the likes of which the neighbors had never seen.

Somehow, the Chicago landlord representative and Harold made a deal for us to move 90 miles north to a farm on Highway 69, ten miles from the nearest village and 30 miles from a town of any significant size, even for Iowa. So the move was done, not easily, but done. This time equipment was transported by tractor and wagon as the old truck could not be made reliable. And there we were out on the flat peat bed lands near Big Wall Lake.

Once again we lived in an old and very drafty house. When the wind blew, which was most of the time, the curtains actually drifted out from the windows even though they were "tightly" shut. There was no running water, so I could not use my washing machine. It was back to boiling water to do laundry in the old way.

The land was fertile. It was peat. Crops grew well here. I helped Harold till the land. After one windy early spring day when I drove the tractor back and forth in the field all day, the wind blew the peat dust across the fields, my skin reacted and I was burnt a beet red like having a sunburn.

That summer, in one of the typical Iowa thunderstorms, a tornado spawned nearby and, only a quarter of a mile away, destroyed the neighbor's barn. The storm occurred in the night, but we were spared. The wind moved two of our buildings slightly on their foundations and stuck straw and sticks of wood into trunks of trees. A few small trees were blown down in the grove, but the house was spared. Perhaps the drafty old house let just enough air through to avoid destruction.

This farm was infested with garter snakes. They were everywhere. They curled up on the seat bench of the outhouse. They hung in the trellis where I grew climbing roses. They crawled in the grass of the lawn. When my son was mowing the lawn one got caught in the reel of the mower and was cut into several short lengths. We always had to be on the watch to avoid these pests.

At the end of the year the farm was sold and we were required to move once again. This was bad news for us as we had invested so much effort and money at several farms to improve the land and buildings. This time, out of frustration, Harold and I made the decision to leave farming and take on a different career. An auction was held and all of the machinery required for farming was sold. It was another sad day.

We were able to rent a house nearby. It was an unused structure, but in reasonable condition. It was positioned by an old wagon trail of the pioneering days. Tracks were still visible from the old wagon route. There were some strong advantages to this house. This house had hot and cold running water. And, wonder of wonders, it had an indoor bathroom complete with toilet, tub and sink. It was wonderful. For the first time in my life, at age 40, I had indoor plumbing! The electrical service was underpowered, and I had difficulty using my washing machine. The landlord said, "No problem," and put a penny behind the fuse! It's a wonder we had no fires.

The water heater was gas fired, but operated manually. That is, we had to turn it on to have hot water and turn it off when we were done. One day our family went to town on a shopping trip, and left the water heater on. When we returned several hours later, we discovered the error when steam poured out of the cold water faucets. Our guardian angels were busy in our lives!

Harold pursued carpentry, working with a builder who built farm structures. I returned to teaching in a one room rural school. The school was situated on an open prairie with no trees to break the wind. The winter months were very cold. The oil fired heater could not produce enough heat to counter the prevailing winds.

Harold enjoyed his new occupation, but the carpentry business was seasonal, and in an effort to improve our lot, we once more moved to yet another rented home. This time we found ourselves living "in town" for the first time in our lives. We were on the southeastern outskirts of Des Moines, but it was an urban community. This home was an older structure, but well kept for its age. We were, however, back to the days of the outhouse.

We lived in the former home for the caretaker of a city park dedicated to a large collection of lilacs. For a few days in the spring, with a gentle breeze in the right direction, we lived in heaven. If the wind shifted to the opposite compass point, we were then down wind of the city dump where garbage and other trash was burned continually. What a contrast!

Living here was good. We were near Danish relatives again, and enjoyed the reunion of the extended family. Here we also reacquainted ourselves with former friends from the Scotch Ridge area. Perhaps we hadn't much money in the pocket, but we at least were wealthy with friendships and family.

This house was scheduled to be demolished, so we lived there for only a short time. Then, after renting farms and houses for twenty-five years, we finally purchased our first home of our own (and the mortgage company). It was a house and lot in the city. Now we had property that we could work on for our own benefit that could not be sold out from under us. It was the biggest change in our life that we had ever made. It was good.

This did not stop our wandering ways, however. After a number of years we moved again to be nearer our grandchildren. I think our early years prepared us for these changes. Harold and I moved a number of times even after this latest transition. We never feared changing addresses. Now, I live in a wonderful apartment, alone, but surrounded by good people and many friends. I often wonder if we missed something by not setting down roots very early in our married life, or did we find treasure that would have been otherwise undiscovered? Regardless, we lived a good life, and it has given me much about which I can consider and write.

AH, THOSE STOVE PIPES

When I was a young girl in the early part of the 20th century, stove pipes and stove pipe wire were standard household items. In those days central heating was not common, and homes and public buildings were heated in the cold weather with the cook stove in the kitchen and a free standing heater in another room.

Our farmhouse was pre central heating. A basement furnace was unthinkable where we lived. No, we had a space heater. A space heater sat on the floor and rested on a metal square underlain with asbestos. The heater needed to be at least two feet away from the wall for fire safety.

Some people had ornate black heaters trimmed in large amounts of chrome-like metal, probably nickel. Ours was newer and was finished in enameled metal to 'fit in better' with the rest of the living room furniture.

To get the greatest amount of heat from the stove and to vent the smoke, there was a series of fitted stovepipes that led from the stove to the chimney, which was located in the upstairs hallway.

The cook stove was usually near a chimney and required only a short run of stove pipe. The heating stove often sat in the center of the living room or parlor, and required many lengths of stove pipe to connect it to the chimney across the room, and sometimes to an upper floor. These lengths of stove pipe were held securely in place with stove pipe wire.

In many homes it was a common practice to store the heating stove in an outbuilding during the summer months, and to move the stove indoors during the winter months. It happened twice a year. It was inevitable. Those stovepipes pipes had to either go up or come down. Fall meant UP. Spring meant DOWN. It was an agonizing task no matter how we did it. This was never a clean task. It meant installing or removing lengths of stovepipe to connect the stove to the chimney. When the pipes were taken down in the spring often the wire could be left dangling from the ceiling, then reused the following season.

Stovepipes vented the smoke and soot from the heater that stood in the middle of the room. It was fired with either wood or coal. Both left a goodly amount of soot in the pipes. If there was a choice of which time of the year was best for stove piping it would probably be the fall season. At least the pipes would be free of soot.

Stovepipe wire was an important item wherever stovepipe was used. This fine wire bore the responsibility of cradling the black tin stove pipes, often in long lengths, which connected the stove and the chimney. This wire was fine, pliable and easy to handle. Hooks were attached to the ceiling. A length of wire double the distance from ceiling to stove pipe was then placed into position, one for every two lengths of stovepipe. One end of the wire was attached to the ceiling hook, swung down and around the black tin stove pipe, and up and around back to the ceiling where it was attached.

Stovepipes were made of blue-black thin sheet metal. Stove pipes came in measured lengths with one end crimped so that it would fit into the second length of pipe. Several lengths of pipe could be used. If the heating stove was situated in the center of a room it would necessitate several lengths of pipe. Every other length of pipe needed to be anchored with a length of wire. Also there were the elbow pieces of pipe to allow the pipe to angle into the stove or chimney.

On our heating stove where my husband and I lived, he first inserted the piece that fit onto the stove. Next was a short piece with a weighted flapper that controlled the amount of draft. Then, two straight lengths of pipe extended the pipe vertically to a little over 12 inches from the ceiling. Then an elbow was fitted to the upright pipe and a third length was fitted into the elbow. This third piece was horizontal to the ceiling. So far, so good!

To keep the pipes from falling, the third length had to slip through a loop of stove pipe wire hanging from the ceiling. Then two more lengths were added through wire loops, and then another elbow.

Now the pipe needed to go through the ceiling. An ornate wrought iron floor register with a hole in the center just big enough for the pipe to slip through was already on the opening. This decorative device kept the stovepipe away from the wooden framing of the house for safety. It also allowed some heat to rise through the grillwork to the second floor. It wasn't much heat in the cold spells, but it helped a little.

Very steadily, so that the already precarious line-up of pipes would not teeter and fall, the next pipe was fitted through the ceiling to the floor above.

This flimsy arrangement was not 100% successful and often there was a loud crashing followed by some well-chosen expletives that my husband saved just for these occasions. This was the worst in the spring when the pipes were full of soot. What a terrible mess that was!

316

When the downstairs pipes were securely hung, the next effort was in the upstairs hallway. There, two more lengths of pipes were added in an upright position being very careful not to disturb the placement down below. Again, another elbow was added, followed by a straight piece of pipe that went into the chimney.

Chimneys were made of brick and often did not extend to the lower level of the house. Instead, the chimney stopped about halfway down the wall in the upstairs hallway. A hole for the pipe was let into the chimney at that location. In the warmer season, when the chimney was not used, the chimney hole was covered with a pretty tin cover with a painted picture in the center. When the stovepipe was installed, this cover was removed and a brass ring was placed in its stead.

One summer a screech owl somehow got into one of the chimneys and could not get back out. We heard the commotion behind the decorative plate during the night. What a racket! The next day my husband put on a heavy leather coat and leather gloves. He carefully opened the plate and reached in to retrieve the poor frightened bird. After a few tries, and with a great fluttering of soot and feathers, he was able to get the owl firmly gripped. The owl was then taken outside and released to find his way again.

Another summer a swarm of bees thought that the chimney that served the kitchen cook stove would make a lovely place to set up a hive. The chimney was completely plugged by the swarm of bees and I could do no cooking. My husband was in Chicago selling livestock, and I was at a loss as to what I should do. About then, the oil delivery man showed up to fill our gasoline and oil needs. His name was Elmer Cawelti, for the record. He was very kind to help me. He found a large quantity of sulphur and kerosene soaked rags. He donned hat, gloves and netting that he had brought, climbed up to the peak of the roof two and a half stories high, stood up to reach the top of the chimney and dropped the sulphur down the flue. He then lit the rags soaked in kerosene and dropped them in on top of the sulphur. The sulphur ignited and soon a thick cloud of yellow smoke billowed into the sky. It killed or dazed all of the bees. We then had to clean out the chimney from inside the house getting soot and bees all over. What another mess!

When the last length of pipe was carefully fitted into the chimney, the complete line up was ready for inspection. Each piece needed to fit securely into the next piece. When all was ready, the heater could be safely used. Care had to be exercised, however, that the fire not be too hot. If that happened, the pipes would turn cherry red, and there was great danger of setting the house on fire.

The fully exposed stovepipe would allow us to use almost all of the heat of the fire in the stove. When the fire was started there would be heat both downstairs and some upstairs. It served its purpose well.

Stove pipe wire served many useful purposes beyond holding the stove pipe lengths. We often used a piece of it to mend broken items, or to hold other items together. But no use carried more responsibility than securely holding the stovepipe. Any failure to do so was a huge mess at least and a dangerous fire at the worst.

LIGHTING THE FIRE

As a new bride I was anxious and determined to prove my proficiency in running a proper house. After all, I was 23 and had worked in several households to learn the ways of the times.

Our 1880's vintage little white farmhouse had no running water, no central heat, no telephone, and no bathroom. In that regard it was like most other farm houses of the era. But I was so excited about being a newlywed setting up my own home that the lack of these unimaginable modern conveniences never entered my mind.

I came down that first morning dressed in a neatly ironed gingham dress ready to make that very first breakfast. My husband was already in the barn doing chores, and I wanted everything ready when he came back in.

I walked towards that beautiful little white enamel cook stove standing at one end of the small kitchen. It was a Montgomery Ward special, purchased at the price of twenty-five dollars. The floor of the kitchen slanted a full six inches from east to west towards the back door and right to left facing the stove. Therefore, blocking up one end to make the stovetop level had solved that problem.

The Montgomery & Ward special

The first thing to do was to light a fire in the stove. I lifted the front round lid on the stovetop and noticed some ashes in the firebox. I used the handle from the stove lid and inserted it inside a little door that opened to the ash pan. I shook those ashes down into the pan by moving the handle back and forth until the grates were clean.

Next, very carefully so as not to raise any dust, I pulled the ash pan out, carried it to the kitchen door, and carried it outside to an area far enough away from the house that the ashes wouldn't blow back in again.

It was early on a warm June morning, and the grass was wet with dew. Walking in the grass made my shoes very wet, so I took them off before going back into the kitchen. With the ash pan back in place I now needed some newspaper, which I crumpled up and placed in the firebox.

Next, I needed the kindling. I walked out to the woodshed to gather a handful of thin pieces of wood, which I deftly split with the axe standing nearby. I took these back to the house. I placed the kindling into the fire pot and took a wooden match from the new match holder mounted on the kitchen wall. The match holder advertised the local feed mill in a nearby town.

I struck the match, touched it to the newspaper, slid the lid back on the open space and raced back out to the woodshed to get some larger pieces of wood. In order to do all of this, I had to slip my shoes on and off at a rapid pace so that the fire would not go out before I got the next fuel on.

Coffee. Oh, yes, now I needed to get the water. The water pump was down at the windmill. I picked up the empty water bucket, put my shoes back on, and raced to the windmill. Vigorously, I pumped the handle up and down until the pail was full of cold well water. I had to carry this heavy pail back to the house. In my hurry some of the icy-cold water spilled over into one of my shoes.

I noted that the blue smoke was trailing out of the chimney lifting lazily up into a brilliant morning sky. Inside the kitchen I dipped water from the pail into the teakettle and placed it on the stove, which was getting hotter and hotter. However, by now I needed to put more wood into the firebox. It wouldn't hold more that two or three pieces of firewood depending on the size of the pieces.

With the coffee pot filled with cold water, I put in the right amount of coffee grounds. I had just freshly ground the coffee beans in the grinder mounted on the wall. In a few minutes the coffee pot began to percolate, and the aroma of fresh coffee filled the kitchen.

I put several thick slices of bacon in the brand new iron skillet and set the pan on the cook stove to cook. The eggs were also ready to fry, and, quickly, I set the table for two at our new kitchen table with the matching chairs.

I was so proud of my accomplishment when my husband walked in. He noted that I was going stocking-footed, and I had to explain about my incident with the water bucket on the way back from the windmill.

Now this was the tale of getting the fire started for breakfast. This routine was repeated for the noon meal, the evening meal, and so on. In the winter we didn't let the fire go out during the day. I brought in a basket-full of wood at each visit to the woodshed to eliminate so many trips.

When corn-shelling season came there were fresh dry corncobs to use for starting the fire. I would bring in a bucket of cobs at a time to use, both to start the fire and sometimes to use as regular fuel. Cobs didn't last as long and the fire had to be more carefully watched.

There were times when there was a shortage of fuel and I gathered cobs from the feed floor where the hogs had eaten the corn from the cobs. These cobs were not as clean and it was a more hateful job to gather and use them.

In the wintertime, we had a heating stove in the living room. Then it was double the work to keep the grates clean, ashes hauled outdoors and to keep fuel on hand when the weather was bad. I must observe that the house was cozy in cold weather. Not so in the summer when the weather was hot and humid.

THE GREAT DEPRESSION

The Great Depression of the 1930's came on the heels of the Roaring Twenties. During the 1920's there was excitement and prosperity throughout the country. World War I, the war to end all wars, had ended and the euphoria of peace and wealth reigned.

The things I remember most about the Twenties were people trying to do the Charleston, the change in dress styles such as dresses getting shorter, and the excitement of the new Ford cars. Our hired man had a Ford Roadster with a rumble seat, which caused quite a stir. My mother had her hair bobbed; a major departure from wearing it in braids and was ostracized by her two sisters-in-law for doing it. And the fashionable black and purple bloomers we wore under our dresses were the height of fashion. Bloomers had elastic both in the waist and around each leg. The expression "Oh boy," was big at the time.

Soon after the stock market crashed in 1929 hard times came and it seemed the world had stopped. Banks foreclosed on the farmers, jobs were hard to find, prices dropped on goods and field crops, and there was much sadness across the land.

My parents must have gone bankrupt, because all of a sudden when I was thirteen years old, there was a farm sale including most of our household goods. The folks rented a Victorian house in Cedar Falls at 18th and Waterloo Road. They brought two beds, a table, chairs, and items such as cookware, dishes and bedding. There we were. Dad didn't have a job. There was no income. Dad finally got a job at the John Deere factory painting tractors. He would come home with green and yellow paint all over his clothes. He got forty dollars a week out of which the rent had to be paid and groceries purchased.

I turned fourteen during the fall we moved into town. I was old enough to work and was sent out to find what work I could. The neighbor next door worked in the Black Hawk County courthouse. They at least had money, so on Sunday afternoons I washed dishes from their Sunday dinner, and probably the breakfast dishes, too. I got 35 cents each Sunday for doing that.

I got a job in the local sweet corn factory during the canning season. My job was operating a machine that filled cans with corn, standing with my shoes in salt brine that leaked onto the floor. One day I cut a finger on the machine and wore a bandage on that finger. This was before band-aids, so the bandage was a narrow strip of a plain piece of cloth wrapped around the finger, the end of the cloth strip was split lengthwise and then tied around the finger in a square knot. Somehow, the bandage must have come loose, because later that day I noticed it was gone. It was most likely lost in a can of sweet corn. Imagine opening that can! If the inspector came around I had to hide, because I was not old enough to be working there

I also ironed white shirts for Hans Holst. The shirts were starched on the collar, cuffs and down the front. He was a very large man and it took me a long time to iron each shirt. I got fifty cents for half a day's work.

When I wasn't working for those people, I worked part time half a block away at a filling station pumping gas. This was literally pumping gas! Gas was pumped into a glass cylinder on top of the pump by moving a lever back and forth. Then, using a hose, I could fill the tanks on the cars. There was a small grocery in connection with the station so I worked the store too. I would sneak a candy bar every now and then.

The Rock Island steam locomotives ran on their rail line about a quarter of a mile from our house. I would take the coal bucket and walk along the tracks picking up coal that the firemen had spilled when shoveling coal into the firebox on the locomotive. I walked along the tracks many times. One time I was near the middle of the railroad bridge when I heard an approaching train. The bridge was very narrow, and there was not room on the bridge to be out of the way. I was in trouble. I had to run towards the oncoming train in order to get off the bridge and to safety. It was a close race, but I made it!

During the school year I walked from home to the college campus in all kinds of weather, a walk of approximately three miles each way. One winter's day I used a dime from my income to buy a ticket on the City Bus. When I stepped off the bus I slipped into a deep icy rut under the bus. I was quick enough to drag myself out to safety before the bus moved. In those days the streets were not plowed for snow. The two sets of tracks became deep ruts and were frozen. I remember that day well.

There was one year I had just two dresses to wear to school. And we girls had to wear rayon stockings that were always getting runs in them. I spent many evenings darning stockings either to hook each thread back or to just sew up the runs.

I was taking Home Economics one year and the teacher had us write down our daily intake of food for a class project. When she read that I got half a cup of milk a day she was upset. She didn't realize that we couldn't afford to buy more than one pint of milk a day for the four of us.

On Saturdays I cleaned house at Axel Holst's house. I probably got fifty cents for the day's work. When his wife was killed in a train crossing accident, I took care of the eight-year-old daughter as well as keeping the house and doing the cooking.

There were High School athletic events that cost ten cents to attend. I never attended any of those events both because I couldn't spare the money and I couldn't walk that far to attend.

At home mother canned lots of applesauce when she could get the apples. One winter we ate mostly home made bread, baked beans and applesauce.

At home, my brother, Hilmar, and I played lots of card games as well as board games. I think that is how I learned to do mental arithmetic. Once in a great while Hilmar and I would walk down town to the Regent Theater and take in a movie for ten cents apiece. That was a journey of two or two and a half miles each way to the theater. I remember Rin Tin Tin films especially.

We had neighbors down on the next street who were called Holy Rollers. We could hear them carrying on through the night on summer evenings.

One Sunday, Harold's folks, my future in-laws, came to visit us. I know I baked a cake for the occasion. They must have proposed a plan for the folks. Harold's father was renting the adjacent farm where there was a vacant house. The folks then moved out to that house and I went to live with a farm family a mile or so west of the college on 27th street. I finished my senior year there, working before and after school and weekends for fifty cents a week. There again I walked back and forth to school in both cold and hot, wet and dry weather.

CROWS

My husband Harold enjoyed telling and retelling the following true event:

When he was a young man and still living on the farm with his folks, he was walking out to bring in the cows when he came upon two pheasant roosters facing each other in the green pasture behind the grove of trees on the farm. Like two bullies in a schoolyard these young cocks were nodding their heads and stamping their feet anticipating a fight to prove which was better. They ruffled their neck feathers, kicked with their claws what dust there was and eye balled each other to see who would be the first to attack.

High in one of one of the maple trees growing in the grove, a crow watched the two birds below. He, in his crow wisdom, anticipated that an interesting scrap was at hand.

Silently, the crow spread his wings and dropped to the ground, landing a few inches behind one of the pheasants. He crept up slowly and deftly pecked the tail of one of the cocks, and then quickly flew back to his perch in the treetop to observe the reaction.

The pheasant, irritated by the tug on his tail, leapt forward in surprise. At once the two birds jumped at each other as if to fight. But the fight did not occur.

The crow, watching from his vantage point and not seeing the action he wanted, quickly flew down again and crept up behind the second pheasant, pecked him on the tail and flew back to his perch.

The pheasants spurred into action, and pecked at each other in a brief flurry. But the fight was still not too serious.

Then for the third time the crow flew down and nipped the tail of the first pheasant. The two cocks fought until one of the cocks flew away.

Do crows laugh to themselves when they have outwitted someone else? This crow seemed to be pleased with the commotion he had caused.

Here is another incident:

On our farm we had a row of raspberry bushes growing in the lower yard. As the season wore on the berries ripened and smaller birds helped themselves to the bounty.

In the surrounding tall trees a family of seven crows watched and took note of what was happening. Fresh fruit was a treat, but how could they get it?

One at a time the crows each tried landing on the branches as had the smaller birds, but their weight made the branch bend very low and frightened them away. After several attempts one crow jumped onto a branch of ripe berries and stood on the branch, holding it near the ground, while the other crows ate the ripe berries. This attempt worked well and soon other crows took their turn at standing on other branches so their friends could dine on the luscious fare.

I never did have a camera ready to record events such as these.

BAND CONCERTS

On Wednesday nights during the summer we would often go to Dike, a nearby town of about 300 souls, for the band concerts. The citizens of Dike had formed a band as early as 1900, when the town was incorporated. They must have been fairly good as they had been written up in both the Cedar Falls and Waterloo newspapers.

To make a stage for a concert, the band brought in a hay rack from a nearby farm, strung a light bulb on a pole on each of the four corners of the hay rack and put folding chairs on this platform where the band members sat and played. Some of the audience sat on the grass in fair weather, but many of those who had driven in to town remained in their cars with the windows rolled down.

Dike was a small town and there were not too many members in the band. Walt Jacobsen played the accordion. Hans Petersen and Albert Knudsen played trumpets, but I don't remember whom the drummer was. There was probably a fiddler in the group, too. After the band played a piece the audience seated on the grass would applaud in the usual way, but the people sitting in cars would toot their horns in appreciation. It made a very raucous noise. Some people sat on wooden benches in front of the nearby stores. Benches were made from a wide plank for a seat nailed to two end pieces for legs and braced across underneath.

After the band was through playing their concert, which was not very long, the audience walked to the corner drug store for a nickel ice cream cone.

These were the days before television and air conditioning. Radios were few, and the programming was not very entertaining. On hot summer nights it was a good pastime to go to town and hear the band, and it was fun to get away from the farm. It was an opportunity to see and talk with people we didn't usually see while on the farm.

I don't recall if the band was very good or not, but it was great entertainment and much good conversation. We knew all the audience members. No one was a stranger. The band enjoyed the opportunity to perform, the audience was very forgiving, and we all appreciated their efforts. It was an enjoyable event when the pace of life was slower than now. More than anything it brought all of us closer together in the tapestry of life.

ENTERTAINMENT

1. May Baskets

Cash money was scarce during those Depression Years. We could not afford to buy anything beyond the bare necessities, and sometimes not even that. So what was there for us to do for entertainment? We were fortunate. We learned to be creative in searching for ways to entertain ourselves.

There were five families in our neighborhood that thought up the idea of hanging May Baskets. We would make it more interesting if four of the five families would plot which night they would gather to hang baskets at the fifth farm house.

There was much planning and secret plotting to carry out the plot. Each household brought out sheets of tissue paper or other suitable paper and began making baskets. There was much laughing and joking as plans moved on.

The game would need to last all through the month of May. This is how it was done:

Someone would telephone one of the other families and make plans for an evening of fun and mischief. The family selected to receive the May Baskets would not know or even suspect the time the other players had chosen to make their surprise visit. Of course, it had to be done after dark. Then, by telephone or secret meetings in neighbors' yards, the plot was completed. It was decided that the four families would quietly park their cars at a distance from the fifth family's farm so there would be no suspicion of the planned evening. So with freshly baked cakes and May Baskets in hand we drove off. Lights had to be turned off some distance away from the selected farm.

Prowling around in a farmyard after dark made the game more interesting. We had all lived around farm machinery and small buildings enough to know the hazards of doing this foolish game. We were out for a good time. That was all that really mattered.

Carefully and quietly someone in the group would place a May Basket on the front porch of the suspecting family. Then he or she would knock very loudly on the front door and shout, "May basket!" He or she, too, then needed to find a hiding place.

Quietly and cautiously everyone else was hidden by now. The host and hostess were obligated to find each one of us. We hid behind trees and buildings. Seldom did we hide inside any of the buildings.

When everyone had been found, we were invited into the house carrying the treats we would share around the coffee table. There was lots of laughing and good conversation to complete the evening.

Many members of the group were very creative in making their baskets. Some used colored tissue paper ranging in colors from pink, to yellow, to green and blue. Following are the directions for making a basket that resembled a paper umbrella:

Directions for one basket:

1. Roll an old newspaper into a tight cylinder not more than ½-inch across. Wrap this with colored tissue paper. Next, cut two 18-inch squares of colored tissue paper. Fold in half, and then in half again. With scissors fringe the cut edges of the squares.

2. Unfold the tissue paper, then place one end of the cylinder into the center of the square. Bring each corner of the square up to a point on the cylinder. When the basket is completed it resembles an umbrella.

All of this preparation could be time consuming, but we had lots of time to do things. It was a simple and an entertaining thing for grown adults to do.

Other baskets were made from construction paper folded into boxes, trimmed, with a handle added.

2. Birthdays

Birthdays were more of a family reunion in my husband's family. There were several uncles and aunts, and many cousins.

Summertime birthday parties were fun because people could sit outside in the evenings and enjoy visiting. Down on the farm, a light cord was strung out onto the lawn so that visitors could see to sit outside after dark.

It was with much anticipation that Grandmother watched the country road at the end of the long lane leading to the farm, to see who would come for her birthday. The house was ready, the lawn and yard were combed to perfection, and the big coffee pot was already filled for the occasion.

Soon, whole families arrived. The women were dressed in their brightest cotton dresses. The men likewise wore clean overalls and shirts for the occasion.

The men gathered out on the lawn where they sat in a circle of folding chairs. Sometimes a box of cigars was shared among the men. The sweet, pungent smell of cigar smoke wafted across the yard. Everyone was content.

Discussions ran the gamut from farm prices, to the weather, to who had gotten a piece of new machinery and the merits thereof, to politics and jokes. There was a wonderful bonding of the entire group as they discussed the pros and the cons of each subject. They shared their varying experiences, opinions and viewpoints of each topic with much sincerity.

The women stayed in the house, as it would not be too long before they would begin making sandwiches. They would cover the bread with butter and a variety of cold meats and cheese. These were arranged on large plates and placed on the dining table.

There were a variety of cakes to be cut. These often brought on a discussion of recipes and an exchange of each. A stack of trays was set at one end of the table.

Two of the aunts each had a dozen oblong rectangular trays, which they proudly shared for parties. However, there was always a bit of discussion after the party to make sure that each of the two got their own trays back. One set was carefully marked on the bottom of each tray with a red dot of nail polish.

When the coffee was boiled on the cook stove and the homemade root beer was brought up from the cellar, the men were summoned to come in and fill their trays. The women watched the plates of food on the table so that they were always filled.

When the men were served then the women took their turns at the festive table.

What was significant about these events was how everyone came together to visit, criticize, discuss or otherwise keep a flow of conversation continually going.

When everyone had eaten their fill of sandwiches, cake and coffee, the group left for their homes talking about when it would be birthday time again.

3 Radios

My first memory of a radio was in the 1920's when the entire neighborhood was invited to gather at the country school for a chance to see and hear this marvelous new invention.

A wire had been strung from a telephone pole out on the road to the schoolhouse, then fed through one of the windows and connected to the radio. That was the aerial.

It was a rainy night with a steady downpour of rain outside, but that did not stop us from coming. We were told that there were three possible radio stations that would be in our range. Those stations were in Pittsburgh, Chicago, and Denver. These cities were all a great distance from central Iowa.

That evening the reception was so scratchy that it was difficult to determine what was being presented. We listened with hushed amazement to the static and muffled sound for a while and then went home, somewhat disappointed.

Once we visited Dad's cousin, Herman Henningsen, who had a radio with a large speaker horn attached to produce a bigger sound. It was mounted to the top of the wooden box containing the radio works. Otherwise, the cousin would have to listen with earphones.

By turning various knobs he was able to get sound from it. The reception was better at varying times of the day, nighttime being the best.

A few years went by, and then my brother was making crystal sets in cigar boxes. He was able to pick up distant stations. He moved a steel point from place to place on a coil of wire in the crystal set until he could hear a station. He did this for several years.

It was not until after World War II that we owned a radio. It was a large upright cabinet that stood on the floor. There were several dials on its front. We often listened to "Amos and Andy", a popular program at that time. Our very young children were convinced that there were tiny people inside the set doing the talking.

I remember one clear summer night when the moon was full that I stood quietly out in the farmyard with my parents. Overhead was a wire strung between the hog house and the barn that carried electricity for the lights. As we stood there we heard the faint sound of music coming from that wire. We heard the music only that one time.

Until that time the only news available was through the daily newspapers. Now with radio the world opened up for us. We could now listen to music, drama or news from places far away from home. Radio entertainment allowed us to "see" scenes and events in our mind's eye. They were far more detailed than similar scenes on early television. In those days our imagination was well developed at an early age.

SATURDAY NIGHT

Saturday night in the 1930's was the night of the week to which we looked forward all week long with great excitement. Freshly bathed and all dressed up in a clean print dress for me and clean bib overalls for my husband, the two of us loaded the 30-dozen egg case into the back of the car and drove off to town.

We parked the car close to the grocery store, unloaded the eggs and brought them in to the grocer. He took the eggs and set them in the back room of the store. Ten cents a dozen! We were thrilled to get the money.

I purchased the groceries I thought I would need for the coming week, packed the groceries into the now empty egg case, and accepted the rest of the money in change we had coming from the eggs. My husband was then able to buy a new blue chambray shirt or a new pair of overalls with the money we had gotten back. Many times we bought nothing.

The men liked to gather at the implement dealer's store, where they could hear the news of the week and pick up other information. A good hour or so was spent in renewing acquaintances and cautiously meeting newcomers. It was also a good place to admire the latest in farm equipment. It was always fun to dream of operating all these machines.

Women tended to gather at the dry goods stores or the 5- and 10-cent stores. Often they met neighbors or friends whom they had not seen for some time. The women, too, would admire the latest dress patterns and fabric selections. They, too, would dream of wearing the latest fashion wear.

There was a popcorn stand at the corner of Main and 4th Street. It was doing a good business at the rate of a nickel for a bag of hot buttered popcorn. We could afford this little pleasure.

Later in the evening when all shopping was finished we enjoyed going in to the brightly lit Greek candy kitchen. We walked past the long counter of glass covered with fine chocolates of every kind and even a few colored candies. We chose to go back and sit at one of the wire-legged ice cream tables with matching chairs, and place our order for a 25-cent banana split. Not only did we have ice cream, but for a whole five cents dropped into a slot on the player piano, we could enjoy fine music as we ate.

This story may seem strange in the 21st century with all the many things there are to do at home or in the bright lights of the city. These were different times. The myriad forms of entertainment that we are now able to enjoy were not available at all. On rare occasions a traveling entertainment would make an appearance, such as a circus or Sousa's band, but these cost money which we often did not have.

These Saturday night excursions were a welcome change from the otherwise quiet of the farm. What a wonderful way to spend a Saturday night in town.

Funerals were very much a part of our lives. They were sad occasions, but life is little without some humor. The following fictional conversation involves the local busybodies who attend almost every funeral.

FUNERAL HOME

It was a warm sunny afternoon in the Midwest. The good citizens of this community lived their modest lives being the good neighbors that people were in rural areas such as in this small town. People shopped on Saturdays, went to church on Sunday mornings, rested and visited Sunday afternoon and tended to their work the rest of the week. When the daily newspaper was dropped in the mailbox, husbands sat back and read the news. Most news happened elsewhere. So there was no need to get too excited about what was happening in the other parts of the country, or the world for that matter. Most people referred to it as a 'decent place to live and bring up kids.'

Social events were observed with graduations, weddings, funerals and birthdays. That was about the most excitement that ever happened around there. The saying went that "people pulled together whenever needed."

But on this particular day people were gathering to mourn the accidental death of one of their good citizens. By twos and in threes, friends stepped softly into the local funeral parlor. The nondescript fragrance of flowers filled the room. Wreaths on wire stands and huge baskets of floral arrangements filled the entire area around the casket. Through the inadequate speakers a gloomy arrangement and a recording of "Rock of Ages" and "Abide With Me" wafted among the guests in every room. The recording had been played far too many times, and the mighty Wurlitzer had lost its luster.

In the dimly lit room a dark red mahogany casket rested on a shiny metal stand. Inside the coffin lined with white shiny satin lay the body of a man well known in the community. His hands were neatly folded across his chest in the customary manner. He was laid out, as they say, in a fine suit of clothes, a white shirt and a silk tie. He was better known wearing work clothes than he was dressed in such a fine manner. His closed eyes and waxy face betrayed his usual happy laughing grin. Over half of the casket was covered with a blanket of flowers.

Two women, in their late sixties came in arm in arm quietly towards the casket and stood there, quietly assessing the entire situation. Each clutched a white linen handkerchief tightly in one hand. Their faces were equally somber as they dabbed at their eyes as they "paid their respects."

One woman whispered to the other after pausing to "have a good look" at the body. "He sure looks natural." she said.

After a sigh the other one said, "They sure did a good job on him. It's hard to believe he's really gone."

Back and forth the whispered conversation continued.

"I can't believe it really happened. I think it's just terrible the way things went."

"You'd think they could have done something."

"He's going to be missed all right."

"You could always count on him when you needed something."

"I wonder how that poor wife of his is going to get along? There's still one or two of his kids living at home. I wonder if he had laid away much money and all."

"Well, there's never enough, you know."

"It's sure too bad."

"I wonder what she's going to do now that he's gone. Maybe she'll have to sell the place."

"Ya, you never know when these things are going to happen. You can be tending to your business one day and the next thing you know you're gone. Just like that. Like this man, for instance. He worked every day of his life. Never drank or got into any real kind of trouble of any kind that I know of."

"Well, there was this one time when something really did happen. You know I really shouldn't say it, but it's true. Now don't repeat a word to anyone will you?"

"Oh, no, I won't breathe it to a soul."

"Well, there was that one time many years ago. I don't remember just when or what year it was. It was before he got married. Well, oh I really shouldn't say anything at all. Him being dead now and all. Let's just forget it."

"Please, tell me. What did happen? I don't know a thing about it."

"Well, there was these two young guys, barely dry behind the ears. Well, it was Saturday night. Everyone you knew was in town. It was hot like today. People were talking and wiping the sweat off their faces. Everybody was having a good time."

"Well, here comes these two young squirts driving that old Model A. The one laying right here in front of you and another guy. And I'll tell you right now that other guy wasn't worth nothing. You could tell the minute you laid eyes on him, you knew right then he'd never amount to a hill of beans. And he sure didn't."

"Well, they were driving back and forth up and down Main Street honking their horn and then they'd gun the engine and pop the exhaust. Not this guy here, but the other one riding along with his one leg hanging out over the door of the car and an empty glass booze bottle rolling down the street behind them. First thing you know they came speeding right up to the end of the street and out of town they went as fast as the old car would go. The next thing we knew, fire bells ringing and we knew something was wrong. We all just stood there looking at each other and we didn't know what to do."

"No-o-o-o-o!"

"Yes—oh, I really mustn't say anything at all. It's just too terrible to even talk about."

Stepping up behind the two women a man in a business suit tapped the two women lightly on their shoulders and asked them to please step aside. There were other people who wanted to "pay their respects:"

By that time several members of the family had gathered in the large room. Handkerchiefs were dabbing at noses. A few coughed quietly. People stood in small groups whispering quietly to each other. The room was soon crowded with friends and neighbors. Everyone was shaking hands and nodding their heads. No one really knew what to say. Men put their hands in their pockets and women looked for more tissues in their hand bags.

The two women who had been busily talking to each other, signed the book and moved towards the door.

"It sure feels good to get out in the air."

"I'll finish the story some other time. I don't think I should tell it now. Besides that happened a long time ago. Let's go home."

ARMISTICE DAY—NOVEMBER 11, 1940

It was another beautiful warm day, completely out of character for the season. It had been like that all fall. Even the apple trees, which had already shed their leaves and gone dormant for the winter season, were beginning to bud again.

Harold and I, with our six-month-old baby girl, were living on one of the two Walter's farms adjacent to Grandfather Petersen's (Harold's father) farm. This day was my 26th birthday, and I was trying to get the house ready for my birthday party that evening.

Towards noon on Nov. 11 the sky began to turn gray, and then the sky became darker. The wind suddenly changed. The warm southerly wind began blowing cold out of the northwest. Harold's first thought was there must be some kind of a storm coming and that the herd of cattle he had out on the pasture on the far west end of the farm should be brought home to the farmyard.

Then there was a burst cold of wind and the sky got even darker. Harold, the hired man and Grandfather, who was visiting there at the time, jumped into our old truck and headed across the fields to bring the cattle in from the far pasture. The pasture was almost a mile away bordering the mile road to the west. The men got out of the truck shouting and waving their arms to get the herd to turn towards home. Instinctively, the cattle bunched up with their heads down in an effort to keep the herd warm as they normally did when there was a storm. The men worked and worked, shouting and running back and forth trying to get the stubborn cattle moving towards home. They pushed and they prodded the reluctant beasts to get them moving towards the farm buildings and shelter. Finally, and with much bellowing, they slowly began to move.

Now it was beginning to snow a little. Between the farm buildings and the pasture there was a small plank bridge over a narrow creek that both the cattle and truck were to walk and drive over. That didn't help the situation. After what seemed like a very long time, as the wind was blowing harder and harder, the cattle finally crossed the bridge, followed by the truck, and got back into the yard next to the barn and to safety. Everyone knew a storm was brewing. Grandfather took the truck and drove to his home as fast as he could.

Meanwhile, I kept looking out the kitchen window to see if they were coming safely home from the pasture. By now I knew a big storm was coming, and I was concerned that they be home soon. My birthday party plans were soon far from my mind.

It began to snow very hard and the wind blew even harder. Our house had no back porch. When we opened the kitchen door we were outside, so it was not unusual for us to leave our overshoes outside whenever we could. My overshoes were in the grass just beyond the cement steps. This storm brought so much snow and left such huge drifts that I didn't find those overshoes until the following spring when the snow finally melted. Harold did have to dig his way through the deep drifts to the barn to do the chores twice daily. Because of the warm fall and severe winter, all of the apple trees died and had to be cut down the following summer.

November 12, 1940

Of course there was no birthday party that evening. No one traveled for days. Most of the time we three just sat in the house keeping warm next to the stove and listening to the howling wind outside. The November 11 storm became legend in the upper Midwest. We were fortunate to have survived, with livestock and family secure.

WWII MEMORIES

World War II brought many adjustments from the pre-war years of the 1920's and 1930's in the way we lived and those items for which we yearned. In the 1920's, after World War I, our parents enjoyed prosperous years of farming. We could afford the occasional comforts and even luxuries of life. With the Great Depression of the 1930's, our families had nothing. Even on the farm where we could raise our own food we struggled to put meals on the table regularly. During the time in these years when my family had to move off the farm to live in a rented housein town we frequently went hungry at mealtime and cold in winter time.

When my husband and I married in the late '30's we were just coming out of the depression years. There was opportunity to make a living while farming. World War II brought us back to the years of the depression in a sense. We had to "make do" without many things, or substitute as best we could. The war was very demanding. Our country became the source of food and clothing for much of the world. We raised a family of four children, farmed without much needed help and listened anxiously to the daily war news. It all changed us in one way or another.

"War brides" who wanted white wedding gowns went to army surplus stores and, when they could be found, bought nylon parachutes from which they cut and sewed wedding gowns.

Sugar rationing was severe and made cooking and baking much more difficult. Men who had been working all day in the fields had big appetites when they came in for meals. They were accustomed to having a hearty piece of pie for dessert regularly. Jams and jellies were impossible to make when sugar was so scarce. There were ways we could use corn syrup for sweetening but the results were not the same. Desserts became a very special treat, or they became disappointing. Sugar was available on the Black Market if one knew where to go and whom to contact, but buying on like that was expensive and unpatriotic.

We received stamps for gasoline rationing. Farmers were allotted separate fuel to run farm machinery because they were raising food to feed soldiers as well as the people on the home front. This fuel had to be kept separate from that used in automobiles. We were required to keep careful records, and these were checked from time to time.

Sheer stockings were in high demand and not often available. When women got word that a shipment of rayon hose had arrived in certain department stores, they quickly drove to town where they stood in line to buy at least one pair. In those days there was a seam down the back of the stocking which we watched carefully to keep them straight. If there were a small snag, we would painstakingly pull the fine threads to the inside. When stockings were not available, some women took to drawing the seams on the backs of their legs to imitate sheer stockings.

When I was pregnant I craved chewing gum, but it was not available.

On the farm, my husband often began work at 4:00 A.M. and during the harvest seasons often worked until 11:00 at night. The usually available hired men had been sent off to fight in the war. Everyone got very tired and worn out from the stress of the work and the news of all the men killed overseas. Men at home anxiously wondered if they would be called next to serve in the army.

Nothing was thrown away. Even junk was carefully collected, and we reused everything we could. Scrap iron in any form became valuable to the war effort. The machines of war required lots of iron. Old farm machinery, old automobiles, old fence wire, tin cans and anything else we could find was gathered together. From time to time a truck came by to load up the scrap metal and haul it away.

World War II involved everyone in the nation. We all made sacrifices for the combined war effort. Since we had just emerged from the Great Depression of the 1930's, it was relatively easy to do. Our farmers did their work very well and selflessly as they fed and clothed much of the world in those years. We as a country have not made such selfless efforts during any armed conflict since.

RAILROAD FAIR

When our oldest children were very small, Harold, my husband, shipped two truckloads of beef cattle to the stockyards Chicago. While he was there he heard about the Railroad Fair and went to see it. The fair was held by the shore of Lake Michigan. He had been so impressed that when he came home he sent the two kids and me to Chicago via the Illinois Central train. The train was very convenient since we were able to board it at the station in Cedar Falls and step off the train at the Union Depot in downtown Chicago. In Chicago we had a room at the old Conrad Hilton hotel, which was very near the railroad station, and then we must have taken a taxi or streetcar to the railroad event.

The railroad fair was a massive effort. There were many displays of the actual engines and cars of railroad history in the United States.

All of the cars and locomotives in the pageant and on display were antiques – the real items. The largest steam locomotive ever built was on display. Abraham Lincoln's funeral train was on display. The steam engine that held the world speed record was also there. The "Tom Thumb", with its open cars, had been restored just for this event. Locomotives from the Civil War were on display. There were many other locomotives and train cars also. The children and I stood in long lines waiting to see some of the pieces on display.

Later we attended a pageant or program that told the history of the settlement of America and how the railroads were a part of that history. It was the highlight of the fair. Actors reenacted the various events such as driving the golden spike in a variety of tableaus. Even a demonstration of hand-pumped fire brigades being replaced by steam powered pumpers was in the show. We sat in raised seating like bleachers facing Lake Michigan and listened and watched the panorama unfold before us. During the telling of the story, many of these trains rolled across the "stage" under their own power. The stage was a large flat area flanked by large panels on either side. There were several sets of rails on the stage. Even the earliest engines in American history ran under their own power in the tableau. It was a remarkable event. Moving all of these huge pieces on and off the stage was a massive effort of coordination and required a lot of rail sidings off stage.

After the show we took the train home again. It truly was a remarkable event likely to never be seen again.

RAISING CHILDREN

Those readers who are parents know of the many adventures involved in raising children. I am sure you could easily write your own collection of stories, and perhaps you should so that you, too, might remember those unique episodes of life. These stories of happenings that took place in our life are only a few of many, most now long forgotten.

When our son was 16 months old he had a life threatening event. I was doing the family washing on the back porch. Our son was hungry and I gave him a graham cracker which I assumed was not harmful. A piece of cracker lodged in his windpipe. I saw him choking and picked him up by the legs and shook him violently all the time praying to God that his life would be spared.

He then was able to get just a little air into his lungs. We rushed him to the hospital in Cedar Falls where the doctors said there was nothing they could do for him. His lungs would have to be pumped and that had to be done at the University hospital in Iowa City. In our rush we were able to get a few extra fuel stamps. By that time Pete Jensen, a friend in the county sheriff's office, heard of our plight and the state patrol waved us by as we hurried the almost 90 miles to Iowa City. When we arrived at the hospital the doctors refused to do anything until Harold laid cash in front of them. We then went on to the next step where again Harold had to put down cash if we wanted help. All this time I was holding a limp body wondering if he was going to live or die.

Our son's lungs were pumped and he was placed in a crib covered with sheets and a steamer was set up sending steam into this tent. Antibiotics, namely penicillin had not been discovered yet.

I sat beside our son's crib for three days, and on the third day having not heard anything from him all that time he sat up in bed, pulled the sheets apart, looked at me and said, "Hoo, hoo." That was the best sound I could ever hear. Soon thereafter, Harold came after us as he had had to go home to tend to the farming. It was a very happy trip to know we were all going home again.

Again when our son was six months old he got the Whooping Cough. I think he contacted a germ one day when we were in Cedar Falls as I heard another child coughing while there. Again, there were no antibiotics. All summer long we kept him in bed with us because every time he coughed I had to hold his stomach in to keep him from tearing the inside of his abdomen. In fact, when I was very tired it was easiest to let him lie across my stomach so I would awaken whenever he started coughing.

342

This farm where we lived at that time had no septic system, which was common in those days. The drain pipe from the kitchen seeped through the ground just outside the back door of the house. Our children both got impetigo on their skin from the drainage water just outside our kitchen. That meant more trips to the doctor.

There were some good things to remember from the time we lived on that farm. Harold and I took our children to Waterloo about four o'clock one morning to watch the Ringling Bros. & Barnum & Bailey's Circus unload from their train, parade to the vacant ground and set up the big top with the use of elephants. That is another event that today's children will never see.

Our daughter attended Greeley School P. S. #8, a rural school west of Cedar Falls. One evening in the late 1940's we were there for a program. The teacher had a tape recorder which we saw and took turns using for the first time. We each had a turn taping our voices and listening to the recording. It was a marvelous device, and really the first venture into the world of electronic toys.

I attended a Ladies Aid meeting at the Rasmussen's farm just up the hill about a quarter mile from the schoolhouse. Our son was three and a half years old and he was attending the meeting with me. While we women were standing for prayer, he quietly slipped away from me and went down to the school and walked inside where our daughter was in class.

We held a birthday party for our daughter one year which was done in a circus theme. Harold and I made a tent over the dining table with red and white striped fabric built over the top of the table to look like a tent. I baked animal cookies and had them setting around a cake in the center to look like a Merry-go-round. We used a Christmas tree holder to hold up the center pole of the tent.

Our son's birthday was in January, the middle of the winter. Harold took the children for a ride on a bob sled pulled by a team of horses. The children were bundled up and didn't mind the cold. Even then, in the late 1940's the bobsled was unique to the children. They had a great time.

343

Our twin daughters were born while we lived there. While waiting in bed for about two months before they were born our son and I built several things with Tinker Toys. We enjoyed that.

One day, our oldest daughter was carrying a glass Crisco jar. She dropped it and cut her buttocks badly and we took her to the doctor for that. A few stitches later all was well. At an early age, our twin daughters got into the mouse poison. I watched anxiously to see if I really needed to take them to the doctor. I had talked to the doctor over the phone about the situation. Apparently no harm ensued, as they are alive and well today.

The kids had a lamb named George. George was a survivor after being born on a very cold night, brought into the house and kept warm by the cook stove. We had guests that evening for a card party. While the card party was going on the lamb got warmed up and began bleating. That lamb became a bottle baby and later a nuisance. He was constantly at the back door wanting to get in and dropping the little pebbles of manure just outside the back door. Harold finally got so disgusted with him after he grew up and he went to market one day. I presume someone enjoyed George as lamb chops.

Being invited to the Black Hawk County sheriff's residence for a meal was a highlight. This was a large building next to the courthouse. The front part of the building was a residence and had a façade of a very lovely home. In the back part of the building was the jail, full of iron bars, cells and sometimes a few prisoners. Pete, the sherrif, and Karen lived there and we had the best meals there. The children had more fun playing in that house. The kids were into doing skits and collecting money for the shows. I think one of our daughters still has the handkerchief with the money they collected for the show.

After the war in 1947 Grandmother and Grandfather Petersen wanted to visit Grandfather's uncle Hans Lausen who lived forty miles east of Calgary, Canada. An account of Hans Lausen's early settlement in Canada can be found in the book named ON THE BOW.

With a one-wheel trailer behind the car, Harold, two children and the grandparents and I drove off towards Canada via Winnipeg. It was in Winnipeg I bought the little wheel I use for cutting strips for pies. From Winnipeg we drove on graveled highways all the way across Canada. We ate at several Chinese restaurants as I remember.

We arrived at a relative's farm out on a barren prairie. The wheat fields were ready for harvest. There was irrigation and so we saw and ate spectacularly large vegetables. Cabbage heads were immense in size. We said it wouldn't do to tell about it when we got home as no one would believe us. But the soil was new and grew wonderful crops.

Harold, the kids, and I drove on to the mountains as Grandmother's heart would not be able to take the altitude. We went to Banff, saw a movie star there, went on to Jasper National Park, saw railroad tunnels through the mountain where we saw the mighty steam locomotive coming out of a tunnel as the caboose was just going into the tunnel some ways below. It was a good trip. Our two children sang SIOUX CITY SUE all the way to and from Canada.

When we lived on Scotch Ridge Road the children went to a country school where a Mrs. Hastie, a very jolly soul, was teaching. We were a Danish family living in a solid Scottish neighborhood. The people were kind but nevertheless we really felt like outsiders. It was our first home outside the Danish community of our ancestors.

The most fun the family had while living on Scotch Ridge was going to Indianola on Saturday nights. We drove our car to town and parked just off the town square. With agreement of when and where to meet again, we all did a lot of shopping and talking as we went our separate ways. The kids were free to walk around the town square, going in and out of shops freely and when the shopping was done we went to the A & W for those good hamburgers and cold root beer. We did not have to worry about our children that someone might do them harm.

One day the twins watched a red fox jumping in the grass out in the pasture. They were disappointed as they watched because the fox was not wearing colorful jackets as foxes do in story books.

Raising children brings both pain and joy. No matter the era, some things seem to remain the same. These tales are only a sample of all that has happened. Your tales will be much the same, and no doubt very entertaining.

FAMILY PET TALES

All of us remember our pets, past and present, for the joy of having them, for the grief they caused us at various times, for the love they gave back to us, for the sorrow at their death and for the friends they were to each of us.

These are a few things that have come to my mind. You will have many more.

For a time, our kids had a green parakeet which all of us adored. He was very noisy at times but that was OK. One day the piano tuner came and the cage was sitting nearby. The piano tuner proceeded to move up the scale on the piano keys as he worked along. The parakeet attempted to follow the notes. As the notes got higher and higher, the parakeet was jumping from one foot to the other attempting to reach the high notes.

At another time, the kids had a white rabbit. It was a real beauty. One night a pack of dogs tore the cage open and killed the rabbit. This caused great sorrow of course, so a funeral ceremony of sorts was prepared. The bunny was buried in a white shoebox out in the garden.

Lassie was a very good family dog, born on our farm. She was very affectionate and served as a sort of guard dog. I can't tell all the stories about Lassie, but there was the time when we lived on a farm, we raised a few turkeys. Lassie took it upon herself to guard those birds. The turkeys would graze along the highway and Lassie stayed right beside them. One day a motorist stopped, and probably considered picking up one of the birds. Lassie would not allow it and the motorist drove on.

For a time my husband and I kept a full-grown Doberman Pincher dog as a favor to a relative. He loved the open yard and fields, and loved to chase small animals. He chased after a jack rabbit one day, and was gaining on the speedy critter. Just as he was about to clutch the rabbit in his jaws, the rabbit ran through a small opening in the wire fence. The dog did not see the fence and hit it full tilt. He was dazed for some time, but it did not deter his interest.

One day he chased a gopher to its hole in our lawn. The dog began digging after the gopher mid morning and did not give up until the afternoon. It took four wheelbarrows full of dirt to refill the hole. I don't think he found the gopher.

The cats learned to tease the dog unmercifully. They knew how far from safety they could stretch out in the sun. If the dog gave chase, they would quickly duck into a hole in the barn wall or climb a nearby tree. If in the tree, they would only climb a few inches higher on the trunk than the excited dog could possibly reach. Try as he might, the dog never did reach the cat.

One time when our son and his family came to visit us, they brought along their pet dog, Hansel, a dog about the size of a German Shepherd. Our white cat, TC, was not aware of Hansel's arrival. TC was in the garage, which was piled high with a variety of lumber. When our son opened the door, Hansel bolted ahead into the garage. When Hansel spied TC and TC saw the dog, a great chase began. TC, in desperation, scrambled over the stacks of boards trying to escape as Hansel gave chase. TC somehow found his footing and flew all around the walls of the garage, sending everything to the floor that was in his path in an awful, noisy clatter. Hansel cheerfully and enthusiastically gave chase after his "new-found" friend! How can we ever forget that mad race?

There is no end of the things to tell about Talcott, or TC as we like to call him. He could get into more scrapes and come out alive. One time he must have gotten into a scrap with a raccoon, as he returned all muddied and bloodied with a torn ear and missing patches of fur. I set him in a laundry tub downstairs and he thankfully let me bathe him. He came out of that OK, too.

Then there was the time when our daughter kept TC at her apartment in the Twin Cities. When she put him on a leash outdoors he would just stand there straining himself at the end of the leash.

Then one time he got away, and we all mourned his loss. You would think he was one of the family, as we all felt so badly at his loss. Our daughter advertised the missing cat in the papers, and we called rescue leagues, but it was no use. He was gone. Then one day we got a call from someone on the other side of the Mississippi river several miles away. They had seen a white cat living in a neighbor's garage. It was a rainy foggy night when we drove to the people's house to lay claim to our cat. He had gained nearly two pounds and was used to drinking whipping cream. There was great joy when he returned.

Rover, our pet dog of unknown lineage, and TC did all sorts of things to write about. We were living on a farm, when Rover developed a sore right foot that was so bad he could hardly walk on it. Our daughter was there, and called the vet on a Saturday forenoon to check Rover's foot.

We drove to the vet's office. Rover, our daughter and I got out of the car and walked Rover to the vet's office. Rover walked without any problem. The vet asked why we had brought him in as there was nothing wrong with his foot. We were embarrassed when we found that Rover just wanted the attention. There was nothing wrong with him. He just liked to get a ride in the car.

On an earlier farm (we rented several around the Midwest), we had bottle-fed a new lamb that was rejected by its mother. We kept it next to the cook stove for warmth. One night, when we had a card party, the lamb began bleating in a loud voice surprising everyone. The lamb grew quickly. Since it had bonded to the kids, the lamb preferred sitting just outside the back door bleating for attention. As lambs do, he left a collection little black dots of manure on the step until it was hard to keep from stepping on them. One day Harold had enough. He picked up the lamb, put it in the truck and hauled it off to Waterloo to the slaughterhouse. That was the end of the lamb business for us.

Pets of all types were always part of our life. They were fun and they were frustrating, not to mention expensive at times. New puppies and kittens were a joy. We mourned each of them when they were killed, or when they died after a long life. But we always enjoyed having them with us.

"...'TIL DEATH DO US PART."

The above words are so casually spoken and accepted during the marriage vows when we are young and don't think of such things. But then when death separates us the impact is too much to assimilate or even try to absorb. It is cruelty at its worst. To be suddenly cut off from love and affection for each other is cruel. And there are no real solutions. So we live day by day in a sort of vacuum trying to project an image of happiness and satisfaction for what we have and enjoy. The loss of a lifelong friend and lover is a very sad situation.

Visualize a road that never ends. When a lifelong partner has died, the surviving partner has to keep plodding down that now lonesome road day in and day out. Things never seem to get better.

I have been alone five years now and I miss my husband Harold more than ever. Whenever I am with any group of friends or family there is no one there to afterwards share any of the fun and laughter that come so easily for others.

For example, when I am on a plane the tears come so easily. There is no one to share the small talk of events just enjoyed while being with my daughter and son-in-law. There is no one to hold my hands in his warm hands as we fly along over the clouds.

Again, I go out to eat with the family. There is no close partner sitting beside me at the table. There is no one like that with which to share small talk or even to sample each other's food. There is little joy or satisfaction in watching the others across the table sharing their bits of conversation. No matter how much I enjoy the company of others, it's just not the same.

Harold, a few months
before he died

Now, when I attend an event, again there is the loneliness of not having someone with whom to share ideas, thoughts, or even the humorous situations that can appear. As much as I talk with people, there is no one with whom to share those quiet, sometimes intimate, conversations that husbands and wives do.

I go about day in and day out thinking of how I could have been a better wife or a better partner in different ways. Death has parted us and it is so unending.

I appreciate having a caring family, a good place to live, and I am provided with everything I need including many, many friends who keep in touch with me.

I have so much to be thankful for and I am thankful, but there is always that void of having a warm loving person with me sharing all the day to day events, and sometimes the disasters to share and work through together.

The faith of knowing that there is life after death is reassuring. I am happy that Harold is enjoying that peace. I believe that there is a day when we will see each other again in that peace that knows no end.

In the 1980's, in my early 70's, I had both knee joints replaced in a simultaneous surgery. The surgery was performed by a father/son team, and it took three years to convince the medical authorities that they were not being billed twice. This fictional account is based on my experience, and hopefully will encourage others to do difficult things with bravery.

OLAF

He and Stina had eaten supper early that evening and Olaf ambled back down to the barnyard to finish up some chores. Stina had watched him as he left the house and slowly walked the familiar grassy path to the barn. She carefully noted that Olaf wasn't walking as fast as he used to and that there was a noticeable limp to his stride.

It was a still beautiful evening. The wind barely turned the windmill wheel with its slight squeak at each turn. Maybe next year he could get up there and give it a greasing. The western sky was turning from light pink to a deeper rosy orange and that would finally turn purple as twilight moved on.

Olaf slid the big barn door shut, slipped the latch into the slot, and walked over to the nearby wooden barnyard gate. As he leaned over the top rail he hit his sore right knee on the board that braced the gate. The pain shot up through his whole body. Muttering a few choice, impolite words he rubbed his leg with one hand and clutched the gate post with the other gnarled hand. He'd just stand there a little while and it would go away.

Old Buster, his faithful black and white shepherd dog looked up at him sympathetically. 'It'll be all right in a few minutes,' he thought.

Well, anyway, the last bale of alfalfa hay was stacked away in the haymow. He was lucky to get the hay cut, baled, and put away in the barn without a drop of rain on it. 'Makes a man feel good,' he thought to himself. He stood there awhile thinking first about one thing and then another. It had been a very hot day and he was tired, sweaty, and ready to sit down and call it a day.

Olaf watched the cows switch their tails and shuffle their hooves to keep away the flies. Then slowly one by one they ambled off into the lush green pasture.

His lean body and slightly stooped shoulders perhaps leaned heavier than usual against the gate. The old gray barn cat brushed back and forth against Olaf's neatly patched overall legs. Buster spied the cat and gave chase nearly toppling Olaf who had relaxed against the gate to ease his discomfort. The cat scrambled to the top of the gray weathered wooden post and hissed furiously at the yapping dog below.

"Dat's enough, Buster. Leave the cat alone. We'll go back to the house and call it a good day"

Christina or 'Stina' as Olaf and the neighbors called her was a buxom, blue-eyed woman who was willing to do her share of the farm work and be a good helpmate. She was also known as a strong-willed person who could hold her own. Now beyond her youth as well, she sighed as she thought of what she needed to do for Olaf.

Many years ago, now, Olaf and Stina had been able to find a good fertile piece of farmland. It wasn't too many years before they were able to buy the land and call it their own. They had raised two boys, one named Svend and the other Chris. Chris, the oldest, was called to the War and never returned. He had been killed in action trying to help a comrade. They had buried him up in the cemetery behind the church. Svend graduated from the University and had a good business going in the Cities.

Olaf had always hoped that Chris or Svend would take over the farm when he and Stina could no longer farm the land. If only one of his boys had stuck around somewhere in the area. Then his son could help farm the land and then he and Stina could live in the house and stay on the farm. But it didn't work out that way.

Up in the house, Stina had washed and put away the supper dishes and had neatly stacked them in the cupboard. When the floor was swept she picked up the wet dishtowel. She took it with her out to the back porch, took hold of two corners and snapped it before hanging it on a short clothesline that stretched between two porch posts. With a handkerchief she kept in an apron pocket, she wiped the sweat from her face. Then, removing her apron, she hung it carefully over the porch railing.

Setting her plump self down on one of the rocking chairs, she began rocking back and forth. Stina had been thinking all day, and even for a few days before that, but tonight she was really going to say something to Olaf about her plans. She brushed a few strands of hair, neatly tucking them back of her ears. Her gray-white braid she had so deftly pinned up with a few hairpins this morning was beginning to come undone. Stina still liked to pin her hair up in braids each morning as she had done ever since she was a young girl. Drops of sweat stood again on her rosy cheeks. Clasping her hands together she began rocking faster and faster. Now and then she would glance in the direction of the barn to see if Olaf was coming.

"Olaf?" Stina always said his name with a big lilting upswing at the end. "Olaf? You comin' up soon? It'll be dark first thing you know."

"Ya, I'm comin';" Olaf called back. He sighed a big sigh as he wiped the sweat from his face with an already slightly damp red handkerchief. Ya, he was thankful for all that the land had given him and Stina in the long years they had lived here.

Olaf took off his old straw hat and fanned himself. There wasn't much of a breeze tonight. Already the mosquitoes were beginning to come. He swatted one on his left arm. 'Suppose I'd better go up to the house,' he thought.

Olaf had a cane there by the barn. He took his cane and began walking. Old Buster, the dog he'd had for many years got up and walked along side of his master. Olaf looked down at the dog, patted him on the head saying, "Good old dog. We gotta go in now." The dog wagged his tail and trotted right along with Olaf.

As she rocked back and forth, her hands twitching in her lap, she watched Olaf and Buster walking slowly towards the house. It seemed to Stina that he walked slower than usual. Of course, it had been a really hot day. Good for haymaking as they say. But yes, he was more stooped and limping some.

Now you wouldn't want to say that Stina was a schemer, but she had her ways with Olaf from time to time. And as a rule she was able to work things out. Stina had been mulling over a plan in her head for a few days. Tonight, yes, tonight she was going to do it. She would say it out plain to Olaf what she was going to do. So there, too!

Olaf pumped a cup of cold water from the hand pump that was close to the porch steps. "Ah, that was good." He carefully eased himself down on one of the steps, trying not to show the pain that shot through his knee. Stina noted the expression of pain that flashed across his face, but said nothing. Buster lay down close beside him panting as he stretched out on the green grass.

There was a long silence as both sat thinking, trying to feel cool in the warm summer air. Olaf had seen Stina's hands moving in that certain way which often meant something was brewing in her mind. Stina was waiting for the right moment to spring her idea on Olaf.

Stina looked at him and started out by saying, "Olaf, you been limping some lately, don't you tink?"

"Oh, I don't tink so. Vy?" came his slow cautious response. 'Oh, no. Not again,' Olaf thought to himself.

"Ya, you walk like you been hurtin' some in dose knees. Ain't dat right?"

"Dey don't hurt anymore dan dey ever did. So yust forget about it"

"Olaf, I tink you ought to see a doctor."

Olaf turned around and looked right at his wife and blurted out, "Vat in de vorld for? Stina you can get more ideas in your head. I am not going to see any old doctor. So now it's settled."

Stina, noting that her timing was slightly off, quickly changed the subject.

"Olaf, I made some nice oatmeal cookies this afternoon. Let's have a cup of coffee before we go to bed." And she got up from her comfortable rocker and opened the screen door, holding it until Olaf got there.

"Now ain't dis yust nice?" she said, trying to calm Olaf's irritation. "Ve can have a cup of coffee and yust enjoy ourselves. Don't you tink?" The screen door slammed shut behind Olaf when he came in trying not to limp. Yes, he was ready for coffee, but not for an argument.

Stina took the pot of coffee from the cook stove and poured a big mug of coffee for each of them.

Silently they sat there eating and drinking until the plate was half empty. Olaf tipped back on his chair and slipped his fingers between the straps of his well-worn overalls.

Now Stina would make her second try.

"You know your sister Lydia. She lives down der in the Cities. Vy don't I give her a ring in the morning and talk to her about you seeing a doctor?"

Olaf straightened his chair as the two front legs hit the floor with a thud. "Now don't let's get Lydia mixed up in dis. Besides, der's nothin' wrong with me. I ain't sick, and I don't vant to see any doctor and dat's dat."

"I heard somebody talkin' about how they can do somethin' for bad knees," Stina persisted.

"Oh, where'd you hear that?" Olaf countered.

"Well, I was talkin' to Catherine in town one day and she said that she knew someone who had even got a new knee and it turned out real good."

"Talk, talk, talk. I don't need nothin' done and dat's dat!"

"Well, I tink!" Stina retorted.

"Tink nothin'," Olaf snorted. "I don't want to hear anymore about it. Do you hear? I'm hot and I'm tired. I yust want to rest a little."

Stina knew the signals and knew it was better to quit the subject while she felt she was a little ahead.

With finality Olaf pushed his cup aside, got up from the table, and shuffled off to bed. It was hard for him to go up the stairs and Stina was well aware of it.

He dropped his overalls beside the bed. Having forgotten to take out a pair of pliers it made a loud thump when they hit the floor. His blue cotton shirt was hung on the end of the bed. Oh, for a good night's rest after a long hard day.

Stina cleared the table, made sure the screen doors were hooked tight for the night, and quietly went off to bed. She hoped that there would be a little cool breeze.

"Good night, Olaf."

There was only a grunt for an answer.

Early the next morning Olaf got up. He had had a restless sleep. His legs were hurting but he sure wasn't going to let Stina know how he felt.

Well, Stina hadn't lived with Olaf for nearly fifty years without knowing what was going through his mind more or less most of the time.

She listened as Olaf quietly got up, went downstairs and, without banging the screen door, he went out to do the morning chores. Buster was wagging his tail when Olaf came out and walked quietly beside his friend of many years. Occasionally the dog would lick Olaf's hand and Olaf patted his head in return.

It wasn't long before Stina was dressed and downstairs. She would make a quick phone call before starting breakfast.

Lydia, Olaf's sister, was awakened much too early. She hardly ever got up before eight o'clock.

Lydia answered in a sleepy tone of voice. "Hello?"

"Lydia, it's me, Stina. Lydia, I got to ask you something. Lydia, are you all right? You don't sound too good. Ya, I know it's kind of early, but we get up early out here in the country."

'Lydia, You know how it is with Olaf. Can't tell him anyting. Especially when it comes to taking care of himself. His knees are getting' awful bad, you know. I tink ve should do something about it. Vat do you tink?'

Stina paused for a moment, listening to Lydia yawn.

"I tink you should get ahold of a good doctor down dere. Somebody dat knows something about knees and all dat. I don't know anyting about getting' ahold of somebody down dere. Vould you help me?"

Without waiting for an answer, she continued, "I read in de paper one time how dey can fix up knees pretty good now. Maybe, you could find a doctor for Olaf and let me know. Ya? You tink you could do dat for me? You can call me back sometime and let me know. Now, you'll do dat, won't you?"

Stina made her good byes and quickly got at the breakfast. She'd make it especially good this morning.

Olaf figured by now Stina had forgotten her hair-brained idea about doctors and all. He finished the chores and went back to the house, where he could smell the delicious breakfast. He washed his hands at the wash basin, and sat down carefully at the table.

There wasn't anything said about a phone call or anything else for that matter. "Looks like another nice day, ya?" Stina ventured.

"Looks like it. Maybe I'll go out and look at the fence on the back forty today," was all that Olaf volunteered to talk about.

Well, the day wore on and Lydia didn't call back. It wasn't until afternoon of the next day that the phone rang and Stina raced to pick up the receiver.

"Hello, oh is dat you Lydia. Vat did you find out? Did you find someone? Did you have any trouble finding someone?"

The questions came in an excited rush, and Lydia was having a hard time getting a word in edgewise.

"Stina, I made an appointment for you. Two weeks from Thursday the nineteenth. I hope that works out for you folks. It was the soonest I could get him in," Lydia replied.

"Vell, now I tink ve can vork dat out real good. I von't say anyting to him right away. Kind of surprise him you know?" Stina responded gratefully.

"Dat's awful nice of you to do dat for us. Tanks, I'll bring you something from da farm. And you know I'm no good at driving in de city. Maybe it's alright if ve come to your house first and den you could help us find the doctor's office?"

Well, Stina and Lydia visited a while longer. It would now be up to Stina to convince Olaf he needed to see the doctor.

Days went by and nothing was said about old knees, doctors, or anything that related to any medical care. On rainy days Olaf took time to sit in town at the local implement store and visit with his neighbors. Olaf was well liked in the community. Those who knew him always considered him honest and dependable. He could be counted on if someone needed advice or help.

Now the two weeks were going by quickly. How would Stina approach the subject again?

One day while she and Olaf were sitting at the dinner table Stina casually said, "Your sister Lydia called."

"Oh, what'd she want?" Olaf asked innocently.

Stina blurted out, "She has made an appointment with a doctor for you."

Olaf let out a groan.

"Now vait yust a minute." Stina quickly said, noting his discomfort. "Lydia said she has found a good doctor that can see you day after tomorrow. So dat's dat." Stina wiped her face. 'What was going to happen next,' she thought.

Olaf jumped up from his chair and shouted, "I'm not going to see any doctor. Butchers all of dem. I don't vant anyone to touch me."

The rest of the day, and all of the next, passed in chilly silence between them. An occasional glance or sigh tested the quiet evenings.

Thursday morning arrived bright and sunny. Olaf came down stairs reluctantly dressed in a clean and freshly starched shirt, his good suit pants, and shoes sparkling black. He slid into the easy chair next to the radio, already resigned to endure this unpleasant trial.

Stina was rushing around like a chicken with its head cut off. Fresh eggs from the henhouse were packed away in a basket, as well as a jar of fresh cucumber pickles wrapped in newspaper to keep the jar from breaking, and a pint of fresh cream. Lydia would be well rewarded for her trouble.

She had put on her best dress 'cause she was going to the City and you had to dress up to go there. 'They're all so fancy down there', she thought. Then she hustled Olaf and herself out to the old Buick that was parked in the shed next to the barn.

"I'd better drive." She said. "You're too nervous to get behind the wheel."

With a lurching start she backed the car out of the shed, turned it around, and headed for the gravel road that ran past their house. Half a mile away they'd get on the highway. No words were spoken until they were well down the road.

An hour and a half later Olaf and Stina could see the skyline of the Cities. Olaf slid further down into his seat. It made him half sick just thinking about what was going to happen to him.

It had been a tense drive all the way down here. They had made only one wrong turn, but soon found their way back to the right street. Thankfully, Stina drove right into Lydia's driveway without any further problems.

Lydia saw them come and ran out to meet them. Stina got out first. Taking her basket in one hand she met Lydia with a warm hug. Olaf slid out of the car straightening his legs and sighing thankfully that they had come through all the traffic without any serious incidents.

Olaf had brought his favorite walking stick with him just in case. He wasn't used to walking on sidewalks. It might come in handy.

Lydia noticed his slightly unsteady stride and nodded knowingly at Stina. Olaf's hand was sweaty and clammy as he shook Lydia's hand.

"Come in. Come in. Come in." Lydia invited. "You must be starved after that long drive. Did you have any trouble finding the place? Was there a lot of traffic?" Lydia kept right on talking as they went into the house.

Olaf and Stina were seated at a table loaded with all kinds of food. And Olaf was hungry. He hadn't been hungry at breakfast time. How could he? After the second and third helpings of sumptuous food, as Lydia liked to display her flair for baking and cooking, Lydia looked at the clock and announced firmly that they had better be going.

A long sigh and a groan was all that Olaf could offer after thanking his sister for the meal.

They settled into Lydia's smaller car and took off for the doctor's office. Escape seemed impossible for Olaf. 'His knees didn't hurt anymore. Could just as well have been home getting some work done,' he thought bravely to himself as he tried to ignore the stinging in his knees. 'He had just been sitting too long, that's all.'

The three of them walked down a long hallway at the Medical Center. Lydia walked in front, Stina came panting behind, and then Olaf limping along in the rear.

Lydia looked at the sign on the door and all three walked in. Olaf surveyed the whole room. So many people in uniforms. Several people seated were waiting their turn to see the doctor. There were sounds of paper fluttering and machines typing away. It was all too much. Why had he ever given in to coming here?

Olaf and the two women sat down quietly glancing at other patients. As they waited Olaf's hat kept sliding off his knees, where he nervously played with it.

A charming young woman approached Olaf and asked, "Are you the gentleman waiting to see the surgeon?" Olaf nodded glumly, his worst fears looming in his mind. "I need to have you fill out this page. You can stay right there and when you have finished bring it to me, please."

"Now why do they need all this stuff for?" Olaf breathed under his breath. "I can't answer all these questions. Here, Stina, see what you can do with it?"

The clipboard with most of the questions answered was soon returned to the desk. The doctor would see Olaf in a few minutes.

Nervously Olaf sat there turning his hat 'round and 'round, crossing one foot over and then the other.

"Olaf, you need to go to the rest room?" Stina inquired. "Yust go out that door and down the hall. You can see the sign on the door."

'Well, it was good to get out of there even for a brief time,' Olaf thought.

Soon Olaf returned and before he could get sat down the nurse came and led him into a small room. 'Oh, what was going to happen next,' was all that Olaf could think of. He sat there with one hand covering his face, lamenting the fact that he had ever been talked into coming here in the first place.

The door opened and there stood a tall, big man smiling down at Olaf.

The doctor offered his hand to Olaf and with a grin said, "Hello. I'm Dr. Stundberg, and you must be Olaf. You look like a Norwegian. Are you? That's what I am."

Well, that much made Olaf feel a little better. He took a deep breath and nodded.

The doctor looked at Olaf's chart and said, "Looks like you've got a little problem with your knees. Is that right?"

"There isn't much wrong with them. Just gettin' a little old maybe. Ain't as young as I used to be." He felt much more relaxed now. Maybe the doctor was all right.

"Let's see you stand up," the doctor asked. Olaf complied and the doctor, after feeling his knees said, "Seems to me your knees are so far apart a hog could run between them. I think we'd better take an X-ray." Olaf smiled and chuckled.

Well, from then on, one thing led to another. The next thing you know Olaf was scheduled for surgery, and all Olaf could think of was what was going to happen on the farm if he wasn't there to take care of things.

Ten days later Stina and Olaf sped down the highway to Lydia's again and then off to the hospital. Things were happening faster than Olaf could comprehend.

In the next few days, Olaf was getting visits and cards and flowers and attention he had never know before. The nurses at the hospital waited on him as though he were a celebrity. Olaf had made friends with the doctor and looked forward to his daily visits. He even stopped worrying about the farm for a time.

Twelve days later Olaf was home in his own house and his own bed. Neighbors from all around flocked in to hear about his new knees.

"Ya, dere's notting to it. Should have done it long ago. Good ting I made up my mind to get it done." Olaf laughed and enjoyed all the attention he was getting. "Should have made up my mind long ago to get it done. But you know how it is. I needed to be here to look after Stina and all. You should see dem nurses," Olaf winked at the men that sat there listening to him go on and on about his experience at the hospital.

Out in the kitchen Stina was visiting with the women telling them about all the trouble she had had even getting him to see a doctor. She'd never want to go through that again.

So that's how Olaf got his new knees. He continued farming for many years after that. And Stina kept right on getting Olaf to do things he didn't always want to do.

GROWING UP DANISH

As one of the hundreds and hundreds of grandchildren born to Danish immigrant grandparents who came to the U. S. in the 1880's these memories I have from growing up on a Midwest Iowa farm were special. However, there are hundreds and hundreds of tales that can be told about others who grew up in the same era as I did. These have little to do with being Danish.

When the Danish immigrants came to the U. S. they envisioned prosperity and the dream of establishing a new Denmark. Under their vigilant care and tutelage they did and we did our best to uphold their visions and dreams. My paternal grandfather came from Stubbum, and my mother's grandparents spoke of Haderslev often.

Some of the immigrants, especially from the very southern part of Denmark came as sixteen year old boys. Upon reaching that age they were required to serve in the German army under the leadership of Kaiser Wilhelm, who in the 1860's was busily unifying the many Germanic states. Without consulting the Danes, the Kaiser considered the southern district of Denmark as part of Germany. Not only did they have to serve in the army, but they paid a fee to serve. Their evenings were spent knitting woolen socks for themselves, and otherwise caring for their uniforms. The possibility of finding a new life in Americas was very appealing to them. Many, as my grandfather did, left the army and took passage on ships sailing to the U.S. arriving in Ellis Island. From there they went by rail to various parts of the country where they already knew people who would meet them and give them a home until they could get on their own.

A few Danes had emigrated earlier and wrote home with glowing accounts of the new land. Steamship lines and railroad companies advertised the virtues of settling America "…where the streets were paved with gold." The availability of land was likely the biggest incentives for coming to America. Homesteading was probably the biggest attraction. The thought of eventually owning a piece of land was very appealing.

Others came to seek their fortune by laboring for other people. Many had a trade that they could use for their income. For example, we had a good man, Thorvald Petersen, who was an accomplished blacksmith. He ran a flourishing business until the farmers began using tractors instead of horses. His profession was mainly shoeing horses. He kept his business going sharpening plowshares in his forge and making things of beauty from wrought iron. He even was the factory dealer who sold my father his brand new Harley-Davidson motorcycle in 1912. Even though he was an accomplished artisan with iron, his retirement meant the end of smithing in that community.

Some immigrants found work in the lumber camps along the St. Croix River as my husband's grandfather and his brother-in-law Jacob Bergstrom did. They lived in an area known as Clifton Hollow in Wisconsin is just north of Hastings, Minnesota.

Much of Denmark was an agrarian society so the skills of the immigrants suited them well as they were farmers and dairymen by trade from Denmark.

The voyage across the ocean was a tiring and an anxious event. Some endured terrible storms in the crossing that tossed the small sailing ships like corks. Most had never been away from home before. Their foremost thought at the time was thinking about the time when they would become wealthy. Then they would return to their Homeland to relate the wonders of this new country and some would come back to marry the sweetheart they had left behind.

Some men brought their brides with them. Others came alone with thoughts of becoming wealthy, then to return to the Home Country to marry their loved one and bring her back to this country. Still others came alone with thoughts of adventure.

Two or three couples would settle several farms in a vicinity where they would establish their new home. They would then be able to share help and continue their friendship.

It would not be long until the thought of building a small church became necessary. Meeting in homes was not fulfilling enough. Most of these churches were built of lumber, painted white, and well adorned with beautiful woodwork on the interior. Churches were built within their own close community. Fredsville was just such a church. Danish pastors came to serve in the new churches. Dressed in their long black robes, their pale faces seemingly bobbed above the stiff white ruffled collars. Every Sunday morning they reigned over the congregation from their pulpit.

As the years went by there were several large families living near in the Fredsville community. Babies arrived at regular intervals.

Some families had twelve or fifteen children. The community of Danes grew rapidly. In a farming community this also provided cheap labor. At a young age the girls helped with the house work and the boys did much of the farm work. The thriving community maintained their customs from Denmark. Customs were carried over into the church, the homes, and other social events.

Hardships were overcome. Sickness and death took its toll. It did not deter the convictions of carrying on traditions.

Although our family spoke English fluently, we always spoke Danish at home and at church and were reprimanded if we did not do so. Living in a home where Danish was spoken and lived I was not allowed to play with one neighbor's children. They were English and were Methodists besides. So I didn't get to play with them. There was another family in the neighborhood that had lot of children and they were fun. I used to play in their hay mow where they had fresh sweet smelling slough hay. The problem there was I got head lice one time and my mother washed my head with kerosene. That took care of that problem.

Over the years since the late 1880s the patriarchal Danish farmers cultivated and harvested excellent crops from the rich black soil unique to the area. Likewise, the Danish women were ever faithful to the work of the Danish church. Monthly meetings were held in the homes. Along with the daily work of a farm woman there was the frenzied house cleaning to have the house in close inspection order. Even the baking to serve the guests was on a competitive basis.

Each Christmas the Ladies Aid diligently donated a small sum of money to the "Seamen's Mission", perhaps a thought for those who fished the North Sea out of Denmark, or perhaps a gesture to the sailors who brought our ancestors to this country.

At a very early age I learned my "Fader Vor du som er I Himmlen…" (Our Father, Who Art in heaven…). It was about the time I was four or five years old I became concerned wondering if my dog could understand me if I spoke English to him.

Danish families were so accustomed to speaking only in the Danish language that it was not too unusual for some to not be exposed to the language and customs of America. My husband did not speak a word of English when he first attended the public country school.

After World War II a need for change became obvious. The old dream of a new Denmark faded away and the lure of the cities took many of the new generation away from the farms.

The Danes are a stubborn lot of people. It has been said "…that you can always tell a Dane, but you can't tell him much!" In a fit of patriotism, the governor of Iowa at the outbreak of World War I decreed that all churches must use the English language, on the theory that "…God cannot hear prayer spoken in a foreign language." The Danes and others protested vehemently, and the decree was scrapped. In spite of their efforts in maintaining the old memories of home, the language and customs have faded from generation to generation. Like many immigrants who held tightly to their memories, the language and customs remained static. In the old country, life moved on. So with time it is the natural order of things that these things fade into distant memory.

Much of what has been written here is to record what life was like as I remember it as a second generation Dane born in America. Perhaps I am still growing up even at age 90. I learned to meet life's challenges with grit and good humor. As was said often, "No use crying over spilled milk."

Growing up Danish is a misnomer. Most of these stories relate life that many others have lived as well. I hope you have been entertained by these recollections, and that they will have reminded you of your own memories of life. Now, in this melting pot called America, some old traditions are forgotten. Events in life have less and less to do with ethnic ancestry, but rather to do with what our parents and grandparents taught us about how to deal with life.

All I can say is, "Til-lykke!" *(Good luck!)*

ABOUT THE AUTHOR

Born in rural Iowa in 1914, Elna Petersen has lived a long and varied life. She has been child, wife, homemaker, teacher, survivor and widow. There were few toys or books available in her childhood, and fewer playmates. Adults were busy for long hours each day. She spent time on her own, observing daily life or imagining distant places. Listening to her parents and grandparents telling stories was an almost daily form of entertainment  and taught her wisdom as well. In this environment she learned her independent attitude and the art of telling stories.

Her interest in writing grew out of her teaching background and her innate ability to spin tales to her children, grandchildren and great-grandchildren.

She began writing late in life – in her 70's – when she finally had time to do so. Now beyond her 90th birthday she continues writing in spite of diminished eyesight. True to her grit and determination, she lives independently in suburban Minneapolis, surrounded by the memorabilia of life represented in these stories.

Printed in the United States
39967LVS00006B/79-153

9 781420 888836